You hope you know who your friends are, but in a case like this one, it's hard to know who to trust!

I0672301

Welcome to Deer Creek!

This is the fourth book by Karin Richardson about Ruth Ann and her friends in Deer Creek, Colorado. At first glance, it's a peaceful little town in the Rocky Mountains, but in reality, it's plagued by a series of mishaps centered around a mystical aquamarine necklace. This time Ruth Ann has to solve a mystery in a remote mansion, complete with hidden passages and inexplicable deaths! And the strangest thing of all is that the mythical blue stone in the necklace has turned bloody red!

Readers say ...

When does the next one come out? I'm ready!

So many twists and turns! This is a great read and perfect for a rainy day.

Jaw Dropping – kept me on the edge of my seat!

This book was so suspenseful from start to finish. The voice of the characters was so strong I felt like I was right there with them all searching for the necklace! Awesome, quick read!

Couldn't put it down!

I loved this book. Every time I thought I had it figured out there was another twist and turn. A great read and now I anxiously wait for the next one!

Love the dialogue between characters. Keeps you guessing. It kept my interest to the very end.

A charming mystery!!

A great read. Perfect for a book club. Looking forward to the next one in the series!

Great read!! Love Ruth Ann! Can't wait for the next book!

Karin Richardson's Deer Creek Series ...

BLOOD

ICE

A Deer Creek Mystery

By

Karin Richardson

BLOOD ICE is also available as a Kindle edition
from Amazon.com

10 9 8 7 6 5 4 3 2 1

ISBN 978-1-57550-114-7

Printed in the
United States of America
Cover Art by Johanna M. Bolton

The fourth book in the series is dedicated to the two strongest, kindest women in my life.

My mom, Nancy,
and
my grandmother, Ruth Ann.

It was because of them I was introduced to Blue Ice.
I miss them dearly and know they are watching over me each and every day.

Also, a huge thank you again to
Wilma and Johanna for all your hard work!

BLOOD ICE

The recipe is on page 136!

ONE

"That Thanksgiving meal was the best one I've ever had!" I declared, rubbing my painfully bloated stomach, regretting that last bite of stuffing.

"Thanks Ruth Ann," Inga responded enthusiastically, standing at her rare spot at the dining room table. "I feel honored that you let me join you at the table for your holiday meal!"

"You're family," Prunella stated. "Of course, you and Sherman would sit with us. Where else would you be?"

"Well," Sherman began to say, "we are only staff." Sherman was correct, but their duties went far and beyond that of *staff*.

We had just returned from a grueling adventure in Jamaica where my long-time boyfriend, John Wilkinson, was kidnapped. John is the Chief of Police in Deer Creek, our rural mountain town. Getting himself kidnapped was an embarrassment for him and he made us all swear to never bring it up again!

That's a difficult task since word spread as fast as the stomach flu in our small town. It began when John surprised me with a romantic getaway in Jamaica to an all-inclusive resort. He surprised me with the trip the week before Thanksgiving. My immediate reaction was, "We can't go away now!" But I didn't have the heart to say those words, so I hurried and scurried to find the time to go.

I own Ruth Ann's Antiques on Main Street. It was the start of the holiday season and I didn't think it was wise for me to go on the trip, but I had bugged John for so long to go away with me, how could I say no? I left my store in the extremely capable hands of my assistant, Meme. She's young, but the best employee an owner could hope for. So, that part of the plan was taken care of. Now, on to my family. This may take some explaining, so sit back and relax a little while I provide a brief synopsis of my growing family.

I've been a widow for many years. I moved to Deer Creek with my twin daughters, Lynne and Nancy, after my sister, Irene, convinced me to leave the hustle and bustle of life in California. She felt it was best to get away from there after my husband was killed in a horrific plane crash. It was one of the best decisions I've ever made. Life in Deer Creek has been a blessing. I am fortunate to not have to worry about money, so once the girls were on their own, I chose to open my very own antique store in the heart of town. I hired an architect and had a Victorian house built to house my store. It's my passion, and I'm lucky to have it. My daughters are also still in town. Lynne owns Sinful Sweets, a bakery only two doors from my store. Sinful Sweets is the best bakery in town and she is constantly busy. She's about to open another store inside the town's one and only resort, Deer Creek Resort. She's got Balls will be a specialty store serving chocolate cake balls that are unique and very popular around here. It took a lot of convincing from me to get Lynne to open this new store. I silently funded the store so it wouldn't wipe her out financially, but I told her I would not interfere with her business whatsoever. I have to remember that in the coming days.

Nancy is my other daughter. She's currently a history teacher at the high school. Nancy is the quieter one of the twins. She is smart, serious, and still single like her sister, Lynne. I've tried over the years to change their marital statuses, but was flatly told, "butt out"! Both of my girls rent apartments not far from my ranch home off Main Street.

My sister, Irene, and her husband used to live here, but left for the warmer climate in Arizona last year. I didn't blame her since it has always been a secret dream of mine to move to a warmer climate in my second half of my life. I'm in my mid-fifties, and truly despise the long, cold winters, but my family is here.

And, in a wild, complicated twist of fate, my family recently grew. A few months ago, I inherited a priceless necklace with a rare aquamarine stone. The necklace was said to be cursed; anyone who came into contact with it was either killed, hurt, or kidnapped. The first person severely injured was my dear friend, Doug. He's the president of the bank in town and was the first recipient of the necklace. A mysterious package, addressed to me, was sent to him at the bank. He was very suspicious of the package, but before he could contact me, he was beaten and hospitalized by a group of criminals trying to get their hands on the necklace. Despite Police Chief John's direct orders, I got involved trying to recover the necklace. John was furious, but I needed to seek my own justice after what they did to poor Doug.

Unfortunately, I was kidnapped and taken to Alex Eklund's mansion just outside town. Alex is a very wealthy Swedish shipping magnate. After kidnapping me, Axel drugged me and flew me to his home in Stockholm, Sweden, which is where I met my new-found family. Yes, it sounds shocking to most that I would find family after all this, but I warned you it was complicated.

Axel kept me prisoner in his huge Stockholm estate. Ironically, he wasn't a cruel kidnapper. In fact, he was gracious and let me have full freedom *inside* his home. I was still confused about what was happening to me, but I'm a quick learner. I investigated the entire estate and uncovered a mysterious woman being held prisoner in the attic. Her name is Prunella. She is Axel's second wife, and the biggest shock... a distant cousin of mine! She is much younger than me, not much older than my daughters. Axel is much older than her, and if I had to guess in his mid to late sixties. As time went on, I learned, listened, and gained their trust. Prunella knew all about the priceless aquamarine I had inherited.

In fact, Prunella and her lawyer, Michael Svenson, were the ones who originally sent Blue Ice to Deer Creek. Prunella and Axel were at odds. Axel thought Blue Ice was his and Prunella believed that I was the rightful owner. After a long, hard battle the crooks who stole my necklace were killed, and Prunella and I got our Blue Ice back. I convinced Prunella, and her housekeeper and butler in Sweden, Inga and Sherman to move back to Deer Creek with me. They agreed, and we thought life was going to be free of crime, but it didn't last for long.

Once back in Deer Creek, Bert, Axel's Deer Creek butler, didn't take kindly to Sherman. Bert was grumpy, loyal to Axel, and a royal pain! Sherman was sweet, loyal to Prunella and had been recently exposed as her great uncle. That's a long story, so just take my word for it!

Unfortunately, the necklace, Blue Ice, was once again the focus of another group of criminals. Prunella's estranged husband, Axel and his henchmen returned to Deer Creek. John and I were terrified about what they would do to get the necklace back.

Once again, after too many murders, including poor Bert's, I kept Blue Ice and Axel and Prunella even reconciled! We even gained Alex, another family member at the end of this adventure when he unexpectedly showed up at the estate and claimed he was the rightful owner of the gem! I knew he wasn't a threat with his kind brown eyes and youthful stance. He wasn't a murderer, just a confused young man who recently lost his last remaining relative, his mother. We graciously brought him into our household and even convinced Axel to hire him as he rebuilt his shipping industry.

This is about the time in my story when John surprised me with a trip to Jamaica. He thought I needed a break from a month full of murders, kidnappings, and unbelievable stress. He was correct! I also wanted to get him away from one of his detectives, Judy Lynch. I haven't mentioned her yet because, well, I just don't like her. John is a friend of her family and she was working in a nearby city. Unfortunately, when my family brought crime to our normally safe town, John thought it best to bring Judy in to help. His staff was small, and he needed her help. I hoped she would leave after things settled down, but no such luck. She was hired as a full-time detective. Judy is younger, about mid-thirties, full of energy and a know-it-all! She flirted with John all the time. She was shocked when John took me away to Jamaica, and I hope it proved to her we were unbreakable as a couple. Time will tell, I guess.

We're almost caught up! Before John and I took off for our romantic getaway. Prunella and Axel convinced me to wear Blue Ice on my vacation. I thought it was a rushed, peculiar decision since we were finally free of danger with our necklace, but I acquiesced.

When we arrived in Jamaica, a terrible mix-up in our reservations left us stuck at a run-down "resort" on the beach. The place was owned by a lunatic woman named Martika and her husband, Carlos. We discovered that Martika had blackmailed Carlos into marrying her and forced him to buy the resort. Trouble started the first night, when at dinner, our waitress, Isabella, ran away from us in complete horror when she noticed the necklace I was wearing. Martika tried to play it off, but she told me that Isabella thought I was wearing a cursed gem and couldn't wait on me. I was intrigued and had to know why these random Jamaicans recognized my necklace and thought that Blue Ice was cursed.

So, while John was out paddle boarding, Isabella and I headed to her grandmother, Meme's shack. Meme was what most people called a 'witch' doctor. Meme confirmed that my necklace was cursed, and I would never be out of danger until the curse was broken. Unfortunately, Martika, who I later discovered was Isabella's half-sister, was greedy and wanted the gem for herself. She had John kidnapped while he was paddle boarding, and left me to rescue him. With the help of Carlos, Isabella, Meme, and a doctor named Joseph, we were able to begin the search for John. I was so distraught and scared that I contacted Prunella and Axel and they joined me down in Jamaica, with Alex, Inga and Sherman tagging along to help.

After a long battle, we were able to rescue John safely. Meme, due to her advanced age and health, did not survive. Before she passed, she was able to rid the gem of its' curse. But she warned me that once she did so, the owner must choose good or evil. I naively believed that we could finally be free to wear Blue Ice and not worry anymore.

Before we returned to Deer Creek, we were able to convince Isabella and Carlos to join us. Isabella readily jumped on our invitation to come to Deer Creek since she didn't have anyone else she knew of alive in her family, but Carlos took more convincing. His wife, Martika, was killed in the battle, and his friend, Joseph also lost his life. Even though his marriage to Martika was a sham, he still lost people he had known for a long time. Martika, Isabella, Carlos, and Joseph were all raised together in a small village not far from the resort we had occupied.

Now, back to Thanksgiving!

TWO

We just finished Inga's first ever Thanksgiving meal. She had a lot of help from my daughter, Lynne. I was still on the 'outs' with my daughters since I didn't ask for their help down in Jamaica. "I would never put your lives in any danger!" I shot back at them.

"Oh, but it's okay to put Prunella's life in danger?" Nancy snapped.

Prunella quickly added before Inga or Sherman could complain, "Don't forget Inga, Sherman, Alex, and Axel, too!"

"Yes, yes, I didn't mean to exclude them," Nancy replied, curtly. "Sorry, Prunella. I didn't mean to sound rude, but I'm just so tired of my mother getting into trouble."

"Trouble?" I questioned her, a little irritated now. "I didn't exactly ask for this."

Axel quickly intervened. "Nancy, your mother isn't to blame for this last escapade. It was my fault."

"Your fault?" she asked Axel.

"Yes. I'm the one who convinced your mom to bring the necklace. It was stupid and dangerous of me, I'm sorry."

"Axel," Prunella spoke before Nancy had a chance. "You mean *our* fault. I went along with the scheme, too."

"What scheme?" Lynne asked, instead of her twin, Nancy.

I hadn't told my daughters about Axel and Prunella's financial situation. Axel desperately needed money to rebuild his business, so he and Prunella worked with Martika to have the necklace stolen out of my room. There wasn't supposed to be any danger and Axel would get the insurance money he needed to reignite his shipping empire. He was going to get a lot of money from Martika, too. She wanted Blue Ice so badly, that she agreed to pay Axel a huge amount of money.

I caught Axel's eye and shook my head. Of course, my daughters both caught my reaction and immediately called me out. "Spill it!" Nancy demanded, and Lynne nodded vehemently, agreeing.

"Let me, Ruth Ann," Axel said. "It wasn't your idea."

"Go ahead, but girls," I said, turning my attention back to Lynne and Nancy. "Please don't judge too harshly."

"The reason why John got kidnapped, and your mother was put into danger was solely my fault."

"How?" Lynne asked, with keen interest.

"I had been spending every moment trying to get all my money unfrozen from my past indiscretions so I could re-open Eklund Industries back in Stockholm. I was pardoned, but apparently, it takes a while to get *all* the assets back in my name. You need to understand; it wasn't just me being greedy. I wanted the hundreds of my employees to get back to work so they could be paid. I admit, I didn't like not being in control of my company or my money, but I would never put anyone's life at risk."

"But you've done exactly that before," Lynne added, crossly.

I threw a nasty glare toward my daughter, and she threw her arms up in the air out of frustration. "Well, he did!"

"Let me continue, Ruth Ann. It's okay if she's angry at me. I'm still furious with myself."

"Go on," I said.

"When we heard about your trip with John, Prunella and I were truly happy for you both. That's about the time a strange woman showed up at my estate."

"I remember her!" Sherman blurted. "She was very rude. I told her you didn't see visitors, but she shoved me aside and marched right inside your office."

"I know," Axel said. "I was on the phone when she stomped in my office."

"Go on, *please*," Nancy begged.

"Yes, it was Martika. She didn't give me time to kick her out before she mentioned our necklace. She went on so quickly that I did all I could to follow her."

"She's the one who suggested the necklace be stolen from me, right?" I asked.

"Yes. At first, I flatly refused, but she kept going on and on and after a few times explaining her plan, I started to think it might be possible."

"You were willing to part with our necklace for good?" I asked him, stunned.

"Yes. That necklace hasn't exactly been a bright light shining positively in this family, has it?"

"No, it hasn't," I replied, solemnly. I raised my head high and quickly added, "But look at all the family we've discovered along the way!"

"Yes, that's been wonderful," Prunella said, looking around the room at her husband, me, Lynne and Nancy, Inga and Sherman, Carlos, Isabella, and Alex. John had been here for a little while and had barely eaten when Judy called him away on police business. She probably made up the call to get him away from our dinner!

"Please get back to your explanation," Nancy requested.

"Well, once Martika assured me there would be no danger, I brought Prunella into the library and explained everything."

Lynne, Nancy, and I turned to Prunella in astonishment. "I've heard this before, but I still can't believe you went along with the plan," I said, hurtfully.

Prunella lowered her head and barely got out, "I'm...I'm so sorry. I was trying to make everyone happy, but I blew it."

"Yes, you did!" Nancy snapped.

"Nancy!" I yelled. "Don't talk to her like that. She was put in a difficult position. Yes, seriously wrong decisions were made, but we're all alive and enjoying our first holiday together."

"I'm sorry, Prunella. I'm just frustrated. I didn't mean to suggest you would do anything to harm my mom."

"Thank you, Nancy. I would never do anything to hurt any of you!"

Finally, we were getting past this. I just wanted to put it behind us when Inga threw open the dining room door carrying a large silver tray full of pumpkin and apple pies, whipped cream piled high in a china bowl, and of course, a large plate of Lynne's balls.

"Ooh, that looks delicious," I said, hoping to brighten our moods. "Lynne, what kind of balls did you make?"

"Pumpkin spice, ginger, and I threw in some cookie dough balls."

"There's always room for dessert, and especially chocolate!" I said, laughing.

Inga put the platter on the dining room table and started serving pieces of pie and passing around the large bowl of fluffy, delectable whipped cream. I grabbed the plate of balls and grabbed one of the pumpkin spice balls. I'd tasted them before when Lynne made a batch for our town's mayor, Henry Hamilton, and his snooty wife, Lulu. I popped the entire ball into my mouth and immediately tasted its strong cinnamon and pumpkin flavors. Most of Lynne's creations were dipped in a rich, dark chocolate, but these were coated with a sweet, white chocolate. "These are better than the first batch you made, Lynne."

"Thanks. The batch for the Hamilton's was my first attempt. Now I'm used to making them so they're getting more and more fined-tuned."

"I assume these will be at your new store when it opens next week?" Alex asked Lynne.

"Yep. I'm going to run the pumpkin ones until Christmas."

We sat in silence as we filled our already stuffed stomachs with pie, chocolate balls and coffee. "I can't eat another bite!" Prunella declared, wiping her delicate mouth with her napkin. "I need to move around and settle my stomach."

"I'll join you," I said, pushing my chair in as I stood up and waited for Prunella. "Girls, will you help Inga clean up, please?"

Inga said, "I don't need any help. It is my job, remember."

Both Nancy and Lynne insisted on helping Inga with the cleanup. A Thanksgiving meal is a messy one to clean. I left Alex and Axel deep in conversation, and Carlos and Isabella clearing dishes and bringing them into the kitchen where Inga, Nancy, and Lynne waited. Sherman followed Prunella and me into the foyer.

"What are you two really up to?" Sherman asked with his accusatory, squinty eyes.

"Up to?" Prunella inquired. "We're stuffed and want to walk around the place for a bit. Nothing's going on, Sherman."

"Oh, okay. I need to get used to the calm around here, I guess. We've been on the go trying to solve murders and kidnappings. I'm not used to the quiet."

Prunella grabbed my arm and laughed. "Get used to it, Sherman. The curse was broken, remember?"

I suddenly felt a chill rush through my entire body. I knew that feeling. There couldn't be any reason for it, right? We'd retrieved Blue Ice and it's safely nestled in the brand-new vault in Axel's office. He wanted to make sure the necklace couldn't be stolen from us ever again. I didn't even know the code yet, which made me ask Prunella, "Hey, do you know how to open Axel's new fancy safe?"

"Me?" she asked, innocently. "What made you ask that question? Are you worried about something, Ruth Ann?"

There was that chill again. I shivered, and briefly caught a shimmering red glow in Prunella's eyes. I was too quick to turn away, because when I looked again her eyes had returned to their normal baby blue. "What's wrong, Ruth Ann?" she asked, concerned. "Do you know something I don't?"

I shook my head and said, "I'm fine. I think I ate too much. That's all."

"Oh, okay. But if you're worried about the necklace, I can

have Axel give you the code so you can check on it whenever you'd like."

"That would be nice, Prunella."

"Let's walk each of the three floors. I need to move!"

We hiked up to the second floor and briskly walked to the other end, where my bedroom was located. It took every ounce of determination to not whip open the door and plop down on my bed. You may be wondering why I have a bedroom in their estate when I live only twenty minutes away? It was Prunella's idea to have a room, decorated by me of course, ready for whenever I'd like to stay.

"No, Ruth Ann," Prunella sternly said. "I know you want to go in and nap. That's the last think you should do."

"I know. It's just that eating all that heavy food made me so tired. Don't worry, I'll keep walking."

We walked back down the hall, passing Prunella and Axel's room, Alex's room, and at the other end of the hall, Carlos' room and Isabella's room. "It was nice that you and Axel let Isabella and Carlos have a room on the second floor."

"I couldn't put them up on the third floor. That's where Sherman and Inga's rooms are, and you know…"

"Bert's and Helena's *were*," I finished for her.

"Yes. We need to rip those rooms apart and re-decorate them."

"I agree. Nobody wants to stay in a room where both of them lived."

"And were murdered."

"They weren't killed in their rooms, though," I said. "Poor Bert was burned to death at the resort, and young Helena met her death in that horrible room in the basement."

"She was young, but not innocent," Prunella snapped, quietly.

"No, she wasn't." I knew it was still a sore spot with Prunella. Helena had a brief interlude with her husband, Axel. She even went and got herself pregnant. I knew Axel was originally accused of her murder, but thank heavens, it wasn't him. He wanted to send her back to her hometown in Mexico and raise their baby. He was willing to financially support them both, but that was never to happen.

"Let's go up to the third floor now," I said quickly, changing the topic. "I'll race you up the stairs!" I said, trying to lighten the mood even though she would beat me hands down.

Prunella laughed and rushed to the main staircase. "Hey, that's not fair. I'm in heels and you're not!"

"Really?" I questioned her, smiling. "I'm twenty years older than you so the two balance each other out."

We each took a side on the wide staircase and on the count of three took off up the stairs. Surprisingly, I beat Prunella. "Just lucky," I said, watching Prunella try to catch her breath. Strangely, I wasn't out of breath at all.

"It's the heels," she said. "My feet wanted to slip out of my shoes."

"Excuses, excuses," I said jokingly, grabbing her arm and walking down the third-floor hall.

We walked past Inga's room, and then Sherman's room. Both doors were shut and any light that would've come from the bedroom windows didn't and left the hall very dark, and creepy. "I don't like it up here," I said.

"Too many bad memories."

"I guess," I said as we walked past Helena's room. "Her room used to be such a cheery place when she was alive."

"It's because she had it painted a bright yellow. It gave the illusion that it was always sunny in there."

"Kind of ironic, isn't it? She acted sweet and innocent, and even decorated her room like a young girl, but deep down she was far from innocent."

"I know you're still upset about the whole Axel and Helena thing, Prunella. You've got to put it out of your head as if it never happened."

Prunella's disposition took a change for the worse. Almost yelling, she exclaimed, "How am I supposed to do that? My husband had a disgusting affair with the girl and got her pregnant!"

"Calm down, Prunella. It's not going to make things any easier. I know it's got to be very difficult for you, but if you can't let it go, maybe you should seek some help." I didn't know how that advice would go over, so I stopped talking and looked into her eyes to see if the strange flash of red would appear. Once again, those sweet blue eyes had that momentary flash of red. I have to admit, it scared me more each time I saw it.

"You think I need therapy?" she snapped, clearly unhappy with my suggestion.

"There's nothing wrong with professional help," I replied. "I've gone many times."

Prunella looked at me as if I was crazy. She rolled her eyes and asked, "You've been to a shrink?"

"Why the hostility? Most people I know have had some kind of therapy. It's always good to seek someone objective, and having your husband cheat on you qualifies as a good reason."

"Out of the question. I'll deal with it in my own time."

"Fine, but don't snap at me about it again," I replied, curtly. I knew she could use some help, but until she was ready to admit it, therapy wouldn't work anyway.

"I won't."

"Can we just get moving again? I'm still full and quarrelling isn't making me feel any better," I said, walking down to the other end of the hall hoping she would follow. Once I hit the end of the hall, I turned around and noticed Prunella wasn't behind me. Where did she go?

I rushed down the hall and looked over the railing, but she wasn't heading down the stairs. Maybe she didn't go down yet, so I walked back and reached for the door knob on Inga's door. It wasn't locked so I pushed open her door and didn't see any sign of Prunella. Inga's room was neat as a pin. She had a large bed without a fluffy, patterned comforter, just a tan down blanket spread over the bed. I closed the door and went to Sherman's bedroom. His door was locked. Figures. He didn't trust anyone, and I don't blame him. Nobody's been who they're supposed to be around here!

Next room was Helena's. Her door was wide open. Aha! Prunella was probably inside tearing the room to shreds. I walked in and even though it was dark outside, it looked cheery and bright in her room. "Prunella?" I called out, looking around the untouched bedroom.

"I'm in her closet," she bellowed from inside the large walk-in.

"What on earth are you doing in there?" I asked, walking over to the opened door.

"I've got too much energy so I thought I'd pull her clothes down and throw them into this box."

I looked at the floor and found two large cardboard boxes. "Oh, I guess that's a good idea."

"Why would we want to hold on to any of her belongings? It's time to clean up this room, and maybe re-decorate it." Prunella's head popped up and glanced my way. "Hey, why don't I give you full control on this room and Bert's. You could bring everything over from your store."

"I guess I could," I said, blown away by her sudden cheeriness.

"Of course, we'd pay you for the furniture and accessories."

"Oh, I wasn't implying you wouldn't, Prunella. I can see why you want to re-decorate. These rooms could be filled someday, right?"

"With whom?" she asked, confused. "We only use this floor for staff, and I think Inga and Sherman are enough help for us, don't you?"

"Yes, yes," I repeated. I looked around the room and started imagining what I could do in here. "You know, it could be fun for us to bring some new stuff in here. What do you want to do with the furniture that's in here?"

"Throw it out!" she exclaimed bitterly.

She was sure up and down with her emotions. If that doesn't

suggest she should get some professional help, I didn't know what could. "I think a better idea is to donate everything to a good charity."

"Oh, yes, that would be the right thing to do. Most of this stuff is brand new."

"It's all in good shape. I figure Bert's room is the same. A bed, dresser, couch, and some tables and lamps."

"Yes, but his room is dark and a bit depressing. Bert was a grouch and his taste reflected his personality."

"Prunella!" I bellowed. "Don't speak badly of the dead!"

"Sorry," she replied, but I could tell she had no remorse. Bert was quite cruel to her, but even she used to stick up for him. What is with her sudden personality change?

THREE

We spent quite a bit of time in Helena's room. By the time we were finished, all that was left was the mattress, metal frame, and the brightly flowered couch. If I would've let her, Prunella would've ripped the cushions off the couch and burned them.

As we shut Helena's door, I noticed Prunella snuck something into her pants pocket. I was about to ask, but decided she would tell me it was none of my business. We left the boxes and piles of linens on the floor near the door and headed to Bert's room. She moved quickly and thoroughly packing as much as she could. We didn't speak while we worked, but when we finished my stomach sure felt a whole lot better. In fact, I could've slipped down to the kitchen and grabbed another piece of apple pie, but I didn't.

"Now what?" I asked Prunella as we walked downstairs. "If you'd like me to leave, just tell me."

Her head whipped around and she spat out, "Now why would you ask a question like that? I'm not mad at *you*!"

"I...I wasn't suggesting you were, but if you're tired I can take the girls and head back into town."

"No, I think you all should stay here tonight. We could start decorating for Christmas tomorrow. Isn't that what you do around here?"

"Yes, but I didn't know you had any decorations."

"Of course, we do. Axel said he bought and stored everything we would need in the basement. We can go down there and take a peek if you'd like."

I stopped on the last step and stared straight ahead. The front door was there for me to run out, but I couldn't do that. I had to face my fear and go down into the dreaded basement.

Prunella sensed my reluctance and quickly said, "Oh, I'm so sorry, Ruth Ann. I forgot about when you were held prisoner down there in that awful room."

"It's also where John and I found Helena shackled to the same wall, but she wasn't as lucky as me. I wasn't murdered there."

"I've got a better idea. I'll have Axel, Alex, Carlos, and Sherman go down there and bring everything up. We can have them dump it all into this massive foyer," she waved her arms in a great big circle as she spoke.

"That would be great, thanks. I really don't want to go down there unless I have to. Too many nasty memories down there."

"I'm sorry," she said back in her normal voice. No red flashes in her eyes or curt tone in her voice. Maybe she just needed closure with Helena and Bert and she would be alright. Or…maybe not.

We headed into the kitchen and found Inga, Nancy, and Lynne working hard to wash and dry the dishes. Isabella and Carlos were diligently packing leftovers into containers.

"Wow, look at all of you!" I said, feeling a tad guilty that I wasn't helping.

"We're almost through, Mom," Lynne said, wiping the large turkey pan dry. "We can go home soon."

"Prunella wants us to stay overnight. Are you girls in?" I asked, looking for Prunella to confirm, but she wasn't behind me when I looked back. "Hey, where is Prunella?" I asked.

"We have no idea, Ruth Ann," Carlos replied for the group. "She never came into the kitchen."

"Huh," I muttered. "Maybe she went to look for Axel."

"And Alex!" Inga added. "He disappeared with Mr. Eklund into the library instead of helping us in here."

"Oh, well, I'm sure Axel needed him for some reason," I said, wondering what was going on. "I'll go and check."

"Wait, Mom," Nancy called before I left the kitchen. "I think Lynne and I are going to call it a day. I'm tired, stuffed, and I have to go to the high school tomorrow to grade tests."

"Tomorrow?" I asked, oddly. "But there's no school the day after Thanksgiving."

"I know, that's why I want to go!" Nancy said, laughing. "I won't be bothered."

"Makes sense to me," Inga said.

"And I need to get into my bakery before the sun rises. I have a ton of baking to do. Plus, my store opens in less than a week. I need to go home and go over numbers and make sure I have everything I need to open on time."

"I thought it was all ready to go, Lynne?" I asked, confused.

"It is. I just want to double and triple check everything. I don't want to upset customers or Carol and Dick over at the resort."

"Carol is ecstatic you're opening soon. She thinks it'll help their business, too," I said. Richard and Carol run Deer Creek Resort, the one and only ski resort in town. Their busiest season is winter, and I'm sure Carol thinks opening a sweet shop next to their gift shop will be quite profitable for everyone.

"Well, Lynne and I drove here together this morning, so we're going to head out if it's okay with you all?" Nancy asked, looking around.

"I'm good," Inga said. "I've never had so much help! Thanks, girls."

I left Inga, Carlos, and Isabella in the kitchen while I escorted my girls to the foyer. Sherman suddenly appeared around the corner close to Axel's library. "Sherman!" I cried out. "You startled us."

"Sorry, I was just checking around to make sure everything's cleaned up after our meal."

I so wanted to call him out, but refrained. Sherman was on the opposite side of the dining room lurking around the library. Knowing Sherman as well as I do, I knew the only 'work' he was doing was eavesdropping. I waited until he escorted the girls to their car and came back in. "Brrr," he said, shivering. "It's really cold out there!"

"It usually is this time of year, Sherman."

"What's your problem, Ruth Ann?" Sherman asked, snappily. "Is Inga upset because I wasn't in the kitchen drying dishes?"

"Why don't we forget that and get to the real reason why you were listening in on Axel and Alex."

"And Prunella," he accidentally slipped and said.

"Ah, you have been snooping, haven't you?"

"I don't snoop. My job is to make sure Mr. Eklund's needs are met. So, I made sure I stayed near in case he needed me."

"Nice try!" I said, smirking. "Why don't we skip your excuses and tell me what you *think* is going on in there."

"I told you, I'm here waiting," I stopped him by raising my hand and saying, "Knock it off, Sherman. We've been through enough lately. Maybe you think something bad is about to happen."

"You're right. Haven't you noticed *anything* strange going on the last two days here?"

"What are you talking about?" I asked, baffled. "We just got back home and I thought all our energies had been devoted to getting this meal off on time."

"Don't lie to me, Ruth Ann!" he barked. "You've seen it too, haven't you?"

I truly didn't know what he was referring to until I remembered the strange look in Prunella's eyes. That red flash of light that came and left so quickly. It was a chilling, scary stare from her, but I was almost positive she had no idea she was doing it.

"Ah, you do know what I'm talking about," Sherman repeated. "I could tell a lightbulb went off in your head."

Do I admit I knew what he was talking or let him bring up the strange red flash? I think we were both being silly, but I didn't want to cave first. "You tell me what you think you know, Sherman."

I saw him wrestling with his answer when he finally said, "Fine. I'll go first. Prunella has been acting strangely ever since we left Jamaica. I thought she was recovering from that traumatic ordeal, but her mood has been so…off."

"How do you mean?"

"She's been up one minute, and the next…she snaps. I don't mean the regular kind of crabbiness one gets when tired or hungry, but a scary, evil kind of change in her. I've seen the weirdest thing, too with her. Her eyes," he stopped, closed his mouth tightly and shook his head.

"I know what you want to tell me, Sherman," I said, trying to help him continue. "I want to hear you say it, though."

He took a deep breath and said, "I've seen her eyes change color several times, and each time it's when her mood changed from good to…"

"Evil!" I blurted out of thin air.

"Yes, thank you, Ruth Ann. I didn't want to use that word, but that's what I feel when I see those red eyes."

"I thought I was imagining it, Sherman. But now you tell me you've seen it, too."

"What do we do, Ruth Ann?" he asked, quietly. "We can't bring it up to her because we don't know how she'd react."

"I know. I don't know what to do."

"You must have an idea, Ruth Ann," he said. "Our sweet Prunella has turned into some kind of demon."

"Don't be ridiculous, Sherman!" I snapped. "I'm sure there's a simple explanation. Maybe she's under the weather and her eyes are bothering her. It could also be why she's been so moody."

"You think she's pregnant?" Sherman asked, throwing me

completely off guard.

"Pregnant?"

"I'm trying to think of something good, instead of…"

"Don't use that word again, Sherman. I know what you're thinking," I said.

"You must be thinking it, too or you wouldn't have said that. You think there's a chance something happened to her back in Jamaica with that witch doctor."

"Witchdoctor!" A voice shouted behind us. I forgot we weren't alone and quickly turned to see Isabella standing near the staircase.

"Isabella!" I said, elbowing Sherman in the side.

"Hey," he said, seeing the frozen expression on the poor girl's face. "Oh, Ms. Isabella. We didn't know you were here."

"He didn't mean anything disrespectful about your grandmother, Isabella," I said, trying to deflect our blunder.

"I clearly heard Sherman use the word 'witch doctor'."

"He was wrong in using that word. Your grandmother was a kind, loyal, intelligent woman. She broke the curse on my necklace and saved our lives."

"She did!" she snapped, turning her gaze on Sherman. "She wasn't a witch doctor, Sherman. Please don't use that term again."

"I'm sorry, Miss. I didn't mean anything ill-mannered, I was just explaining to Ruth Ann about the strange look in…"

"Sherman!" I interrupted immediately before he could spill about Prunella's red eyes.

"Oh, yes, um, I was just reminiscing about what happened back in your home."

"You both are lying!" she exclaimed. "Why don't you just tell me the truth? I'll find out anyway."

"That's right!" Sherman bellowed. "You have those powers like your grandmother."

"Exactly, Sherman," Isabella said, obviously trying to scare Sherman into confessing everything.

"Why don't we put this conversation on hold until later. I'd like to check on the others in the library. Can we talk later, Isabella?" I asked, hoping she would accept my suggestion.

"I'll go with you, Ruth Ann," she said, walking toward the double doors. "I want to see how Prunella's doing, too."

"Huh?" I asked, wondering how much of Sherman's and my conversation she heard.

"I'm very aware that Prunella's being acting differently ever since we boarded the plane to come back to your home. I'm pretty good at sensing things, you know."

"Yes, you are," I said, remembering that Meme, her grandmother, knew what thoughts were inside my head just as I was thinking them!

"I'll open the doors so the both of you can enter. I'll follow to see if anyone wants anything." Sherman didn't wait for us to respond, but tapped on the library door and waited for a response.

Once we heard Axel say a distant, "Come in," we entered into the cozy, spacious library with a roaring fire heating the entire room.

"What are you three doing in here?" I asked as soon as we were a couple steps inside the room.

Prunella was sitting on one of the two chairs that faced Axel's massive desk. Alex was in the other chair. Axel stood and invited Isabella and me to come closer. "Alex and I were just going over some work, and Prunella's just hanging out," he said.

"Prunella," I said. "You were right behind me when I went into the kitchen, but you didn't come in. Why not? I thought we were going in to check on everyone."

"I didn't feel like it."

Axel's was stunned and glanced my way. "Um, Prunella. You didn't have to snap at your cousin."

Prunella sat upright in her chair and said, "Oh, I'm sorry. I didn't mean to snap."

"It's okay, Prunella," I said, walking closer to the desk. Isabella was right on my heels, staring directly at Prunella. I knew she sensed something odd was happening to Prunella.

23

Axel hurried to the other side of his desk and stood over his wife's chair, blocking Isabella and me from getting too close to Prunella. It was that exact moment I knew for sure something was very wrong, and Axel knew it too.

FOUR

"Prunella, dear, why don't you go up to bed and I'll be up in a couple minutes," Axel suggested, with extreme compassion in his voice.

She glared at him and retorted, "I'm not tired. Don't tell me to go to bed like I'm a child, Axel. I can stay up as long as I want!"

I could see the worry in his eyes, and even Alex appeared uncomfortable. He unsteadily stood and excused himself from the library feigning he was hungry again and wanted another piece of pie.

Sherman followed Alex to the door, but instead of leaving with him, he shut the door behind him and came back to the desk where we were standing around Prunella. Axel was clearly making excuses for his wife's behavior, but I wasn't going to take it.

"Prunella, may I ask if you're feeling okay?" I thought it was the least offensive comment I could make.

Prunella flew from her chair and stomped toward the door. "I feel fine, and I wish you all would stop asking me that!" And there it was again, the sudden flash of red in her eyes. Sherman, Axel, Isabella, and I all saw it. Prunella turned on her heels and disappeared out of the library.

"What was that?" Sherman hollered. "That's not right!

Something's seriously wrong with my great niece!"

Axel ignored Sherman and went back to his desk and wearily plopped down in his chair. I desperately wanted to speak to him privately so I asked Sherman and Isabella to give us a moment alone. "It's my niece," Sherman protested, but Isabella gently took his arm and led him out of the library.

"Not now, Ruth Ann," Axel spoke, exhausted. "Can we talk in the morning?"

"No."

"I didn't think that would work," he said, sitting up a little straighter in his chair. "And before you go after me, I'm brutally aware of the change in my wife's mood."

"And the eyes, don't tell me you didn't see her *red eyes*!"

"I saw them, and it's not this first time either."

"Me, too."

"So, I'm waiting for your insightful reasons why my wife has become some sort of evil person."

"Don't use that word!" I snapped. "I hate that word."

"And I know why."

Did I want to go there tonight? I didn't think I had the strength to pursue this topic right now. Maybe he was right. We should sleep on it and talk in the morning, but then we would run the risk of others overhearing. With that thought, I hurried over to the library door and as Axel intently watched, I threw open the door.

"I knew it!" I yelled. "Sherman, get out of here!"

Sherman stormed off toward the kitchen and I slammed the door and walked over to Axel, who was grinning at how I caught Sherman in the act of eavesdropping. "That lightened my mood a little," he said. "You know, I'm very aware that he does that all the time."

"How could you not? He's about as inconspicuous as a rhinoceros's stampede!"

"Good description, Ruth Ann."

"I'm tired, too, Axel. However, we need to discuss what we

26

think is happening to Prunella."

"Yes, we do," Axel replied, leading me over to the couch facing the fireplace.

"When did you notice a change in her mood?" I asked him, plopping down on the couch and grabbing the afghan that was thrown over the back of it. It was warm in front of the roaring fire, but I couldn't rid myself of the intense chill that kept running through my body ever since I saw that peculiar look in Prunella's eyes.

"At the airport in Jamaica."

"Really?" I asked. "Today was the first time I've noticed it."

"You've been busy the past two days since we've come back. I'm around her all the time," he said, appearing exasperated with his young wife. "I hide away in here just to avoid her." He held up his hand to stop my protests and added, "I know it sounds horrible, Ruth Ann, but she's kind one minute and horribly mean the next. I don't know what's wrong with her, and it scares me."

"Me, too," I said. "Do you think this has anything to do with what happened in Jamaica? Or maybe she's not feeling well and doesn't even realize it."

Axel studied my expression keenly. "Wait a minute," he said. "You think she might be pregnant, don't you?"

"It's a possibility. Look at her mood swings, and her appetite is worse than ever. She claims she's starving, but she barely eats enough to stay alive."

"You forgot one important thing, Ruth Ann," he looked toward the door to make sure nobody had entered the library. He whispered, "those freaky red flashes in her eyes that come and go when she's having one of her little tantrums."

"Maybe we should ask Doc Albert," I suggested. "He may have a medical reason why her eyes keep giving off those red flashes."

"Hey, great idea, Ruth Ann. Can you call him right now?"

"It's Thanksgiving night, Axel. I don't think I should interrupt his holiday."

"But, what if he's working at the hospital? You could call over there and see if he's there, and then ask him."

"I guess it wouldn't hurt," I said. "But, I need to get my cell phone and it's upstairs in my room."

"Use my phone," he said, reaching into his pants pocket and pulling out his cell phone.

"I don't know his number."

"It's in my contacts," Axel said, surprising me.

"Why would you have Doc Albert's number in your phone?" I asked, curiously.

"I've seen him for check-ups. Nothing sinister about it, Ruth Ann."

"Oh, okay. Can you pull it up and hit the button? Hand me the phone after you hear it ringing." Axel nodded and pushed a couple buttons, and a few seconds later handed me his cell phone.

"I put in on speaker so we both can listen," Alex said.

"Shirley," I said, scowling. "You're working on Thanksgiving, huh?" I waited for one of my least favorite nurses to explain why she was stuck at the hospital on a holiday. After a few, painstaking seconds, she finally asked me why I was calling the hospital. I asked her if Doc Albert was in, and she asked why I wanted to know. "Because I need to ask him something, Shirley. Do you mind getting him if he's available?"

Shirley huffed and put me on hold. I looked at Axel and gave him a thumbs up. "She's getting him, I think."

"Great. We need to rule the medical side of it out," Axel said, nervously.

A couple minutes passed, and finally a voice came back. "He'll be right with you, Ruth Ann," Shirley barked. "You know he doesn't have time to socialize when he's at the hospital. We're very busy with accidents tonight!"

"Shirley, how do you know I'm calling to socialize with Doc Albert?" I asked aggravated. She was really beginning to irritate me.

Before Shirley could answer, another frantic voice came on

the line. "Ruth Ann, is everything alright?"

"I'm fine, Albert," I answered quickly. "I'm sorry to bother you, but I have a question for you. It's a medical question."

"Fire away, Ruth Ann. You've been through so much the last couple months that I wouldn't doubt you had questions about your health."

"It's not about me, Albert," I stated.

"Okay," he said, doubting my sincerity. "Why don't you just ask me your question?"

"Is there any medical reason why a person would have red flashes in their eyes?"

"That's your question?" he retorted.

"Yes, but please, I really want to know," I begged.

"Oh, let me put your mind at ease. It's probably a common floater or flash. It's harmless, Ruth Ann."

"It is?" I bellowed. "I am so glad we called. Seeing those red flashes in Prunella's eyes have really freaked us out!"

"Whoa, wait a minute," Doc Albert replied. "Did you say *you* see the flashes in Prunella's eyes?"

"Yes, but you just told me they are harmless."

"No, no, that's not what I meant, Ruth Ann. I thought you were referring to an individual seeing red flashes in their *own* eyes."

"No, Albert. A number of us here at the estate have witnessed Prunella's mood swings, and when she's mad her eyes throw off the scariest red flash. It's as if her eye color changes to red, and then when she calms down they go back to light blue."

"That's not normal, Ruth Ann," Doc declared, obviously perplexed. "Maybe you should bring her in and I could examine her. She may have picked up a local virus or something while in Jamaica."

"What do you mean by *or something*?" I asked him, worried about what he was implying.

Axel looked frantic and asked Doc Albert, "Do you think my wife is sick?"

29

"I didn't say that, Axel. I just want to examine her and maybe draw some blood. She could've picked up a local bug."

"I don't want it to be anything serious," he said.

"I don't know anything yet, Axel," Doc Albert added. "Can you get her to see me tomorrow?"

"Albert," I interrupted. "She's very hostile right now. When I've asked her if she was feeling well, she snapped my head off. How can we get her to agree to come in and see you?"

"Figure it out, and I'll plan on seeing her tomorrow. How's late morning?" he asked.

"We'll do what we can, Doc," Axel said and ended the call.

"Well, I'm not tired anymore, Ruth Ann," Axel said, worried. "Now we need to come up with a plan to get her over to the hospital tomorrow morning."

"I've got it!" I exclaimed. "Why don't we *all* go to see Doc Albert in the morning?"

"Huh?"

"We tell her each of us have to have a quick exam and blood test after what we've been through in Jamaica."

"Hmm," Axel said, thinking hard. "Not a bad plan, but she'll catch on. She's pretty smart."

"Yes, but if I go in first to see Doc Albert, and then Inga and Sherman, Alex, and you, and then…"

"Prunella," he finished for me. "Obviously, Carlos and Isabella don't need to be checked. They lived their entire lives there until now. Are we actually going to get examined by Doc Albert?"

"No, unless you want a blood test," I answered. "I just had one recently so I'm fairly confident I'm all right."

"Sounds like a plan. Do we tell her tonight or tomorrow morning?" he asked.

"Tomorrow morning, early," I replied. "I'll come rushing down the stairs into the dining room at breakfast and pretend it was already a planned appointment, but I forgot because of the holiday. The look on Inga and Sherman's faces will show her they're totally surprised, too."

"You do have a devious mind, Ruth Ann," Axel said, smiling and taking hold of my hand and giving it a tight squeeze.

"Thanks, I guess," I replied, waiting for him to release my hand, but he didn't. I thought it was a kind gesture at first, but now I was feeling a bit awkward, so I pulled away as politely as I could. "I'm going to get some sleep."

"I'm glad you decided to stay here, Ruth Ann. I don't like you driving all the way down the mountain in the dark. It could be icy out there."

"I'm used to it, but walking up the stairs and crawling into bed sounds more appealing to me right now." I stood up and said goodnight to Axel and headed into the abandoned foyer. What a shock, Sherman wasn't there!

I went straight to my room without bumping into a soul. I was tired, aggravated and feeling a little guilty about tricking Prunella into going to see Doc Albert in the morning. She will be furious with me if she finds out, but there wasn't a choice. Something very strange was happening to her.

FIVE

I immediately fell asleep, but woke suddenly in the middle of the night. I looked over at my nightstand and the clock was flashing four in the morning. I rolled back over and tried to fall asleep again, but my mind was racing with strange thoughts about Meme. Not my assistant Meme at the store, but Isabella's very old grandmother who lost her life shortly after breaking the curse on our now famous necklace, Blue Ice. I had a pang of guilt over her death until I remembered it was Meme who begged me to let her break the curse. She had been waiting for that moment her whole life. I had to let her do it, but then her words came back to haunt me. "After I break the curse, the gem will be cleansed. However, you will have to decide the fate of the gem now. It can be used for evil or for good." What path will the purified gem take? I assumed we'd chosen good, but something about Prunella's look made me doubt my assumption.

I laid in bed staring at the ceiling, trying to clear my mind. At about five I pulled myself out of my warm bed, threw on the robe I left at the bottom of the bed and walked into the dimly lit hallway. I walked downstairs and made my way into the kitchen. A cup of hot tea was in order and possibly I'd be able to go back to sleep.

I pushed open the kitchen door, and was surprised when I saw Isabella sitting at the island on a tall stool. "Isabella," I called out, quietly. "What are you doing down here?"

"I couldn't sleep so I thought we could enjoy a nice cup of

tea. The kettles on the stove, ready for you to pour yourself a cup."

I walked over not paying attention to her words. I stopped as I grabbed a mug, realizing what she just said and asked, "Hey, what did you mean by 'we'?"

"I knew you were coming down here, Ruth Ann."

"Oh, I get it. You read my mind like your grandmother used to, right?"

"Yep. Don't freak out. I don't always read your thoughts. Just when there's a strong force that allows me in. You were thinking hard up there, weren't you?" Isabella asked.

"Yes, Isabella, I was. I keep going over what happened back at the resort in Jamaica. I'm not afraid, that's not it. I'm just trying to figure out if I noticed a change in Prunella's personality before we hopped on the plane to fly home. I have racked my brain, but I didn't see it. Axel did. He noticed it before we left Jamaica."

"He's her husband, Ruth Ann. You've been through a lot. You had so many distractions down there and now up here. Today was the first time you settled down and that was when you noticed Prunella's strange behavior and her unusual eyes."

"I guess, but I still should've been more aware."

"Give yourself a break!" Isabella exclaimed, in a quiet voice. "What else was on your mind?"

"Why are you asking me? You already know the answer."

"You were thinking about my grandmother and her last words, weren't you?"

"Yes," I replied, solemnly.

"You have no reason to feel guilty. She was very weak and old when you arrived. In fact, I have to thank you."

"Thank *me*?"

"Yes. You gave her a renewed sense of energy when you brought your necklace to us. It was her last dying wish to break that curse and you allowed her to do it. I should be thanking you!"

"No. I was selfish and it cost people their lives."

"Selfish?" she quipped. "That's the most ridiculous thing I've ever heard. You had no idea why Prunella, Axel, and Martika conned you into wearing the necklace on your vacation with John."

"You have a point, but still," I stopped and took a sip of the hot, soothing tea.

"Let it go, Ruth Ann. I know what else is weighing heavily on your mind."

"Yes, I'm sure you do. Your grandmother's last words. They haunt me, Isabella."

"You're terrified that Prunella already chose the wrong direction for your necklace, aren't you?"

"Well, those red eyes are disturbing, Isabella. Don't you think so?"

"They're odd, but she hasn't really done anything yet," she said.

"She's been so moody, and when she's angry her gentle, loving blue eyes transform into red, threatening, evil eyes."

"Be careful using that word, Ruth Ann," Isabella said, seriously. "Evil may be a slang word in the states that could describe many things, but for Carlos and me, it's a heavy, dangerous word implying action needs to be taken or one can die."

"Die?" I cried. "I don't think it's that bad." I waited for Isabella to agree with me, but she remained quiet. "Do you?"

"I'm definitely concerned, Ruth Ann, but we need to wait and see. All we can do is watch Prunella closely, and if she shows any further anger or strikes out at any of us, we need to look deeper into what might have happened to her down in my country."

"Yes, yes," I agreed. "We're all going to go to see our local doctor in town this morning."

"All of you?" she asked, confused. "Are the others showing strange signs, too?"

"No, Axel and I knew Prunella wouldn't agree to an exam and blood test, unless everyone pretends to have one, too. So, Inga and Sherman, Alex and Axel, Prunella and I are going into town later this morning to see Doc Albert. But only Prunella will actually get examined."

"How are you going to pull that off?" she asked, interestedly.

"I mean she's been pretty steadfast about feeling okay. In fact, she gets quite insulted when anyone asks how she's been feeling."

"I know," I said. "But if she thinks *all* of us are getting examined in case we picked up a local virus, I think she'll go along with it."

"Good luck with that one!" she said, smirking. "Does Sherman know about this yet?"

"Nope. Axel and I aren't telling anyone so they will be surprised with our plans."

"Ah, good plan, Ruth Ann. I think it'll be good to rule out any physical issues with her, and if it comes out okay, and she's still acting weirdly, then I'll look into other ideas."

"What do you mean?" I asked, concerned. "You think she's been cursed or some other bad mojo has been inflicted on her?"

"I don't want to comment on what I think just yet. Let's get past the doctor's visit and see what he says."

I watched Isabella's concerned expression intensify. I knew she had a feeling about what could be wrong with Prunella, but she obviously wasn't ready to share with me. We finished the rest of our tea in silence, and then I told Isabella I was going to try and get a little more sleep.

"I'm sure you'll rest now," she said as if she knew I really would, making me even more uneasy.

I headed upstairs and down the long hall past Carlos', Isabella's, Prunella's and Axel's and Alex's bedrooms. Everything was silent as I hurried down the hall and into my room. I quickly shut the door, feeling slightly rattled there might be evil lurking in the halls.

Isabella was correct. I laid down on my bed and within a couple minutes I fell fast asleep. I don't recall any bad dreams or horrible fears of what could be happening. I woke up to Inga banging on my door. "Inga!" I hollered from my bed. "Please stop yelling. I'm awake now!"

Inga threw open my door and rushed inside. "What took you so long to respond, Ruth Ann?"

"What are you talking about?" I sat upright in bed and raised my arms up to stretch. "I didn't sleep well so I went down and had some tea early this morning. I came back up to get a little more sleep." I looked around the room and noticed a bright light trying to peek in from the heavy velvet curtains. "Hey, what time is it anyway?"

"It's 10:00!" Inga relied. "Everyone's had breakfast and Mr. Eklund's been pacing around his office demanding I go and wake you. He said we all have an appointment soon, and you needed to fill us in on it."

I hopped out of bed and scurried around the room looking for the clothes I laid out the night before. "I didn't know it was so late! We need to hurry."

"Hurry for what?" Inga asked, confused. "Everyone's asking lots of questions, Ruth Ann. Where are we going?" "Go downstairs and tell the others to meet me in the dining room. I'll be down in less than five minutes." I picked up my clothes from the floor near the couch and headed for my bathroom. I stopped before Inga left the room. "Hey, is there anything left to eat?"

Inga glared back at me and snapped, "All that's still edible is cereal. The eggs, toast, and bacon were eaten or thrown out."

"Can you throw some bran flakes into a bowl for me, please? Oh, and a small glass of orange juice..." Inga huffed and nodded. She disappeared after slamming my door shut.

"Geez, it's not like I asked her to make me a stack of pancakes!" I exclaimed to myself.

Within five minutes, I was in the dining room shoveling cereal into my mouth. The only ones present were Inga, Sherman, and Alex. "Where's Prunella and Axel?" I asked.

"They're coming," Sherman said, tersely. "Do you need Carlos or Isabella?"

"No, but where are they?"

"I'm not their watchdog, Ruth Ann," he snapped. "Probably somewhere around here."

What was with him? I shrugged my shoulders and by the time I was done with my cereal everyone I needed was here. "So, we're going to take a quick trip into town in a few minutes," I said, waiting for the protestations and questions. I held up my hand to stop them and continued. "Look, I talked with Doc Albert yesterday and he suggested we have a quick examination and possibly a blood test after our trip to Jamaica. He said we spent time in the jungle, ate strange food, and had a traumatic experience."

"I feel fine!" Inga bellowed. "I don't need no doctor!"

"Well, you don't have a choice," I said, but the nasty glares continued. "Look, I have to go through it, too."

"What about John?" Alex asked. "He was down there. Is he going to be there?"

I quickly made a mental note to text John before anyone else asked him. I knew he would have a million questions about why we're pretending to be examined, except for Prunella. I didn't want to alarm him or trigger red flags that our problems were continuing, but I couldn't lie. "Well?" Sherman asked, waiting for my answer.

"John?" I repeated. "Of course, he'll be checked out. He was kidnapped and went through more than any of us!"

"Oh, then I guess it's okay with me," Sherman replied.

"I'm good with it," Alex said, and Inga nodded in agreement.

"What about you two?" I asked, directing my attention to Axel and Prunella. I watched Axel hold out, acting out his reluctance. Good job, I thought, but answer already.

"Prunella, you okay with it?" he asked her. "I guess it wouldn't hurt to have a quick examination."

Prunella stood next to her husband watching us intently. Was she buying this or was she suspicious? Finally, after what seemed like an hour, she said, "I'm good. Let's go."

Phew, she bought it and within a few minutes we piled into Axel's largest limousine and headed down the mountain and into town. "It's beautiful out here today," Prunella said, cheerily. She was in a great mood, which made me wonder if this was unnecessary.

"It is," I answered. "Last night's little snowstorm covered the ground, and the trees look like a picture on a postcard. How are the roads, Sherman?" I asked him.

"They've been treated. No problems so far!" he called out from the driver's seat.

We sat in silence looking at the beautiful scenery. "I'm surprised Doc Albert's working the day after Thanksgiving, Ruth Ann." Prunella said.

"He always works. I'm glad he finally hired a couple young doctors to help him at the hospital. It was too much work for him."

"He's not getting younger," Axel said.

"He's my age!" I snapped. "I'm not that old."

"No, no, that's not what I meant, Ruth Ann," Axel quickly replied. "I just meant he's not a young doctor who can work seven days a week."

"Oh, well, I have to agree with you on that," I said. "I'm thankful I decided long ago not to open my store today. I know it's a huge shopping day, but not here in Deer Creek."

"So, Meme has the day off, too?" Inga inquired.

"Yes, with full pay of course."

"That's very nice of you," Prunella said.

There she went again. Being nice and friendly and worrying about my assistant Meme. Maybe I was imagining her bad moods and the whole red eye thing, but the others noticed it too, so I shot my guilty thoughts down. "We're almost here," I said to the others. "Who wants to go first?"

"I will," Alex said.

I had filled Doc Albert in on Axel's and my plan. He knew that he was going to pretend to examine the others, but not really do much. We decided it best to not fill them in on our scheme since it would be highly unlikely it wouldn't be leaked to Prunella. "Great," I said. "Then why don't Inga and Sherman go, and Axel and Prunella after that."

"What about you, Ruth Ann?" Prunella suspiciously asked me. "You're being examined too, right?"

"Of course. I figured I'd go last."

"Oh, well, that's okay," she said, resolutely.

Sherman flew through town, a little too fast for me, but he was probably anxious about getting an exam. "Lynne's place is lit up," Inga stated. "Maybe after we're through we could stop by and grab a treat."

"Sounds good," I said, always willing to drop by and see one of my daughters.

We arrived at the small, local hospital, and Sherman dropped us off at the front door. We entered the waiting area, and Claire Owens was working the reception desk. She smiled enthusiastically as we walked up to her desk.

"Hi," she said, cheerily. "Doc Albert's waiting for you."

"Great. Can Alex go in first?" I asked Claire.

"I'm sure that's fine. Let me call back and see if he's ready." Claire picked up her phone and a minute later one of the double swinging doors leading from the waiting area to the examining rooms flew open. It wasn't Doc Albert who walked to meet us, but Shirley, his snappy, rude nurse.

"Hi, Shirley," I said, trying to appear excited to see her. "Ready for us?"

Shirley ignored my question and demanded, "Prunella. Doc Albert would like to see you first."

"But, but, we agreed that Alex would go first," Prunella cried out. "Can't he go before me. I'm a little nervous."

Shirley shook her head and replied, "Nope. Doc told me who to ask for."

Prunella desperately looked in my direction and I had to think of some way to diffuse the situation. "Look at it this way, Prunella. You'll be all done and can sit and relax while the rest of us have to be nervous while we're waiting our turn."

"That makes no sense, Ruth Ann," Sherman bellowed, but I jammed my elbow into his side.

"Shut up, Sherman," I whispered. "If Prunella's nervous, you just made her more nervous!"

"Oh, sorry. I'm sure it's just a simple check-up. Don't worry, Prunella. I'm sure you're the healthiest one of all of us!"

I wanted to scream at him, but figured it wouldn't help, so I halfheartedly agreed. "Go ahead, Prunella. Just get it over with."

"Will you go with me, Ruth Ann?" she pleaded. "I've always been terrified of doctors."

Axel nodded his head slightly giving me permission to accompany his wife. "Sure, I'll go with you, but if Doc Albert asks me to leave, I'll have to go, okay?"

Prunella's scared, pale face bobbed as we headed with Shirley through the swinging door into the stark, white hallway.

"In here," Shirley barked. "Doc Albert will be with you shortly."

Prunella and I entered the spacious examining room, and Prunella said, "She's not very nice."

"No, she isn't. She has never liked me very much."

Prunella hopped on the exam table and asked why. I answered truthfully, "Because she thinks she and Doc should be a couple. You know, the doctor and the nurse. How perfect it would be..." I laughed and added, "But I kind of ruined that for her."

"How?"

"Doc's single, and he proclaimed that the only one who could change his status would be me."

"Doc Albert proposed to you?" she asked stunned, but calming down since the attention was off her.

"I didn't let him get that far. I knew what he meant, but I told him we were better as good friends. He was disappointed, but I think he's never really given up hope. When Shirley became his nurse, she thought she could distract him from me, but he never showed any signs of romantic feelings for her."

"And that made her blame you, right?" she asked.

"Oh, yes. Plus, I told Albert that Shirley was a mean, cold-hearted..."

"Ruth Ann!" Prunella bellowed, stopping me from completing my sentence.

"Well, she is!"

Prunella and I were laughing as the door whipped open and Shirley appeared. For a split second, I thought she had overheard us, but she only came back to take Prunella's vitals. "I forgot," she snapped and grabbed Prunella's arm and wrapped the blood pressure cuff around her skinny arm.

"Hey, not so tight!" Prunella complained.

"Sorry, you have such a small arm I wanted to make sure I get an accurate reading. We want to make sure everything's okay since you came back to the States."

Prunella eyed her suspiciously. "What do you mean by that?"

I quickly interrupted and answered for Shirley before she blew it. "She didn't mean anything by it, Prunella. You need to calm down or your blood pressure will be high and Doc Albert *will* think something's wrong."

"Oh, you're right, Ruth Ann," Prunella said, immediately taking a few, slow breaths to calm down.

Phew, another slip-up averted. Shirley gave me a funny glance, but didn't say another word. "Okay. Doc Albert's on his way now."

As Shirley exited, Doc Albert entered. "Hi, there," he said, merrily. "It's nice to see the both of you safe and unharmed."

"Of course, we are, Albert," I said.

"Ruth Ann," he transferred his attention to me. "You've really got to stop getting yourself into these situations. It's not safe."

"It's not like I do it on purpose, Albert."

He ignored me and turned to Prunella. "So, can I ask you why Ruth Ann is in here?"

"I'm, I'm a little nervous," she said, meekly. "Is it all right she stays with me?"

"I don't see why not as long as you gave permission."

"Thank you," she said, shyly. "Why did you want us to get

examined, Doc Albert?"

Doc Albert looked at me and I did a quick shake of my head to remind him of our agreement. A light bulb went off in his brain and he quickly replied, "Oh, yes, yes, Prunella. We need to make sure none of you caught a strange bug while you were roaming through the jungle."

"Fine, but can we get it over with? I'm not good in doctor's offices."

He grabbed her arm and put his fingers on her wrist to take her pulse. "Why not? I'm not going to hurt you. I just want to give you a clean bill of health."

"I had some bad experiences when I was younger," she said, surprising both Doc and me.

"Huh?" I asked, interestedly. "You've never mentioned that to me."

Prunella appeared nervous and uncomfortable. "Let her be, Ruth Ann. Her pulse is racing, and I'd like this brave, beautiful woman to relax."

"Thanks, Doctor Albert," Prunella said.

"Please, call me Doc or Albert."

That seemed to calm her nerves a little because she smiled sweetly at him. "I will. So, what do you need to do to me?"

"I'll check your vitals and look inside your ears, nose, and mouth…listen to your lungs and heart…feel your tummy for any strange bulges."

"Excuse me?" she asked unnerved. "Strange bulges?"

"Don't worry, it's just a standard exam, and then I'll draw some blood."

"Is that really necessary?" she asked, scared.

"Yes. That's how I'll know for sure that you didn't pick anything up from your trip."

"It's no big deal, Prunella. I have blood tests all the time it seems."

The rest of her exam went along quickly and in silence. Doc said he'd be right back and I said, "That wasn't too bad, right?"

"Nope."

Shirley came in with Albert and he told us that Shirley would be taking her blood. "Everything looked good, Prunella," Doc Albert told her.

"Great!" Prunella replied, happily. "You're not leaving, are you?"

Doc looked at me and back to Prunella. "Why, yes. I'm done here until your blood work comes in."

"What about Ruth Ann's exams…and the others?" she asked, confused.

"Oh, yes. I'm doing theirs. I'm just done with yours."

"Why don't you do Ruth Ann's right now. She's here and I can stay with her while you examine her."

"Oh, I… I guess that would be okay," he said, looking desperately in my direction. I too was trying to figure a way out of it when I thought…just go along with it."

"You know, it's a great idea, Prunella. Albert can give me my quick exam right now, too."

Doc Albert shrugged his shoulders and waited for Shirley to leave with the vials of Prunella's blood. She stopped and stuck her head back into the examining room. "Doc, should I come back and draw Ruth Ann's blood?"

Doc and I knew we were caught. I had to go along with the plan and have my blood drawn. I nodded in Albert's direction and he said, "Yes, give me a few minutes and then come back in."

Doc asked me to hop up on the table and he started with my pulse. "Hmm," he said quietly, but loudly enough for me to hear.

"What's the 'hmm' for Albert?" I demanded. "Something wrong?"

"Wrong? No, it's just funny that's all. Your pulse is racing like Prunella's was."

"Is that a big deal?" I asked, suddenly worried.

"No, no, I'm sure it's just a coincidence," he said, turning serious as he continued his exam.

"Ouch!" I cried out when he pushed on my tummy. "Not so

hard, please."

"That spot was tender?" he questioned me. "Have you had a stomach ache or pain since you've been back? Or any problems going…"

"Albert!" I bellowed. "Please, that's private!"

"Oh, sorry, but have you?"

"No, not that I'm aware of. I haven't had my normal appetite, but we've only been back two days, and I've been busy."

"So, no stomach aches or pains?"

"A little nausea, but nothing that has stopped my day to day activities."

"I'm sure it's nothing. I'm going to get Shirley back so she can draw your blood." Before he walked out he asked Prunella, "Have you had any nausea?"

"Now that you've mentioned it, I guess I've had a little like Ruth Ann. Are we sick?"

"Don't worry about anything. I'm sure it's just from the trip and all the craziness you went through down there. The blood test will be in tomorrow, so it will tell me more."

Suddenly, I became more and more concerned. Doc decided it was best to really examine Alex, Axel, Inga, and Sherman. None of them had any signs of stomach distress or racing pulses. I asked if he was going to call John in and Doc Albert told me he definitely was. "You haven't talked to him lately?" he asked, curiously.

"Yesterday, he was at Axel and Prunella's for the beginning of our turkey dinner, but he was called away. I haven't heard from him since."

"There was a bad accident last night," Doc replied. "I have two of the victims here as patients. I bet he was busy with that."

"Was he here?" I asked.

"Yep. In fact, he was supposed to be here right about now. I'll go check." Doc left us in the waiting area and I noticed the group was anxious to leave the hospital. "C'mon, Ruth Ann. Can we go now?" Sherman asked, irritated at the delay. "It's bad enough they had to poke and prod me all over!"

"Please, Sherman. It couldn't have been that bad," I said, shrugging off his complaining disposition. "I just want to see if John's here."

A minute later, the double swinging doors flew open and banged the walls on the other end. Claire Owens, the receptionist almost fell off her chair. "John! Can you please not whip open those doors? You'll scare everyone in here."

"Oh, sorry, Claire." He turned his direction to us. "Hey, Doc told me you were here. He told me I needed to hang out a few extra minutes and get a quick exam."

"Yes, John. Doc felt it was necessary. He checked each and every one of us out, too." I looked at him and subtly nodded to confirm I wasn't pretending anymore. I could tell he wanted to ask more questions, but Prunella was standing with me. "Just do it. It's not that big of a deal."

"Fine. Will you be here when I'm through?" he asked me. "I'd like to talk with you."

Sherman protested. "Can't you come up to Mr. Eklund's estate later to talk to her?"

"I may go home, Sherman," I said, wanting to see my daughters and go home.

"No, Ruth Ann!" Prunella shouted abruptly. "You have to stay with me until we get our blood tests back." I whipped around and her eyes turned red, scaring everyone. I didn't want anyone to warn her, but I sure wished Doc Albert was here to see them.

"Hey!" Inga thundered, loudly. "Did you see…"

I cut her off as fast as I could and shouted, "Let's go! John and I can catch up a little later, can't we?" John didn't know how to respond. He was caught off guard by the sudden need of an exam and watching Prunella's baby blues turn devilish red!

SIX

I hurried everyone out of the hospital and ordered Sherman to get the limousine. Axel pushed me to the side and said, "What was that about?"

"I don't know. I just said that I'd like to go home and Prunella went berserk."

"It's getting worse, isn't it?" he whispered in my ear, causing the others to become suspicious.

"What are you two whispering about?" Sherman demanded, out of place. "I thought we were done with secrets."

"Sherman, shut-up!" Axel snapped, but too late. Prunella noticed and she insisted we tell her.

"Fine," I said. "I just told Axel I was thinking of going home and you became upset with me. I wasn't trying to make you angry."

"I'm not angry," she said, back in her normal, sweet voice. "I didn't mean to snap. I would like you to stay with us since we have to wait for the blood tests, and it was obvious you and I have different symptoms than the others."

"I have an idea," Axel said. "Why don't we stop by Ruth Ann's so she can get whatever she needs and then we'll head back to the estate. Doc Albert said he'll know within the next twenty-four hours."

I felt a rush of anger. Why did I always have to stay there? What's wrong with sleeping in my own bed and coming back to their estate tomorrow morning? "Fine," I conceded. "But I want to grab my own car."

"Oh, that's right. You drove with your daughters yesterday," Inga said. "I'll drive with Ruth Ann so she's not alone."

"I can handle it, Inga, but that's fine if you want to."

We drove in silence the six blocks or so to my home. It felt like I hadn't spent any time there the last few months. Axel opened the door for Inga and me to get out before Sherman could complain about doing it. "You won't be long, will you?" Prunella asked, nervously.

"No," Inga answered for me. I nudged her and told her it was my house and I was the one who had a few things to grab. "Sorry, Ruth Ann. I was just reassuring Ms. Prunella we'll be right back."

"It may take me a little while, Prunella. I'm sure Inga and I will be up there within an hour."

"Oh, okay," she said, yielding.

"You'll be fine, Prunella. You have Axel, Sherman, and Alex," I said, wondering why Prunella was being so needy.

"Don't forget Carlos and Isabella are up at the estate waiting for us," Axel said. "We'll hold lunch for you."

"You kind of have too, Axel," I said, jokingly. "Inga's with me!"

"You're right!" he said, laughing. "I forgot. So, we will have to wait until you get back."

Sherman drove off right after Inga and I entered my house. "Oh, it's so good to be back here!" I stated. "I miss my little house."

"It is quite small, Ruth Ann." Inga marched into the kitchen and started snooping. "You don't have enough room to entertain a lot of people, do you?"

"I don't need to," I said, curtly. "My family's small and if I need more space, I'll go to the resort."

"Oh, that makes sense," Inga said, filling the teapot with water. "I'll make us some tea while you pack what you need. We have to talk."

I agreed. Inga and Prunella go way back, and Inga was very protective of her. "I don't need a lot. Just some fresh clothes and toiletries."

I walked across the great room and down a hall to the master bedroom. There were only two bedrooms in my ranch, but I didn't need any more. My master was huge and when I spotted my bed, I wanted to run over and jump in. However, this wasn't the time, so I opened my closet and pulled out enough clothes for the weekend. I wasn't sure when I'd get back here, but for sure by Monday because Meme and I had to open my antique store for the busy holiday season.

"Tea's ready!" Inga hollered from the kitchen.

"Coming," I called out, carrying a small suitcase. I walked over to the tall island and noticed Inga had put out two cups of steaming tea and a couple biscotti. "I forgot I had those," I said, reaching out for one.

"They're not bad for store bought," Inga replied, taking a bite out of the hard treat.

"I bought them at our local grocery store that Chris Jenkins runs. She buys top of the line products and they're usually quite good."

I took a few sips of my tea and watched as Inga stared at me. I knew she wanted some answers regarding Prunella's devilish eyes and the escapade this morning at the hospital. "I know you see me staring at you, Ruth Ann. I need to know what's going on with Ms. Prunella!"

"To be honest, I don't know," I said, biting into the chocolate half of my biscotti.

"I know you know more than I do," Inga declared. "Spill it!"

"Actually, Axel and Isabella noticed before me that Prunella was acting oddly."

"And her eyes, what's going on with her eyes?"

"I know, it's quite disturbing, Inga."

"Did she catch something down in Jamaica?" Inga asked, worried.

"That's what I'm hoping the blood test might reveal, but I'm not so sure it's just a physical condition."

"What do you mean, Ruth Ann?"

"I keep going back and forth about what happened down there. Meme warned me that once the necklace, or I should say the gem on the necklace, was rid of its curse, whoever had possession of it could choose its destiny."

"Huh?" Inga asked, looking totally baffled.

"Before Meme did her incantations, that necklace brought us a lot of grief. You agree so far?" Inga nodded. "Good. There was evil associated with the gem. After she broke the curse, the gem was cleansed, so to speak."

"Oh, I get it!" she exclaimed. "Meme handed over a blank gem. If the person who takes it over wants it for evildoing, then that's the course the cleansed gem takes, right?"

"Yep."

"Hey, wait a minute…you think Prunella is evil?"

"No, no, that's not what I believe." I said, hearing how bad that sounded. "I'm just telling you that Meme's last words were to make sure the necklace falls into the right hands so there would be no more grief associated with the piece."

"And you're worried that Ms. Prunella took a hold of it and wants to use it for bad and not good?"

"Yes, but I'm not sure she even knows, Inga. I think something happened to her down in Jamaica. I just don't know what or how!"

"Isabella should be able to answer that question."

"She's aware of what's going on, but she wants to wait to make sure it's not something medical."

"And if her blood test is clean?"

"Then you and I corner Isabella and Carlos, and force them to tell us what could have happened to our sweet Prunella."

"I'm sure glad that blood test isn't taking long," Inga said. "But why didn't the rest of us have a blood test? Maybe we caught a virus or were bitten by some strange insect."

"I did have a blood test, Inga."

"You did?" Inga remarked, surprised.

"Prunella insisted Doc Albert examine me while she was in the room right after her exam."

"But you didn't have to have your blood drawn."

"It would've looked suspicious if only Prunella did," I said, not divulging the real reason Doc Albert drew my blood. If she knew I had a racing pulse and tummy distress like Prunella it would only worry her. Until the test comes back, I'm staying quiet.

"Makes sense," Inga admitted, and changed the subject. "Are you done? I think we should get going. I have to come up with lunch as soon as we get back and it's late already."

"I'll help you, Inga," I said, waiting for her to laugh. I wasn't the best cook, but I'm capable of making a sandwich.

"Maybe," she said, surprising me. "I think I'll put out cold cuts, you can't burn those!"

"Very funny, Inga," I said, grabbing my purse and suitcase and walking out to the garage from the kitchen. "Let's go."

I drove up the mountain, like I normally do, but with Inga grasping the center console and passenger door handle with white knuckles. "Really, Inga. I'm driving perfectly safely, so knock it off."

"I can't remember being in a car with you driving before," she said, trying to release her grips. "You drive fast!"

"I'm used to it, Inga. We'll be fine."

Within twenty minutes, I pulled my bright yellow SUV around to the front of the estate and we hurried up the stairs and inside. Inga disappeared into the kitchen to start lunch. I was about to follow when Axel summoned me into his library. "Shhh, Ruth Ann," he said, softly. "I don't want anyone else in with us."

I couldn't resist, so I walked into his library and Axel gently shut the door. "What's this about?" I asked, curiously.

"She's not the same person anymore, Ruth Ann," he said, wearily sitting down on one of the chairs in front of his desk.

"Did something happen after Inga and I left all of you?"

"Yes. Sherman was driving us back home. Alex and I were in the back of the limousine with Prunella. She was whistling one minute, and then the next she was yelling at the two of us."

"About what? Did you or Alex say something to make her upset?"

"We didn't say one word!"

"Then what happened?" I asked, concerned.

"She started accusing Alex and me of leaving her out of my business. She said it was just like before, right after we got married."

"Wait, what?"

"Yes, she said it won't be long before I lock her in the attic like I did when she thought I was trying to kill her!"

"That's crazy," I said, wondering if I misunderstood what he was saying. "Why would she say that? Did you joke about it recently?"

"I would never joke about that terrible time in our lives. I have no idea where those words came from. We never talk about that dark time in our life. I think she's starting to imagine things."

"No," I said, but without conviction. "Maybe she dozed off and had a nightmare about that time. When she woke, perhaps she was confused about where she was."

"NO! She wasn't sleeping or dozing! Prunella was sitting whistling a cheery tune, and then she turned to us with those horrendous red eyes and started accusing Alex and me of trying to push her away and kill her!"

"Kill her?" I said, trying to grasp his words. "Something's terribly wrong with her. Where is she now?"

"She locked herself in our bedroom and said the only person she wants to see is you, Ruth Ann."

"Me?" I asked baffled, but then inquired, "What did Alex think of her outburst and accusations?"

"He took it in stride. He's a good kid, but I'm pretty sure he's rethinking moving here right about this time."

"I'm sure he isn't. We've all seen Prunella's odd behavior.

51

I'm sure he's noticed it, too."

"I hope so."

"I should go up to her," I said, standing up from the chair next to him.

"Wait a minute, Ruth Ann," he said, looking worn and tired. "I know this may sound strange, but maybe she's noticed I haven't been as devoted to her as I used to be. I've been distracted with my business and trying to get it back up and running. Also, she may have misinterpreted a few words I've said about you."

"Me? What have you said about me?"

"Nothing bad, Ruth Ann. I've mentioned how strong you've been through the last couple months, and what a trooper you've been, and I've even said you have to be smart because your antique store is very profitable."

"That's not anything that should upset her. In fact, I would think she'd be happy you said all those things about me."

"Well, I might've mentioned that John is a fool for not running off and marrying you because you're the perfect catch."

"You said that?" I exclaimed, flattered but also uncomfortable. "I, I don't know what to say…"

"It's the truth, Ruth Ann," Axel said, suddenly standing very close to me. "I've had feelings for you that I can't explain. I'm so sorry to load this on you, but maybe Prunella's sensing my affection toward you."

I was speechless. Axel had feelings for me! What does one say when a person surprises you with feelings you didn't even know he had? "Umm, umm, I don't know what to say, Axel."

"There's nothing to say. That trip down to Jamaica messed up more than just Prunella!"

"Maybe that's it, Axel!" I exclaimed. "Prunella's behavior and your supposed feelings for me…what will be next?"

We stood in silence waiting for the other to speak. Finally, after several awkward seconds, I said, "I should go to her. Let me find out what she's thinking."

Axel, rocking back and forth said, "Yes, go and see if she's calmed down. Let me know what she tells you, please." He walked to his desk and sat down. "I'll stay in here tonight."

"That's ridiculous!" I said, exasperated. "There are a million bedrooms in this place. Just pick one!"

"The only ones open are on the third floor. That'll confuse everyone."

"Hey, there's the guesthouse down the path behind the garage. You could sleep there if you felt it absolutely necessary."

"I'm not leaving this house. I feel like something is brewing and I need to be near."

"Maybe I should call John," I said without thinking. "We can fill him in."

"Oh, yeah, that'll be great, Ruth Ann. John would knock me unconscious if he found out I had feelings for you!"

"*Supposed* feelings, Axel. I think something's off with all of us. Once we figure it out, we'll go back to normal. I think the only person you want to be with is Prunella. She's been difficult lately, and you're frustrated. Give it time and I bet you'll forget about this sticky situation."

"It's not a sticky situation, Ruth Ann!" Axel backed away and started pacing near the fireplace. "I think I started having feelings for you the day you and that security guard were caught at this estate."

"Paul," I mumbled.

"Yes, that's his name! I wasn't myself back then, but I knew the minute we talked, we had a connection. You felt it, didn't you?"

"I, well, I...don't know! I've never thought of you in that way, Axel. You kidnapped me and flew me to your estate in Sweden. Yes, you were always kind and respectful, but you did kidnap me!"

"I know. I was a horrible human being. I get that, but even then, I knew I had strong feelings for you. I just didn't know what they were until now."

"It's been a tough time, Axel. Let the dust settle and wait for

Doc Albert's test results. If we're clear of any problems, then we'll get Isabella and Carlos involved. How's that? Can you stop talking nonsense until we get this resolved?"

Axel muttered quietly, "It's not nonsense. I know how I'm feeling. I feel guilty, too."

"Guilty?" I cried out. "Yes, you should! Prunella is the love of your life. You're just confused. Who would pick a woman in her mid-fifties over a beautiful, much younger woman?"

"The heart wants what the hearts wants," Axel muttered. "You should go and see her. She's waiting for you."

"Where's Alex?" I asked, suddenly worried he may know too much.

"He took off as fast as he could when Prunella starting accusing me of throwing her into the attic."

"Oh, probably a good thing," I replied. "I'll go and check on both." I headed for the library door when Axel stopped me, again.

"You're not going to mention any of this to Prunella, are you?"

"Of course not! It's nothing real anyway." I turned to leave, but hesitated and told him, "Wait until you see either Prunella or me before deciding on where you're going to sleep."

"Excuse me?" he asked, embarrassed.

"Oh, that's not what I meant, Axel!" realizing he thought I was suggesting he would sleep in either Prunella's or my room. "I just thought I could convince Prunella to let you into your room with her."

"Oh, okay. I'll stay put."

I took off as fast as I could. "Wow, that was really uncomfortable!" I said to myself, but I wasn't alone in the foyer. "Sherman!" I exclaimed, startled. "What are you doing here? Were you lurking around listening to our conversation?"

"Me, no. I just came out of the kitchen and walked over to see if anyone needed anything."

"Oh, as long as you weren't eavesdropping."

"Nope."

This time, I believed him. If Sherman overheard any of my conversation with Axel, he would've blown a gasket. He questioned where I was going, and I told him to see Prunella in her bedroom.

"What's wrong with her? I saw her bolt up there not too long ago, and I asked her if anything was wrong. She wouldn't answer my question."

"She and Axel had a little fight. Nothing big," I added before he could demand what the argument was about.

"So, you're going up there to smooth things over?" he inquired.

"Yes." I didn't want to utter another word. Sherman was the last person I'd want to know what was really going on. Not that I actually knew!

SEVEN

I slowly went up the stairs to the second floor. What was I going to say to her? She's acting irrationally and maybe she'll lash out on me, too. However, I didn't have a choice. I had to confront Prunella and explain to her that Axel loves her and would never lock her up again. I walked down the hall and came to her closed door. Just as I reached a hand out to knock, the door across the hall flew open.

"Alex, you scared me!"

"Sorry, Ruth Ann. I thought maybe Prunella was leaving her room."

"So you know she's in there?" I asked, curiously.

"Yes. I'm sure you already know that she and Axel were having quite the fight before you and Inga got back from your house. I didn't know what to do so I snuck away and came up here. After I went in my room, I heard Prunella stomping down the hall muttering some seriously nasty words."

"Hmm," I said, trying to think fast. "Axel told me she was angry, but there really was no reason for her to be so upset."

"I know. I was in the library when she accused Axel and me of leaving her out of his business. I barely have a foot in the door at his company, Ruth Ann."

"I know, Alex. I feel like some of this is my fault. I'm the one who convinced you to work for Axel, in fact, I'm the one who called and forced all of you to fly down to Jamaica and help save John!"

"You didn't *force* anyone, Ruth Ann. Prunella would do anything for you."

"Yes, the old Prunella would, but this new, peculiar Prunella wouldn't."

"You think that now. She'll get back to her normal self. She's strong and intelligent. I'm sure she's not feeling like herself right now. That's all."

"Hope so," I replied, trying to keep him encouraged, but truly feeling doubtful. "Well, here goes. I've got to go in and see what's in that pretty little head of hers."

"Good luck. If you need me, I'm right across the hall," Alex said, and disappeared into his bedroom.

Once the door shut, I stared at both closed doors. I had a strange thought... if didn't know better, I would say young Alex had a crush on young Prunella, and that would cause Axel to get jealous! Maybe that's not such a bad plan after all. It could push Axel right back into Prunella's arms. That's if she wants him back.

"Come in," Prunella called out from inside, after I knocked on the door.

I grabbed the handle and pushed the door slowly open. "It's just me, Ruth Ann," I said, sticking only my head in.

"Hi, Ruth Ann!" Prunella cheerily called out, sitting on the couch near the door. "I'm just resting before Inga calls me for our late, really late, lunch."

I forgot about lunch! I left Inga in the kitchen to prepare it alone after I promised I would help her. "Maybe we should go down and see if Inga needs any help."

"Why would *I* do that?" Prunella said, snobbishly. "It is her job."

I wanted to reprimanded her for her arrogant response, but thought it would just set her off, again. "We could go down and find out if lunch is ready then."

"I am starved!" she answered, throwing the afghan off her

lap.

"Good," I said, knowing she always said that, but never ate enough to keep a bird alive. "Let's go."

"In a minute, Ruth Ann," she said, patting the cushion next to hers. "Sit down for a minute, please."

Bummer! I had a feeling I wasn't getting out of here without discussing her fight with Axel. I did as she asked and sat next to her. "What's up, Prunella?"

"I had a blow up with Axel before you arrived." She glared at me and added, "What took you and Inga so long? I told you I wanted you here with me!"

"We were only a few minutes behind you, Prunella. Why are you so worried about where I am?"

"I'm not *worried*, Ruth Ann," she said, snottily. "I thought I made it perfectly clear you were to stay here with me until Doc Albert calls with the test results. Is it so much to ask?"

"Whoa, Prunella," I said, becoming irate, but refraining as much as I could. "You've got to calm down. I'm always here for you, but this behavior has to stop!"

She tilted her head like a puppy and asked, "What behavior?"

I never said I was a patient person! I couldn't take it anymore so I came clean with her. "You've been so moody lately. One minute you're cheery and sweet, and the next you snap at anyone around you. I know things have been crazy since you've moved here, and you haven't had a moment without someone getting kidnapped or murdered, but the rest of us aren't behaving the way you are." I watched her horrified expression and quickly tried to mend my words. "I'm sorry, Prunella. The last thing I want to do is make you upset, but if there's something wrong, please tell me!"

Prunella's mouth hung wide open in shock, but after I spat out a meek apology, she said, "I, I didn't know I was behaving so badly, Ruth Ann. I know I've been a little tired and had this upset stomach, but you're making me out to be a monster!"

"No, I'm not, Prunella. You're not a monster, just very moody." I wanted to kick myself for my lack of tactfulness, but it was too late. "You know me. I get right to the point, Prunella. Please tell me what's going on with you."

"Nothing, Ruth Ann, but thanks for pointing out how horribly I've been treating everyone. I'll be sure to watch my words," she said with sarcasm and bitterness. I wish I could've let her open up on her own, but it was too late now. Prunella stood up and walked out into the hallway. I wasn't sure if she wanted me to follow or not when she stuck her head in and said, "Are you coming?"

I nodded and followed her into the hall and watched as she knocked on Alex's door. He opened it up right away and smiled innocently, "Prunella, Ruth Ann. Are you going downstairs to get something to eat? I'm hungry."

"Yes, Alex," Prunella replied kindly, back to her normal self. "Ruth Ann wants to go into the kitchen and see if Inga's made some lunch for us. You want to join us?"

"Definitely."

We walked down the hall in silence. Right before the staircase, Prunella grabbed Alex's arm and intertwined her own arm. He proudly took it and the two of them walked side-by-side down the stairs with me trailing them. It was an awkward moment as we descended. Especially when I noticed Axel standing at the bottom of the stairs intently watching.

"Prunella, there you are," he said, trying to keep his composure even though I knew he was fuming inside. Watching his wife on the arm of a young, good-looking man couldn't have made him feel good.

"You knew I went upstairs to rest, Axel," she answered, tersely. "Now it's time to eat something. Have you eaten lunch yet?"

"Nope. I was waiting for you," he said sweetly, glancing my way with pleading eyes. "Let's go into the kitchen."

"I don't understand why we have to eat in there," Prunella snapped. "We should be lunching in the dining room!"

"It's just easier for Inga, Prunella," I said. "It's a late lunch, and I'm sure she's trying to start preparing for dinner, too."

"Oh, well, that's okay then," she said, marching around the stairs into the short hall that passed the dining room and stopped at a closed door. She pushed it open and we entered the massive kitchen. Inga was standing over the sink, cleaning up dishes when she spotted us.

"Finally," she cried out. "It's almost dinnertime. I wondered if any of you (eyeing me specifically) were going to come in to eat a sandwich."

"Sorry, Inga," I said quickly before Prunella snapped her head off. "It's my fault we're so late to eat. I see you put out cold cuts."

"Yes. Just grab a plate and make yourself a sandwich. I put out some chips and sliced fruit."

"Thanks, Inga," Alex said, not waiting for the rest of us to join him at the island. "I'm starving!"

We walked over and watched Alex pile on ham, roast beef and cheddar cheese slices onto four slices of bread. He made two sandwiches, grabbed a pile of chips, but no fruit. He laughed and said, "I don't have any more room on my plate. I'll come back for the fruit."

"You are hungry," I said, hoping his light-hearted mood would diffuse the tension in the room.

Inga relaxed and smiled. "I like to see people eat healthy amounts." She turned to Prunella and said, "You need to keep your strength up, Ms. Prunella. I would love to see you eat two sandwiches!"

Uh-oh, I didn't see that comment going over well with Prunella, and it didn't. "What's that supposed to mean, Inga? I have plenty of strength. Just because I don't stuff my mouth full of food doesn't mean I'm weak. I mean, look at Ruth Ann…she eats and eats tons of sweets. I think she has sugar flowing through her veins!"

"Prunella!" Axel shouted, angrily. "That was rude and uncalled for."

I was so taken back by her comment, I couldn't speak. How

dare she make that comment about what I eat. I wasn't overweight, well maybe just a little, but nothing that called for her to say I eat too much. She knows I have a daughter who owns a bakery and I test a lot of Lynne's new creations. Before I could respond, Prunella ran out of the kitchen and up the stairs. At least that's where we thought she ran. By the time Axel, Alex, Inga, and I made it into the foyer, she had disappeared.

Sherman appeared out of thin air asking what was going on in the kitchen. He could hear the yelling. "Where'd you come from?" I asked him.

"I was in the dining room with Isabella and Carlos. They were talking while helping me clean the silver."

"Oh," I replied, forgetting all about Isabella and Carlos who just entered the foyer and joined us.

"Why's everybody in here?" Carlos asked, looking around.

"Yeah," Isabella agreed, curiously. "Is something wrong?" She noticed that one person from the household was missing. "Where's Prunella?"

"I think she went to her room. We were just going to check," I said.

"Something's wrong," Isabella said. "What happened?"

"Her mood happened," Inga replied, bitterly. "Can't you tell us what's wrong with her?"

I was wondering when the others would ask Isabella for help, hoping it would be after the blood tests came back from Doc Albert. "Leave Isabella alone," I answered for her. "She wasn't even in the kitchen."

"But if she's as psychic as she claims, then she would be able to know what happened!" Sherman spat.

"I'm not psychic!" Isabella bellowed.

"Then what are you?" Sherman demanded. "You knew everything down in Jamaica when you were working with your grandmother."

"Leave her alone!" I ordered Sherman. I turned to Isabella, Carlos, and Axel and asked, "Can we talk in the library for a moment?"

"Hey, you can't leave us out!" Sherman argued.

"Yeah, no more secrets," Inga said, agreeing with Sherman.

Axel ignored their comments and led Isabella, Carlos and me into the library. Before Sherman and Inga could follow, he slammed the door shut leaving Alex out there with them, too. "Should I have let Alex in?" I asked, knowing it wasn't nice of me to exclude him.

"No. He's new to this family and I don't want to scare him off more than he already is. He's been quite an asset to me with work so I don't want to lose him," Axel said, worried.

"Hey, that's great," I said, hoping we could make this a positive conversation, but I doubted it.

Axel turned to Carlos and Isabella and motioned them over to his desk. He went behind his desk and pulled his chair out to sit. "Ruth Ann, why don't you come around by me and Carlos and Isabella can sit in the chairs?"

"Fine," I said, thinking I was going to be the only one standing, but Axel pulled his chair out for me to sit. I had a sudden feeling of uneasiness being so close to him, again. "Thank you."

"Now. We need to figure this out. I'm getting more and more frustrated with Prunella's behavior. Isabella," Axel looked directly at her. "Can you tell us any reason why my wife is acting so erratically?"

Isabella moved anxiously in her seat. "I really don't want to say anything until her doctor calls with her blood test results."

"Wait a minute!" I exclaimed. "You know that *something* could've happened to her down in your country, don't you?"

"Well, there's a lot of things that might explain her behavior, Ruth Ann. Not all of them involve my homeland."

"What else is there?" I asked, curiously. "We just got back two days ago and she wasn't acting this way before she flew to Jamaica."

"Well, that does narrow things down a bit. Please, can't we wait until tomorrow to have this discussion?"

We weren't able to answer Isabella's question when the library doors flew open and Inga, Sherman and Alex poured in. "She's gone!" they said at once.

"Gone?" I screamed. "Gone where?"

"We don't know," Inga said, out of breath. "After you shut us out of this conversation, we went up to make sure she was alright. Alex knocked on her door, and she didn't answer so I pounded on it really hard, but still no answer." Inga took a deep breath and continued, "I tried to open the door, but it wouldn't budge."

"She must've locked it, but why?" I asked, confused.

"At first, we thought she locked herself in her room and didn't want to answer us. But then Sherman whipped out a set of keys and unlocked the door." Inga looked to Axel and added, "We're sorry to invade the privacy of your bedroom, but we were really concerned for Ms. Prunella."

"It' okay, Inga. Go on," Axel said.

"Well, Sherman unlocked the door and when we opened it we couldn't find her."

"Did you notice anything missing or out of place?" Axel asked, worried.

"Yes!" Alex replied. "The room was in chaos. The couch cushions were thrown on the floor, and the bed was torn apart."

Inga angrily interrupted Alex and said, "And the drawers of your dressers in the closet were opened and emptied on the floor."

Sherman added, "And don't forget the bathroom."

"What about my bathroom?" Axel asked, whipping his head back and forth from Inga to Sherman.

Sherman looked at Alex and Inga wondering who would answer him. "I'll say it," Inga snapped. "I'm not afraid of bad luck!"

"What are you talking about?" I demanded, tired of the bickering between them.

"The mirror was broken and shattered on the floor. They emptied the medicine cabinet and the cabinet drawers," Inga said, eyeing the horror on Isabella's face.

"The mirror was shattered?" Poor Isabella asked, terrified. "That's not good."

Our attention turned to her. "Explain, please?" Axel insisted. "I know breaking a mirror has superstitious connotations, but they're not real, are they?"

"Well, where we come from it isn't good luck."

"That's nonsense," I bellowed. "Whoever destroyed the bedroom, probably threw something at the mirror out of frustration."

"Frustration over what?" Carlos asked, intrigued at the direction I was hinting.

"From not finding whatever it was they wanted," I replied.

"I'm so confused," Sherman said, exasperated. "My niece was acting oddly, I'll give you that, but now you're saying she was kidnapped and whoever took her was looking for something up in Mr. Eklund's bedroom, but didn't find it?"

"Yes," I said. "Maybe there's more to Prunella's mood swings than any of us knew!"

"You may have a point, Ruth Ann," Axel said, suddenly looking more relaxed than any of us. "I was so worried about her, and it might not be because of some strange voodoo or medical virus she picked up down at Carlos' resort."

"Hey," Carlos interjected. "She was barely at my resort. It would be more likely she got bit while running around the jungle or in Felix's place."

"It doesn't matter!" I cried out. "Prunella is missing and we don't know why!"

"Martika's dead, and so are Joseph and Meme," Carlos muttered. "It can't be because of them."

"True, but who else was involved with us in Jamaica?" Inga inquired. "I don't think anyone else besides Carlos and Isabella, but they're with us."

"Are you accusing Carlos or me?" Isabella asked, crossly.

"Of course not," I answered for Inga. "You both have been as confused about Prunella's behavior as we have."

"Yes, you're right, Ruth Ann. I'm the one who told you that if your doctor's blood test comes back good, then we'd have to look at other avenues."

"What's that supposed to mean?" Inga and Sherman demanded. "You haven't told us that!"

"I was waiting until after the blood test results. But now, this has gone in a different direction. Maybe Prunella was acting so moody because she knew someone was trying to get to her."

"For what?" Alex asked, innocently.

"Really? You have to ask," Inga spat out at him. "The bloody necklace!"

"Not that again," he said, miserably. "I haven't been here that long and even I'm sick of that piece of jewelry."

"And I thought the gem was wiped clean of any curses," Inga said, confused.

"Well..." I started to say when the library doors flew open and John and Judy Lynch entered. I was happy to see John, but Judy, not so much.

"What are you two doing here?" Axel said loudly from behind his desk.

"I got a text about fifteen minutes ago and we rushed up here. What's this about Prunella missing?"

I looked around the library and wondered who texted John. I knew he would have to be contacted, eventually, but I was hoping we could've figured more out before he showed up.

"John," I said, going over to him quickly. "Who contacted you? We just discovered her missing."

"I did," Alex confessed. "The minute Inga, Sherman, and I found her room ransacked, I texted John. He responded only with...'on our way'."

"You neglected to mention this to us, Alex," Axel said, bitterly.

"Hold on," John said, gently moving me to the side and walking toward the desk. "Alex did the *correct* thing by contacting me. There's been a crime here, and before the scene has been too

65

touched by all of you, Judy and I can get up there and investigate."

"He's right," I said. "We have no idea what's going on besides her mood swings."

"Doc explained those to me, Ruth Ann. Why didn't you fill me in?" John requested, offended.

"I was going to right after we got her results back from Albert."

"Oh, I guess you assumed there was something medically wrong with her, correct?"

We all nodded. "Anything else strange happen?" Judy asked, directing her question to Axel and not me.

"No. My wife's been extremely up and down with her behavior and…" Axel stopped, looked in my direction and I nodded for him to keep going. "And, she's had these very terrifying red eyes that come and go."

"Excuse me?" Judy asked, almost mockingly. "Did you say Prunella's eyes have changed color?"

"Not permanently, Judy," I said. "Just when she's upset. Her eyes flash to a red color that is very disturbing."

"Oh, did Doc say what could be causing it?" she inquired.

"He didn't have any answers once I told him it wasn't her seeing red, it was us looking at her eyes that see the red flashes."

"That's odd," John said. "Anything else?"

"No," Axel answered. "Except for the fact she's missing now and our bedroom has been ransacked."

"By whom?" Judy asked.

"We have no idea, Judy!" I snapped. "That's for you to figure out, isn't it?"

"Easy, Ruth Ann," John said. "We just got here and are trying to figure it out as quickly as possible so we can find Prunella, safe and unharmed."

"What could be happening now?" I exclaimed. "I can't take any more."

EIGHT

John and Judy left us in the library with explicit instructions not to leave. We wanted to go up with them, but John told us, "No."

"So, did you tell us everything you found up there?" Axel asked Alex, Inga, and Sherman.

Alex didn't answer. Inga and Sherman said they told us everything. I thought that Alex's silence was a bit odd, and I planned on confronting him as soon as I could get him alone.

"Hey," Inga jumped out of the chair and said. "Ruth Ann was about to tell us something about the curse Meme broke on your necklace."

"Yeah, Ruth Ann, why don't you fill us in before John and Judy return," Axel suggested. "What about Blue Ice's curse? Was it actually broken or not?"

Offended, Isabella replied before I could. "My grandmother broke that curse! Are you suggesting that what she did for a living was a joke?"

"No, of course not, Isabella. I was just wondering if something went wrong, that's all," Axel quickly said.

"Oh, sorry. I'm still grieving and feel the need to defend her."

"Nobody's putting anybody down!" Inga bellowed. "Can we just get back to Ruth Ann's explanation?"

Thanks Inga! Here goes, "Right before Meme passed away, she told me something very interesting about the gem." I stopped, held up my hand to fend off any interruptions and said, "Before anyone speaks, yes, the curse was broken. However, there was a little more to it."

"What?" Sherman demanded, anxiously.

"I'm telling you, if you mind not interrupting!" I waited only a second before continuing. "Here it is in a nutshell. Meme told me once the gem was free of the curse, whoever had initial possession could determine the future of the gem."

"Huh?" Inga and Sherman muttered in unison, baffled.

"Oh, I get it. It's like a blank slate. If someone wants to use the necklace for evil it's back to being cursed again, but if the person chooses to use the necklace for good, then it's safe, right?" Axel asked me.

"That's how I understood it." I looked to Isabella for confirmation.

"Yes, but why are you worrying about that? Prunella would never use the gem in a corrupt way. She wanted the curse to be broken in the first place."

"Yes, unless she was *forced* to," Alex added.

"But who would do that?" I asked, confused. "From what I've been told, Prunella was acting oddly back in Jamaica before we left for home. Maybe someone down there influenced her?"

"She was with us the whole time, Ruth Ann," Axel said.

"Or it could be one of us," Sherman said, turning his attention to Isabella and Carlos.

Isabella looked like she was going to cry, but Carlos was furious. I mean really, really angry. "Are you alright, Carlos? Nobody here believes you or Isabella would do anything to Prunella." I turned to Sherman and ordered, "Tell them that's not what you meant!"

"Why should I?" he declared. "We don't really know them very well."

"They saved our lives down there, Sherman!" I cried out. "Why would Isabella and Carlos help us as much as they did just to turn on us?"

"Maybe they can answer that question," Axel intervened, and

suggested.

"Not you, too!" I said to Axel.

"I'm not saying Isabella or Carlos are guilty of anything, but they do know a lot more about this voodoo stuff than we do."

"Nobody said any of this has to do with witchcraft or voodoo, Axel!" I bellowed, trying to get everyone to cooperate. "Maybe somebody totally new has entered our lives and wants our Blue Ice."

"Really?" Inga asked, almost laughing. "I know it's worth a lot of money, but this is getting ridiculous. Not everybody in the world wants to possess your famous necklace!"

She's got a point. The last few months seemed like years. I know it's valuable, but the whole world really doesn't want my necklace, or do they? I thought about Inga's comment and fought internally about it. On one hand, two families had battled over the piece for over a hundred years. And then, the recent escapade in Jamaica threw in a new twist. We realized the necklace was cursed, and broke the curse, but that doesn't mean nobody wants it anymore. There were still crooked lawyers in Sweden, hopefully still in prison, and Isabella's and Carlos' families down in Jamaica. Plus, that doesn't rule out any local criminals after it, too!

"Ruth Ann?" Inga called out my name. "What are you thinking about so intently?"

"Inga's wrong."

"Huh?" she demanded. "What do you mean I'm wrong?"

Axel interrupted and it was as if he read my mind. "I think I know what Ruth Ann's thoughts are." He watched as I smiled and nodded for him to continue. "Just because the curse is broken, it doesn't mean somebody else isn't after the necklace."

"You've got to be kidding!" Inga said, but quickly amended her rude comment. "Sorry about that, Mr. Eklund. I just don't think that's possible."

"Why not?" I asked. "I mean look at all the people who've come into our lives in just that last couple months. Lawyers, jewelers, crooks, healers," I stopped and looked at Isabella to see if it was an offensive term for her grandmother. She smiled and let me go on. "That's just to name a few. Look at Martika. She had no reason to want the gem except to make her rich."

"I think Martika wanted revenge against Isabella and her grandmother for their long tumultuous past," Carlos suggested. "She was very jealous of the relationship between Isabella, her mother, and her grandmother."

"Don't forget our father, Carlos," Isabella added. "Martika and I shared the same father, to remind you all. He cheated on my mother with Martika's mother, and he died because of it."

"Your mother put a curse on him, correct?" Axel asked.

"Yes, but he basically killed himself," she answered. "Martika never got over that and when she came to live with us, she was welcomed in at first, but then she became cruel and took off. I was very close to her years ago, but she didn't ever care for me."

"She wanted a mother and grandmother," I said.

"She had mine, but she never thought she fit in so she went off the deep end, and in the end, she was killed because of it."

"True," I said.

"Why are we talking about all of this?" Sherman exclaimed. "Martika is dead, so she can't be the one messing with Prunella."

"You're right," Axel said. "But, we're trying to show that anyone could enter our lives just to get a hold of Blue Ice."

"Not just anyone this time," I said. "Prunella started acting strangely right before we flew home from Jamaica. So, it tells me it must have something to do with that period of time."

"That was only three days ago!" Inga said. "One of us must've seen Prunella talking with someone we don't know."

"You all are forgetting one thing," Axel said. "It really could be a medical reason and maybe my wife kind of lost it and tore up our room herself."

"No way!" I said, coming to Prunella's defense. "She would've talked to me if she felt so desperate."

"Even if it was a medical reason, Prunella wouldn't have just disappeared," Alex said. "I think somebody took her!"

"So, do I," John said, reappearing suddenly.

"You do?" Inga asked, shocked.

"Yes. That room was a disaster, and I'm pretty sure they were searching for something."

"Why up in our bedroom?" Axel asked, baffled. "It's not like we keep anything really valuable up there."

"Are you so sure about that, Eklund?' John asked.

"What's that supposed to mean, Chief?"

John turned to Sherman, Inga, and Alex. "Did any of you happen to notice the pictures that were hanging on the walls?"

"What do you mean *were* hanging?" Axel inquired, interestedly.

"They were pulled off their hooks and dropped on the ground. To me, it shows someone was looking for a safe up there."

"We don't have a safe in our bedroom," Axel said.

"Yes, you do," Judy replied for John, suddenly stepping inside the library.

Everyone turned toward Judy and John glared at her. "Judy, I told you to get a crew up here to dust and go over every inch of the room."

"I did. They're on their way, John."

"Oh, well, we don't want to say too much," he said.

"It's my house!" Axel bellowed. "What do you mean you don't want to say too much?"

"It's now a police investigation, Eklund. Your wife is missing. Try and focus on that."

"But we need to find out why she's missing, John," I said, worried. "Let's get back to this safe you uncovered in their bedroom."

"Yeah, I'd like to hear about that too," Axel agreed. "I didn't have a safe built into the wall."

"Prunella did," John said.

"If she hired someone to open a hole up in our wall you'd think I would know about it?" Axel exclaimed.

"Why don't I take you up there and show you," John said. "But you have to leave everything the way it is and not touch a thing."

"Let's go," Axel said, hurrying over to the library entrance.

"Hey, can I go?" I asked, curious about the safe, too.

"Sure, Ruth Ann," John said. "But the same rules apply to you, too."

"If Ruth Ann can go, why can't we all go?" Inga demanded.

"No." John turned and whispered something into Judy's ear and then he waved to Axel and I to follow.

I turned to look back as John was shutting the library doors. Judy must've been told to stay and keep an eye on the others. I got a quick glance of Alex's eyes looking down at an object he was holding in his hand. I wanted to yell out and demand to know what it was, but then everyone would hear. I knew something was up with him, and once I came back downstairs I had to find out what he was hiding.

"Okay," John said on the top step just before heading down the second-floor hall. "No touching, taking, hiding anything in the bedroom, got it?"

"Yes," Axel and I said together.

John ripped down the police tape Judy had carefully put up and walked inside Axel and Prunella's bedroom. I had been in there many times, but this time I was shocked. They weren't kidding when they said the room was torn apart. The once spotless, formal bedroom was now in chaos. There wasn't one piece of furniture or accessory in its original place. "Wow," I cried out. "It's completely trashed!" How did they get in here?

"I know," Axel said, stunned. He walked over a couch cushion and tramped through the clothing sprawled on the carpeted floor. "I don't even recognize our room."

"It's just stuff, Eklund," John said, nonchalantly. "I'm sure you'll have this place back to normal once we've released the room."

"Yes, probably, but now I want you to show me this safe."

John walked toward the king-size bed which was previously adorned with a rich emerald green and gold comforter. He stepped on the balled-up comforter next to the bed and went to the far-right corner of the room. "Here," he said, pointing to a hole in the wall.

"What was here?" Axel asked, trying to imagine the room before it was ransacked.

I stepped over clothes, books, broken vases and made my way to the wall. I noticed a medium sized painting not far from the wall, lying on the floor. I bent over to pick it up when John yelled, "Ruth Ann! Don't touch that!"

"Oh, I'm sorry. I was just trying to see what the picture was. It's upside down."

"It could have finger prints. It obviously is the most important piece we have. They had to take it off the wall to get inside the safe."

Axel ignored our conversation and moved closer to see inside the safe. "How did she do this?" he asked, perplexed. "I should've been told about this safe. Why didn't she trust me?"

"Eklund, are you sure you don't remember her or you putting this in?" John asked, implying Axel might've forgotten constructing a safe in the wall.

Axel glared at him and snapped, "No. I think I'd remember."

"Well, she had to have it installed, Eklund. Have you left town recently?" he asked.

Axel slowly turned to look at John. "Are you serious? You know we were all recently out of town, Chief."

"I meant," he said, correcting his question, "Without her."

"Oh, no. I haven't gone back to Stockholm yet. I need to get over there, but we haven't exactly had the time with all the upheaval around here!"

"He's got a point, John," I said, agreeing with Axel. "I have a thought. What if she had it installed while both of you were down in Jamaica?"

"Hey, that's a great deduction, Ruth Ann," John said, smiling at me.

Axel wasn't so happy. "Why would she need to do that? We had no notice when Ruth Ann called panicking about your kidnapping."

"He's got a good point, too, Ruth Ann," John admitted.

"Maybe it was planned all along, Axel," I suggested. "But, why and what she was putting in there? I mean our necklace is in a secure safe in your library."

John suddenly looked frantic. "Hold on a minute. When was the last time either of you saw the necklace in the safe downstairs?"

"Just a couple days ago," I answered. "Right when we got home from the airport, Prunella, Axel and I went straight into the library and locked it up."

"So, neither of you have looked today?"

Axel and I shook our heads. John turned and ran out of the room. "You don't think it's missing, *again*, do you Ruth Ann? I mean this is getting ridiculous."

"I, I don't know anymore. I'm so confused right now I don't know what to think or do!"

We stood silent for a moment when Axel said we should head back down. I was about to follow him toward the bedroom door when a strange sensation rushed through my body. It was a chilling surge of doom starting in my legs rushing up to my head. "Whoa," I said unsteadily, trying to remain standing. Axel hurried to my side to catch me before I fell to the ground.

"Ruth Ann! Are you alright?"

"I think so," I mumbled, shakily. "I had this weird rush of cold air run through my entire body."

"Maybe you'd better sit down," he suggested, grabbing my elbow and leading me to the stripped bed.

"I'm okay, Axel," I said. "I don't feel sick or anything. It was a strange feeling, almost like I had…"

"Don't say it, Ruth Ann," he said, terrified. "Please don't say what I think you're about to say!"

I nodded, "I have to say it. It happened to me when I was

down in Jamaica when John was kidnapped."

"I know, I just didn't want you to say it!"

"You think it has to do with Prunella?" I asked, wondering myself. "John says she's been kidnapped, and maybe I'm feeling her fear."

"No, Ruth Ann. I'm sure it's just adrenaline rushing through your body. You're on autopilot with everything that's happened the last couple months."

"Yeah, you're probably right. Let's go down to the library and see if John got into the safe."

"He can't!" Axel bellowed. "Prunella, you and I are the only ones who know the combination, unless…"

"No, Axel. I didn't tell John the combination."

"Oh, okay. I guess it would be alright for him to know, but nobody else."

He helped me stand, and I was a little uneasy with his gentle grasp, but I shook it off to him helping a middle-aged woman. "I never got a good look in the safe," I said, stopping before we left. "I'm going to take a peek before we go down."

"It was empty, Ruth Ann," he said.

"I feel the need to check it for some reason, Axel," I said, turning around and walking up to the safe. I had to stand on my tippy-toes to see inside, and when I did I was awarded with a significant clue.

NINE

"What did you grab, Ruth Ann?" Axel asked, extremely curious. "I could've sworn it was totally empty."

"Nope," I said, holding a tiny ring in the palm of my hand.

"Whose ring, is it?" he asked, perplexed. "I don't think it's Prunella's."

I had a flashback to one of the huts down at the resort John and I were supposed to stay at in Jamaica. It couldn't be...

"Ruth Ann, you don't look so well. Do you need to sit down?" Axel asked, concerned I was going to faint.

"I'm fine. It's just that...I know this ring, but I have to be wrong."

"What? C'mon, Ruth Ann. Spill it!"

I stared at the cheaply made silver ring with a blue-green stone set in the middle. It was probably nothing of value, monetarily that is. "I have to be mistaken, but I'd swear this is Martika's ring, the one her father gave her. I found it when Carlos and I were looking through the huts trying to find clues to where she was hiding John."

Axel stood silent. "Huh?"

"But, I swear it was left behind when Meme broke the curse. We had that ring with all our other stuff. Meme and Isabella kept their items, and there's no way Martika would have it because..."

"She's dead."

"Yes, she was killed and we saw it happen. There's no way she could've survived, is there?"

"No. Impossible."

"But why would Prunella have this ring hidden in the safe?" I asked, confused.

"I don't know, Ruth Ann. Only Prunella can answer your question."

"No, Axel. There's someone else who knows more than they're sharing."

"Who?" he asked, interestedly.

"Alex."

"Alex? What on earth are you talking about, Ruth Ann?"

"I noticed his odd facial expression when the three of them ran into the library telling us Prunella was missing."

"That doesn't mean anything."

"Well, maybe this will change your mind, Axel. As we left to come up here, I looked back and noticed Alex holding something in his hand and staring down at it. He caught my eye and I knew it was something important."

"Why would he have kept it secret? He had plenty of time to tell us that he found something important up here when we were all in the library with John and Judy."

"I don't know why, Axel. We need to have a private conversation with him, don't you think?"

"Yes, private. Just Alex, you and me."

"Let's go, but how can we get him alone?" I asked.

"We'll figure it out when we get down there," he said, grabbing my hand and pulling me out of his bedroom, down the hall, and he continued to hold on to it tightly as we descended the stairs.

John was at the bottom of the stairs in the grand foyer. His expression as Axel and I held hands was priceless. He just stared, open-mouthed as Axel marched up to him. "Well, did you manage to break into my safe?"

"Uh, I, no, Eklund," John mumbled, trying to regain composure.

I pulled my hand out of Axel's grip and walked past them

both into the library and right to Alex. I whispered, "I need to speak with you."

Alex looked surprised, but nodded. "You want to talk to me alone, don't you?"

I nodded, but Inga noticed. "Hey, what's going on? John won't tell us anything. He practically pulled Mr. Eklund's safe from the wall trying to get in there."

"He was looking for Prunella's necklace, wasn't he?" Sherman inquired.

"You mean our necklace, Sherman!" I corrected.

"Uh, yes."

Isabella and Carlos stood off to the side of the group trying to remain inconspicuous. I saw them out of the corner of my eye, watching me intently. "Would you all mind if Axel, Alex and I had a moment alone?"

I figured the best way to get to the bottom of things was to do it openly. I knew I would get complaints. Especially from John, who was clueless as to what my objective was. "Please. It'll only be a couple of minutes. Why don't you go into the kitchen and grab a bite to eat? I'm sure Inga and Sherman can get something together to snack on."

"Me?" Sherman inquired, angrily. "That's Inga's job!" Inga knew not to argue with me. She was acutely aware that I would tell her everything eventually so she grabbed Sherman by the arm and told him to come with her. "Everyone else, follow me into the kitchen."

John was livid. He demanded to know what I was up to, but I stood my ground and said he would know shortly. He huffed, but agreed to give us ten minutes. If we weren't in the kitchen after ten minutes, he would come in here and break the door down if he had to. "C'mon, Judy," he said, pulling her out of the library. "I am hungry. It's been a longtime since I've eaten."

"That's because we've been working, John," Judy said, sarcastically.

Once we were alone, Axel made the first move. He told Alex

to sit down in one of the two chairs in front of his desk. I sat in the other, and Axel sat behind his desk in a position of authority. I was a tad intimidated by Axel so I waited for him to speak first.

"I think you know why we want to talk with you?" Axel asked Alex.

He looked pleadingly at me. I shook my head and quietly said, "Just start talking."

"I know you think I have an idea of where Prunella is, but I don't."

"What were you holding in your hand when John, Ruth Ann, and I left the library?"

"What are you talking about?" he asked, even though he knew he was busted.

"I saw you and you know I did," I told him. "I don't know what's going on with you, but we need to find Prunella. If you know anything just tell us."

Alex apparently was fighting with himself. Finally, after a minute or so, he said, "Fine. I did find something upstairs, but I don't know what it means."

"Why don't you put it on the desk so Ruth Ann and I can look at it."

He leaned back and put his hand in his front pants pocket. He pulled out a tiny object and laid it on the desk. I couldn't see it clearly so I leaned in and Axel did the same thing from the other side of his desk.

"What is it?" Axel asked.

"I think it's a ring," I said, looking closer at the object. "But, wait a minute…"

"It can't be," Axel said, reaching out to grab the item. He held it in his hand and checked it out. "It looks the same, Ruth Ann."

"Same as what?" Alex asked, uneasily.

"Can I see it, please?" I asked, pulling out the other ring I had stuffed inside my own pants pocket.

Axel reached over the desk and placed the ring in my hand. I closed my fist and sat back in the chair. I was terrified to open my fist and see if it was the same ring that I held in my other hand.

"It's okay, Ruth Ann," Axel said, watching my hesitance. "Just compare the two."

"Two what?" Alex demanded. "I have no idea what's going on!"

"You will in a minute," Axel said, waiting for me.

"Here goes," I said, opening both hands at the same time and staring down at the identical rings. "How can this be?"

"They look alike," Alex said, confused. "What are these?"

"One of them was Martika's," I confessed. "At least I thought it was."

"Why are there two of them?" Alex asked.

"That's the million-dollar question," Axel said. "What do you think, Ruth Ann?"

"I know one way to find out," I said. "We need Isabella and Carlos to get in here. They knew Martika best."

Axel asked poor, confused Alex to go get Carlos and Isabella. "What if the others ask me why?"

"Just tell them to give us a few more minutes and then we'll explain. Don't say anything about the rings, please," Axel said.

Alex hurried out of the library. Axel came around his desk and sat on the arm of my chair staring down at the duplicate rings. "Do you think they're fake? Or that maybe somebody was sending Prunella evil messages with these things."

"What message?" I asked him. "Martika is dead!"

"I, I don't know, Ruth Ann. But I have a feeling Carlos or Isabella can fill in the missing pieces for us."

We sat in silence waiting for the three of them to return. Finally, after a long couple minutes, Alex walked in with Carlos and Isabella. "Okay, they're here," Alex said, walking over to the desk with the two behind him.

"What's going on?" Isabella asked, anxiously. "Alex wouldn't tell us."

"It's okay, Isabella," I said, trying to calm her nerves.

"There's something we need to show you, and you have to tell us the truth, please."

"Of course, Ruth Ann," Carlos answered. "You're past the doubts with us I hope."

"Yes, we are," I said, smiling at him. "But when you see what I'm about to show you…well, you might be shocked."

"I'm getting worried, Ruth Ann," Isabella said. "Just show us!"

I held out my hand and on the palm, lay two identical, cheap rings. "Here," I said, waiting their reactions.

"Oh, no!" Isabella cried out, loudly.

"How did you get those?" Carlos asked, not as shocked or upset as Isabella.

Axel and I noticed Carlos' reaction. Axel jumped on it immediately. "Carlos, you don't seem surprised seeing the *two* rings."

"I am surprised, but it's not like you haven't seen Martika's ring before," he said quickly and smugly.

"I've seen *one* ring of Martika's, Carlos," I said, hoping he would get the subtle hint. "But there are two of them here."

"Why are there two?" Axel demanded. "Isabella, did you know there was more than one?"

"Me, no!" she cried, profusely. "I only know about the ring Martika got from her father." She looked innocently at Carlos and said, "Did you know she had two?"

"Um, she didn't have two," he replied. "Martika's father gave her just the one."

"Enough!" Axel shouted, angrily. "Enough of the cat and mouse game, Carlos. Tell us about the other ring, now!"

Just as Carlos started to sweat a little, the library door flew open and John stomped in with the rest of the group behind him. "You've had plenty of time. Now tell us why the private meeting, and don't leave anything out!"

Axel turned an ugly shade of red. He was about to get Carlos to confess about the extra ring when John interrupted. Now I wonder when we'll hear the truth, because I doubt Axel wants everyone to know about our discovery or should I say discoveries!

Axel took control of the conversation before Alex, Carlos or Isabella blew it. "We were trying to get information out of these two about what they know. Ruth Ann and I think those two have pertinent information regarding my wife's disappearance."

"And do they?" John demanded, looking at Carlos and Isabella.

"Us?" she asked, innocently. "I don't have any idea where Prunella is."

"And you?" John asked Carlos.

"No."

"Then what's with the secrecy in here? I know there's more to this than what you're telling me."

"John," I said. "We didn't want Isabella or Carlos to feel uncomfortable talking about things that could've happened down in Jamaica that may have affected Prunella's behavior."

"What did you learn then, Eklund?" John asked Axel. "I better hear something good or I'll know you're lying to my face!"

"Fine, John," Axel said. "Isabella admitted there could've been a residual effect from breaking the curse on the gem."

"What?" I bawled, confused. I turned to Isabella and tried to plead with my eyes for her to go along.

"Ah, yes, I just said that her behavior is similar to that of a person who has been manipulated by a witch doctor."

"Manipulated how?" he demanded.

"She was acting erratically. Her mood swings were growing worse and whenever she got angry, her eyes turned red. It's not something I haven't heard of before. My grandmother taught me to see the signs, but I've never experienced it firsthand. However, my grandmother and my mother had."

"Your father," I said quietly, remembering what happened to the man after he cheated on Isabella's mother with Martika's mother. He was cursed, and instead of living out the curse, he went into the jungle and let himself get bitten, stung and killed by wild animals.

Suddenly, I realized what Isabella told us was actually the truth. This is what she was going to tell me after the blood test came back. I knew she wanted to divulge the information to me, but if it was a medical condition making Prunella act so oddly, then she wouldn't have had to say another word about it. However, that hasn't happened, even though we still didn't have the results yet. I wish I could call Doc Albert and get a rush on those tests!

John listened attentively. Once Isabella finished explaining, he appeared to calm down. "Oh, why the secrecy? It's not like I wouldn't understand!"

"It's not something most people want to hear, Chief," Isabella said, truthfully. "It means she could be in very serious danger."

"Wait, what?" Axel hollered. "Are you telling me my wife is in danger? But from what or whom?"

Isabella replied, "I don't know that, Mr. Eklund. That's what we need to figure out."

I had that funny feeling rising inside me again. What does the second ring have to do with any of this? I strongly felt the ring and what Isabella confessed were intertwined somehow. Now we need to figure out who, what, why, and where!

"That's not good enough, Isabella" Axel hollered, immediately apologizing to Isabella. "I'm not mad at you. I'm very frustrated, and now my wife is missing!"

"We know, Axel," I said, trying to calm him down. "This could all be a big mistake, too."

"How so?" John asked.

"Maybe Prunella was so angry when she went upstairs she went berserk. She tore apart her room, and emptied whatever she put in the safe and took off."

"Highly unlikely, Ruth Ann," John said. "I don't think even Prunella could've caused that much damage so quickly. Plus, we don't know what was in that safe." John suddenly whipped his head around and faced Axel. "Hey, open that safe of yours!"

Axel stood like a statue glaring at John. I quickly added,

"What John meant to say was could you please check your safe in here to make sure our necklace is still there?"

"Ah, yes, Eklund. Sorry. I almost forgot about the necklace with all these secrets floating around."

Axel walked behind his desk and faced the numerous book shelves. He pulled off one of our family's paintings and gently placed it on his desk. With his back to us, he opened the safe and waved us over. Alex, John, Carlos, and Isabella, and I gathered as close as we could to see him open the safe door. "Here goes," he said with a noticeably trembling hand.

"It's okay, Axel," I said. "I'm sure it's in there."

"Hurry up!" John demanded.

"I can't look," Axel said, backing away and leaving enough room for one of us to step up and look.

"I'll do it," I said, pushing John aside before he took the first look.

"Fine. It's your necklace anyway," he said, moving to my right.

I grabbed the unlocked handle and pulled the metal door open. I had to stand on my tippy toes to see inside. I closed my eyes wishing for the necklace to be inside. "Here goes," I said, opening my eyes and staring inside the safe.

"C'mon, Ruth Ann. I'm going to have a stroke!" Axel cried out from behind me.

"Um," was all I could muster.

"What...what's inside?" Alex asked, just as anxiously as John.

"I can't believe it!" I muttered in shock. "It's gone."

"Gone!" Axel yelled, finding his nerve again. He gently took a hold of my shoulders and moved me into John. I was in such shock I didn't care that I was being moved around like a chess piece.

"Eklund, is Ruth Ann, right?" John asked, trying to put me on his other side so he could look, too."

I walked over to Axel's desk and plopped down on his chair.

How and when did Prunella take the necklace? Or I should ask, was it even Prunella who took the necklace out of the safe? That's a silly question, I said bickering with myself. Prunella, Axel and I are the only ones who can get inside the library safe.

"Maybe she took it out of this safe and put it upstairs in her new safe," Isabella suggested, trying to help.

"Possible, but it doesn't really matter, does it?" John questioned. "It's gone. The upstairs safe was completely empty, right?" he looked at Alex and me. "You two were up there at separate times. Alex, you were up there with Inga and Sherman. Who saw inside the safe first?"

"Um," Alex mumbled. "I did."

"Was it empty like I've been told?"

"Yes."

"Okay." John turned to me and asked, "I know you were with me up there with Eklund, but I ran out of the room before you two. You didn't find anything else up there, did you?"

"You mean in the safe?" I asked him while sitting at Axel's desk, exasperated.

He didn't reply, but stood with his hands on his hips in a defensive manner. Axel was next to him staring inside the empty safe mumbling incoherent words. "Well?" John finally demanded.

"Empty," I replied, lying to him for the time being. I needed to find out more about the two rings before I revealed the information to John. I noticed the smirk on Alex's face. He was happy I went along with him.

"Now what, Chief?" Carlos asked.

John grabbed Axel's arm and pulled him over to the desk leaving Carlos, Isabella and Alex standing in front of the safe. "What was in the safe?" he demanded.

"Nothing. It was a special safe just for the necklace. That's why it's so small. I keep other valuables and papers in a separate safe."

"You have *another* safe?" John asked, surprised.

Everyone stopped and stared at Axel. "Of course, I do. I run a business, and have other valuables."

"I didn't know you had another safe," I said, a bit put off.

"The big question is, did Prunella know about the safe?" John inquired.

"Of course, she did."

"Don't you think it should be checked?" John asked, sarcastically.

"I will when I'm alone."

"Why?" I asked, hurt he had to hide it even from me.

"It's not in here. I would like a little privacy with some things of mine."

"Fine," John said. "Why don't we stay in here while you go check out your little safe."

Axel glared daggers at John, but left the library. While he was gone, I stood and went and checked out the safe again. It really was empty. I didn't know what to think. Did Prunella willingly take the necklace out of there or did someone force her to do it? That's what I needed to know.

"You okay, Ruth Ann?" Isabella asked. "You're quieter than normal."

I actually laughed at her comment. John held his hand over his mouth because he also laughed. "That helped, Isabella. Thanks," I said, feeling my neck muscles relax from laughing briefly.

"I want answers," I said.

"We all do, Ruth Ann," Carlos said.

"Speaking of answers, Carlos," I began. "You were about to tell us something before John stormed in."

"But Axel is gone. I should wait until he comes back."

"What are you mumbling about?" John asked, crabbily. "Are you hiding something from me?"

"No," I replied. "Can't I talk to Carlos without you suspecting anything deceitful?"

"Unlikely you weren't plotting or discussing something I don't know about. Wouldn't it be easier to just tell me about it now?"

"Nothing's going on right now, John," I replied, tersely.

John walked away from Isabella, Alex, Carlos and me. I shook my head signaling we'd discuss the rings later. Just as we were getting antsy, the library doors flew open and Inga and Sherman stomped in. "Well, is anyone going to come and eat? Judy won't shut up, and I'm about to stuff a turkey leg in her mouth to keep her quiet!"

"Ease up, Inga," John said. "She's still eating? I thought she ate when I was in there."

"She did, but she hasn't stopped. That woman has quite the appetite!"

"So," Inga started to say to Isabella, Carlos, Alex and me. "Are you four going to eat and..." she looked around the library and added, "Where's Mr. Eklund? I thought he was in here with you."

"He was," John answered for us. "He went to look for something. He'll be right back."

Sherman got curious. "Look for what?"

"None of your business, that's what!" John snapped. He turned to the rest of us and told us to go and grab some food.

"I've got turkey sitting out so you can make sandwiches. I have enough leftover turkey for us to eat for a month!"

"You'll think of creative ways to cook it, Inga," I said cheerily, walking past her and into the foyer. Isabella followed me, and we walked into the kitchen together.

"I am a bit hungry," I said. "I don't know how with Prunella missing!"

"And your necklace," Isabella added.

"Yes, that too. I can't believe this is happening again. I really thought we wouldn't have any more trouble after Meme broke the curse."

"She broke it, but someone got to it first and cursed it again."

"You really think so?" I asked, discouraged. "Do you think it was Prunella?"

"I don't know, Ruth Ann. I'm concerned that the duplicate ring has something to do with all of this, but what?"

"We need Carlos to tell us, Isabella. I think he knows about the two rings."

"But why wouldn't he have told me?"

"It must be something so bad he didn't want to worry or scare you," I said.

"Great, just great."

We walked over to the island and made ourselves a turkey on rye sandwich. Isabella and I just sat down at the massive wooden kitchen table when everyone, but Axel, appeared. "Axel hasn't come back to the library yet?" I inquired.

John looked worried. "No. He better not have done something stupid like he's done time and time before."

"Wait a minute!" I hollered with a mouthful of food. "You think he took off to find Prunella, don't you?"

"Would you be surprised?" Judy asked, just getting filled in from John on what's been happening. "That man can't be trusted. He never listens to us."

Judy did have a point. I didn't think much of him having another safe, but it didn't cross my mind that he was lying and took off to who knows where. "Maybe the safe's upstairs or in the basement," I said. "Or, or maybe he had to go through the tunnels to the guesthouse."

"I forgot about that place," John spat out.

"What guesthouse?" Carlos asked, curiously. "Why haven't Isabella and I been staying in that place?"

"This house has plenty of space for you and Isabella," I answered. "The guesthouse is pretty far from the main house."

"You mentioned tunnels?" he inquired, interestedly.

"There's a tunnel in the basement that'll take you directly to the guesthouse without having to walk outside."

"Wow, this place is full of surprises," Carlos said. "Why don't we have a look at this tunnel. I'm curious to see one."

"*See one*?" I asked. "You've never been in a tunnel?"

"Nope. There's not a lot of room below ground where we're from," Carlos said, smiling at Isabella. "The sea's underneath us!"

"I'm sure there's room for tunnels, Carlos," John said, mockingly. "What about caves? I'm sure they're plenty of them."

"Well, yes," Carlos answered. "Is a cave like a tunnel?"

"Kind of," I said. "Can we get back to my missing cousin and necklace, please?"

"As far as I can tell Prunella must've been in contact with someone who wanted the necklace. They either drugged or put some type of spell on her and forced her to open the safe and hand it over. They probably grabbed her in her bedroom and tore apart the room before leaving."

"Impossible!" Alex bellowed. "If they were upstairs and then came down and emptied the safe, one of us would've seen or heard them."

"He's got a point, John," I said. "There's quite a few people staying in the house. I doubt Prunella went willingly."

"You don't know for sure," he said. "Maybe she knew her kidnapper and went voluntarily."

"No way!" Alex replied in a hostile tone. "Prunella would never hurt or betray her family!"

"Whoa, calm down Alex," John said, curious at his passionate response since he wasn't her husband.

"We're cops, people," Judy chimed in. "We have to look at all angles, and if there's even a remote possibility Prunella went willingly...we have to pursue that, too."

I glared at her. I knew she was right, but the way she said it irritated me. She was so smug and cold I wanted to slap her. Anyone who truly knew Prunella would know she would never willingly steal our necklace and run off with someone else. It was at that exact moment that I remembered a couple times Prunella went rogue and did kind of, sort of, betray me. It was only last week in fact when she convinced me to wear the necklace on my trip with John to Jamaica. I didn't want to bring it out of the country, but they practically forced it around my neck and told me to enjoy it. However, I came to find out they had a plan with Martika to have the necklace stolen while we were at our resort so they could claim an enormous payout from insurance. Plus, Martika was doubling the amount with her own money so she could possess the gem.

"You're awfully quiet, Ruth Ann," Judy said, sensing my disdain toward her. "You do understand what I said, don't you?"

John stopped me as I jumped out of my chair and lunged at his detective. "Easy, Ruth Ann," he said, embracing me tightly.

"Don't talk to me like I'm a child, Judy!" I said, trying to unclench John's grip on me. "Prunella isn't that kind of person and you should know that by now, too."

"What I know, Ruth Ann," she said, emphasizing my name, "is that Prunella has a habit of being sneaky and she has betrayed you before. Don't get mad at me because I'm the bearer of bad news!"

John released me once he felt my limbs go limp. Judy was right. I really didn't know what was going on this time and a part of me, deep inside, knew Prunella could've done something she shouldn't have. But why? That's the question I need answered. And where did Axel run off to? Could he have been a part of this and left to meet up with his wife, leaving us behind wondering what was going on? I couldn't let my thoughts get the better of me, and said, "Judy, you're a cop and you have to do your job. I get that, but realize I may not agree with you."

"There, see, Judy," John said, smiling meekly. "Ruth Ann can be reasonable."

Reasonable? Why did he say that to her? "I'm always reasonable, John. I would argue with you, but until I know what's really going on, I can't. So, Judy and you need to find them, and fast."

"That's the plan. It just happened, so we need to stay on their trail." John turned and walked over to Judy who was standing next to the island picking on a turkey wing. "Is the team here yet? And if they are, I assume they're upstairs investigating the room?"

Judy nodded with her mouth full. John snapped and told her to get up there and supervise them. He wanted to know the minute they were finished or find something, anything. He turned back to us and said, "So, while they're upstairs, I want to go over what's happened in detail since we got back from Jamaica."

"We've already told you that, John," Inga said.

"All I know is that before Prunella left the island, she was acting strangely. Axel noticed it, but what about the rest of you?"

I admitted I didn't notice it until yesterday. Alex, Inga and Sherman said they noticed it yesterday, too. Carlos and Isabella were silent until John directly asked them. "Well?"

"I, we, I noticed she was a bit bossy," Carlos said. "But, she also begged and pleaded with me to come and stay here for a while."

"Me, too," Isabella said. "She invited us to stay as long as we wanted. It's hard to criticize her after that."

"You didn't answer my question," John said. "I want you both to tell me how she was acting, and if you noticed any change in her demeanor before she left your island?"

Carlos nodded, and Isabella quietly said, "Yes. I did notice her strange behavior."

"Go on," he said to Isabella. "I need details, please."

Isabella glanced my way to see what she should do. We were in the process of trying to figure that out ourselves, and Isabella didn't want to be the one to bring up the two rings and possible connection to Martika. I shook my head and said, "John, leave the poor girl alone. She told you she noticed Prunella acting oddly. That's what you asked. I'm sure she's regretting coming here now."

"Are you?" he asked Isabella, curiously.

"Um, no, sir. I just don't know anything."

"Oh, well, we can discuss it later," he said, noticing Judy walking into the kitchen and motioning with her hand for John to come out to the foyer.

"Phew," Isabella said. "I sure don't want to be responsible for getting us into trouble."

"Trouble?" Sherman bellowed. "What trouble, *Ruth Ann*?"

"Oops," Isabella muttered. "Sorry, Ruth Ann."

"Sherman, I might as well include you and Inga."

"Wait, what?" Inga cried out. "What's going on?" she dropped the dishes she was washing loudly in the sink and stomped over to the kitchen table where we were standing. "Spill it, Ruth Ann! I knew it would be a disadvantage coming into the kitchen to make food while you all talked in the library."

"We didn't have a choice, at first, Inga. Let me explain what's going on before John and Judy come back," I said, sitting down and waiting for everyone else to sit.

"Hurry up," Alex said, nervously. "Your chief pops in and out constantly and usually catches us when we're talking secretively."

Sherman barked, "Then why do we keep secrets from the Chief?"

"Because if we told him *everything* we know the police would take over and leave us out," I answered. "Look at everything we've been through the last couple months. We solved almost all of it."

"Maybe if we stayed out of the way there wouldn't have been so many murders or kidnappings," Sherman declared. "I'm for letting the Chief in on whatever it is you're about to tell us."

"Sherman!" Inga hollered. "Sit down and shut your mouth. You may not want to hear whatever it is they're about to divulge, but I do!"

"Okay, okay," Carlos interjected. "Nobody has to fight. We're all on the same side, remember?"

"Yeah, Sherman," Inga said. "Just sit and keep your mouth shut."

Sherman smacked his lips together and let out a little huff. "Can we get through this before John or Judy comes back?" I asked, looking around the group. "Good." I filled Inga and Sherman in on what Alex and I found upstairs in the safe.

"I remember that ring!" Inga exclaimed. "It was a tarnished, silver ring that Meme needed to break the curse, right?"

"Yes, exactly," Isabella replied.

"But you just said there were *two* of them," Sherman stated, confused. "Who's the owner of the second ring?"

Alex, Isabella and I looked to Carlos. "That's where we left off in the library," I said. "Carlos, will you please explain?"

"Carlos?" Inga called out. "What does he have to do with it?"

"I was her husband, remember? I also knew her for many years."

"So, did I," Isabella reminded us. "We *were* friends and half-sisters."

"We know that," Inga snapped. "But why are you looking at Carlos for an explanation of the second ring? Does he know who it belonged to?"

"That's what we want him to explain, Inga," I said, trying to get us moving. "Hurry, Carlos."

"It's complicated," he said, turning to face Isabella who was sitting next to him at the kitchen table. "I thought for sure you knew."

"Knew what, Carlos?" she asked, confused. "You're scaring me!"

"Well, if it's true, then we *all* should be scared."

"C'mon!" Sherman barked.

"Okay, okay. Isabella and I were raised in the same village as Martika. Nobody knew Martika was Isabella's father's illegitimate daughter until she was much older. Isabella idolized her as a young girl, but I knew the real Martika. She was furious that Isabella's mother cursed their father and forced him into killing himself. Martika's real mother died when she was pretty young. The one thing nobody knew was until Martika's mother died, she and her mother lived just on the outskirts of our village. Isabella's father knew about Martika and gave them whatever money he could sneak to them. But, he didn't regret having the affair with her mother because he didn't end it when he found out she was

93

pregnant with Martika."

"No!" Isabella cried. "I was told my father only cheated on my mother the one time and got the woman pregnant."

"Sorry, that's incorrect, Isabella. Your father didn't end his relationship. He continued to visit Martika and her mother for quite some time, and…"

"And what?" Isabella cried with tears streaming down her young cheeks.

"And…he got her pregnant again."

"Martika had a full blood sister!" I exclaimed, loudly.

"Shhh, Ruth Ann," Alex said, quickly. "Let's get through this story. We don't want them to come running in here."

"Yes. Martika had a full blood sister unlike you, Isabella. You and Martika were only half-sisters."

"I know, but why didn't I know about her and where did she go when Martika came to live with us?"

"Their mom died after she gave birth to Cassandra."

"Cassandra," Isabella whispered. "That name sounds familiar."

"She's younger than you, and you're younger than Martika," Carlos said. "I think she's a few years younger than you."

"So, she would be in her mid-twenties now?" I asked.

"About," Carlos answered.

"I don't believe it," Isabella said. "I'm almost positive I've heard that name before."

"Well, you probably did," Carlos said. "She ran around the village just like you and Martika did years ago."

I watched as Isabella closed her eyes, imagining her youth in the tiny Jamaican village. Suddenly, she popped open her eyes so wide I thought they'd burst out of their sockets. "Oh! I remember a little girl named Cassandra. She was younger than me, and very, very cute. She used to follow my friends and me trying to play with us, but we wouldn't let her. We would laugh at her because she wore such ratty clothes, and her hair never looked clean. In fact, she never looked clean."

"But I thought you said she was cute," Inga said.

"She was. But she was very poor. I mean, we were all fairly poor, but she was literally dirt poor."

"That's horrible," I said, distressingly. "Were you cruel to her?"

"I, I don't think I personally was, but I know we wouldn't let her hang out with us. She was much younger, and you know kids. They can be kind of mean at times."

"It's nothing you can change, Isabella," Carlos said. "We had to survive back then. It's not like here where people have jobs and make a lot money. That wasn't our kind of life. We had to grow and pick our own food. On a good day, we'd get a little piece of meat to serve to our family at dinnertime. Life was different down there."

"I know, but if I knew she was my…"

"Half-sister," I finished for her. "It would have been different, but you can't change what happened, Isabella. What we need to know from Carlos is Cassandra the other owner of one of those rings?"

"Yes. Their father gave each of them a cheap, identical ring. He left them behind, and went into the jungle and died."

"But, wait," Isabella said, frantically. "Only Martika showed up at our door saying she had no parents anymore. What happened to Cassandra?"

"According to Martika," Carlos began, but I interrupted. "Hold on, Carlos. Were Martika and Cassandra close? I mean, Martika wouldn't have left her behind if they were."

"No, not according to what Martika confided in me. Martika admitted that she couldn't stand the 'little brat'."

"She called her younger sister a brat?" I asked, surprised.

"Martika knew from a very young age that they were different. They didn't have a typical family with a mother and father. She knew this man would come around every so often and spend a little time with them, and then he disappeared for long periods of time."

"That's because he had a wife and daughter," Isabella added, bitterly.

"Yes. Martika overheard her parents arguing a lot. She knew when she was a little bit older that her father had another family and that her mother wanted him to leave them, but he refused. She accused him of abandoning his 'bastard children' and that he didn't care for them at all."

"Wow," I mumbled. "Go on, sorry."

"Martika grew bitter and started acting out as a child. That's why she wanted to run around with older kids. She thought she was too mature for kids her own age."

"But what about Cassandra?" Isabella inquired.

"She tried to get close to her sister, but it didn't happen. Finally, when the affair was revealed, her father told them he was never going to come back to see them. He said he had to make things right with his wife."

"But his wife cursed him instead," Isabella said, finishing Carlos' story.

"Yes."

"But how did Martika come to stay at my home with my mother and grandmother?" Isabella asked, confused.

"She lied. She told you her father made her come and live with you once he was dead, but she planned it herself. She abandoned her sister, who was still quite young, and knocked on your door. She wanted revenge against you, Isabella and your mother and grandmother."

"I, I don't believe this, Carlos. Why have you never told me this before?"

"Because I didn't want to hurt your feelings. I knew you looked up to Martika, and this makes her out to be a cold-hearted monster."

"She is!" Isabella yelled. "I hate her!"

"Hated," Carlos corrected her. "She's dead, remember. We saw her killed just a few short days ago."

"But what happened to Cassandra?" I asked, repeatedly. "Did

Martika ever go back for her?"

"Not that I know of. All I ever heard about her sister was that she lived alone in her mother's tiny shack of a house."

"But she was just a child!" I cried. "That's horrible."

"Yes, but why did she end up with one of the two rings?" Inga asked, bringing us back to our current dilemma.

"From what Martika told me, when their father knew he was never coming back, he brought them each a ring. He told them never to abandon one another and whenever they looked at the ring to think of him."

"That doesn't sound like a man who didn't love his daughters," Alex said. "I mean, why would he tell them that and hand them a ring?"

"It's all his fault," Isabella muttered. "If my father didn't cheat on my mother then none of this would've happened. Martika and Cassandra wouldn't exist!"

Sherman interrupted and asked the all-important question, again. "What happened to this Cassandra woman? She apparently is the key to what's happening now."

"Sure sounds like it," I said.

We sat around the kitchen table confused, having no idea where to begin when John came back in the kitchen *and* the back door flew open, startling all of us. "Eklund!" John yelled, angrily. "Where have you been?"

Axel brushed light snow off his upper body and casually walked over to our group sitting around the table. "I told you where I was going, Chief."

"You left the house and we couldn't locate you. We thought you took off like you've done so many times before."

Axel glared at John and came and stood behind my chair. I had that uneasy feeling again, but I shook it off and turned my chair so I could see him when I asked him, "Where did you go, Axel? I thought your safe was somewhere in this huge estate."

"Nope. With everything that's happened to us, I have another safe outside of this house. I don't know when or who will break in anymore."

"Where is it?" John demanded.

"I don't believe I need to disclose that information to you, Chief."

"If you want to remain a free man you do!"

"John," Axel said, smirking. "I doubt you could arrest me for not telling you where I keep my personal belongings. Let it go."

"Enough!" Inga bellowed, exasperated with the petty fighting. "Did you find anything we should know about? You know, like the necklace?"

"No."

"So, it really is missing, again," I said, discouraged. "But this time we haven't a clue where it is."

"And where Ms. Prunella is," Inga added.

John, irritated with us, stormed out of the kitchen to find his partner, Judy.

"Of course," I said quietly, worried. "But Axel doesn't know what we've just been discussing. You know, about Martika and her sister."

"Sister?" Axel exclaimed. "What sister?"

I spent the next couple minutes filling Axel in while Inga, Isabella, Carlos and Alex ate a little more. Once we were through filling Axel in, he walked over to the island and without speaking, made a sandwich and started eating it, mumbling incoherent words to himself.

"What are you blabbering about?" Carlos surprisingly asked. "If you have something to say, say it so we all can hear."

"I'm not saying anything you need to hear. Can't I be ticked off? I can't believe there's another relative after that cursed necklace!"

"Don't say that!" Isabella cried, defending her grandmother's honor. "You know she broke it before she died."

"Sorry, I didn't mean cursed as in hexed, but as in a bloody nightmare of a piece we can't seem to keep from disaster."

"He's right," Sherman chimed in. "I'm too old for this

nonsense."

"You don't need to be involved in this nonsense, Sherman," John barked, entering the kitchen again, but still without Judy. "It's a police investigation now, and you *all* need to let Judy and me do our job."

"Sorry, John," I said. "I can't do that. I'm going to do whatever I can to find Prunella and our necklace."

"Ruth Ann, there's a point where you have to let me handle this. You've been through so much the last couple months that your body is going to shut down."

"I feel great!" I hollered.

"Then why have you been nauseous lately?" he asked, immediately regretting the words after he said them.

"Excuse me?" I bellowed, wondering if Doc Albert's examining room was bugged.

He stumbled on his words and finally admitted, "Doc slipped and told me you haven't been feeling well. He immediately regretted saying it to me, but it was while I was being checked out at the hospital."

"That's confidential information!" I yelled.

"He was concerned about you, Ruth Ann. He didn't tell me anything specific except that you've had a little stomach distress."

"Probably something I ate."

"Then Prunella must've eaten the same thing," John added. "Yes, before you blow another gasket, he told me Prunella has been experiencing the same thing. He was anxious to get the blood test results and see if you and Prunella caught a bug down in Jamaica."

"We didn't catch anything! I feel much better. It was probably exhaustion and now that I've rested and eaten, I'm better."

"You just said what I've been trying to tell you. You're exhausted, and running around trying to find Prunella won't help. I am perfectly capable of getting Prunella home safely."

"And the necklace," Alex muttered, hesitantly.

"Yes, the necklace too," John said.

Judy walked back in and told John that the team left and that they didn't recover anything new. He turned his attention toward us while standing near the kitchen island. "So, who wants to confess?"

"Confess what?" Sherman asked, innocently.

"I know you've had powwows. One of you needs to step up and tell me what you've uncovered so far."

Axel, Alex, Sherman, Inga, Carlos, Isabella and I looked from one to the other. No one wanted to man up and tell John and Judy about the rings. I felt horribly guilty, but something inside me was screaming to keep it quiet for now. "We haven't uncovered anything, John," I finally said. "We're just as baffled as you."

Both John and Judy stood unmoving, staring at each one of us. "I don't believe you!" John declared, angrily. "Every time I enter the room you all shut up, and Eklund disappearing for such a long time makes me even more suspicious."

"We had nothing to do with Axel going to his safe, John," I reminded him. "He chose to keep the whereabouts of the safe from all of us, remember?"

"Well, I know you're keeping something from me. It'll save us a lot of time and maybe a few lives if you, or any of you, open up to me!"

I spotted Isabella's nervousness from across the island. It was time to shut this down and get John and his obnoxious detective out of here for a little while. I didn't want John looking at Isabella or we'd blow it. She wasn't used to lying, not that it was a good thing, but it was necessary for the moment. "John," I said loudly, so he would look my way and not at Isabella. "Why don't you stop wasting your time with us and go out and find my cousin?"

He debated my request. Even if we were holding back information, which we were, he still had a job to do. "I do need to get back to the station to get the results back from the pieces we took out of the bedroom." John turned to Axel and quickly added, "I hope you don't mind that we took a few pieces from your bedroom? We needed to test for fingerprints and there was some blood on them."

Axel and I caught what John said at the end of his statement. "Did you say you found blood?" Axel asked as his face turned white with fear.

"Yes, not much though. We need to see if we can trace it."

"But, what if Prunella's been hurt?" I asked, worried. "Will you be able to figure out if it was her blood or someone else's?"

"It helps that she just gave Doc some of her blood earlier. He'll have that information for me," John said.

"That's a relief," Axel said, but saw my expression of horror. "I meant about them being able to tell if it was her blood or not."

"Oh, yeah, you're right," I said.

"Remember what the Chief just said," Judy chimed in. "It was very little blood. Just a few smears on a couple pictures and a few items that were broken on the floor."

"Whoever took her probably cut their hands on the broken glass from the vases and picture frames," Inga said, trying to keep us calm. "I'm sure it wasn't Ms. Prunella's"

"Hope not," Alex muttered, quietly.

John became agitated and anxious. "I don't have time for this! I'm going to go back into town and check with Doc about Prunella's blood test and the items we took out of here." He turned to Judy and ordered, "You stay here and watch them."

"Me?" she asked, unhappy with his request. "Why do they need a babysitter? I'm a cop, not a babysitter!"

John pulled her to the side, near the door to the grand foyer and whispered a few words to her. I could see the anger rising in her, but John was being tough and didn't let her off the hook. I liked to see John give it to her, but this time it would only hurt us with her here, so I quickly tried to amend the situation.

"John, we don't need to be watched. Judy should go back to town and help you."

John flatly refused and turned to leave, but not before warning us to stay here at Axel's estate. "Where would we go?" I asked him, naively.

John laughed so loud it startled us. "Give me a break, Ruth Ann. I know you well enough to know that the second my truck leaves the driveway, you'll be out the door racing after whoever took Prunella."

"We have no idea where she went, John," I said, truthfully. "But don't expect us to sit here and not do anything about it."

"Oh, I know," he said. "But whatever you do or plot to do, wait until you hear from me. I don't need or want to hear about another kidnapping or find Judy unconscious in the front hall closet!"

"Hey, that's unfair," she cried out. "That only happened once, and it was a long time ago."

John ignored Judy and made us all promise to not hurt, tie-up, gag, chase away or lock-up his detective while he was gone. Judy looked like she wanted to sock him for the implication, but she shook it off and laughed. "Like they would or could do that, John."

"Don't let them fool you, Judy. They've had a lot of practice lately."

Judy scowled and looked at us innocently standing around the island. "I won't be fooled again, John."

"Good, see you all soon."

John took off and left us in the capable hands of his detective, Judy Lynch. What a joke! I wasn't going to let her get in our way at any cost. All we had to do was keep her occupied so we could figure out exactly who took Prunella. So far, the strongest lead was Martika's sister, Cassandra. We needed to get Carlos to tell us more about this mysterious woman.

TEN

We were left alone in the kitchen with Judy. She walked over to the island and helped herself to a plate of food. Of course, Inga let her because she was a bit intimidated by Judy's gun! "I'm starving," she said, her mouth stuffed with turkey. "This job never lets me have a normal schedule."

"That's because you're a cop, Judy. Crime doesn't work a 9-5 schedule," I said, sarcastically.

"I'm aware of that, Ruth Ann," she said, irritated. "While I've got you all, why don't you tell me what each of you think happened to Prunella."

Isabella choked on a carrot, Carlos glared at her, Axel laughed, Alex started pacing nervously around the kitchen pretending to be looking at the knick-knacks on the walls and shelves, Sherman stood frozen with his hands on his hips, and Inga started packing away the food so Judy wouldn't eat it all. "We don't know," I declared, walking around the island to help Inga clean up. I didn't want her looking directly into my lying eyes.

"That's a joke, and you know it!" she laughed, frustrated with our lack of cooperation. "John's gone, so why don't you tell me what's up and maybe I can help."

"Excuse me," Sherman said, but then his voice got much louder. "None of this is a joke, ma'am. My niece is missing and somebody took her! It's not our job to find her this time. Why doesn't the Deer Creek Police Department solve a crime for once?"

"Whoa, Sherman," Judy said, surprised by his outburst. "Have a little respect for an officer."

"He's got a point," Axel interrupted, agreeing with Sherman. "It appears Ruth Ann has been the key person solving the crimes around here. However, I would stress, even to her, that the individuals we've been dealing with have become very violent and I would highly recommend that she backs off a little. I really don't want to see any further murders or kidnappings occur."

"Eklund," Judy bellowed. "It was *you* who started this whole mess in the first place! If you didn't try to kill your own wife and have that cursed, excuse me, bloody necklace sent to Deer Creek, then none of the murders and kidnappings would've occurred in the first place."

Axel quickly responded, "It wasn't me who sent the necklace to this town. It was Prunella and her lawyer. Yes, I wasn't thinking clearly back then, but I think I've proven myself since and I will go to any lengths to protect each and every one of you."

"Axel," I said, interrupting their argument. "Don't listen to her. She doesn't understand our relationship. I don't blame you anymore for what's happened, and you didn't try to kill your wife. Prunella was under a lot of stress back then so she thought it best to protect herself from you. But everything's changed now. You two are married, happily married, and right now all you want is to bring her back home, safely."

"Here, here," Sherman shouted. "Ruth Ann's right. We *all* want my niece brought home safely. So, what are we going to do about it?"

"That's what I asked in the beginning of this exhausting conversation!" Judy hollered. "Can we get back to my original question?" She waited for our response, but nobody budged. "Who knows anything about her disappearance, and the necklace that has once again gone missing?"

"We don't!" I said, exasperated. "Can't you leave us alone?"

"Well, I'll back off for now. Anyway, I've got to call into the station and see if John made it back, and if he found anything out."

Phew. We watched Judy storm out of the kitchen, leaving us alone to talk, finally. "Quick, we need to discuss what we're going to do next," I said. "Who knows when she'll return. She's such a pain!"

"I think you've made it abundantly clear how you feel about her, Ruth Ann," Axel said, smirking. "She's not smart enough to figure it out anyway. She may have the physical strength to fight off a criminal, but she doesn't have the intelligence needed to solve this case."

"I agree!" Inga hollered from the sink where she was frantically trying to clean the dishes. She eagerly wanted to get close enough to contribute to our conversation. "I think we need to finish hearing from your friend, Carlos."

All eyes returned to the young man from Jamaica. He was brutally aware that the information he was about to divulge would be critical in getting Prunella back. Carlos wasn't holding back from us, but I knew there had to be more to his story regarding his history with Cassandra. Maybe he did know where she ended up, and if she held a grudge against Martika or Isabella and her family. That's what we needed to find out, because my cousin's life was on the line.

"I told you what I know about Cassandra," he said, walking back to the long, wooden kitchen table, pulling out a chair and plopping down. "I thought I was coming here to relax and get to know everyone better. This has been the shortest vacation I've ever had!"

"It was supposed to be a fun trip for you and Isabella," I said, sadly. "But it didn't turn out that way, at least not yet. Let's get this solved so we can enjoy showing you both off in town. Nobody has even met you."

"I don't care about that," Carlos barked. "I should've stayed back at the resort."

"No, too many bad memories," Isabella chimed in. "It's good we came here with Ruth Ann and Prunella. I think it's beautiful up here, cold, but a nice change."

"So, let's get back to what happened to Cassandra," Axel said, turning his attention to Carlos. "You said you have no idea what happened to her, right?"

"Yes."

"So, the last you heard or saw of her was through Martika?"

"No, not exactly."

"Explain, in detail please," Axel asked.

"Martika told me the entire story after she forced me to marry her, years after it happened. She said she abandoned her sister and purposely moved in with Isabella, her mother and grandmother. She was out for revenge. Not really because of her father, but because of her circumstances. I think she did love the man, but when she found out he had another family, she went insane."

"Insane with jealousy," Isabella muttered.

"Yes, but I remember seeing her and her sister when I was young. They came into town often. Cassandra would follow Martika around, but Martika didn't want her to. She would have little temper tantrums in the middle of the village. It was odd, really. Cassandra and Martika were beauties. They could've changed their lives and became something other than *bastard* children."

"That's harsh, Carlos," I said.

"But, that's what they were called, Ruth Ann. I don't mean any disrespect. Martika and I were friends when we were young. I actually think I had a crush on her! But then I got to know her as she grew up and she changed. From a sweet and innocent little girl to a bitter, revengeful, b...!"

"Carlos!" I cried out.

"She was pretty," Isabella said quickly. "I envied her in the beginning. I thought I had a long-lost sister who could be my friend. Boy, was I wrong."

"Cassandra was just like her older sister. I saw her grow up, but didn't think much of it. Maybe she moved in with distant family of her mother's. I only remember seeing her living alone in that house just outside of the village. Martika claimed she never went back, but I think she lied."

"Why?" I asked, curiously.

"Because she wanted to wipe out the painful parts of her past and then kill off Isabella and her family, too!"

"She wanted us dead?" Isabella asked, horrified.

"Yes. I'm sorry to repeat that, but it's true. Martika thought she deserved so much more and she would do *anything* to get it."

"So, if Cassandra was like her older sister, you think she could've had the same agenda, don't you?" I asked Carlos.

"Yes. My guess is she became furious with her older sister and followed her life closely. Martika might've tried to kill Cassandra, but it failed."

"Do you think Martika believed she was dead?" Isabella asked, shocked. "I mean, if Martika thought she got rid of Cassandra, then there wouldn't be anyone left in her family that could stop her from ruining my family!"

"This is where it gets foggy," Carlos said. "Martika alluded to many things, but now that I'm looking back, I think she was crazy, delusional even."

"She had to be," Axel said. "Who would go to such lengths to get revenge?"

The minute the words left his mouth he knew what he said resembled his own life. "I know what you're thinking. I was horrible trying to get revenge on Prunella and even you, Ruth Ann. But, I'm different now. I woke up. Martika didn't. She was more disturbed than I was at my worst."

"True," I mumbled. "Go on, Carlos. What else do you know about those two sisters?"

"Well, memories keep flooding back as I'm telling you the story, but what I do know is Martika did have a plot against Isabella, her mother and her grandmother."

"Why didn't you tell me, Carlos? I thought we were close," Isabella inquired, pathetically. "I can't believe you'd go along with her."

"I didn't!" he burst out. "C'mon, I didn't think she was

actually serious when she told me she wanted you dead. I had my suspicions, but when I did a little poking around not too long ago, I couldn't find anything out about Martika's younger sister."

"What did you do?" Alex asked, curious. "Did you visit their old house and see if she was still there? Or if anyone knew where or if she moved?"

"Yes. After Martika blackmailed me into marrying her, I pretended to go along with her in the beginning. I wanted her to disclose as much information as she could, hoping I could get ammunition against her. I listened to her describe her past from her perspective. I knew I had been raised in the same village, but my upbringing was much different than theirs."

"You came from a wealthy family," Axel said.

"Well, my parents were considered privileged in the village."

"Why did you live in such a poor village if your family had money?" Inga questioned, perplexed *and* suspicious.

He saw the look in our eyes and quickly said, "I know what you're thinking. Yes, my parents did have a lot of influence there, but they didn't take advantage of anyone. My father became well-respected through hard work and a lot of luck."

"What did your father do?" I asked.

"He was kind of, what do you call here…a banker. Yes, he took care of the people in our village's money. Villagers trusted my father. He made most of them enough money to survive and keep food on their tables."

"What gave him the qualifications to be a financial advisor to these people?" Axel asked, clearly suspicious of Carlos' father's intentions.

"He went to school. He would take a bus to a school that was very far away. He got a degree in business," Carlos replied, defending his father. "He didn't rip people off if that's what you were implying."

"But he made a lot of money doing it, didn't he?" Axel asked. "So, he must've charged these people quite a fee to keep them 'just making ends meet'. Wouldn't you agree?"

"No, these people would have no money if someone didn't manage it. They were farmers, tradesmen and small business owners. Most of them were uneducated and took over from the generation before them. Times had changed and our village had to keep up with the new world."

"Can we move on, please?" I snapped. "What about Cassandra and Martika?"

Carlos appeared agitated and relieved when I put an end to Axel's incriminations about his father. "Yes. Martika and Cassandra were poor. Martika found out about my homosexuality and threatened to expose me to my parents if I didn't marry her. You have to understand, my parents wouldn't have understood and disinherited me. I needed to keep them happy and…"

"Rich!" Inga balled. "You didn't want to lose what your parents were going to share with you, right?"

"Well, yes. Does that make me a horrible person?"

"No, Carlos," Axel quickly answered. "But while you were trying to keep the peace, Martika and her hitmen killed people. So, you see it doesn't look good for you. You went along with her blackmailing to stay in your parent's will and innocent people died."

"That's not fair!" he cried. "I never meant anyone to get hurt. All I did was marry that woman and convince my parents to give me the money to buy that broken down resort."

"So that's how you bought the resort," I said.

"Yes," Carlos replied to me. "I didn't know her objective then. I found out as time went on."

"You mean about my necklace and how she would do anything to get it?" I asked.

"Yes. At first, I thought she was just a thief. But when she went to Deer Creek to plot the whole thing out with Axel and Prunella…well, then I knew she was dangerous and very, very serious."

Axel stirred uncomfortably. "Can we please skip the lecture about how Prunella and I made matters worse?" He looked directly at me and knew I wasn't past it yet, but it wasn't the right time to hash it out further.

"Yes," I answered.

"So, after she came back from visiting this little town of yours, she filled me in on the plan. She also admitted she had even gone to Stockholm first to find you. She hired those twin hitmen to protect her and go after you and John, Ruth Ann."

"So, she really was planning on killing John and me!"

Axel turned pale. "She was only supposed to steal the necklace out of your safe, Ruth Ann. I feel sick when I think of what could've…" he stopped and that's when I noticed everyone in the kitchen staring at the two of us. Axel looked like a lovesick puppy, and I hoped I didn't return his affectionate gaze.

"Let's move on, Carlos," I immediately suggested. "What else did you learn from Martika?"

"She told me her plan to steal the necklace from your villa. That's why you and John had the nicest villa in our resort, but there was no lock on the door. Martika told me to convince you both it was safe and no lock was necessary."

"John didn't go along with that plan, did he?" I asked.

"Nope. He was a man on a mission to get a lock for your door. I got him one, but what you didn't know was there were *three* keys. I gave John one, housekeeping had one, and…"

"Martika had the last one," I answered for Carlos.

"Yes. She was going to go into your room while you were down at the beach."

"But I wore the necklace the whole time and therefore she didn't find it in the villa."

"Yes. She was livid. She planned John's kidnapping by forcing you to believe John drowned when he was paddle boarding. He was actually forced off the board by her two goons and they placed an oxygen mask over his mouth and took him down the beach. That's why you never saw him come up from the water."

"Sick," I mumbled.

"She wanted you to believe he was dead."

"But she didn't count on Isabella's reaction to the necklace when she saw me and John in the restaurant, did she? Also, she never thought I would pursue Isabella and meet her grandmother, Meme."

"No. That infuriated her. She was just going to force you into giving up the necklace and then let John go. However, she was evil. She hated you now, and wanted you dead, too."

"Me?" I yelled.

"Yes. You messed up her plans. She had already given Axel and Prunella a large sum of money, and now she didn't have your necklace. She was out for revenge and she didn't care who she killed."

"Get back to Cassandra, please!" Isabella cried out. "We know most of this."

"Martika confided in me that she had taken care of her younger sister years ago. She thought she was dead, but Cassandra didn't die. I knew that, but I didn't tell Martika."

"Why?" Alex asked. "Oh, wait. She would go and kill her then, right?"

"Of course," Carlos said. "I only heard she was alive through people back in my village. They told me there was a mini Martika roaming around the village causing trouble. She would drink and flirt with married men. She was trouble, that's what I was told." He quickly added, "It was only rumors, of course."

"But Martika had no idea and you did?" I asked, confused.

"Yes, but that's because I had family back in the village, Martika had no one."

"So, did Cassandra ever come around the resort to see her sister?" I asked.

"I think so. I would see a young woman who looked just like Martika wander around the grounds every so often. I wasn't sure, but if she wasn't her sister, she was a dead look alike. Every time I tried to confront her, she ran off. I thought about going to Martika, but I didn't want her death on my hands."

"So, it's okay that other deaths were on your hands?" Axel snapped.

"NO! I told you I didn't know that she was going to kill people, not really. I thought she was just a big bully."

"Well, we know Cassandra was alive and was sneaking around the resort while we were chasing John and Martika all over the place," Axel said. "She probably caught wind of what was going on and once her sister was out of the picture, she went after the necklace."

"I guess it's a possibility," Carlos admitted, sounding beaten. "I handled everything so badly. If I could've stopped myself from falling for Joseph, maybe I would've had sense enough to turn Martika into the authorities."

"Joseph," I repeated. "He was in her pay until he fell for you, Carlos. He died protecting us, so he's forgiven."

"Yes, but my distraction with him caused you to doubt me, too."

"Just at first. You proved your loyalty over and over," I said, smiling at him. "Let that go, Carlos. We need to find out if Cassandra flew to Deer Creek."

Axel stood up and said he'd be right back. "You're going to make some calls and see if she did leave Jamaica to come here, aren't you?" Alex asked.

"Yep. Everyone stay here. I don't want miss nosy-pants coming back and find us plotting. If I run into her I can tell her I need to make a business call. Actually, it's not a lie!"

Axel rushed out of the kitchen and we remained sitting around the table. Inga finished the dishes, and put a pot of tea on the stove. A few minutes later the whistle blew, startling us. "I'm so jumpy," I said.

"I wonder if Cassandra really did come here to kidnap Prunella," Sherman said. "But, if she got the necklace, why take my great niece?"

"That's what we need to find out, Sherman," Carlos responded. "If she's here and anything like her sister, we should be very worried."

"Great, just great. Here we go again," I muttered, irritated and exhausted at the same time.

We sat in silence for several minutes sipping our tea and munching on the biscotti Inga set out on a plate in the middle of the table. Suddenly, the swinging door* from the butler's pantry flew open and Judy marched in.

"Did you have to force the door open so roughly, Judy?" Inga snapped. "We're all on edge here."

"S-o-r-r-y!" she replied, sourly. "The door was so light it didn't take much pressure to whip it open."

"What are you doing?" I asked her. "Did you speak with John?"

"Yes."

"What's he doing?" I asked, irritated with her lack of seriousness about our case.

"He's working on your case, Ruth Ann. What do you want me to tell you?"

"Let's see…how about what he is actually doing right now to find Prunella would be a good place to start," I said, with an attitude as strong as hers.

"That's police information, Ruth Ann. When we need to fill you in or ask you more questions, we will."

"Enough!" Axel bellowed, entering from the door that led to the foyer. "Leave Ruth Ann alone. She's worried sick about her cousin."

Judy gave Axel a nasty glare, but ignored his comment. She sauntered over to the table and reached over Isabella and snatched a biscotti from the plate. She stuffed the crunchy biscuit into her mouth and chomped loudly, irritating not only me, but everyone else in there. "Do you have any manners?" Axel asked, agitated.

"It's a hard piece of toast! What do you want me to do with it?" she barked.

Alex stood up from his chair and started pacing again. "Can we stop this? I'm sure we're just on edge with everything going on. I hate waiting. I don't have the patience for this."

"What are you so anxious about?" Axel asked Alex. Curious about his reaction.

He stopped his pacing near the massive double ovens and said, "Your wife is missing. I know I haven't known you long, but she's as sweet as they come. I can't imagine how scared she is right now."

Axel studied the young man for a moment before saying, "Prunella's a lot stronger than you think, Alex. I'm sure she knows we're doing everything possible to bring her back home."

"Yes, I'm just not good at waiting, that's all."

I watched as Axel kept a close eye on Alex. Was he jealous of Alex's feelings toward his wife while flirting with me? It's an odd question, but it was the first thing that entered my mind. I experienced a weird feeling of jealousy. What was going on? I didn't have those kinds of feelings for Axel, just John. It's always been John. Well, at least since I moved to Deer Creek.

"Can I ask if John said he's coming back soon?" I inquired of Judy.

"He said he was waiting for Doc Albert and then he'd drive back up the mountain."

"That wasn't so hard to tell us, was it?" Axel asked Judy.

"Oh, well, I didn't reveal any critical information regarding the case."

"It's Prunella's kidnapping!" Inga bellowed. "Stop calling it a *case*!"

"Sorry," she said, lowering her head and marching to the sink to grab a glass.

"What do you want, Judy?" I asked. "Inga just cleaned up the dishes."

"Geez, I just want a glass of water," she snapped. "Is that alright?" she asked, maddened.

Inga marched over to the sink, grabbed the tall glass from her and went to the refrigerator. She opened the door and grabbed a bottle of water and handed it to her. "I'm tired of dishes right now.

Here's a bottle of water."

Judy grabbed it and drank thirstily. "There. Now we wait for John to show up."

I looked to Axel and tilted my head. I wanted to know if he discovered anything about Cassandra's whereabouts. We must've had telepathy because he shook his head and tapped his wristwatch. I knew exactly what he meant. He had made his inquiries, but hasn't heard anything yet. He was probably waiting for a call when his cellphone rang a popular 70's disco song. I nearly jumped out of my chair, and poor Isabella screamed. "It's okay," Axel said, holding up his cellphone. "It's a song Prunella put on my phone so I would know it was…"

Suddenly, it dawned on most of us. I shouted, "Her!"

Carlos and Isabella looked confused. Inga, Alex, Judy and I understood immediately. Sherman, well, he tried to pretend he knew what it meant, but clearly, he didn't. Otherwise, he would've burst out yelling, "Answer it, quickly!"

Judy moved so quickly she nearly knocked over Alex as he stopped pacing near the table. "Hand it over!" she demanded.

"No!" Axel shouted and twisted his body so she couldn't grab it.

"Don't let the call drop," Alex bellowed. "Answer it!"

Axel pushed a button and shakily called out, "Prunella, is it you?"

We stood like mannequins around Axel trying to see his reaction, but he stayed motionless with the phone to his ear listening to the other end. "Hello? Hello?" he cried out. "Please, someone answer me!"

Seconds later, he lowered his arm. "What happened?" I begged. "Did you hear anyone on the other end?"

"No, Ruth Ann. There wasn't anyone on the other end."

"Or, maybe Prunella wanted to speak, but it was too dangerous. She might've been able to make the call just to let you know she was alive," Alex suggested. "It's good news, don't you think?"

"Yes, maybe," Axel said, deflated.

Judy pushed Sherman and Carlos to the side so she could get closer to Axel. "Tell me exactly what you heard."

"Nothing, Judy."

"Think, Eklund. Maybe there was a noise, bang, or even a breath of some sort."

Axel stood and closed his eyes. I could tell he was reliving the few seconds of the phone call. "Think, Eklund!" Judy insisted.

"I called out her name, and when there wasn't a response I listened to see if I could hear anything. I, I remember," Judy cut him off before he could finish and said, "What?"

"Let me think!" he shouted at close range. "I believe I could hear cars or trucks."

"From a highway or maybe a parking lot?" she urgently asked.

"It wasn't too loud, so I think she was calling from a car or maybe from a parking lot."

"She's probably somewhere in town, and the kidnapper might've left her alone for a second!" I exclaimed. "We should go look for her!"

"NO!" Judy hollered. "Let the police look for her. We can probably track her phone's GPS system." She turned back to Axel and asked, "What else? Any cars doors shutting or voices?"

"No, just distant sounds of cars. That's good, right?" he asked, worried. "I mean, if this woman…" Carlos instantaneously cut Axel off, "you mean Prunella, not this woman, right?"

Axel appeared confused, but immediately regained his composure when he realized we hadn't told Judy about Cassandra and the possibility she kidnapped Prunella.

"What's going on?" Judy insisted, suspiciously. "You're hiding information, aren't you?"

"No, Judy," I quickly chimed in. "Don't you think you should call John and let him know what happened?"

Judy nodded and pulled out her cellphone. "I think I should make the call in the foyer for privacy, Judy," Axel suggested. "It'll be too distracting with us talking and trying to figure out where she could be."

"Oh, yes, good suggestion, Eklund," Judy said, turning and leaving the kitchen.

"That was too close, Axel," Carlos said. "I didn't think we were telling that detective about Cassandra yet."

"You're right. I forgot for a moment."

"I don't blame you," Isabella said, sweetly. "You were worried about Prunella and weren't thinking clearly."

"I can't make any slip-ups, though. The last person I want to know what we're doing is that blasted detective. The more I've gotten to know her the more I think she's not all there in the head!"

"She's not that bad," Inga replied, shocking me. "I used to think she was after the Chief, but it seems like she's just trying too hard to prove she's not incompetent. She's made a lot of mistakes in the last couple months."

"She is after John," I amended. "But, John doesn't think of her that way. I don't doubt she's a good cop, but my personal feelings for her get in the way, I guess."

"You have nothing to worry about, Ruth Ann," Isabella said, smiling sweetly. "John would never leave you for someone like her. She's not very feminine."

"I've noticed that lately, too," I said, baffled. "When she first got here late summer she looked different. She put on makeup and did her hair. I thought she was doing it to get John's attention, but maybe when he told her he wasn't interested in her that way, she stopped trying."

"Probably," Axel said. "Who cares?"

"Yeah, let's figure out where Cassandra took Prunella," Sherman bellowed, loudly.

"Shhh, Sherman!" I told him. "If Judy hears loud voices, she'll come running in here."

"Sorry."

We turned our attention back to Axel. Carlos, leaning on the island appearing exhausted said, "So, is that *really* all you heard on the phone?"

"No."

"Axel!" I exclaimed. "Why didn't you say something before?"

"Because of that detective!"

"What did you hear on the other end?" Carlos asked, impatiently. "Spill, please."

"When I called out Prunella's name I thought I heard a weak response. It had to be Prunella, but she was speaking so softly I had a difficult time making out what she said."

"So, you heard Prunella?" I asked. "Thank God."

"What did you hear?" Inga asked, anxiously.

"I thought I heard her say..."

"I don't have much time, but listen, Axel. This strange woman grabbed me out of our bedroom. She wanted..."

"She wanted what?" I hollered, throwing my hands over my mouth knowing I might've just blown it. "Sorry, I'll keep it down. What next?"

"Please, let me get out everything I remember. I called her name after she hesitated and after a pause she said, *"Axel, I'm sorry. I tried to fight her, but she startled me and hit me over the head with a vase. I lost my footing and fell to the ground. When I woke up, she was standing over me with this big thug of a man. She told me to go get the necklace or they'd kill me."*

"I wanted to respond, but I could only mutter her name. I waited for her to go on, and after another pause, like she was making sure the coast was clear, she whispered,"

"I didn't have a choice. I betrayed you and had a secret safe built into our bedroom. I don't know how this woman knew about it, but she ripped the painting off the wall and had the man force me off the floor. He dragged me to the safe and demanded I open it. What else could I do? I tried to ask who she was or why she wanted it, but she wouldn't say until...now.

She's from Jamaica, Axel. She's related to Martika somehow, but she's much worse than her. She makes Martika look like a baby."

"She paused again, but I couldn't ask her any questions. I didn't want Judy to catch on just yet. So, getting the hint, she hurried and went on."

"Axel, I don't know why you can't talk, but obviously, you're being watched. So, this is all I know. It's a woman from Martika's past. She has me and the necklace and we're being held...OH, NO, PLEASE LET ME GO. YOU HAVE WHAT YOU WANT..."

"The call went dead. She must've gotten caught!" he said, terrified. "I was in such shock, I thought I was going to pass out."

"Wow," Inga said, shocked. "She said so much in such a short amount of time."

"She talked very fast, and very quietly. I can't say it was word for word, but pretty close. She just confirmed what we thought happened."

"Martika's sister, Cassandra, kidnapped her and stole the necklace," Carlos stated. "But, who's the guy she referred to?"

"She hired a criminal like Martika did with the Swedish twins," Isabella said. "I'm sure if she's as bad as Prunella just told you, she had the connections to some pretty awful people."

"I didn't like what she said about being *worse* than Martika," I said, nervous. "Martika was cruel, and willing to kill to get what she wants."

"How much worse can her sister be?" Inga inquired. "I mean, you just said Martika killed to get that necklace. What can her sister do that would be worse?"

"She didn't say, Inga," Axel said, horrified. "We need to find her." He walked over to the island and sat down heavily on one of the stools. I couldn't help but feel sorry for him and walked over and gently placed my hand on his shoulder. He reached up with his hand and patted mine briefly. "We'll find her, Ruth Ann. I know I haven't been the best husband, but I don't want anything to happen to her. She's been through enough lately."

"Yes, I agree."

"So, have you, Ruth Ann," Carlos added, becoming angrier

with Axel. "Ruth Ann has been through more than anyone around here!"

"You're right, Carlos," Axel said, calmly. "I didn't mean anything by it when I said Prunella's been through a lot."

"We've *all* been through a lot!" Inga shouted, quickly turning her head in the direction of the door hoping Judy didn't hear her outburst.

"Axel, did Prunella say anything about where she was?" Alex asked. "Did you really hear car noises?"

"No. There was no car noises. I just made that up for Judy."

Sherman threw his hands up in the air out of frustration. "Well, now what are we going to do? We have no idea where this Cassandra woman is holding her captive."

"She couldn't have gone far," I said, trying to think rationally. "I mean it's only been a couple of hours. It's getting late and I want to find her before the day is over."

"I don't know if that's possible, Ruth Ann," Axel said, sounding defeated and unsure of what to do next.

"Okay, we need to regroup before Judy and probably John come in here," Inga said, taking control of the situation. "I think we should split up and look around town. If she has Prunella, I bet she went somewhere familiar like the resort."

"Why would she go somewhere so public?" Alex snapped at her. "I'm sure she'll dump Prunella at a remote location and then get back to her own country."

"We have to stop her before she boards a flight back home!" Isabella exclaimed more loudly than any of us had ever heard. "I don't want to go back. There's too many bad memories still fresh in my mind."

"Isabella," I started to say. "John left to find out if Cassandra entered the country, so I'm sure he knows by now..."

"Knows what?" a voice called out from the back-kitchen door near the butler's pantry.

"John!" I cried out, loudly. "You're back! Did you trace the GPS signal from Prunella's phone?"

"We tried, but unfortunately the signal was blocked somehow." said John as he stomped to the island and joined our discussion. "I heard you tell Isabella I probably already knew the answer to something. What is that something, Ruth Ann?"

"If Cassandra entered our country and made her way to Deer Creek."
"Well, unfortunately, if she did enter the states, she didn't use her real name."

"That makes sense," Axel said. "But, we don't need that information anymore."

John slowly turned his attention to Axel who was opposite of him at the island. "And what do you mean by that, Eklund?"

Axel glared at him, but before he could respond, I said, "We already know that it was Cassandra who took Prunella."

John almost choked on a piece of biscotti he was nibbling. "And how do *we* know?" he asked, demanding to be filled in on everything. "I just saw Judy, and she informed me about the phone call Eklund received. She said you didn't hear anything but car noises." John eyed Axel suspiciously and added, "Did you purposely leave out vital information?"

"Yes."

"John," I said quickly, before he reached across the island to strangle Axel. "Axel was in shock, and Judy was being her usual pain, so we waited to tell you when you came back to the estate."

John thought about my statement for a second, obviously fighting with himself internally about whether he believed me or not. He must've decided to trust me. "Oh, okay, but Judy is a trained detective. It would've been beneficial for Eklund to share everything the minute it happened. She might've asked specific questions that might've helped us locate where Cassandra is holding Prunella."

"Prunella didn't say. She was about to tell him when her kidnapper must've caught her," I said.

"WHAT?" John screamed, causing Judy to whip open the kitchen door to see what was the matter.

"Why'd you scream, John?" Judy asked, gun drawn and ready for battle. "Did something happen?"

"NO, Judy!" John snapped. "Go back and finish what you were doing. I was angry at what Eklund said. No reason for you to pull out your gun." He quickly added, "Put that thing away!"

Judy lowered her gun and placed it back in its holster. I could tell she didn't want to leave, but John gave her a direct order, so she pouted for a moment and headed into the dining room.

"You just did to Judy what you told us we shouldn't have," Inga tried to say, but the words didn't come out right. "You know what I mean. You left Judy out of the conversation, too!" "I'm her boss! I tell her what I need to. Let's get back to the conversation you had with your wife, Eklund," John said.

Axel took a moment to relive the terrifying phone call. When he was done, John didn't even have the heart to reprimand him for not telling his detective. "Um, I'm sure that was hard on you Eklund. If that was my wife," John paused and then said, "or Ruth Ann, I would've panicked, too."

"So, where do we go from here?" I asked, trying to get away from that awkward comment.

"*We* don't, Ruth Ann," John repeated. "Since we didn't get any GPS coordinates, I'm going to have my people search this entire town until we find her. I doubt they've gone far because it hasn't been that long. I'm just worried that Prunella got herself in more trouble after being caught talking to Eklund on her cell phone."

"You don't think they would hurt her, do you?" Alex asked, even though it was Axel's place to ask that question.

"If what she said was true about Cassandra being worse than Martika, then..." John hesitated, swallowed hard and said, "We just need to find her right away. I'll be back," he said, turning to rush out of the kitchen. "I need to talk to Judy and get every cop I have searching the town."

It suddenly dawned on me that if they start a search they would most likely start with my daughters and where they live and work. "John!" I bellowed, stopping him in his tracks half-way out of the kitchen. "I don't want Lynne or Nancy involved in any way."

"We will have to search their places and the bakery unless you have another suggestion of where Cassandra took Prunella?"

I sat on a stool next to Axel and desperately tried to think of what this nasty woman would do. I felt so out of sorts and unable to concentrate when a thought entered my head. "Hey, John. Did you get any of the results from Doc Albert about our blood tests?"

"Yes."

"And..." Axel and I said together. "Did they show anything wrong with Prunella?" I asked.

"And you, Ruth Ann," Isabella reminded me. "You had your blood drawn too."

"Yes, me too."

John reentered the kitchen, exasperated, but he chose to answer our question. "Yes, Ruth Ann. Doc got *both* of your blood tests back."

"And?" Sherman bellowed, frustrated. "Do we have to keep beating around the bush about EVERYTHING?"

"Ease up there, old man," John said, walking over and standing behind the stool I was sitting on. "I need to decide what I can and can't tell you."

"Really?" I questioned him. "After everything we've been through, you still pick and choose what I can and can't know! It's my blood test results. I give you full permission to tell me if something is wrong!"

"I'll tell you about yours, but Prunella's results fall under privacy laws."

"I'm her husband, and I've signed the papers that allows you or Doc Albert to inform me about her healthcare."

"Fine. I'll tell you, and..." he paused, and stared me straight in the face and said, "Only you."

"But," I said, wanting to argue, but knew it would get me nowhere. Anyway, Axel would tell me once John left the room.

"Okay, about Ruth Ann's tests," John said. "Are you sure you don't want to speak privately?"

"You're scaring me, John! Is something wrong?"

"Actually, no. You're fine. Doc said you had some nausea lately, but he's writing that off to the trip and stress. He told me to tell you to pop some antacids and you'll be fine."

"Phew," Inga said before I could. "That's great news."

"Yes, but now I want to hear Prunella's results," Axel said, nervously. "I think it's okay to tell me in front of everyone here."

"No, sorry," John said. "Let's step into the foyer."

John and Axel walked out of the kitchen together. Just as Axel was leaving the kitchen, he turned and looked me in the eyes. I felt a warm rush run through my body. It had to be my anxiety over what could be wrong with Prunella. I so wanted to follow them, but stayed put on my stool. Everyone waited around the island until Axel returned a few minutes later, alone.

He looked a little pale as he stepped back in the kitchen. Inga and Isabella were near the sink rinsing out coffee cups, and Sherman was putting them into the dishwasher. Carlos and Alex were pacing around and around the island making me dizzy. Once we spotted Axel, we stopped and stared waiting for him to speak.

Finally, I couldn't take it any longer. "Well?" I inquired, worried by his appearance. "Did John give you bad news?"

Axel slowly stumbled to the island and grabbed the back of my stool. He pulled the stool next to me closer and hopped up. "C'mon, Mr. Eklund," Inga said, trying not to sound too pushy. "You're making me really worried about Ms. Prunella. If it's that bad, we can help her, whatever it is. I'll donate blood or a kidney or whatever she needs!"

"No, Inga," Axel muttered. "Prunella doesn't need your blood or any of your organs. What she needs is your..." he stopped, shook his head and if I didn't know better, almost wept.

"Oh, my God, Axel," I said, terrified. "You're really scaring me. Please, I can't take this any longer."

"She's pregnant."

Wait, what? She's not dying or sick. I must've misunderstood what he said, but how does one misinterpret one being pregnant? "Pregnant?" I asked, quietly. "Did you just say Prunella is going to have a baby?"

"Yes, Ruth Ann," he said, turning a sickly shade of green. "But, but..." he stopped, nearly falling off the stool before landing on his feet and running out of the kitchen.

"What's wrong with him?" Carlos asked. "He should be thrilled with the news."

"It is odd," I said, staring at the door hoping he would come back.

"My great niece is going to have a baby!" Sherman announced, proudly. "I will be a great-great uncle!"

"But she's missing," Alex stated, bringing us back to reality. "Maybe Axel is worried about her being newly pregnant and kidnapped!"

"That's it!" I shouted. "Axel is worried sick, literally."

John suddenly pushed the swinging door from the butler's pantry to the kitchen wide open. "What's with Eklund? He just ran through the hall and upstairs!"

"You just told him Prunella was pregnant," I snapped. "That's seriously big news, especially since she's been kidnapped by a sick woman!"

"Why would Cassandra be so desperate?" he inquired, curiously.

"Probably because she spent most of her life eluding her evil sister and then found out about what Martika did with us and the necklace," Inga responded, irritated. "He was distraught and sick. Once he told us everything, he ran out of here."

"He told you *everything* I told him?" John asked, inquisitively.

Before anyone could ask what he meant, I quickly said, "Of course he did!"

John, taking this to heart, said, "Oh, so you aren't upset about the other results? I mean, it's pretty strange to not only me, but to

Doc Albert."

Inga, Sherman, Alex, Carlos, and Isabella turned to me. None of them wanted to blow our cover that we didn't know what he was talking about. I couldn't think of how to respond when Alex, thankfully, said, "Of course we're upset. But the primary issue is getting her back so we can take care of *everything* that's inflicting her."

"Oh, yes, good point, young man. I'll just go and see if Eklund is all right."

"Wait!" I cried out. "Let me. I bet he ran up to their bedroom. I'll go talk to him and report back."

John, eyeing me suspiciously, said, "You're going to speak with Eklund in *his* bedroom? Don't you think that's a tad inappropriate?"

"Why?" I asked, seriously. "I've had many talks with him up there."

"*You have?*" John inquired, turning a little green with envy. "You never told me that."

"C'mon, John. It's no big deal." I was truly smiling inside. John was jealous of Axel, causing my recent twinges of affection for Axel to seem a little silly. I must be imagining the feelings I thought Axel had for me. He was just distraught and scared by Prunella's recent health issues. I'm sure when she's found, safe and sound, he will be the proud papa to be.

"Fine, just don't be gone long. I took the tape off their bedroom since the investigators were through. But, the room's still a mess."

"I'm sure Inga and Sherman will clean it up once we're through talking in there, right you two?" I asked, turning my head toward the sink where the two of them were listening attentively.

"Me?" Sherman bellowed. "I'm not housekeeping. In fact, Mr. Eklund never hired a new housekeeper after Helena."

"She was murdered in this house, Sherman!" I protested. "Have some respect."

"I didn't mean anything disrespectful, Ruth Ann," he

commented. "I just think it's time to hire a housekeeper with all the people living in his estate."

Inga shot Sherman a nasty glance. "Really, Sherman! You don't clean a thing. I DO! I DO ALL THE COOKING AND CLEANING. You act like a spoiled, entitled, pompous, pain in the..."

"INGA!" I hollered before she finished her outburst. "I'll help you clean up the room."

Sherman turned his nose in the air and said, "I don't clean up messes. I run the household and order other people to clean."

"Not now!" I snapped. "Sherman, you have no say to whether you clean or not. That's up to Axel and Prunella. Stop being a snob. If we ask you to help clean up that room, you will. Got it?"

He huffed and marched out of the room into the butler's pantry. "Let him go," I said. "Can I go find Axel now, John?"

"Go."

I hurried out of the kitchen before he could change his mind and follow me. I walked past Judy in the foyer as she stood near the bottom of the stairs, texting on her phone. Once she realized it was me she shouted, "Hey, where do you think you're going?"

"Up to see Axel," I said. "Before you say anything else, John told me it was okay."

"Oh, I guess it's fine then." She returned to her phone and I fled up the stairs as fast as I could. I got a little out of breath, but was not going to let Judy see me huffing and puffing. I reached the second-floor landing and hurried down the hall to Prunella and Axel's bedroom.

The police tape was missing and the door was wide open. I stepped inside and looked around at the disaster. "What a mess!" I exclaimed. The room was torn apart from floor to ceiling. I knew it was going to take Inga, Sherman, Axel, Alex and me to clean it up. I wasn't about to ask Carlos and Isabella to pitch in since they were our guests.

Suddenly, the words John asked us in the kitchen about if we knew *everything* that was wrong with Prunella flooded my mind.

Being pregnant isn't something that would be considered 'wrong', unless there was a problem with her pregnancy. That could be what he meant! I needed to speak with Axel and get him to confide in me, but I didn't see him anywhere in their bedroom.

I called out, "Axel, are you in here?" No response. I turned and went back into the hall. I started to walk back to the stairs when a voice called out my name from the other end of the hall. "I'm down here."

I turned and looked down the long, dimly lit hallway and saw Axel's head sticking out of...my room! What was he doing in there? I rushed down and found him sitting on my sofa. "What are you doing in here?" I asked, a little annoyed, but trying not to show it. It was his estate. He could go wherever he pleased.

"I'm really sorry I invaded your private bedroom, Ruth Ann. I went into my room, but I couldn't stand the sight. It's a disaster in there."

Understanding what he said, I responded sympathetically, "It's okay, Axel. We'll get your room cleaned up right away. John said they're done with it, too."

"It's not that, Ruth Ann. I don't know how I could ever sleep in there again!"

"Why? I know we'll get Prunella back home safely. Then you two can prepare for that great news."

"It's not great news, Ruth Ann," he said, looking sick again. "At least not for me."

"I don't understand," I said, totally baffled. "John just told you that you are going to be a father. Aren't you happy about that at least?"

"I would be thrilled if *I* was the father, Ruth Ann."

"What did you just say?" I asked, shaking my head to unclog my ears. I thought I heard him say he wasn't the father of Prunella's baby.

"You heard correctly, Ruth Ann. I can't be the father of her baby. That means..."

"I know what it means, Axel!" I blurted, disgusted at what he was implying. "Why don't you tell me why you think you're not the father, exactly?"

"I'm not, how do you say, capable of producing a child anymore."

A lightbulb went off in my head. Oh, he must've had a vasectomy at some point. "But sometimes those procedures aren't perfect. Maybe they made a mistake and you can still make a baby." I hated to remind him of a recent past indiscretion with his former maid, Helena. "I'm sorry to bring this up, but weren't you the father of Helena's baby not too long ago?"

"Yes, but things have changed since then. I know for a fact I can't make a baby with Prunella or anyone anymore."

"Are you sure? I mean a hundred percent sure?" I asked, dumbfounded. "Mistakes happen all the time."

"No, not with this. Just take my word for it."

"So, if you didn't...then...who...I'm so confused."

"So am I, Ruth Ann," he said, miserably.

We sat on my couch in silence for quite a while. I had so many thoughts bouncing around my head, but my mouth couldn't form a sentence. I stared at my bed straight ahead and thought about where it came from. It was an antique from an estate not far from here. The mattress was brand new, but the frame had to be over a hundred years old. The white iron footboard had bruised my knees and calves endless times, but I loved it anyway.

"Ruth Ann?" Axel called out while I was daydreaming. "Are you alright?"

I refocused and turned my head to see this gentleman staring back at me with his baby blue eyes filled with immense sadness. I looked in his eyes deeply and could almost feel his pain, but that was ridiculous. I was in pain and that must be what I was feeling. His flawless, wrinkleless skin was pale, but so smooth it looked like white porcelain. "I'm fine, Axel. Well, not fine, but I don't know what to think or say right now. I came up here to see if you were alright, and to find out what else John told you about Prunella's blood test results. He alluded to the fact that there was more to her being pregnant." I waited to see if he would speak honestly with me, but he just sat, listening to me. "Or was John referring to the fact that you aren't the father?"

"John has no idea about me not being able to give Prunella a baby."

"Will you tell me what else is wrong with her or would you like that to remain private?"

"What's the point, Ruth Ann? She's been lying to me...I mean to us."

"I don't fit into this equation, Axel. She betrayed you, not me, but with whom?"

"I have some thoughts, but," he stopped, swallowed hard and shut his mouth tightly.

"Axel, you can tell me. I won't be upset, just surprised."

"Aren't you curious how far along she is?" he asked.

"I didn't even think to ask that question, actually. It would make a huge difference as to whom I think might've..."

"Gotten her pregnant, Ruth Ann. You have to be able to say it."

"It's such a shock, Axel. I can't believe she would've cheated on you. Are you sure you can't be the father?" I looked pleadingly at him and prayed I misunderstood what he confided a few moments ago.

"I'm not the father."

"How far along is she? I assume Doc Albert told her and she knew before the blood test. No wonder she was so angry about getting checked out by a doctor!"

"Yes. That's what John told me. Prunella had secretly seen Doc Albert and he couldn't tell anyone about it because of the privacy laws."

"But, Doc told John just a little while ago and he told you," I said, confused. "He broke the doctor/patient confidentiality."

"Not exactly. Prunella's been kidnapped and it's an official police investigation now. Doc did it for official reasons."

"Okay, that answers one of my questions. Now, please tell

me how pregnant she is."

"Brand new. Not even a couple weeks."

"But, we were all together in Jamaica!" I exclaimed. "I don't get it."

"She must've slept with someone down there."

"But how could Doc Albert know so soon?"

"They can tell right away now, Ruth Ann. Special blood tests and all. When Doc Albert ran her blood test yesterday he did a complete workup."

I sat in shock. Prunella was in Jamaica with all of us. The only man that could possibly impregnate her would be Axel, but he's ruled out, Alex, but he's about ten years younger than her, Sherman, he's her great uncle, so that's sick...who else? I thought long and hard and I couldn't come up with anyone else.

"I see you're going through the names of men like I did, Ruth Ann," he said. "I think you've left out a few. It took me a moment, too."

"Like who?"

"Carlos, Joseph, those twins Martika hired, Felix, and the possibility she met someone new."

"That list is ridiculous, Axel!" I ruled out Felix immediately. He was about ninety years old and was killed right after Prunella arrived in Jamaica. Carlos, well, he doesn't even like women, and neither did Joseph. I say 'did' because Joseph was killed trying to protect us. Now the twins Martika hired could be a remote possibility. "Hey!" I bellowed loudly, startling Axel.

"You thought of it too, didn't you?" he asked, smiling weakly.

"When we were held in Martika's house," I mumbled quietly.

"Yes."

"My wife was held in Martika's bedroom, remember?" I nodded and he continued. "She wasn't brought into the kitchen like the rest of us when you arrived with Martika.

"I remember, Axel. Martika took Prunella hostage right before she was killed."

"Yes."

"That would have to be it, Axel," I said. "If she was alone with one of those twins, that means she was..."

"Raped."

"OH, MY GOD!" I screamed. "She didn't betray you! She was violently abused. No wonder she was acting so strangely. It wasn't some new curse. She was assaulted and found out she was pregnant right after we returned home. I bet she went immediately to see Doc Albert to see if her worst nightmare had come true."

"That's what I think happened too."

"It's absurd that Alex, Carlos, or any of the others would betray you so," I said, feeling relieved about that at least. "Do you think that's why she's been so angry since we returned home?"

"Mostly at me, Ruth Ann. Don't you see? She probably felt she betrayed me even though she didn't. She had a horrible crime committed against her. It makes me sick thinking about it. I can't take this!"

I reached over and put my arm around his shoulder to console him. He leaned into me and for that moment I didn't feel at all awkward. It was the right reaction and we were both shocked and horrified at what most likely took place down in Jamaica. No wonder my cousin flashed red dagger eyes at everybody. We all thought the curse was broken and could start a new, happy life. But Prunella was caught up in her own horrific nightmare.

ELEVEN

"So, what do we tell everyone downstairs?" I asked him.

"I'd like to keep the fact that I'm not the father between you and me. John and Doc Albert know she's pregnant, too. But they won't tell anybody," Axel said.

"Maybe his nosy nurse. There's no reason to yet, but if Prunella started going there for prenatal care, then Shirley would obviously know the truth."

"I'm not going to worry about that now. First thing we have to do is find her, Ruth Ann. She's under an insurmountable amount of stress. She was acting erratic the last few days and who knows what she might do to this Cassandra woman."

"You're right! Cassandra should look out for the wrath of Prunella Eklund!"

"Here, here!" Axel bellowed and stood up. He reached out his hand for me to grab and I took it eagerly. "Why don't we burn some of our energy and start cleaning my bedroom. A few minutes ago, I couldn't bear to look at it. But now, I'm feeling much better. I know if we are correct, and Prunella was assaulted by one of Martika's goons, our lives will never be the same."

"Let's take it one step at a time, Axel," I said, releasing his hand and heading into the hall toward their bedroom. "I asked the others to help."

"Sherman agreed to help clean?" he asked, astonished. "I'll bet he put up quite the fuss."

"Oh, yes he did, but I gave it right back," I said.

"I bet you did, Ruth Ann."

We entered the room and found everyone hard at work cleaning the broken glass from the picture frames and shards of smashed pottery. "Were any of those vases worth money?" I quietly asked Axel before the others spotted us standing in the doorway.

"Yes. Most of them were heirlooms and pieces I've picked up over the years at auctions. It breaks my heart they destroyed this room just to get the necklace. Why would they have to destroy everything if they already knew there was a safe?"

"I don't know," I replied, not knowing what to say. Thankfully, Sherman looked up from the ground where he was trying to reach down and grab some loose jewelry.

"Hey, you're finally here!" he bawled. "We've been working hard."

"Looks like you're making headway with this mess," I said, changing the subject so Sherman wouldn't begin complaining, again.

Inga shoved Sherman aside and walked over to Axel and me. "Sherman hasn't done anything!" she snapped. "He just bent over for the first time once he knew you two were here."

"That's a lie, Inga!" Sherman cried. "I've been working as hard as the rest of you."

"I don't care," Axel exclaimed. "I just want it clean so when Prunella comes back it looks like it did."

"We're getting there," Isabella said, smiling. "It's a very nice bedroom. It's so massive and richly decorated."

"Thanks," Axel replied. "Prunella has been itching to redecorate, but it's hard for me to change this room. I like it the way it is." He turned to me and quickly said, "I know you want in on the decorating too, Ruth Ann."

"Prunella and I have discussed a few changes," I responded, thinking back to when we planned an entirely new color scheme to get away from the dark, heavy atmosphere in here. "I think now that this room has been torn apart, it would be a great time to bring in some lighter, happier colors."

Axel groaned, but smiled. "I agree."

We spent the rest of the evening cleaning and straightening. It was quite late and John had not come upstairs to check on us. "I wonder what's going on with the investigation?" Alex asked, nervously. "We haven't seen him in a couple hours."

The time did pass, but it was a good thing. If we sat around it would've driven us crazy waiting for news. I looked at the sparsely furnished room and shook my head. "This is pathetic! All that's left is the bed and the couch. They broke everything else, including your nightstands and chairs."

"I know, but I'm too tired to think about it, Ruth Ann," Axel said. "I think we should all go back down and grab a bite to eat, and find John and Judy."

We agreed we needed to eat so we stepped into the hall, climbed over the garbage and headed downstairs. Axel and I were first to descend, and then Alex, Isabella and Carlos followed. I noticed Inga and Sherman bickering quietly at the top of the stairs. I could barely overhear Inga snapping at Sherman and ordering him to clean the mess in the hall. "But, what am I supposed to do with all of it?" he complained. "I can't carry this stuff downstairs!"

"Call someone to get it cleaned, Sherman. You can make a phone call, can't you?" she said, insultingly. "I've got to feed everybody, so I don't have time to do it!"

She hurried down the stairs leaving Sherman staring down the hall at the pile of garbage bags and broken furniture. He mumbled something inaudible and marched out of sight.

"He's a pain," Inga snapped as she passed the rest of us on the way to the kitchen. "He should retire and move somewhere warm!"

"Inga!" I shouted. "Sherman is a part of this family. I agree about the retiring part, but he'll never leave us."

"Great, just great," she muttered, entering the kitchen through the foyer entrance.

After Inga and Sherman went their separate ways, Axel pulled me aside. "I need to speak with you quickly before we go and eat."

I nodded and told Isabella, Carlos and Alex to go ahead into the kitchen. They looked at us strangely, but did as I asked. "What is it?" I asked Axel as we stepped into his library.

He shut the door behind me and inquired, "Isn't it odd that none of them questioned us about our conversation earlier in your bedroom?"

"I think they were so busy cleaning your bedroom that they momentarily forgot. Don't think that will last. Inga's pretty sharp and will hit us with it once we're sitting down eating."

Axel looked saddened. "Oh, I guess I was hoping they would let it be for now and concentrate on finding Prunella."

"Fat chance!" I chuckled. "This is the nosiest group of people I've ever been around."

"Including yourself?" he questioned.

"Yes, including me."

We left the library and walked into the kitchen to find Isabella and Inga hard at work putting out leftovers, again. It's only been a day since Thanksgiving and I'm already sick of turkey. It's the second time today and I wasn't in the mood for more turkey. I left Axel at the kitchen table with Alex and Carlos and went to help them.

"What can I do?" I asked Inga, who was bent over opening a cabinet under the island and pulling out a large silver tray.

"You can put the turkey on the platter, Ruth Ann. I'm warming up the potato and broccoli casserole, and I have Isabella stirring the Cherry Whip Jell-O."

"Mmm, I do love that Cherry Whip Jell-O," I said, now looking forward to eating. "I've been making that dish for over twenty years."

"You gave me the recipe, Ruth Ann," Inga reminded me. "It's easy and a huge crowd pleaser."

CHERRY WHIP JELLO

1 – Can Cherry Pie Filling
12-ounce container of frozen whipped cream (thawed)
1 – large can crushed pineapple, drained
1 can – sweetened condensed milk
(I use fat-free to try and keep fat & calories down
a little on this recipe)
1 – cup sour cream
mini marshmallows

Mix all the ingredients in a large bowl, adding mini marshmallows last. Use as many as you like! I use about a half a bag unless doubling the recipe and then I use more.

Cover and let sit overnight in the refrigerator. Serve, and wait for all the compliments you'll receive on this easy side dish.

Once we put out a substantial amount of food on the island, Inga called the men over to grab a plate and help themselves. Sherman had not returned yet, and I was getting worried about him. I knew he wouldn't attempt to carry down all the garbage in the hall. But then, where was he? I told Inga I was going to look for him when she spat out, "He's fine, Ruth Ann. I'm sure he's still trying to figure out who to call to haul that garbage away."

"I'm going to check on him anyway," I said, walking out of the kitchen into the foyer.

I stood alone in the massive grand foyer looking for him. There wasn't any sign of him so I forced myself to walk up to the second floor to take a look. Once I stepped onto the landing I glanced down the hall and spotted the pile of garbage. "Sherman, are you up here?" I called out, loudly. No answer. I suddenly felt an odd sensation in the pit of my stomach. "No, it's nothing," I said out loud. "I'm just hungry."

I decided he was probably up on the third floor in his room, sulking after Inga embarrassed him about getting rid of the garbage. I marched up to the third floor to tell Sherman not to worry about it.

Sherman's room was the second room on the left after Inga's. It was dark in the hallway, lit only by small sconces in between the bedrooms. "I'm going to tell Axel he should put brighter bulbs up here. It's kind of creepy!"

I walked past Inga's room and came to Sherman's. The door was closed, and I grabbed the knob to see if it was locked. The door must've been slightly ajar because a gentle touch opened the door enough for me to peek in and discover Sherman wasn't inside. I figured I would go and check the second floor again to see if he was working on the pile of garbage. I went back down to the second floor and marched up to the pile of garbage. I noticed that Axel and Prunella's door was shut. There was still no sign of him and I was about to turn around and leave when something made me stop. "Sherman?" I whispered, feeling myself begin to shake from head to toe. "This is nonsense." I lifted my hand to knock on the door when I heard a noise.

"Sherman! If that's you playing a trick on me it's not funny!"

Another barely audible grunt came from the other side of the door. I should've turned and ran downstairs to grab Axel or one of the others, but did I? Of course, not. I reached my trembling hand up to the large brass doorknob and tried to turn it. Subconsciously, I hoped it was locked.

I turned the knob and gently tried to push the door open enough for me to stick my head in, but the door wouldn't budge. "What's going on?" I questioned. Something was on the other side of the door blocking me from opening it. Against my better judgement, I pushed a little harder and was able to open the door about two inches. I stuck my face as close as I could and got my nose and one eye in. It was pitch black in there.

With a trembling voice, I called out, "Sherman...are you in there?"

Just as I thought I heard another grunt, a hand grabbed me on the shoulder and forced me back. "What the...?" I cried out.

"Ruth Ann! What are you doing?" Axel asked, right before I swung my fist at whoever was touching me.

"Oh, it's just you, Axel," I said, trying to slow my heart rate down a smidgen.

"What's going on?" he demanded, looking terrified. "Is something wrong?"

I explained that I went to look for Sherman and couldn't find him so I thought I'd check up here to see if he was still cleaning. "That's when I felt a bit uneasy, Axel. I thought I heard a grunt. I know I should've run back down and grabbed you, but, well...you know me. I'm too impatient to wait, so I reached out to open the door, but it wouldn't budge. It's as if something's on the other side of the door. That's when you showed up."

Axel looked at the door and gently moved me to the side. He tried to open the door with no luck. "Back off a little, Ruth Ann. I'm going to give it all I've got." He took a step back to gain momentum and hurdled himself up against the door and pushed with all his might. The door moved, but whatever or I should say whoever was on the other side let out a loud, painful moan.

"Somebody's on the other side of that door, Ruth Ann," Axel said, nervously. "You stay back while I go in. If there's any sign of trouble...run and get help!" He turned slowly and made me promise to get help. I nodded, mostly out of fear, and watched as he forced himself through the partially open door.

Once again, I was alone in the hallway. What could be happening inside the room? I didn't have to wait long when an arm appeared through the opening and then Axel's head stuck out. "Give me a second to move him and then you can come in."

"What do you mean by *move him*?" It had to be Sherman, but why was he lying on the other side of the door moaning?

Within a few seconds, the door fully opened and Axel grabbed my hand to pull me in. I reached around the wall and flipped the light switch. The room illuminated brightly and I had to close my eyes to adjust for a moment. When I opened them, the sight I saw wasn't what I expected at all.

TWELVE

"Sherman!" I cried out, falling to my knees and reaching out to the unconscious man lying on the floor. His wrists and ankles were tied with rope, and a black sock was stuffed into his mouth.

Axel pulled the sock out of his mouth as he bent over his butler. "He passed out right after I came in, Ruth Ann. I think it was more from fright then injury."

"What happened to him?" I asked, terrified. "Is he hurt or bleeding anywhere?"

"I, I don't know yet. You turned on the light, and I found him on the floor. I must've forced his body to move a little when I pushed in the door."

"You didn't have any choice, Axel," I said. "We had to get inside."

Axel nodded and reached out for Sherman's wrist. A moment later, "he's alive."

"I saw his chest rising and falling so I figured that much." I looked Sherman over from head to feet. "I don't see any blood or cuts on him."

"I'm pretty sure he was just scared and passed out," Axel said as Sherman started to come to.

"Sherman!" I called, grabbing his arm and jiggling it. "You need to open your eyes for us."

"I'm awake, leave me alone," he snapped with annoyance. "Why are you waking me up? I'm tired from working so hard in Mr. Eklund's bedroom!"

"Sherman," I said, tapping his face to get him to open his eyes. "You aren't in bed. You're lying on the floor near the door of Axel's bedroom. Don't you remember what happened to you?"

He quickly came to and opened his terrified eyes. He noticed Axel was on his other side and tried to sit up. "Hold on there, Sherman," Axel said, gently holding him by his shoulders to keep him on the floor. "We need to make sure you're not hurt anywhere. Are you in any pain?"

"Yes!" he stammered, holding his hand on his head. "I forgot for a second, but I was attacked!"

"Do you know who did it?" I asked.

"I, I can't believe it, Ruth Ann. I must've imagined what happened to me. Maybe I blacked out and didn't see what I think I saw."

"Sherman!" Axel retorted. "Please, I know you're in pain and scared, but what are you mumbling about?"

Sherman looked to me and then to his boss. "No, no, I won't incriminate..." he stopped, and then I realized he was referring to Prunella. I don't know why that thought popped in my head, but I knew that's what he meant.

"Sherman," I started to say. "It was Prunella, wasn't it? She hurt you."

Axel quickly responded to me, "What are you talking about, Ruth Ann? Why would you accuse Prunella of doing something so...so violent?"

"Because she did," I said. "Didn't she, Sherman?"

He looked at me with distraught eyes. "Yes."

"Impossible!" Axel shouted, and painfully, with aging knees, stood up to get away from us. "She was kidnapped earlier today and...and she's pregnant!"

"It was her, Mr. Eklund," Sherman murmured quietly, afraid of his boss's reaction. "I saw her with my own eyes."

"Enough!" I said, irritated. "Axel, come back and sit down with us. Let Sherman tell us what happened."

We helped Sherman stand and led him to the couch. Axel let

go of him a little too soon and Sherman dropped down hard. "Hey, I've been hurt. Ease up a little, please."

"Sorry, old man," Axel said, appearing to enjoy himself a little.

"Please stop!" I exclaimed. "Sherman, don't let Axel rile you any more than you already are. He didn't mean the 'old man' comment, so let it slide."

Sherman grumbled, but acquiesced. Axel eased up on the poor guy and sat on one side of him while I sat on the other. "Okay, start at the beginning please."

Sherman rubbed his head an exaggerated amount of times I thought, but finally, he spoke. "Inga left me on the second floor with that mess in the hall. I had no idea who to call to get it cleaned up and hauled away."

"Don't worry about that, Sherman," Axel said. "I can handle getting it cleared away."

"Oh, thank you," he said, surprised. "So, I walked back to your bedroom after stepping over the piles of garbage and started pacing inside thinking about who to call and how to get your room back in order. I was so frantic that I didn't notice..." he stopped, gasped and turned a sickly shade of green.

"Sherman! What's wrong? Are you going to be sick?" I asked, worried about him.

He tried to speak, but there weren't any words coming out of his rapidly, moving mouth. He looked in such distress that Axel leaned over and slapped his cheek.

"Ouch!" he hollered. "What'd you do that for?"

"You were having some sort of anxiety attack, Sherman. No words were coming out of your mouth. What on earth freaked you out so much?" I asked.

"I, I don't know how to say it."

"Spit it out," Axel said, exasperated with his butler.

He turned his head toward Axel and said slowly, and very bitterly, "Are you aware of the secret door in your room?"

Axel looked at me nervously and saw the astonished look on

my face. "Wait, what did you say, Sherman?" I asked, stunned.

"There's a secret opening in the wall and part of it slid open as I was pacing in here."

"Axel..." I called out, hoping he would respond to Sherman's claim.

"Yes, the wall does open into a tunnel," he admitted, ashamed. "I, I didn't tell anyone before because, well, I really don't know why I haven't told anyone."

"Did Prunella know about it?" I asked, angry about just finding out this piece of information.

"I didn't think so."

"Obviously, she did!" Sherman snapped. "She marched right through the wall, and I thought I was seeing a ghost! It scared me so much I fell to the floor...AHA! That's what happened to me."

"What, what?" I asked, impatiently.

"Once I fell to the floor, Prunella rushed to me with the scariest, wildest expression on her face I've ever seen."

"Were her eyes red?" Axel asked, uneasily.

Sherman's dumbfounded expression led me to believe he had never seen Prunella with those red eyes of hers before. "Yes, but...why? What's going on with her?"

"She's been acting strangely. We're all aware of that," I said.

"And the whole pregnancy thing," Sherman added. "Maybe something's wrong with her and she's gone off the deep end." He turned to me and asked, "Can being pregnant cause such a severe reaction?"

"I really don't know, Sherman."

"You both are hiding information about my great niece from me, aren't you?"

"No, Sherman," I replied immediately, lying. "What else could we possibly know?"

He looked from me to Axel and back to me. "I don't know, but I just know you are."

Axel stood up and walked over to the secret wall. He ran his fingers along a seam in the wall. I've never noticed it before, but why would I look at seams in the wallpaper? It didn't take him long when I heard a slight click. Sherman's eyes popped wide open and he unsteadily stood and pointed. "There it goes! The wall is sliding open."

"I see that, Sherman." I watched in amazement as the wall creaked and moaned and slid to reveal a door-sized opening. "Wow, was this something you knew about when you purchased the place, Axel?"

"Yes," he replied quite fast. "It was actually one of the reasons I bought this place. That and the fact that it's very secluded, but still fairly close to town."

"And don't forget, you bought this place to rob me," I said with a slight taste of bitterness in my mouth. "You came here to steal my necklace last summer. I can't believe it hasn't been that long and we've come so far. You should've spent the rest of your life in prison, Axel. But look at you, free, and a big part of my life."

"In a good way I hope, Ruth Ann," he added, smiling sweetly at me from the tunnel opening, hoping I would forgive him again.

I wasn't sure how he meant that, so I took it as a *friendly* comment not a romantic one. "Yes, Axel. We've worked through our issues and all of us have become one big, friendly family."

"Yes, we have," he replied, appearing a little dejected. Maybe he was referring to my use of the word *friendly*.

"Can we get back to what happened to *me*?" Sherman cried out. "I was assaulted by my own flesh and blood and you two are reminiscing!"

"He's right," I admitted. "I really want to hear the rest of what Sherman said happened, but that tunnel is also making me very curious. Where does it lead?" I asked Axel, ignoring Sherman's open mouthed reaction.

"Later, Ruth Ann. Sherman's right. Let's hear what happened and then we'll take a little stroll inside the tunnel."

"I'm not going in that dark, dirty, tunnel!" Sherman bellowed. "I'm injured."

"Yes, yes, we know, Sherman," Axel said pacifying him, even though we both knew he wasn't horribly injured. Most likely, he was so frightened that he passed out and was not physically harmed. Prunella would never do that!

"She did what?" I shouted after Sherman described what happened. I was shocked and appalled at his account of what my cousin did to him. "Prunella doesn't have a violent bone in her body!"

"Well, now she does," Sherman announced.

Axel, not interrupting during Sherman's description of what transpired, finally spoke up. "So, let me get this straight. My wife barreled out of the tunnel and stormed over to you with glaring red eyes and picked up the lamp and hit you straight in the head?"

"I picked up the broken lamp base to add to the pile of garbage in the hall," he described walking over to the middle of the room where he found the lamp base. "The lampshade had already been tossed. I saw her appear out of the wall, and remember, I thought she was a ghost at first."

"Sherman, please," I begged. "You know your niece, she's not dead so therefore she's not a ghost!"

"Well, she caught me off guard. I dropped the lamp base and I could see her gaze follow the piece as it fell to the floor. She stomped over with such ferocity that it scared me. She bent over, picked it up and whirled it in the air saying the most horrible things. Then she hit me. That's all I remember."

"Wait, you said she spoke to you, Sherman," Axel said, trying to figure out if Sherman's story was true or not. "What *exactly* did she say?"

Sherman shook his head. "I, I can't remember exactly. I remember her saying horrid things to me."

"Come on, Sherman," I said. "Please, think hard!"

Axel and I were both standing just inside the tunnel opening and Sherman was only a few feet away. He was afraid of the tunnel, that was obvious, but curious enough to not let us go without him. He started rubbing his head and shouted, "Here,

here's the lump she gave me!" He pointed to the spot on the side of his head. I couldn't help myself so went over and reached up to feel this supposed lump. I still was pessimistic about his story.

I looked disappointedly at Axel and replied, "He clearly has a lump on his head."

"Maybe he got it when he fell to the floor."

"I can hear you, you know, and I didn't get the lump that way. She hit me, and very hard. Hard enough to cause this lump and render me unconscious for a little while."

"I'm finding this hard to believe," I said, and before he could argue I held up my hand and quickly added, "I'm not saying you're lying, Sherman. I believe what you said happened. I'm finding it extremely difficult to believe Prunella could be so violent."

"Finally," Sherman spat out. "I was beginning to think you'd never believe me. I wouldn't lie about this."

"You're right, Sherman," Axel said, submitting. "I was only questioning you because I can't understand why my wife would do that."

"That's what's so confusing," I said. "If she saw Sherman, why knock him on the head?"

"She wasn't acting like herself, Ruth Ann," Sherman said. "She was wild, almost manic. I didn't recognize her at all. Those searing red eyes were glaring at me like I was a murderer and she had to kill me. I will be haunted by this forever."

"Stop being so dramatic!" I said, agitated with him. "She's not herself. Something is horribly wrong with her. Maybe Cassandra put some sort of spell on her."

"Excuse me?" Axel asked. "You think that woman caused Prunella to become violent?"

"She's Martika's sister. What do you think?" Sherman replied for me. "She probably practices voodoo and witchcraft."

"That was Meme's family, Sherman," I said. "Martika didn't have any powers like Isabella, her mother or her grandmother."

Axel reminded us that just because Martika didn't have special powers doesn't mean Cassandra couldn't.

Axel asked Sherman, "Did Prunella call out your name or did she march over and attack you?"

"Good question, Axel," I exclaimed. "Maybe she was so out of her mind she didn't know it was even Sherman."

Sherman looked upset. He walked closer to the tunnel opening and said, "Sorry, she called me her Uncle Sherman."

"She did?" I asked, stunned.

"Yes. But she said it mockingly. Like she was making fun of me."

I had no words. What was going on? I thought Prunella was kidnapped by Cassandra to get the necklace. But if Cassandra has the necklace, why kidnap Prunella? And why did Prunella attack her great uncle and make fun of him? "I'm so confused," I said, feeling miserable. "We have to admit Prunella hasn't been herself since we returned from Jamaica. Now, we find her and the necklace missing. The most probable suspect is Cassandra, Martika's long lost baby sister. But, the most interesting part of this is Prunella turning on us and attacking Sherman. It's as if she *wants* to hurt all of us and force us out of her life!"

"No way, Ruth Ann," Axel said, calmly. "I'm sure there's some logical answers to your questions, but I don't know how to find them."

"What about your chief?" Sherman asked.

"John?" I questioned him. "He won't give Prunella any mercy once he finds out what she did. He'll think she was in on it with this Cassandra person."

"You think?" Axel asked me, a little surprised by my coldness toward John. "He knows how much she means to you, Ruth Ann. I'm sure he'll see that something must be going on to make her turn violent."

"I don't want to risk it," I said with conviction. "I'm going to get to the bottom of this without him or Judy."

"And I'll be right next to you," Axel declared.

We looked at Sherman wondering if he felt as strongly about rescuing Prunella without the help of the police. I glared daggers until he finally caved. "Fine!" he stammered. "But if it doesn't go as planned, I'm out."

"Good. What's our first move?" I asked Axel. "I think we should fill in Carlos, Isabella, Inga and Alex. What do you think?"

"I think we should take a little stroll through the tunnel to see if we spot any signs of activity, and then have a little chat with the others."

"So, we're agreed not to tell John or Judy what happened to Sherman?" I asked them.

"Yes," Axel answered, and looked at Sherman. "Well?"

"Yes," he responded, with much less enthusiasm.

THIRTEEN

"Where do the tunnels lead?" I asked Axel curiously as we stepped inside the pitch-black tunnel.

"All over the place," he replied, grabbing a flashlight that was attached to the cement wall just inside the opening. "This will help," he said, turning on the light. "Before you chew me out, Ruth Ann, I'm painfully regretting not telling you about these tunnels."

"Don't forget about the tunnel that goes from this house to your guesthouse," I reminded him.

"Yes, but you already know about that one."

"Can we get a move on?" Sherman cried loudly. "I could use some pain medication for my head. It's throbbing!"

"Maybe you should go up to your room and take some medication. You can go to bed. It's late anyway," I suggested. "Axel and I don't need your help walking through the tunnels. If we find anything we promise to fill you in."

I could practically see the wheels in his brain spinning. Sherman was torn between going to bed and hoping this was just a nightmare, and... his nosy curiosity about what was inside these tunnels. One clearly outweighed the other because it didn't take him long to respond. "I'll go up to my room. I'm too old for this anyway. Plus, my head really does hurt!"

"Maybe we should call Doc Albert," I said, worried he might have a concussion.

"NO!" he bellowed, and then grabbed his head in pain. "I don't need a doctor. I just want to take a pill and go to sleep. Wake me when this nightmare is over and my niece is back in her right mind."

We left Sherman and headed to the right, which was the only direction we could go in the tunnel. "It looks like we're heading toward the other bedrooms, mainly mine," I said, feeling uneasy.

"Yes, it goes to the end of this hall and then there's a choice to either go up to the third floor or down to the main level. And from there, more choices."

"Let me guess, to either sneak around the main floor or go deep into the basement."

"Yes," Axel replied. "It will take you into the tunnel that leads to my guesthouse."

"How convenient," I said, a tad irritated. "I wish I knew about these when I was trying to escape from you a few months ago."

"I'll bet you do," he answered, chuckling a little.

"Hey," I exclaimed when a troubling thought crossed my mind. "If you can sneak into any of these bedrooms, well, then you could've..."

"Don't go there, Ruth Ann," he said, interrupting me. "I never peeked on you if that's what you were about to imply. I am still a gentleman, even though I've strayed from right and wrong before."

"Thanks for being honest," I said, believing him completely. It would take a total creep to watch people inside their private bedrooms.

"The one thing you can't argue about is that I've always been honest with you." He rubbed his head with one hand and added, "I don't understand what effect you have on me, Ruth Ann. You actually *make* me try to be a better person."

"I'll take that as a compliment," I said, just as he stopped, ran his hand along the wall and found the knob he was searching for.

"Here's your room."

The wall moaned, wobbled, and shakily opened to reveal my bedroom. "This is amazing," I said, still a little upset I never knew about the tunnel. "I can't believe these tunnels really exist!"

"I didn't see any clues along the hall yet, have you?" he asked, curiously.

"No, but I have to admit I was too busy trying to figure out where we were. I'll pay better attention now. We need to find out where Prunella and Cassandra are hiding out."

"I still can't believe she's turned on us, Ruth Ann."

"Maybe she was drugged and didn't have control of her actions," I said, hoping there would be a rational explanation once we found her.

"She's pregnant, remember? I doubt she would take a drug, willingly."

"She might not have had a choice, Axel. Maybe it was forced down her or even injected."

"That would be horrible!" he said, terrified. "There could be another explanation though."

"More than one I think," I said, considering other reasons that might cause Prunella to rebel.

"She may be under a spell from Cassandra. Cassandra certainly understands curses and spells well."

"I am blatantly aware of that, Axel," I said, remembering Meme and all the wild experiences I had when she was trying to break the curse on Blue Ice.

"You think there's another explanation?" he asked, curiously.

"Only one more, Axel," I said, not wanting to say out loud what I was thinking, but I had to. "That she willingly *chose* to betray us and hurt Sherman."

"I would argue with you, but I had the same thought, too."

"I find it the least likely, Axel. I think that she was put under some type of trance and acted out what Cassandra told her to do."

"Of the three explanations, that's the one I hope is true. It removes the chance of her being drugged and harming her baby, and it rules out that she's totally turned on us."

I nodded and stepped inside my bedroom. We took a quick look around, but didn't find any sign that Prunella or Cassandra had been hiding out. We went back inside the tunnel and came to a dead end. "Hey," I said loudly, causing my voice to reverberate back. I lowered my voice and continued. "I thought you said there were choices when we came to the end of the hall."

Axel didn't speak, but shined the flashlight on the wall opposite the bedrooms and said, "There." He pointed to a quarter size button and grabbed my hand for me to push. "You do it this time. You should know how these buttons work."

I reached over my head and pushed the button. A smaller opening appeared out of nowhere and he stepped inside the dark hole. "Come on, Ruth Ann. I'll shine the flashlight so you can see where to step."

I waited for him to light the way and then I stepped over a small threshold. A dark, narrow stairway was in front of me and Axel was standing on the top step. "Okay, be careful. The cement stairs aren't even and outside of my flashlight, there's no light."

"I'll be fine," I answered confidently, even though I really wasn't. "Just keep the light on the stairs so I don't fall into you and we both go tumbling down."

"I'll catch you if you trip," he said, smiling. "I would take your hand, but it's easier if you put your hands on each wall and guide yourself down. It gets pretty steep until we get down to the main level."

He wasn't kidding! I followed the dim light and carefully took each step one at a time with both feet landing on a stair before taking the next one. The steps were cracked in places with bumps and loose pieces of cement. I almost tripped as we were about halfway down, and had to grab the wall to catch my balance. He was right, it was easier holding onto the wall as I stepped down.

"Almost there, Ruth Ann," he said only a few steps ahead of me. "I haven't seen anything at all."

"Me either," I said. Not that I could've seen anything anyway, but why would they leave something behind?"

153

"When you reach the bottom, you'll be surprised at where we are."

I was completely turned around. We could end up in the library or the kitchen for all I knew. "Finally," I said, stepping onto firm, flat ground. "Doesn't the tunnel go around the main level?" I asked, noticing we were standing in a small box of a room.

"No. The tunnel only runs along the walls of the second and third floors. Once we get to the main level you can only go out into the butler's pantry or continue into the basement."

"The butler's pantry!" I exclaimed. "So, that's where we are."

Axel shined the light on the wall in front of me and I almost spotted the big button. Once my eyes adjusted, I saw the button. "Should I push it?"

"Not yet. The others will probably hear and I thought we'd check the rest of the tunnel first."

"Don't you think we should let them in?" I asked, baffled. "I mean, if we come across Cassandra, she may have hired men and we could get ourselves caught."

"I didn't think of that," he admitted. "Maybe we should grab the others."

He let me push the button and I waited as the wall moved open. "Hey," I called out, excitedly. "There isn't an opening on the other side."

"You'll be amazed at how this one works, Ruth Ann," he said, stepping in front of the opening and forcefully pushing the wall in front of him.

"What are you doing?" I asked.

"Watch."

The second wall slowly opened like a normal door. Axel stepped into the butler's pantry and told me it was clear to come in. "Look at that!" I said, surprised. "The door is a built-in buffet!"

"Yep. The cabinet looks like it's built into the wall, but it's not. It opens up into the tunnel."

"Very clever. Nobody would ever think to look there," I said, and then suddenly the swinging door from the kitchen flew open, startling me half to death.

"Ruth Ann!" Inga bellowed, wielding a large marble rolling pin.

"Put that down, Inga," I snapped. "It's just Axel and me."

"How was I supposed to know that? We were in the kitchen waiting and waiting for you when we heard this strange noise in here. I grabbed the first thing I could find."

Just as Inga lowered the rolling pin, Carlos stuck his head in. "Everything all right in here?"

"Yes, we're coming into the kitchen," Axel said, walking past Inga and me.

"But, where did you come from?" Inga inquired perplexed, as she noticed the buffet out of place. She was about to grab the back of the buffet that was sticking out from the wall and examine it when Axel interrupted her.

"We'll explain in a minute," Axel said, grabbing her by the arm and pulling her away from the cabinet.

"Where's Sherman?" Inga asked.

"He went to bed. We need to explain that, too," I said, stepping into the warm kitchen and seeing Isabella and Alex standing in the middle of the room.

"He's all right, isn't he?" Alex asked.

"Yes, yes," Axel said, walking over to the island and asking Inga if she could get him some water.

Inga rushed over and grabbed a cold bottle of water from the refrigerator. "Would you like a glass?"

"No, I'm just very thirsty." He turned to me and asked, "Aren't you thirsty from being in those tunnels?"

"Tunnels?" Inga barked, frustrated. She turned and looked back in the butler's pantry, figuring out that the buffet was a hidden entrance.

"Let him explain," I said, before the others could complain.

We stood around the island with Axel. Inga was standing near the sink, leaning and waiting for his explanation. I let Axel do the talking until we got to entering the butler's pantry, and then I blurted out how the buffet cabinet opened.

"Amazing," Carlos said. "This place is so massive, and with secret tunnels. We don't have places like this in my country."

"None of us knew about them, Carlos," I said, but quickly adding, "Except for Axel that is."

"And obviously Prunella did, too," Inga said, upset and hurt. "What's going on with her? She attacked Sherman and took off, leaving him to die."

"He wasn't going to die, Inga," Axel declared. "I'm not sure exactly what happened, but he does have a prominent lump on the side of his head."

"So, she really did hit him with a lamp?" Isabella asked, horrified. "She can't be in her right mind." A second later, Isabella mumbled quietly, "I wish my grandmother was here."

Inga jumped down her throat immediately and demanded, "You think Ms. Prunella's under some kind of voodoo spell, don't you?"

Isabella looked scared. "I, I really don't know."

"We're wasting time," Axel snapped impatiently. "I think we should *all* go and check the tunnels. We need to pay close attention for any clues that they've been there. We need a couple more flashlights, Inga. Do you know where more are?"

"Of course," she replied, opening a wide drawer in the island. She pulled out two more flashlights and handed one to Alex. "Here, you hold one and I'll keep this one," she said, clinging to it.

"Let's go," Axel said, turning and heading back to the butler's pantry.

"This is so cool," Carlos said, impressed. "I really may consider staying in this country if I'm able."

"Of course, you can!" I said, enthusiastically. "I would love it if you remained in Deer Creek. We can figure out a new career for you, too."

"Easy, Ruth Ann," Axel said. "Let's get through one thing at a time."

I noticed Carlos' expression fade, but Axel was consumed

with finding Prunella and not worried about trivial matters like Carlos' new career. I wanted to explain to Carlos, but didn't want Axel getting irritated with me. I waited for Axel to go into the tunnel and push the button that led to the basement. Inga was behind Axel and Isabella, and Alex followed Inga. I pulled Carlos to the rear and whispered, "Don't take Axel's response personally. He does want you here, he's just worried about Prunella."

"I know that," he replied. "But I don't think he's as worried about his wife as much as *you* think he is."

"What?" I hollered, causing everyone to stop and turn their heads to look at me.

Axel hollered up from the front of the line, "Everything okay?"

"Sorry, it's nothing," I quickly responded. Carlos gave me a slightly irritated look, but didn't say a word. We started down the stairs to catch up with everyone else at the bottom of the steep, damp, cement steps. I was happy when we made it to the bottom with nobody toppling down on another.

"There's no way we could find any clues," Inga snapped. "It's too dark. I think I'd like to take one more trip up those stairs and shine the light on each step. The first-time down I was too busy trying not to fall."

"Go ahead," Axel said, standing in a small corridor in the basement somewhere.

"Where are we?" I asked Axel. "Please don't tell me it's that secret room where Helena was murdered!"

"No, Ruth Ann. We're on the other side of the wine cellar where the entrance to the tunnel is located. It will take us to the guesthouse."

"Oh, that makes sense," I replied. "I'm going to take a good look in the cellar. Anyone else care to join me?"

I waited for an answer, but the others remained silent, except for Inga who started back up the stairs. I think they were waiting for Axel to open the door into the wine cellar. Finally, Carlos walked around me and stood by Axel. It was a tight room, with only enough room to breathe. A moment later, Axel pointed to the button on the wall and Carlos reached up high and hit the button.

Axel stood in the doorway and allowed the rest of us to step into the wine cellar. "I'm going to wait for Inga," he announced.

Carlos, Isabella, Alex and I walked around the sizeable cellar. Against the cement walls were shelves filled with every kind of wine imaginable. He had quite a collection, but the funny thing was I didn't recall him drinking much wine. I spotted the shelf that pulled away to reveal the secret door that opened into the other tunnel. I didn't want to disclose that yet because I wanted to keep everyone's attention focused on looking for clues in the cellar first. On the surface, I didn't notice anything out of order.

"What are we looking for?" Isabella asked confused. "There's just shelves of wine in here."

"Look for anything like a small piece of jewelry or maybe a balled-up piece of paper. It could be really tiny," I said, checking out each shelf. "Most of them are still dusty."

"Not these," Carlos announced near the shelf that opened up secretly. "These are totally free of dust, and there aren't as many bottles stored here. Why's that?" he asked, suddenly very curious. "Somebody must've just put these bottles in here. I think that could be something, don't you think?"

"Very clever of you, Carlos," Axel said, stepping into the cool cellar. He looked my way and said, "Ruth Ann must not have told you about that particular shelf."

Carlos looked at me and waited for my response. I was planning on telling them, but wanted to exhaust the search for clues in here first. "Well, Ruth Ann?" Carlos inquired.

"That wine shelf hides the opening to the tunnel that leads to Axel's guesthouse."

"Why didn't you mention that when we came in here?" he asked, a little annoyed with me. "Don't you trust me?"

"Of course, I do," I answered. "It wasn't that at all. I wanted all our attention on this room first, and then I was going to disclose that other opening. But, you figured it out anyway."

"Well," he said. "I didn't figure it was a shelf that would open to a tunnel. I just noticed it was different than the others," he said, humbly. "Let's go check it out!" he said, anxiously. "Is it like the tunnel we just left?"

"This is why I didn't want to mention it too soon. We need to finish with this room first," I said, exasperated.

"Ruth Ann's right," Axel said, walking over to me and standing quite close. "Check every square inch, and if we don't see anything except for dusty bottles of wine, then we'll head into the next tunnel." He turned to Carlos and added, "And to answer your question, no, it's nothing like the dark, uneven tunnel we were just in."

Carlos, Isabella and Alex looked strangely at Axel until he finally said, "It's really bright with fluorescent lights and white cement walls; totally opposite of the one we just came from."

"At least we'll see where we're going," Alex responded. "I bet they took off toward that guesthouse of yours. I'm kind of anxious to see it, too."

"It's just a big log cabin, Alex," I said. "It's beautiful, of course, but there aren't any secret tunnels or rooms outside of the entrance to the tunnel in the basement." I hesitated, turned back to face Axel and asked, "Are there? I mean I didn't know about these tunnels."

"No, nothing secretive about the guesthouse," he replied, crestfallen. "Are you ever going to forgive me about not telling you about the tunnels?"

"I'm not upset, Axel. I just don't want any more surprises. That's all."

"Oh, well, you should be happy to know that I am not aware of any other tunnels or secret rooms. However...,"

"However, what?" Inga snapped, suddenly appearing in the cellar.

"I was just telling Ruth Ann that I do not know about any other secret rooms or tunnels in the guesthouse."

"Oh," she said, smiling oddly.

"What's your problem?" Alex asked Inga. "You look funny."

"Do I?"

"What is it, Inga?" Axel inquired, with his hands on his hips, becoming impatient.

"I found something."

"You did?" I blurted out, loudly. "What did you find? I didn't see anything when we were coming down the stairs. However, it was dark and those stairs were difficult to maneuver."

Inga waited until all of us were giving her our full attention. She reached into her dark gray apron and pulled out a shiny object. She closed her hand around it making a tight fist.

"Come on, Inga," Axel said, irritated and quite anxious. "What do you have in your hand? I saw a glimpse of something shiny."

"I found a piece of jewelry!"

"Oh, don't tell me it's that Blue Ice necklace?" Carlos asked, cynically. "I can't imagine any of them would drop that as a clue!"

"Give me a break!" Inga exclaimed. "Do you think they would leave that lying around?"

"Then what did you find and where?" I asked, getting more and more interested and more and more annoyed.

She walked into the middle of the cellar and we formed a circle around her. Axel, Alex, Carlos, Isabella and I stood still waiting for Inga to reveal her discovery. Once we were in place, she raised her arm to shoulder height and turned her palm up and slowly opened her fist.

"I can't see, what is it?" I demanded, standing on tippy toes. "Lower it, Inga."

"Fine," she said, deflated by our lack of reaction. She lowered her arm and I inched a little closer.

"It's a silver necklace!" I shouted, causing my voice to echo.

"Not so loud, you'll cause these old walls to cave in!" Inga bellowed, just as loud as I did.

"It's not that old of a house, Inga," Axel reminded her. "Can you hold up that necklace so we can see what it is, please?"

She grabbed the shiny silver chain and a small charm fell toward the floor. "It's a circle!" Alex cried. "What's on there?" Axel walked to the necklace and bent over to grab the charm, but still letting Inga keep the chain in her grasp. "Is there something written on there, Axel?" Isabella asked, quietly, but eagerly.

"I found it! Why aren't you asking *me?*" Inga snapped, irritated that we weren't giving her the credit she was due.

"I'm sorry, Inga," she said, sweetly. "I assume you know what's on that charm?"

"Yes, I do. It's a letter."

"Letter what?" I asked, excitedly.

"C," she replied. "The round silver charm that's attached to this chain has a letter 'C' engraved in it."

"Cassandra," Carlos said, even though we all knew the answer.

"So, they were in the tunnels and made it down here," Axel said, sadly. "I guess I was hoping Sherman imagined the whole thing."

"He didn't imagine that lump!" Inga replied.

"He could've fallen and dreamt that Prunella came in and bashed him in the head," Alex said.

"That didn't happen, Alex," Axel said, obviously upset about his wife. "We now have proof." He took the necklace from Inga and looked at it closely.

"Can I see it?" Isabella inquired. "Maybe I can tell where it's from."

"How?" I asked, curiously. "It looks like a plain, silver initial necklace."

"Please?" she asked Axel, again. "You never know."

Axel reached his hand out and Isabella gently took it from him. Her reaction once the piece of jewelry touched her hand shocked us more than words can describe.

FOURTEEN

"Isabella!" Carlos cried, falling to his knees to catch her as she dropped limply toward the floor.

"Why did she pass out?" I asked, alarmed.

"Did you see that?" Inga roared. "The minute that necklace touched her hand she went pale and fell to the floor!"

"We saw her, Inga," Alex said, rushing over as we stood over Isabella. "Wake her up! It's scaring me."

Axel grabbed her limp wrist and took her pulse. "It's very fast. She's alive, but something shocked her so terribly that she passed out."

"The necklace!" Inga said. "It had to be the necklace!"

"We won't know until we rouse her," I said, reaching down and kneeling on the hard cement floor. It hurt both my knees, but it didn't matter. I grabbed her shoulders and gently shook her and called out her name. Nothing.

"Why won't she wake up?" Carlos screeched, panicking. "Something is very wrong."

"Give her a moment," Axel said, calmly. "Ruth Ann, take the necklace out of her hands."

I nodded and let go of her shoulders and reached down to open her clenched fist. "She has quite the grip," I announced, trying to pry open her fingers. Finally, after a little more effort, she released her fingers and the necklace fell to the floor.

"Look at her hand!" Carlos exclaimed, pointing toward her

palm.

We all tried to get close enough to see what Carlos was talking about, but I was the only one who was able to grab her hand and turn it over. "Oh, my God!"

"What, what, Ruth Ann?" Inga insisted.

"Her hand is burned!"

Inga moved me aside brusquely, causing me to land on my behind. "Hey, Inga!"

"She's right," Inga declared, ignoring me. "But it's not just burned," she turned pale herself and backed away. "Something very weird is going on here!"

Axel and Carlos couldn't take it anymore. Axel moved Isabella to a sitting position while Carlos grabbed her hand and took a look. "Inga's right. That necklace burned the letter 'C' into the middle of her palm."

"That's ridiculous!" I hollered. "How could a charm on a necklace cause a burn? Maybe her hand scraped the floor and turned red."

"And imprinted the letter 'C'?" Inga spat out sarcastically.

"Well, there has to be some rational explanation," I said. "We need to wake her up!"

Axel and Carlos held her in a sitting position for a few more minutes. Finally, Isabella's eyes started to flutter. "Isabella," I called out. "You need to wake up!"

She reached with her good hand and rubbed her forehead. "What, what happened to me?"

"You fainted," I answered. "Do you remember falling?"

"No," she replied, weakly. "I would like to stand, please."

"In a minute," Carlos told her, holding her down by her shoulders so she wouldn't try and stand. "Let's make sure you're okay first."

"I'm fine," she said, putting her burned hand on the hard floor, but stopping in pain. "What the...?" she looked at her hand and we thought she was going to pass out again. "No, I'm fine. What happened to my hand? Why is there a letter 'C' on my palm?" Her horrified stare will always be implanted in my memory. It was at that exact moment I knew she was aware of what was going on with Prunella and Cassandra. I told myself to let her regain some strength before I confronted her, but, well, that didn't quite happen.

"Knock it off, Ruth Ann!" Carlos barked, shielding Isabella from my abrupt questioning of his close friend.

"Put your arms down!" Isabella snapped at Carlos. "I don't need protection from Ruth Ann. She's right. I've had an idea of what's been going on ever since I saw those red eyes of Prunella's."

"You did?" I asked, baffled. This was the first time I ever heard her admit to it. "Why haven't you told us?"

"Ruth Ann. You just chewed me out because you figured out that I knew what was wrong with Prunella. If I would've talked to you about this before Prunella was taken hostage by Cassandra, you would've told me I was crazy and that all this 'voodoo' and 'witchcraft' stuff was nonsense!"

"No," I said, but then thought twice. "Maybe I would've said you were imagining things and reminded you that Meme broke the curse, so there had to be some other reason why Prunella was acting so erratically."

"See," she said.

"I don't care who told whom!" Axel snapped, angrily. "What do you know about Prunella and this other woman, Cassandra?"

Isabella was frightened by Axel's outburst. "Easy on her, Axel," I said. "She just regained consciousness. Let her stand and get her bearings."

Axel nodded, and he and Carlos helped her to a standing position. Isabella confirmed that she was ready to confess what she knew. "Can we get out of this cellar first?" she asked. "I don't like the feeling I get when I'm in here. Something bad happened either in here or not far from here."

"Nothing's happened *in here*, Isabella," I said. "You probably are referring to a room not far from here. Axel's housekeeper and

...," I promptly shut my mouth before I could add 'mistress'. I noticed Axel's horrified stare, but I quickly recovered. I was held captive in a room down here in a few months ago, and Helena, the housekeeper, was also found murdered there not long ago." Before Isabella fainted again, I hurriedly added, "None of us were responsible. The murderer is long gone so don't fear him."

"Oh, I guess that must be what it is," Isabella said, shivering a little. "It is cold down here. Maybe we could go inside that bright tunnel you told us about," Isabella said to Axel. "It's got to be better in there."

"Fine," he said, walking to the shelf and moving it out about a foot. "We enter through here."

Axel went first. He pushed a door open behind the shelf and stepped into a small, dark room. It wasn't large enough for all of us, so he continued through another door. The light bled into the small room and I could see into the tunnel I remember so vividly. Lynne was found in this tunnel not long ago, too.

"There," he said, after we all were inside the tunnel. "Tell me what you know. I hope it's fact and not one of those feelings you and your grandmother have or had," he said.

"It's fact," Isabella said. "I might as well just say it. I know about Cassandra and she's evil."

Carlos turned on her and bellowed, "Why didn't you tell me when I was explaining about her?"

"I, I didn't want you to know that I knew her."

"Wait, you just said you *knew* her," he said, catching Isabella's word. "You two were acquainted?"

"Yes. We were friends, actually. We weren't far apart in age and when she used to run around town, well, I befriended her."

"You two were friends?" I exclaimed, shocked. "Why didn't you just say so? It's okay that you and Cassandra were friends when you were younger."

"Not just when we were younger," she admitted, lowering her head out of shame. "I was in contact with her up until when you and John showed up at Carlos and Martika's resort."

"No way!" Carlos cried out. "But how, why?"

"She didn't want anyone to know she was hanging around the resort. I kind of took her in."

"She was *living* with you?" he asked, astonished.

"Well, I hid her in my room at the resort once in a while."

"But those rooms are so small. They're for staff and there was just a small bed and a dresser in each room. You had to share the bathroom and everything else with the rest of the staff," Carlos said, confused. "How could you sneak her in without anyone knowing?"

"She made me!" Isabella cried. "She was terrified that her sister, Martika, wanted to kill her so she made me hide her."

I couldn't help but ask the obvious question. "Why would she hang around a place where her sister wanted to kill her? Why didn't she just leave?"

"She told me she wanted to help her sister, but it would take time for Martika to accept her. Cassandra believed Martika loved her deep down, but had some delusion about wanting to kill her."

"I'm so confused," Carlos said, agitated and hurt by Isabella's betrayal. "You're telling me that Cassandra hid in your room and was planning on 'persuading' Martika not to kill her?"

"I guess that's one way to put it," Isabella said. "She was my friend. I couldn't abandon her. She wasn't always nice to me, but she made me believe I owed her, and that I had to help her."

"How did you owe her?" I asked, trying to get to the truth. "Did she do you some sort of favor in the past?"

Isabella looked scared. I didn't want to waste time on the past, but it might explain why Cassandra took Prunella and turned her against us. "It's okay, Isabella. You need to tell us *everything*. It's important that we understand Cassandra's motives."

"I guess so," she said, still looking unsure. "I didn't think any of this would affect our futures, but it has. I only hid her in my room to keep the peace, not invoke violence. However, it appears I was mistaken. Cassandra's worse than her older sister!"

"Why are you saying that?" Axel stammered. "Do you think

she'll harm my wife?"

"She already has," Carlos replied, angrily. "She kidnapped her and obviously put a spell on her. That's why she's been acting so oddly and flaring those evil red eyes of her!"

"She's not evil!" Inga hollered. "It's not her fault any of this happened."

"And don't forget she's pregnant," Alex reminded us. "None of this is good for her baby."

"Don't you think I know that?" Axel snapped. "No matter what, I don't want any harm to her or that baby!" "You're referring to *your* baby as 'that baby'! She's pregnant with *your* child," Alex said, emphasizing it was Axel's baby as if he was suspicious that it wasn't.

Axel quickly corrected his last statement. "I didn't mean anything by it, Alex. I'm angry, terrified, and helpless right now. I don't know where or how to find Prunella and Cassandra."

I decided to intervene and get Isabella back to her story. "Enough! Isabella, please continue. Why do you feel you owe Cassandra? Did she save your life or something?"

"No. I, I helped Cassandra when she was a teenager and I shouldn't have. I was very wrong in ever helping her. I thought she would be grateful, but she twisted everything around and made me think I was the one who should be grateful to her."

"Nothing you said makes any sense, Isabella," Axel said, confused and relieved to get Alex off his back about the paternity of the baby. "How did you help Cassandra when she was a teenager?"

"I taught her things that my grandmother taught me. I felt sorry for her because she was abandoned not only by her parents, but also by her older sister, Martika. I thought she was helpless, but it was just an act. She was a good manipulator."

"Just like her older sister!" Carlos said, clearly bitter about how he also was fooled. Carlos was forced into marrying Martika and buying a run-down resort or she would expose the fact that he was gay to his extremely traditional parents. He didn't want to upset his family so he went along with Martika's demands until he couldn't take it any longer and joined forces with John and me.

"Martika was a horrible woman!" Carlos declared. "I'm glad she's dead. If Cassandra is half as bad as her older sister, I hope she meets an early death, too!"

"That's cruel, Carlos," I said. "Maybe Cassandra's just out for revenge of her sister's death. It doesn't mean she should die, too. However, life in prison may be a possibility with what she's done."

"Stop it!" Isabella cried, loudly. "You all don't get it. Cassandra's much, much worse than her sister. She's been out for revenge since she was a teenager and she wanted to learn not only what I knew from my grandmother, but much darker, dangerous forms of witchcraft. She didn't want to help people break curses like my grandmother did, but place terrible curses on people, especially her older sister."

"So, she didn't want to slowly make peace with her sister?" Axel asked, confused from what Isabella told us a few minutes ago. "I thought you let her live with you so she could get back into Martika's life."

"Yes. That's what she told me. I begged her to tell me the truth. I reminded her of all I taught her years before, and she assured me she didn't want any harm to come to her sister. She said she was going to try and become best friends with her, not harm her."

"And you believed her?" I asked, baffled. "She conned you into believing her, didn't she?"

"Yes," Isabella replied, solemnly. "I really thought she had grown up and didn't want to do any harm. At the time, I didn't know she had sought out others who knew such black magic."

"How did you find out?" I asked, curiously.

"While we were with my grandmother just before she died, she told me to be extremely careful about Cassandra."

"Meme knew about Cassandra?" I questioned her, shocked.

"Yes. She knew I had tried to teach her some spells years

ago, but I didn't know if it worked. Maybe it didn't, but my grandmother told me she was very dangerous and informed me she had found out from Felix that Cassandra had sought out some of the seedier people in my grandmother's profession. He told her to warn me just in case."

"In case what?" I asked.

"In case Cassandra might try something against our family. But I told my grandmother she would never harm us. She was my friend and I was the only one who didn't judge her. I was horribly mistaken. Cassandra and Martika are just bad people who were abandoned and left to fight for themselves. They found comfort hurting others and I'm afraid Cassandra is here to not only hurt Prunella, but me, too."

"But, you were there for her. Why would she want to hurt you, Isabella?" I asked.

"Right after my grandmother died and I was about to come here with all of you, I had to confront Cassandra. I told her that my grandmother warned me about her and that infuriated her. She said she's never done anything to me and it was crazy of me to doubt her. She became so angry it scared me. I was happy to leave and go as far from there as possible. She screamed and hollered that I better not leave her, too, and that she was happy Martika was dead. She threatened that this wasn't over, not until she said it was."

"Why didn't you tell us this?" Axel hollered, clearly upset. "Maybe we could've prevented this maniac from coming to Deer Creek! Prunella is her victim now and her life is in danger!"

"I didn't think she was serious. I thought she was just mad at me for leaving her like her parents and sister did. I never knew she was aware of the necklace and how far Martika went to get a hold of it. I think she's continuing Martika's mission to possess your Blue Ice. I believe she thinks it has great powers."

"That's gotta be it!" I blurted out, my voice echoing deep into the tunnel.

"Not so loud!" Inga snapped at me. "If they're around, they definitely heard you."

"It just hit me," I said, excited. "I bet Cassandra watched Martika closely and found out she was after this mystical Blue Ice gem that possessed great power."

"But it doesn't," Inga said, confused. "I thought it was only cursed."

"It was," I said. "But Martika obviously thought there was more to it, and when Cassandra found out about it, she was determined to beat her sister to the gem."

"She died, Ruth Ann," Alex reminded me.

"And once Martika died, we came back home to Deer Creek with Isabella and the necklace. Cassandra was furious, so she hopped on a plane, hopefully alone, but it sounds like she got help, and flew here."

"You don't think..." Axel's pale expression said it all. He was worried the twins that Martika had hired in Sweden and brought to Jamaica somehow got out of jail and were now assisting Cassandra.

"It is possible," I muttered, not wanting to admit it out loud, but didn't have a choice. We had to cover all possibilities.

"NO!" Axel bellowed. "If they are here, then Prunella might know who..." I quickly interrupted him by shouting, "Stop!"

"Stop what?" Carlos cried out. "What are you two babbling about?"

Isabella gazed deeply into my brown eyes as if she was trying to read my mind. I could tell the exact moment she knew what I was thinking. A light flickered in her eyes. "Isabella," I said very, very slowly. "You're doing it, aren't you?"

"Doing what?" Carlos cried out, again. "What is going on? I feel that you, Axel and Isabella know something, and you don't want to tell the rest of us!"

"Hey, he's right," Inga protested. "We need to share *all* information."

"She's right," Axel admitted. "I think I need to tell them."

"Are you sure?" I asked, apprehensive about their reactions.

"Knock it off you two!" Alex interjected. "I may have an idea about who Cassandra came here with."

"She brought men with to help her recover the necklace, didn't she?" Inga demanded. "I knew it, I just knew it. She is just like her sister who had those two Swedish..." she stopped. I could see the lightbulb go off in her head. Inga slowly turned her head and stared directly at me. "She got those twins out of jail and brought them up here, didn't she?"

"That's my guess, Inga," I said, truthfully. "I don't know for sure, but it makes sense. Those two knew everything since they were working for Martika until she got killed."

"But, how did they get free?" Isabella asked, becoming hysterical. "They were locked up!"

"I'm sure it's easy to get criminals like that out of jail," Axel said.

Carlos barked back at Axel, "I guess you would know!"

"Hey, how did you know?" I asked, stunned at his accusations toward Axel. I tried to think back to our time in Jamaica when Carlos and I ran around looking for John. Maybe I did fill him in on Axel's shady past, but it wasn't the right time to throw it in Axel's face. "Forget it, Axel. Carlos is just frustrated. He didn't mean anything by it."

Axel and I looked at Carlos and waited for him to respond. "Right, Carlos? You're just anxious, and blurted it out by mistake."

"No, I didn't," he declared. "But, Ruth Ann's correct. This isn't the time, but if those two goons did get out of jail, we need to find out immediately. They were totally devoted to Martika, and if Cassandra convinced them to help her, we know they're only after the necklace for themselves."

"They couldn't possibly have any connection to that crooked lawyer in Sweden, could they?" Inga asked, troubled.

"Svenson," I mumbled. "Steven Svenson. He was the nasty cousin of Michael Svenson, Prunella's lawyer."

"Yes," Axel replied. "But Steven's in jail over there. He has no power anymore."

"Are you totally sure about that?" I asked him.

Axel thought about it long and hard. "Impossible."

"I think we should look into it. We need to find out if the twins escaped or were released, and find out if Steven Svenson is still locked up in Stockholm." I waited for Axel's response, but it was Carlos who responded for him.

"Of course, he'll check, Ruth Ann. I met the twins, and they were bad enough, but this Svenson character sounds even nastier."

"He was horrible," I said, thinking back to how he had poor Helena and Bert murdered so viciously.

"This can't be happening all over again," Inga said, a terrified look on her pale, rigid face. "Ms. Prunella's pregnant. This can't be good for her baby."

"No, Inga, it isn't," Axel agreed.

FIFTEEN

We stood silent inside the tunnel for a few minutes soaking in the information we had just discussed. Finally, knowing time was of the essence, I blurted, "I think we need to investigate the tunnel to see if we find any clues leading to Prunella. This is Axel's estate and he knows all the ins and outs of the place. We need him to stay with us." I looked around at Inga, Alex, Carlos, Isabella and Axel waiting for one of them to argue, but nobody did. "Okay, if we come up empty, I think Axel should go back to the main house and check his contacts in Stockholm to verify whether or not Steven Svenson is still in prison."

"But, Ruth Ann," Axel said, wanting to argue with me.

I held up my hand and said, "We need to know, Axel. I also think Alex should go upstairs and check on Sherman. He's alone in his room, and after Prunella attacked him, we need to protect him, too."

"Prunella would never hurt Sherman!" Inga snapped.

"But Inga," I said. "Prunella's not in her right mind. We really don't know who we're dealing with at the moment."

"She's got a point, Inga," Axel agreed. "I think Ruth Ann's got a plan we should try. We'll search the tunnel and make our way to the guest house..." Axel stopped, frantically looked around before saying, "Did you hear that?"

"What?" I asked, having no idea what he was referring to.

Suddenly, the bright-white fluorescent lights flickered and

cracked, scaring our group. "What's going on...?" Isabella asked, anxiously.

"I'm not sure," Axel replied. "Maybe there's a short in the wiring or..." Unexpectedly, blackness surrounded us. "Nobody move!" Axel hollered, his voice echoing deep into the tunnel. "Does anyone have a cell phone so we can turn on the flashlight?" All at once, several lights shone in the darkness. Carlos, Alex and Inga turned on their phones. "That helps," Axel stated. "Now, either we innocently lost power or..." Once again, Axel was cut off mid-sentence. A loud, ear-piercing, high-pitched ringing blared throughout the tunnel.

"Cover your ears!" I screamed, quickly raising my hands to cover my own ears.

"What's going on in here?" Carlos hollered over the painful screeching noise.

"I don't have any idea!" Axel yelled.

Alex shouted right in Axel's face, "Do you have a speaker system installed in the tunnel?"

"No!" he barked, stepping away from Alex. "You screamed in my face. That wasn't necessary!"

"Sorry," he snapped, sarcastically. "I wanted to make sure you heard me."

I was about to step in to break up their bickering when the sound ceased. "That's good," I said, but I spoke too soon.

"I think someone's about to speak," Isabella announced, predicting what was to happen.

We looked up to the ceiling and around the walls trying to see something in the dark tunnel.

Out of nowhere, a woman's voice blared through the tunnel. "I think it's Prunella's voice," Axel said. "But, where's it coming from?"

"Shhh," I said. "Let's hear what she's saying!"

A sickening, disturbing cackle sounded throughout the tunnel. Prunella must've had speakers installed recently. "That's not her," Inga demanded. "She doesn't sound like that."

"Shhh," I bellowed, once again.

"Yes, Inga, it's not your pretty little Ms. Prunella's voice you're listening to."

"I told you so!" Inga smarted.

"So, you finally made it down to the tunnels. Not the smartest group of people if you ask me."

Axel interrupted her banter and yelled, "Who are you?"

"You already know the answer, Mr. Eklund!" Silence ensued until the mysterious voice realized Axel wasn't going to respond. *"Please, let me introduce myself...I am Cassandra. Yes, you already figured that out, but now you can officially know you were correct. I am or was Martika's long-lost, pathetic little sister who poor Isabella took in as her trusted friend. Didn't you Isabella?"* The voice halted, waiting for Isabella to respond. But when she didn't, Cassandra's voice raised to an ear-piercing level again. *"Answer me, you little brat!"*

Before Isabella could answer, the lights flickered and turned back on. The blinding, instant brightness took us by surprise, but we quickly recovered. I looked down the tunnel to make sure nobody was coming at us wielding a weapon. I then looked at Isabella and noticed her face was flooded with tears. The poor girl was shocked and devastated by Cassandra's words. I reached over and put my hand gently on her shoulder and nodded. I whispered, "Just answer her. We need to go along with her for the moment."

"What was that, Ruth Ann?" Cassandra yelled through the speakers. Or at least we thought it was speakers.

I shook my head at Isabella. I wasn't going to respond, but Isabella should. I gave her a little shove to get her out of her state of shock. She shook herself and wiped her tears with her trembling hands, "Why are you doing this, Cassandra? You and I were friends. Why would you say that I'm pathetic?"

"Finally, the little cry baby speaks!"

"Knock it off!" Carlos hollered, angry. "Why don't you go home and leave us alone?"

"That was never a home for me. Once my dear, dead parents

abandoned me and Martika was killed, I had NOBODY!"

Isabella stood straight and clearly said, "You had me."

"You? You abandoned me too. You left me alone and came here to live with these, these traitors!"

"Why would you call us traitors?" I couldn't help but ask.

"Shut up, Ruth Ann! I don't want to hear from you yet. I'm talking with Isabella, and nobody else. If anyone else says a word...your precious Prunella will die."

"We promise," Isabella quickly responded, for all of us. "Nobody needs to die. There's been enough of that, don't you think, Cassandra?"

"Are you referring to my nasty sister and horrible parents? Or your beloved grandmother?"

"All of them. Your parents weren't horrible. Yes, my father had an affair with your mother. You and Martika were my half-sisters. I would never hurt a sister of mine no matter what she did."

"LIAR!" she hollered. *"You murdered my sister!"*

"No, no, I didn't. She died doing horrible things to these people that didn't deserve it. I didn't kill her!"

"A technicality, dear sister. She was only trying to get her hands on that precious Blue Ice, and instead of her being punished for it, she was murdered."

"But she killed for it, too," Isabella pleaded. "Is that why you're here?" She dared ask. Silence. I wondered if Isabella pushed her too far asking about the necklace.

Isabella obviously got her confidence back because she continued speaking to Cassandra. "If you already have the necklace, why take Prunella prisoner?"

More silence.

Isabella looked at me and I looked at Axel. He shrugged his shoulders and we stood still until the lights went out and blackness surrounded us again. A few, harrowing seconds later the speakers blurted out Cassandra's terrifying laughter. Her voice bellowed, *"Come and find me...come and find me...come and find...Prunella and her precious necklace...I dare you to find us!"*

"She's horrible!" Inga whispered, disgusted.

"I think you're safe talking as loud as you want now, Inga," I said. "She's off on her sick game and taunting us to come after her."

"We have to!" Carlos exclaimed. "We have to get Prunella away from her, and those twins."

"If the twins are here," Axel reminded us. "We don't know that for sure."

"We don't have a choice but to push forward."

"What about splitting up?" Axel suggested. "I think Alex should go back and check on Sherman."

"Me, why me?" he barked. "I don't want to go alone. That lunatic could be hiding out anywhere."

"I don't think they're back in the big house," I said. "They're somewhere in front of us toward the guest house."

"I agree," Axel said. "We need to find the speakers and see how they installed them. Then we head up to my guest house and look around. They probably won't be there when we show up."

"Where would they go?" I asked, confused. "Would they go back to the big house?"

"That's why I don't want to go alone!" Alex bawled, clearly scared to wander the bigger house alone.

"We need Carlos and Inga with us," Axel declared. "Just in case we need some strength."

"What about Isabella?" Alex inquired. "Can she come with me?"

"No," I said immediately. "We need her to deal with Cassandra." I turned toward Alex whose cell phone flashlight was dimly illuminating his face. "It'll be fine, Alex. They're not after you. Grab one of Axel's guns in the house before you check on Sherman. You can catch up with us in the tunnel if Sherman is willing to come."

"He won't have a choice, Ruth Ann," Alex said, angrily. He clearly didn't like being sent away.

"We need you to go because you can handle yourself if

anyone is in the house. You're smart and strong and Sherman needs you to be tough on him. Make him come back into the tunnel," I said, hoping my compliments would do the trick.

"Alex," Axel interrupted. "I keep an extra gun in my library. Let me tell you exactly where it is, and the ammunition for it."

Axel whispered in his ear, and Alex nodded up and down so fast I thought his neck would snap. "Why the secrecy?" Inga demanded.

"Just in case Cassandra and her men are eavesdropping, Inga. Better safe than sorry."

"Oh, that makes sense."

"Alex, don't go anywhere but into the library and up to Sherman's room," Axel insisted. "We'll be in this tunnel for a while, so I'm sure you'll be able to catch up with us. I just don't like leaving Sherman all alone. He comes across brash and tough, but he's just a big, wishy washy, gentle old man."

"Fine," Alex replied. "I don't like it, but I see why I am the one who should go." With that, Alex turned and headed back inside the door that took him through the wine cellar.

"Okay, I feel better that Alex is going to get Sherman. We shouldn't leave anyone alone," Axel said, turning his attention to the tunnel ahead. "Now, we need to slowly walk forward and look for any clues."

"Like speakers and wires?" Isabella asked.

"Yes. There might be other things in the tunnel too. Just keep your cell phone lights close and look up and down everywhere."

Axel led the way with Inga in the rear since she was tougher than most. If anyone snuck up behind her I would almost feel sorry for them!

Not everyone had a cell phone. I didn't have mine, and Isabella didn't have one either, making it difficult to find any clues in the tunnel. Isabella and I walked side by side trying to use the light from Axel's cell in front of us and Carlos' phone behind us. "I can't see anything!" I said, exasperated. "I'll just keep an eye out for anyone coming at us, and Isabella can be the lookout behind Inga."

"Sounds good to me," Isabella answered, taking a step back to walk behind Carlos and right in front of Inga."

"I don't need any protection!" Inga snapped.

"It's not for your protection, Inga," I replied. "It's just to warn us."

"Oh, I guess that's a good idea."

With limited light, I couldn't see much ahead anyway. We were getting close to half-way through the tunnel when Axel stopped suddenly, forcing me to ram into him. "What'd you do that for?" I asked, irritated.

"I found something," he said, bending over and picking up a small object from the cement floor."

"What...what did you find?" I asked, anxiously. "Is it a clue?"

Axel held a tiny piece of paper close to his face so he could see it better. "It's a boarding pass stub."

"Whose?" Carlos asked, stepping up to Axel's side. "Cassandra's?"

"Nope," he said. "I don't believe it!"

"What?" Carlos barked, reaching his hand out to grab the paper.

"Here," Axel said, handing it over before Carlos ripped it to shreds trying to get it out of Axel's hand.

"He's right," Carlos muttered quietly. "It is a boarding pass stub from the airport in Stockholm!"

"No way," I bellowed. "Whose name is on it?"

Axel put a hand on Carlos' shoulder and said, "Let me. I should be the one to tell her."

"It's Steven Svenson, isn't it?" I bellowed loudly, knowing the answer before he told me.

"Shhh, Ruth Ann," Isabella said, gently. "Whoever it is, we can handle them." She saw the look of horror on my face and added, "Who is this man? I knew he was a crooked lawyer, but did you also say he murdered people?"

"Yes! He stabbed a poor young Helena countless times and had poor Bert, the other butler, burned to death and hung out for everyone to see at a Halloween party!"

"Hold on a second," Inga said, stepping closer. "Mr. Eklund never said it actually was Steven Svenson's ticket."

"She's right, and it isn't," Axel said, still appearing pale and troubled.

"Then whose?" I demanded.

"It's for Jacob Svenson," Axel said. "I totally forgot that Steven had twin nephews and, and..."

"No way, it can't be," I said, when a lightbulb went off in my head. "The twins that Martika hired in Stockholm and brought to Jamaica!"

"Yes, Ruth Ann," Axel said, horrified at the revelation.

"That means," I began to say, but swallowed hard. "That means Prunella's b..." Axel quickly stopped me from finishing my stupid announcement. "That means Prunella's in the hands of those twins, again."

I recovered, realizing that I almost blurted to everyone that Prunella's unborn child was fathered by one of Steven Svenson's twin nephews. I wanted to turn and run away. Far away from here so that I could somehow ignore what was happening to our family.

Inga called us out. "What's going on? We already guessed that the twins from Jamaica were probably here helping Cassandra, but you two look like a ghost appeared out of thin air! Spill the truth!"

Axel discretely shook his head at me. I knew before he alerted me that I wasn't going to divulge the truth about the paternity of Prunella's baby, and that it couldn't possibly be Axels.

"I clearly heard Ruth Ann say something about Prunella's baby!" Inga spat out, accusatorily.

"I didn't say anything about her baby!" I replied, lying, but for a good reason.

"Inga, let it go," Carlos said, trying to get us moving. "Whatever it is, it doesn't matter. We need to hurry and find

Prunella. We know for sure that Cassandra has the twins helping. Who knows what they'll do to poor Prunella. We need to rescue her now!"

"I agree," Isabella said, staring directly into my eyes as if she knew what had transpired between Axel and me. "Can we keep going and see if we find anything else?"

"Yes, good idea, Isabella," Axel said, regaining his composure. "I still haven't seen any speakers, but there have to be some. How else would she be able to project her voice?"

"It's odd," Carlos said, shivering a little. "Maybe she has some strange power and was able to speak without the power of a speaker."

"Nonsense!" Inga responded bluntly. "We just can't see them in the dark. I'm sure there's a bunch of speakers somewhere in here, but it's too hard to see with these cell phone flashlights."

"She's probably right," Axel said, aiming the light down the tunnel. "We're getting close to the other end of the tunnel where we enter the basement of the guest house. I think we should push on."

We marched silently down the tunnel. We didn't hear anything more from Cassandra or find any other clues. Finally, about ten minutes later, we reached the end of the tunnel and the opening to the guest house basement. "Let me go first and check it out," Axel said. "I know how to get in there, unobtrusively."

"But, what if Cassandra has a guard waiting for us?" Isabella asked, worried. "I don't like this. I have a very bad feeling something is wrong, deadly wrong."

SIXTEEN

"Stop being so dramatic," Inga exclaimed. "They won't kill Ms. Prunella. She's their hostage."

"Exactly!" Carlos declared, abruptly. "But why would they still need her if they already have the bloody necklace? Think about it!"

"I, I don't have any idea," I replied, honestly. "If she helped them take it, why take her? What does she have that they want?"

"Finally, we're thinking sensibly," Carlos said. He turned to Axel and asked, "Don't you have any idea? She's your wife!"

Axel replied, "There is no reason they should keep her. Unless they want something else and we just don't know what it is yet."

"I wish we could talk to her again and she was willing to answer some questions for us," I said, but then that lightbulb went off in my head again. What if they were keeping her because Jacob (or his twin brother whose name we don't know yet) found out she was pregnant and put it together. I doubt Prunella would've admitted to him that he was the father, but if she wasn't in her right mind, who knows what she might reveal. I looked up to find everyone staring at me.

"What is it, Ruth Ann?" Carlos asked, concerned. "You look deep in thought. Did you come up with a possible motive?"

"Me?" I asked, innocently. "No, I was just racking my brain like you were."

I noticed Axel's squinty-eyes glare at me. He must've read my mind or already figured it out himself. Now, I don't mean literally read my mind like Isabella and her grandmother could, but I felt fairly confident Axel thought along the same lines as I did.

Inga, clearly agitated, pushed me aside and stood next to the opening of the tunnel. "Let me go. If there's a guard there I can take him. I can't stand waiting out here knowing Ms. Prunella's in there!"

"No, Inga," Axel said. "I'm going first. You can follow me, but the rest of you wait here until we call you inside."

Nobody argued. Carlos, Isabella and I waited while Alex led Inga through the small door into the basement.

"They'll be right back," I said nodding quickly, assuring Carlos and Isabella, and even myself.

"I hope so," Isabella said, anxiously. "I told you I have a bad feeling. Something's gone wrong."

"What?" I demanded. "Can you feel it or are you seeing something?"

"I have a strong sensation of doom running through me. I've had it before and I was right."

"When?" Carlos asked, interestedly. "Back when we were chasing Martika at my resort?"

"Well no, but I had strong feelings then, too. This was a long time ago with my father."

"When he was killed by snakes in the jungle?" I asked, immediately regretting my decision to bring up that nightmare.

"Yes. I knew when my mother cursed him that he wasn't going to live very long." Isabella closed her eyes. I could sense she was reliving that event. "He walked into the jungle and I vividly remember the exact moment I was overtaken with feelings of his death."

"But, you weren't in the jungle when it happened, Isabella," Carlos said. "How would you know?"

"Because I was," she admitted, shocking us.

"What?" I bellowed, stunned by her announcement.

"I understood why my mother cursed him. He cheated on her with Martika and Cassandra's mother. I was young, but my grandmother warned me about my mother's anger against my father. She said whatever curse my mother placed on him, it would be cruel."

"What did you do?" I asked, not being able to resist.

"I followed him as much as I could without getting caught by him or my mother. Once he left my mother and she cursed him, I knew bad things were going to happen. But I didn't think he would give up on life and basically throw himself into the jungle to wait for a wild animal to kill him."

"Don't tell me you watched your father die!" Carlos blurted out, horrified.

"Not exactly. I remember being home getting ready for dinner when a strong sensation ran through my entire body. I thought I was going to die. It was horrible. I didn't know what was happening to me. I was a young girl and didn't understand these new powers of mine. My grandmother told me I was smart and should be open to my powers, but I didn't take her too seriously at the time. I told my mother I needed to go outside and burn off some energy before dinner. She didn't think much of it so I ran to the small room in the village where my father lived in after he was kicked out of our home. I looked everywhere for him and finally ran back outside and asked everyone I saw if they had spotted my father. A man near our village's drinking well told me he saw him head into the jungle. He told me where and I ran after him.

"Did you find him?" I asked, even though I knew the answer. Her story had Carlos and me totally captivated.

"Yes, but it was too late. He was dead. He was strangled by a snake, and I saw bites all over his body. I will never forget the look on his face."

"Don't relive it, Isabella," I said, appalled. "Put it out of your mind."

Her eyelids flew open to display huge, frightened eyes. "I can't. The image of my father will never leave my mind." She lowered her head and sobbed into her hands. I wrapped my arms around the poor girl and let her weep until she was done. It didn't take long, she appeared so meek and timid, but I truly believed she was fierce and strong on the inside. Isabella's head popped up. She wiped away her tears and said she was fine. "It's in the past, Ruth Ann. I just wanted to let you know how I know about my sensations, and that they are real."

"We believe you," Carlos said. "Nothing we can do now, but wait."

I wasn't going to argue with her. She and her grandmother had proven to me that they had supernatural powers. I saw it with my own eyes when Meme broke the curse on my necklace while on her deathbed. It was an amazing experience that I will never forget. The shadow images of all the people who had come in contact with my necklace flittering around the room as if they were being expunged from the gem. It was terrifying, yet exhilarating at the same time.

"I hope they hurry back," Carlos said, nervously. "I don't like being trapped in this tunnel."

Suddenly, out of nowhere, the fluorescent lights flicked on. "Wow, that hurts my eyes!" I bawled, covering my eyes to adjust to the brightness.

"Who do you think turned them on?" Carlos inquired. "I sure hope it was Axel or Inga!"

"We're about to find out," Isabella said, pointing a shaky hand toward the small opening.

The door opened to reveal Inga's head. "It's okay," she said. "Nobody's down here, but you'll never guess what we found."

"What?" I quickly asked.

"Come in here first," she said, pulling her head back inside the basement.

"Ruth Ann, you go first. I'll give you a hand to get you in," Carlos said. "Then I'll help Isabella."

We made our way up the steps and through the door into the basement. "Ah, it's warm down here," Isabella said. "That tunnel was getting pretty chilly."

"It's heated, Isabella," I said. "But, you're probably still in shock from passing out."

"Maybe," she said, throwing her arms around her body and shivering. "This is really a nice basement."

"Nothing but the best for Axel," I announced, seeing him walk toward us from the other side of the room near the staircase that went up to the main floor of the guesthouse. "I forgot we entered the tunnel through a trapdoor under the bar stool."

"Ingenious," Carlos said, looking around the room. "Eklund, you really are loaded, aren't you?"

"I make a comfortable living, Carlos," he replied. "Did Inga show you what we found?"

"*Show us*?" I questioned.

Axel stepped lightly even though the entire basement was carpeted. "I don't want to be heard just in case someone's upstairs."

"You didn't look up there yet?" I asked, worried. "What if they are up there?"

"I did a quick look, but nobody is around. But, it looked like they were here."

"*Were*?" I asked, deflated. "Where did they go now?"

"One step at a time, Ruth Ann," Axel said, turning to Inga. "Show them."

Inga pulled out an object from her housekeeper's apron. She held up a tiny doll. "Wait, you found a doll?" I asked, confused. "What's the big deal about that?"

Isabella made her way over when she heard Axel asking Inga to show us what they found. One look at her pale face, and I knew that it wasn't just an ordinary doll. "She's going to pass out again!" Axel yelled, grabbing a hold of her shoulders before she keeled over.

"She did pass out!" Inga hollered, slapping her empty hand over her mouth. "Sorry, I shouldn't have yelled, but I can't believe she passed out, again."

"She caught site of the doll," Carlos said, kneeling on the floor and taking her gently from Axel's grasp. Axel stood up and looked intently at me.

"It's not just a doll, Ruth Ann. I gather you've figured that out already."

"Can I see it?" I asked, holding out my hand.

Just as I reached out to take the doll from Inga, Isabella's eyes popped open and she exclaimed, weakly, "No, Ruth Ann. Don't touch it!"

"But, why?" I asked, confused. "It's not going to hurt me."

"It can and it will. Leave it alone!"

Inga suddenly realized that the doll she was holding wasn't safe. She threw it on the floor and stepped back. "What's wrong with it? I thought it was just a silly doll left behind as a clue from Prunella. Are you saying it's not an innocent little doll?"

Isabella sat up and apologized for passing out again. "It obviously scared you so much you fainted," Axel said. "But you need to tell us why."

"It's not an ordinary doll," she replied, staring at the object just a few feet away from her. "It's a voodoo doll."

"A what?" I exclaimed.

"It's voodoo," she repeated. "Not the good kind, either."

Inga looked from the doll to Isabella. "There's a *good* kind of voodoo doll?" she asked, puzzled.

"Oh, yes," Isabella stated, perking up. She pushed Carlos away and an abrupt change of energy surged inside her. She was excited, almost frantic. "My grandmother used voodoo dolls."

Before she could continue, I found myself appalled and hastily said, "That's horrible, Isabella! I thought you and your grandmother broke curses and healed people. Now you're telling us that your grandmother practiced voodoo?"

Isabella looked angry with me. She snapped, "You're wrong, Ruth Ann. We didn't do anything cruel with these kinds of dolls. We used them for good."

"Voodoo dolls can be a good thing?" Inga asked, totally

freaked out by the thought that she was holding a piece of voodoo. She rubbed her hands on her apron to clean them, but realized that wouldn't be good enough. She quickly disappeared into the bathroom, and then we heard the rush of water. We waited for her to return before Isabella continued.

"That won't do you any good, Inga," Isabella stated.

She snapped at Isabella and reminded her, "You told Ruth Ann not to touch it. I had the thing in my hands!"

"You're saying only *I* shouldn't touch it, right Isabella?" I asked, trying to reassure Inga.

Isabella vehemently shook her head. "No, no. Anyone who touches it could be affected by it."

"What do you mean by that?" Inga barked. "Are you telling me I'm going to get cursed or sick?"

"No, it just means that they will know you've touched it and there's a slight chance you'll have the same reactions as the person it was made for."

"That's ridiculous!" Axel chimed in, laughing in disbelief. "It's just a doll, Inga. There's no such thing as a voodoo doll. That's just in the movies."

"You're wrong, Mr. Eklund," Isabella answered. "They are very real and can be very dangerous."

"I believe her!" Inga exclaimed, terrified. "What do I need to do to now?"

"Nothing you can do, Inga," she responded, matter of factly. "Once the doll has been destroyed, then you'll be free of any powers associated with it."

"Aren't these voodoo dolls supposed to represent a human being?" Axel asked, trying to get attention away from Inga's rising anxiety.

"Yes," Isabella answered. "Who do you think it looks like?"

"I'm not touching that thing again," Inga snapped. "You all can take a closer look at it."

"I will," Isabella said, getting on her hands and knees like a toddler and crawling to where the doll lay.

Axel, Carlos and I slowly met up with her, closely watching Isabella's expression to see if she showed any sign of dread. Once we noticed she was calm, we bent over to see it closer. "It's definitely a woman," Axel said, eyeing the long, yellow hair on the doll."

"Yes," Isabella said, sadly. "My best guess, it's Prunella."

"Why would you say that?" I asked. "It could be me!"

"Ruth Ann," Inga cried out from several feet away. "It can't be you because you have brown hair!"

"Does it have to look *exactly* like the recipient?" I inquired.

"Pretty much, Ruth Ann," she replied. "Plus, not to be mean...this doll clearly has a younger appearance to it."

Well, I thought to myself. I'm not exactly ancient, but I did kind of agree with her when I looked more closely at the doll. "Sorry," Isabella said. "I wasn't trying to be disrespectful."

"I know," I said, admitting she was correct in her assessment of the doll's age. "From what I see, the doll has long blonde hair, a slim body, and blue eyes. It clearly can't be me." I waited for someone, anyone, to tell me that I wasn't old or fat, but nobody spoke up. "Hey, wait a minute!" I exclaimed. "If we have this doll and it's supposedly for Prunella...doesn't that mean we can make her do things with it?"

"Yes, can we?" Carlos chimed in, excited with the thought.

Isabella stood, not picking the doll up, ignoring Carlos' and my question, said, "Why was it left behind?"

Clearly her question was rhetorical. She knew none of us understood anything about voodoo dolls! We stood in silence, waiting for Isabella. "I don't get it. If Cassandra was using the dark arts, then she would have to keep the doll close to her." She added, "it's as if she abandoned it hoping we would find it."

So, Isabella answered Carlos' and my question. The doll had to be in the possession of the person who made it or put the curse upon it. "Do you think Cassandra did it on purpose?" I asked, perplexed.

"Maybe they were in a rush," Carlos said. "They knew we

were coming and had to leave in a hurry."

"Possibly," Axel said. "I think we should see if anything else was left behind. Maybe it'll tell us where they disappeared."

In my head, I thought...here we go again. This reminds me of racing from the main house through the tunnel into his guest house over and over. I wasn't thrilled to repeat history. In fact, it completely angered me so I said, "I'm not going to let them play cat and mouse from house to house. We need to come up with a better plan."

"Any ideas, Ruth Ann?" Axel asked. "All we've heard is Cassandra's voice in the tunnel, and this doll," Axel said, kneeling down to pick up the doll.

"STOP!" Isabella cried, loudly. "If we're going to take it, at least put on a pair of gloves and stuff it inside a bag."

"Does that really make any difference, Isabella?" Axel asked, surprised at her suggestion. "I mean, if it's a real voodoo doll, I'm sure it doesn't matter what we pick it up with. Plus, I don't care anymore. Let me be the one to hold it."

"I already touched it." said Inga. "Maybe I should hold it since it's already been in my hands."

"Yeah," Carlos said. "Why risk the rest of us?"

Inga glared at Carlos, but he had a point. Inga had already held the doll in her hands. I walked over to her and quietly said, "He's kind of got a point, Inga. I highly doubt anything will happen to you anyway."

Inga replied sarcastically, "So, better safe than sorry, right?"

"Sorry," I said, truly meaning my word.

She marched over to the doll. She bent over and brusquely picked it up and shoved it into her apron pocket. "There, it's done."

Isabella's pale face revealed her concern for Inga. She saw me staring at her and said, "We didn't have any choice."

"So, now what?" Carlos asked, trying to get us on track. "We need a plan now."

"Any suggestions?" I asked everyone.

"I think we should head back and get Alex and Sherman," Axel suggested. "We need to stick together and think smartly about our next move."

"What if they left some other clue behind?" I asked. "Maybe a quick run through upstairs?"

"I already did that, Ruth Ann," Axel said. "It was empty, but I could tell they had been hiding here. The place was a mess upstairs."

"How so?" I asked, curiously. "Maybe there's something in that mess we can use to track them."

Axel shrugged his shoulders and headed up the plush carpeted stairs that led into the kitchen. I went behind Axel, and then Isabella, Carlos and Inga followed. He was right. I stepped inside the brightly lit kitchen and understood immediately what he meant by a mess!

Ordinarily, the tiled floor was spotless. Now it looked like a garbage dump. There were empty beer bottles, fast food wrappers, and remnants of eaten food everywhere. I stepped carefully to avoid slipping on the spilled condiments on the floor. "This is disgusting!" I cried out, just missing a half-eaten cream filled pastry.

Inga's expression said it all. She was furious. "I'm not cleaning this up!"

"Nobody's asking you to, Inga," Axel quickly replied.

"Why would they treat the kitchen like this?" Inga asked, stunned. She walked over to the large kitchen island and picked up a half-full gallon of milk and put it into the refrigerator behind her. She went back and grabbed an empty jug of orange juice and was about to put it into the garbage can. "What's the point?" she clamored, putting it back on the island. "There's no room in there, anyway."

"Well, I guess it shows they used the garbage can at first," Carlos said, mockingly.

"They couldn't take the garbage out and put it in the trash cans outside?" Inga snapped. "Imbeciles!"

"Let it go, Inga," Axel said. "Wait until you step into the great room."

"No," I interrupted before Inga could respond. "What did they do out there?"

Before Axel answered, Inga marched out of the kitchen and down the hall past the dining room and into the great room. We heard a loud scream and went running after her. "Look at this room!" she shouted, fuming mad. "What vermin!"

I passed the dining room and only had time to peek in, but I spotted filthy dishes everywhere on Axel's beautiful mahogany table. I shook my head and hurried into the great room to find Inga bending over picking up newspapers, pillows, and blankets that were tossed on the ground.

"Well, it appears we know where they slept," Inga barked as we caught up with her.

"Looks like it," I said, grabbing a stack of loose papers from the ground.

"Hey, Ruth Ann," Carlos said just as I was setting the stack of papers on a coffee table in front of the leather couches. "What are those papers you're holding?"

I looked down, mad at myself for not paying closer attention before I dismissed them. "You're right, Carlos. I should see if there are any clues in them."

Axel hurried to me after hearing what Carlos said. He stepped over a wool blanket thrown on the floor and held out his hand. I handed a few papers to him and a few to Carlos. Inga and Isabella were oblivious to what we were doing. They were busy picking up large pillows and more empty beer bottles from the floor so that no one got hurt.

"Hey, look at this!" Axel called out, causing Inga and Isabella to stop what they were doing.

"What? Did you find something in one of the papers?" I asked, eagerly.

"Yes, I think so!" he replied, excited. He threw the other papers he was holding onto the table which irritated Inga. She rushed over and straightened them before turning her attention back to us.

"Tell us, Axel," Carlos pleaded. "We need something to go on or we're doomed."

"Don't be so dramatic, Carlos," Inga said, sarcastically. Carlos shot her a nasty glare before turning to Axel.

"I think it's an itinerary."

"An itinerary?" I questioned. "You mean as in a *travel itinerary?*"

"Yes."

Carlos, unable to help himself, grabbed the sheet of paper out of Axel's hands. I understood his anxiousness, but he could've ripped it and then we'd be in trouble. "It's fine, it's fine," Carlos said, showing us he didn't hurt the paper.

"Read it," Inga snapped.

"It sure is an itinerary for, no wait..." he stopped speaking and had a puzzled look on his face. "I don't get it."

"What is it?" I demanded this time. "Is it a for a trip or not?" "No, it isn't."

Axel looked disgusted and tried to grab the paper back, but Carlos pulled away from him and kept studying the piece of paper. "I saw it. It sure is an itinerary for a trip!"

"No, Axel," Carlos cried. "It's an itinerary *from* a trip."

"From?" I asked, baffled. "You mean it's just an old itinerary and has nothing to do with Cassandra?"

"Oh, I'm pretty sure it has everything to do with her," he replied.

"Explain, please," Isabella said, joining us near the coffee table. I noticed didn't stop cleaning until all the pillows, bottles, and remnants of filth were neatly off the floor. I quickly surveyed the room and noticed the pillows were neatly placed on the loveseat and the blankets were nicely thrown over the back of the couch. In addition, she had completely filled a large black plastic garbage bag with trash.

Carlos held his hand high, signaling us to give him a minute more to read the paper. "Okay, this is what I read. Cassandra, and the twins, left Jamaica the day after Thanksgiving. They made a stop before coming here."

"Where, where did they stop, and is it important? Maybe it was just a connection," Inga said, irritated that we might be making a bigger deal about this than warranted.

"Hey, think about it. They left the day after we did!" I said, excitedly. "That means they've been hanging around and watching us for days."

"No, Ruth Ann," Carlos said. "Don't you want to know *where* they stopped on the way here?"

"I guess so," Axel said. "Just tell us, Carlos. You're dragging this out longer than needed. Just spill it!"

"New Orleans," Carlos said with a smile on his face, hoping we'd get it.

"New Orleans?" Inga asked with a dazed look on her face. "So, what?"

There went Isabella again. She went pale and dropped on the nearest couch. "Now what?" Inga asked, tired of Isabella's fragile psyche and fainting spells.

"Is she okay?" Axel asked, concerned. "This is happening too often."

"I didn't faint!" she bellowed, weakly. "I just understood what Carlos said."

"What, what did he say?" Inga asked, totally confused still. "Am I missing something?"

"Yes," Carlos replied. "New Orleans, think about it."

"About what?" I asked, still as puzzled as Inga.

Isabella sat straight up, no longer pale, but she did have a worried look on her face. "That's where she had the voodoo doll made."

"How on earth would you know that?" Axel demanded.

"Because," she began. "I know for a fact that those dolls can be bought and personally made in the Bayou."

"How do you know that?" I asked, curious to hear more.

"My grandmother told me. We can do it where we come from, but Cassandra clearly stopped in New Orleans to make the doll Inga has in her pocket."

We turned our attention to poor Inga. She was staring down at her apron and wishing she had never touched that doll. "What if she had others made?" Inga asked, wondering if one of us would start acting strangely.

"I'm sure it's possible," I said. "Why just Prunella?"

"Because she's the only one so far who's been acting erratically."

"But why her? She's pregnant with Axel's baby!" Inga howled.

Axel and I quickly shot each other a look, but this time we got caught. "Hey," Carlos cried out loud, pointing to me and then Axel. "What was that look for?"

"What look?" I quickly asked. "There was no look."

"Don't lie to us, Ruth Ann!" Carlos snapped. "The minute we asked why Prunella would be kidnapped and brainwashed you two shot guilty looks at each other."

"No, they shot the look *after* we said that she was pregnant with Axel's baby," Inga corrected. "Is there something we should know about her pregnancy?"

"No, Inga," Axel said. "We know as much as you." Well, that did it. Axel just told a monstrous lie, and I had two choices. Either tell the truth or keep the lie going about the paternity of the baby. Whatever I chose, it would be wrong and could affect our relationships and trust. I was about to tell the truth, but my inner voice stopped me. It wasn't my place to tell who the baby's father was. That was up to Prunella and Axel. So, there it was. I left the lie as is and confirmed what Axel had just told Inga.

"We found out she was pregnant when all of you did. Prunella hasn't even told me herself yet. I don't know anything. If there was a funny look, it was just worry that this vicious woman has taken our poor Prunella hostage. Pregnant and all!"

"Oh," Carlos and Inga said in unison.

195

"Can we get back to the itinerary we found?" Isabella asked, eyeing me oddly. She knew I just lied; I could feel it in my bones.

"Yes. So, they stopped in New Orleans," Axel stopped and looked at Carlos. "How long were they in New Orleans?"

"Two days," he said, looking at the sheet of paper. "Then there's a flight to Denver, and a car rental receipt attached to the back."

"A car rental?" Axel said, slowly. "That means we know what they're driving!"

"Yes!" Carlos said, excited. "That's a great clue."

"What kind of car did they rent?" I asked eagerly.

"A 2015 black sedan," he replied. "It even gives the license plate number!"

"That's terrific!" I shouted. "We can find them if they're still around town."

"That's a big if," Axel said, suddenly depressed. "What if they went back to Denver and caught a flight out of here?"

"Maybe there's another itinerary in those papers," Inga said, bending over and picking up the pile of papers she just straightened out.

"I doubt it," Axel said. "How would they know how long they'd be here? They probably had an agenda, but didn't know how long it would take."

"I'm sure they planned on coming here, grabbing Prunella and the necklace, and heading back to Jamaica," Isabella said. "That's what I would do."

I shot her a shocked look. Would Isabella do something like this and turn to the dark side? No, I'm sure she was just speaking hypothetically.

"I didn't mean I would do it, but that's what I would plan if I was Cassandra."

"You didn't know any of Cassandra's plans, did you?" Axel asked her, suspiciously.

"Of course not!" she cried. "I told you she was furious with me for leaving her. Why would she tell me what her plans were?"

"Leave her alone, Axel," I said, quickly. "Isabella is and always will be on our side." I smiled at her, hoping it would make up for the lie I told a few minutes ago.

"No, I've always worked on the good side of the supernatural and spirits. Many people from my country practice a crueler version of what I do, but I've never and would never do that! Cassandra sought out very horrible, evil people to teach her how to practice the dark arts. That's why she's doing what she is with Prunella and all of us. She's bitter, angry, revengeful, and she's probably enjoying every minute of it!"

"Wow, those are some strong words, Isabella," Carlos said. "But all very true."

Inga dropped the papers back on the table, ignoring most of what we were talking about and reported, "Nope. No itinerary to return to Jamaica in that pile."

"Thanks for checking, Inga," I said. "But we do have a car we can look for now."

"If they're still around town," Axel reminded us. "Why hang around if they got what they want?"

"Because she's playing an evil, sick game," Isabella said. "I bet she's still here. However, I really think she didn't mean to leave this doll behind. I think we should figure out a way to let her know we found it and are keeping it with us until she turns herself in."

"Why would she care?" I asked.

"Because that doll still holds a lot of power for her with Prunella," Isabella replied.

"Hey," I blurted, loudly. "Can't we use the doll to reprogram Prunella ourselves?"

"That's a great idea, Ruth Ann," Axel exclaimed.

"It doesn't work that way. Sorry you guys," Isabella said, sadly. "It only works for the person who created it, and for the person who had it made.

"So, what you're saying is that the only person that can control it is Cassandra and the person who cursed it?" I asked, suddenly having an idea.

"Yes," Isabella answered.

"What if we contact the person who made the doll?" I asked, excited. "Then she can remove the curse over the doll and Prunella would go back to her normal, sweet self."

"Hey, yeah," Inga said, thrilled.

"Think about it, Ruth Ann," Carlos interrupted. "How are we going to locate this 'witch' person who made the doll? We don't know any information."

Deflated, I said, "You're right. I got excited for a moment."

"Not exactly," Axel said. "What if we find something that shows where she got it? I mean, I doubt Cassandra knew where to go without directions, right?"

"Yes, I get what you're saying. Maybe there's a piece of paper with directions to who they saw down in New Orleans," I said, back to feeling excited and hopeful.

Isabella was the first to respond, "It's a long-shot, but we should look through everything before we head back to the main house."

We agreed to keep looking, but not take too much more time at the guesthouse. Inga and Isabella took the great room, including the filled garbage bag. Axel and I went back into the kitchen while Carlos searched the dining room and bathrooms. I asked why we didn't check upstairs and Axel told me he had already been up there and knew none of the visitors had even stepped up the stairs. It was completely clean and free of garbage!

SEVENTEEN

It didn't take long when Isabella and Inga walked into the kitchen shaking their heads. "Nothing," Inga said, discouraged. "Anything in here?"

"Nope," I answered. "Poor Axel even went through the disgusting garbage can and I went through the garbage on the floor. We didn't find any papers in here. Maybe Carlos had better luck."

Just then, Carlos entered the kitchen, smiling broadly. "Did you just ask if I had better luck?" He paused for effect and added, "Well, I did!"

"What did you find?" I asked, praying that it would lead to the person from whom Cassandra bought the doll.

"It's a map, drawn in pencil."

"There's a map giving us directions to where to find this woman?" Axel asked, stunned.

"Or man," Isabella corrected him. "It could've been a man that made the doll, too. It's not just women who work in this business."

"It is a business, isn't it?" I asked.

"Yes, Ruth Ann," Isabella replied. "We do need to make money, too. We have to eat and have a place to live just like the rest of you."

"Good point," I said.

"So, let's get back to the map, please," Axel said,

impatiently.

Unfortunately, Carlos was about to drop an unexpected bomb on us. "It's not to a man *or* woman's place in New Orleans."

"Oh, no," I said, exasperated.

"It's a local map."

"A *local* map?" Axel questioned. "Where and whose?"

"I don't know," Carlos answered, shrugging his shoulders and holding the small, torn piece of paper.

"Let me see it," I said. "I've lived here longer than any of you."

Carlos handed it to me and I was thankful that I could see the details of the map without my glasses. I saw the crude drawing of a mountain with a road up the mountain. There was a large square with an 'X' at a location that I strongly assumed was Axel's estate. There was a smaller 'x' located where the guest house is located. I explained this to the group and we all agreed.

"However, there's another 'X' not far from town, Ruth Ann," Axel pointed out. "Where is this?" he said, putting his index finger on a spot past the town's school campus.

"There's nothing over there," I said, confused. "The school campus is at the end of town. Beyond that is just woods and empty land."

"There has to be something there," Inga said, pointing her finger on the paper. "There is a clear 'X' marked there."

"I know, but I can't picture it. Maybe it's where they were going to stay, but they ended up in the guest house."

"Maybe, but it's something we need to check out. Maybe that's where they went," Carlos stated, excited. "Let's go!"

"We should head back to the house and check on Alex and Sherman. I'm surprised they haven't caught up with us yet," I said, suddenly feeling anxious and shaky.

"What's wrong, Ruth Ann?" Isabella asked me, clearly seeing a distressed look in my eyes.

"Nothing. I just had a funny feeling that's all."

"About Sherman and Alex or the mysterious 'X' on the

map?" she asked.

"I don't know," I admitted. "I'm okay, let's get out of here."

We hurried down the stairs into the basement, and back inside the tunnel. The lights were brightly illuminating the tunnel, and none of us dared to question how they turned on. I was secretly hoping Axel had flipped a switch or fixed the fuse. We ran through the tunnel as fast as we could. When we arrived at the end, Axel reached to open the door that leads into the wine cellar in the basement. Then, suddenly, the door flew open toward us!

"Alex!" Axel yelled, nearly getting hit by the door. "Why did you do that?"

None of us cared about Axel's complaint after seeing the look of horror in Alex's eyes. I walked around Axel. "What is it?" I asked Alex, knowing something had gone terribly wrong.

Alex was out of breath and he panted heavily trying to get his words together. "It's, it's, Sherman."

"Sherman?" Inga asked, pushing me aside after hearing his name. "Did you just try and say something about Sherman?"

"Yes, Inga," he replied, catching his breath.

"What happened to Sherman?" I asked before Inga could.

He shook his head violently. "No, no, you need to come with me. I can't say it out loud."

"Knock it off, Alex," Axel bellowed. "Just tell us what happened. We thought you and Sherman would've caught up with us by now. A lot has happened and we need to get out of here."

"Axel," I said, turning away from Alex's shocked expression. "We need to let Alex fill us in on what happened before we leave."

"We're just wasting time!" Axel cried out.

Alex shook his head in disbelief at Axel's coldness. He turned and headed into the wine cellar. We followed and watched as Alex marched out of the cellar and into the large, open room. "Follow me."

We did as he asked and went up the stairs into the kitchen. I expected to see Sherman sitting at the island or kitchen table glaring at us as we entered. "What took you so long?" Was what I expected to hear, but Sherman wasn't in there.

"Where is he?" Inga demanded.

"Just come with me," Alex said, his breath back to normal. He headed out of the kitchen and into the hall that led to the grand foyer. He didn't stop there. He marched up the stairs, waiting for us on the second-floor landing.

"He's up here?" Axel asked, confused.

Alex didn't stay on the second-floor landing for long. He took off to the third floor toward Sherman and Inga's rooms. I hoped Sherman was in his room waiting to tell us some new, wild story of what happened to him while he was alone. I also knew he would be furious with us for leaving him alone in the house.

"Why's he in his room alone?" Inga asked, baffled. "Did he fall and hurt himself and that's why he didn't come with you to find us?"

Alex still didn't speak. He hurried down the third-floor hall and passed Inga's room, and then the late Helena's room. The next door was Sherman's. The door was shut and Alex hesitated in front of his room. Finally, he said, "I think Axel should go in with me alone."

"Why?" Inga and I demanded at the same time. "If Sherman's mad at us, I think we should all go in," I insisted, wondering why Alex was being so mysterious.

Axel must've picked up on why Alex was so insistent about only the two of them going inside. He turned to me and said tenderly, "Let me go ahead in. If Sherman's mad I can defuse him a little. I'll bribe him with a trip to back home to England for a long, well-deserved rest.

"Fine," I said. "But don't leave us hanging out here for too long. I think it's silly, but I'll agree for now."

Alex opened the door just enough to slide his body through. As Axel went in, he didn't open the door any farther. "That's strange," I said. "They must not want us to get a peek inside the room."

Carlos suggested, "Maybe it's the other way around, Ruth

Ann. It's possible they didn't want Sherman to see us standing out here looking in!"

"Good point," I replied.

Inga, not as patient, said, "Well, I'm giving them about two minutes, and then I'm storming in. If this is Sherman's way of getting attention, he's wasting our time finding Ms. Prunella!"

"They won't leave us out here for long," a quiet voice said from behind. It was Isabella. "They know you and Ruth Ann are eager to see Sherman."

"Yes, she's right, Inga," I said, smiling at Isabella. "You've been awfully quiet. I almost forgot you were still here."

Isabella lowered head, and I got the feeling she knew more about what was going on. "What's up, Isabella?" I asked her, curiously. "Do you know why Alex only wanted Axel to go inside Sherman's room?"

Isabella turned a little pale, but not to the point of passing out. She shook her head and said, "No, no. I, I don't want to say anymore, Ruth Ann."

Inga glared at her and spat out, "What's that supposed to mean?"

"Easy with her, Inga," I said gently, so Isabella wouldn't get too freaked out by Inga's outburst. "Isabella is sensitive. She might sense Sherman's anger or pain. Who knows what he did in there while he was supposed to be sleeping."

Isabella eyed me suspiciously. I knew something was amiss, but I didn't want Inga to worry until we had all the facts. We waited in the hall for what seemed like an eternity. Inga angrily paced up and down the hall not saying a word, but huffing as she passed us. Carlos sat down and leaned against the wall opposite Sherman's door. Isabella and I stood in front of Sherman's door.

"I can't take it anymore," I said, anxiously. "I'm going to knock."

Just as I reached my hand to hit the door, Isabella grabbed it and pulled it back to my side. "No, Ruth Ann."

Initially, I was irritated at her for stopping me, but then I looked into her kind, soft, gentle eyes and my anger melted. I backed away and nearly tripped over Carlos' feet. "Sorry," I said, feeling flustered.

Carlos stood up and decided it was time to end all of this. He didn't care what warning Isabella gave me or the fact that Inga nearly ran right into him. He grabbed the door handle and pushed the door all the way open. "I'm going in. If you want to keep waiting, that's your prerogative."

My curiosity won over, and as soon as the door was opened, I peeked around Carlos to see what was going on inside that room. It didn't take long for a yell to resound from the other side of the room. It wasn't Sherman's voice or young Alex's, but it was Axel's voice that yelled, "Get out!"

Carlos refused and snapped back, "No! We've had enough. Tell us what's going on in here!"

I couldn't see past Carlos since he was standing directly in the doorway blocking my view. I was about to step inside when the door slammed shut. "Hey, what'd they do that for?" I demanded, almost getting my face hit by the door.

"Just open the door, Ruth Ann," Inga said, angrily. "I didn't hear them lock it."

I reached for the door handle when I heard loud voices from inside. Instead of interrupting and having Axel yell at me, I leaned the side of my head against the door and tried to hear what they were yelling at each other about. Inga and Isabella took a spot on the door to do the same. "Can you hear anything?" Inga asked with her head just above mine to the right.

"No, but be quiet! They aren't happy in there."

Isabella asked quietly, "Have any of you heard Sherman's voice?"

Inga and I pulled back from the door and realized Isabella might have a very good point. "No, in fact it's been Axel, Alex, and now Carlos," I said, baffled. "You don't think Sherman's missing or hurt again, do you?" I specifically asked Isabella since she seemed to sense something wasn't right in there.

"I, I don't know for sure, Ruth Ann," she replied. "I think there is something very wrong though."

Inga exclaimed, "That's it. If something is wrong with Sherman, I'm going to find out right now. This isn't fair leaving us out in the hall!" Inga didn't wait for our objections, but reached and opened the door handle. She stepped inside and motioned for me to follow. Isabella and I entered behind Inga to find Axel and Carlos standing face to face with red faces and arms swinging in an attempt to get their points across. They weren't fighting or yelling loudly, but it was clear they weren't happy with one another.

"What's going on in here?" I demanded, startling both of them.

"You shouldn't be in here, Ruth Ann," Axel said, turning toward the three of us standing by the door.

"Enough, Axel," I said, exasperated. "Where is Sherman? Did he wander into the secret tunnel?"

Carlos and Axel turned toward Sherman's unmade bed where Alex was hovering. "No, Ruth Ann. Sherman hasn't gone anywhere."

Inga ran over to the bed and shoved Alex aside. "What's wrong with him?" she demanded, pulling the sheet from his covered head and body.

"Oh, my God!" Isabella yelled frantically. "He's dead, isn't he?"

"What are you talking about?" I asked, practically laughing at the absurdity of her comment.

Inga turned toward me and told me to come next to her. I started to walk, but my body felt like it was moving in slow motion. I had the strangest feeling rushing through my body. As if I was being transported into a deep, dark tunnel of despair that wouldn't any sound emerge from my mouth.

Isabella saved me by holding my arm and leading me to Inga. Axel, Carlos and Alex watched intently as I passed the three of them to get to the side of the bed where Inga was waiting. "It's okay, Ruth Ann," Inga said, holding her hand out for me. "I'll help you."

I let go of Isabella before I reached the bed and grabbed Inga's cold, shaking hand. "Is he...?" I couldn't say the word. Inga's strong, but trembling hand gave me support while I looked at the lifeless man lying in his bed. I stared for what seemed like an eternity before I said, "This can't be happening. It's Sherman! He shouldn't have died alone!"

"We don't know what happened to him, Ruth Ann," Inga said.

"Ruth Ann," Axel said, now standing next to me. "It looks like he passed away peacefully. I think he died in his sleep. He wasn't a young man, remember."

"Oh," I said, not knowing why.

"There aren't any signs of foul play," Axel said. "Alex found him like this when he came to check on him."

Inga's head whirled around to face Alex "But, if he was dead when you came up here, why didn't you hurry and find us? You were gone a long time before you ran into us in the tunnel!"

Alex looked worried. "I tried to revive him, Inga. Really, I did."

Axel said, "Alex, please tell the women what happened when you came up here."

Alex looked strangely at Axel. "You mean *everything*?"

"Yes, Alex, tell them exactly what you told me."

"Okay, here goes," Alex said unsure. "You told me to go back and check on Sherman because he would be furious if we left him alone in this house."

Alex continued, "I wasn't thrilled walking around this empty house myself so I did what Axel suggested. I grabbed one of his guns from the library. It was loaded and ready to fire if necessary."

I glared at Axel, shaking my head for him leaving a loaded gun accessible to anyone who found it. Axel sensed my agitation and quickly said, "We have no children living here. It was safely hidden away and I told only Alex."

Alex continued before I could respond, "I quickly went up to the third floor. All of a sudden I had a terrible feeling inside that something had happened up on the third floor."

"Why?" I asked, curiously. "Did you hear anything while you were on your way up?"

"No, no, nothing like that. I just had a funny feeling inside. You talk about how you've had these feelings of doom. That's exactly what I had! Maybe I'm more like you than I thought!"

"Go on, Alex," Axel said, trying to get back on track. "Get to when you came inside Sherman's bedroom."

"I didn't waste any time after I retrieved the gun. I walked down the hall and noticed it was extraordinarily dark. I looked around and noticed a few of the hall sconces had burned out."

"Sorry," Inga said. "I noticed those too, but I haven't had a chance to change them."

"Wow," I said. "I didn't even notice that when we were in the hall."

"So, what?" Carlos snapped. "Can we get a move on, please! We're in a room with a dead man!"

"Don't be so tactless when you're referring to Sherman!" Inga replied, angrily. "He was a close friend. No, he was family!"

"Yes, Inga, he was," I said, smiling at her. "He really was family. He was Prunella's great uncle."

"I've known him a long time. I don't want to be in here either, but we need to finish hearing Alex's story."

Alex took that as his cue. "I wasn't sure which room was his, so I opened up Inga's and your late housekeeper's doors first. Finally, I came to Sherman's, at least I thought it was his, and grabbed the handle. The door was locked."

"Locked?" Axel asked, confused. "It wasn't locked just now."

"No, because I broke into the room. I probably broke the lock in the process."

"Who cares?" Carlos snapped, again. "When you opened the door, did you find Sherman dead in his bed?"

Inga glared daggers at him, but Alex ignored her. "I entered his room and it was pitch black. I reached around to flip on the light switch when..." he stopped, turned to Axel and asked, "Are you sure you want me to tell them this part?"

"Yes."

Carlos, Isabella, Inga and I looked at the two of them. What were they talking about? Why wouldn't Alex be able to tell us what happened next?"

"Okay," he said, hesitantly. "I flipped on the light switch and before I was able to look over at Sherman's bed I heard a rustling noise and a sudden screech coming from the direction of the secret tunnel." Alex stopped speaking and watched our reactions.

"Somebody ran out of here just as you entered the room!" I exclaimed, excited. "That means they probably heard you working on the lock and had time to open the secret door and get out."

"That changes everything!" Carlos spoke up. "Somebody killed him!"

"Wait, wait," Alex said. "Let me finish this part before I have any more interruptions. Please," he said, pleading with us to keep quiet until he was finished. "I ran over to the wall just as it closed. I couldn't figure out how to open it so I thought it best to get to Sherman."

"He was still in his bed?" Inga asked, even though Alex begged us to wait until he was done explaining.

"Yes," Alex responded without reprimanding her. "I rushed over and he was lying in his bed as if nothing had happened. He looked so peaceful, I thought he had slept through it all!"

"But he wasn't sleeping, was he?" I couldn't help but ask.

"No. I was about to go back to the wall and find the button when I felt the need to take his pulse. I don't know why, but I figured he couldn't possibly have slept through everything." He stopped and waited for us to ask any questions, but we didn't. We were stunned and horrified that our dear friend was dead. "I reached up and pulled the sheet down from his shoulders and found him lying flat on his back with his arms neatly at his side. I didn't think anything of it, but now I have my doubts that he died peacefully in his sleep."

"Because he was too neatly laid out, right?" Axel asked.

"Yes. His eyes were closed, but he appeared so...so stiff I guess is the word." He saw our shocked looks and quickly said, "Sorry, that was inconsiderate of me. I just didn't know any other way to put it."

"Go on, Alex," Axel said, soberly.

"Well, I took his pulse. I knew then that he was gone. It was obvious."

"Then what did you do?" Inga asked, eagerly.

"I placed his arm next to his side just like I found him."

"Did you call the police?" Carlos asked.

"No. I wanted to find all of you."

"But, that couldn't have taken as long as you were gone, Alex," I said. "We were in the tunnels and the guest house for quite awhile. What took so long?"

Alex looked guilty, but answered, "It took me awhile to come up through the house and find the gun. Then I rushed to the third floor and I'm sure it took me several minutes to get inside his bedroom. I don't know. Once I found Sherman dead, I paced awhile trying to decide what to do. I worked on that wall for a while, but still couldn't find the damn button to open it."

Axel walked over to the wall and within a couple seconds opened the wall with a tiny push of a button. "You probably didn't pay attention to where it was last time, Alex," Axel said, defending the distraught young man.

I wasn't so sure. Something struck me the wrong way. If I would've found Sherman dead, I would've run as fast as I could to find us.

"I know what you are thinking!" Alex cried out, staring at each one of our accusing glares. "I didn't do anything wrong!"

"Nobody's blaming you for anything," Axel said, quickly. "We're just trying to figure out a timeline, that's all. *Right*, Ruth Ann?"

I realized I was the one causing the tension. "Of course, I

don't think you had any part in Sherman's death. I'm just confused at how this could happen."

Inga's tempered flared. "Um, we're forgetting one very important part. How did Sherman die? I think somebody killed him and when they heard Alex coming into the room they took off. But who?"

Axel was the first one to speak, "Maybe it was my wife."

"You're crazy!" Inga yelled, completely out of place. "I'm very sorry to sound disrespectful Mr. Eklund, but what you accused Ms. Prunella of is totally, without a doubt, wrong!"

"Think about it, Inga," I said, not wanting to think the unimaginable.

"Not you, too!" Inga shouted out of exasperation.

"Look, Inga," I began to explain. "I can't believe these words would ever come out of my mouth, but you have to remember that Prunella isn't herself. She's under some kind of spell or whatever you want to call it. She would never hurt Sherman unless she wasn't herself."

"Or was forced to," Carlos added.

"Yes. He's right," Axel agreed. "We don't even know if Sherman died from natural causes or not. We haven't thoroughly checked him over yet."

"But, we would have to call the police and wait for the coroner to do an autopsy. We don't have that kind of time!" I said, frustrated. "Did you check him to make sure there weren't any signs of foul play?"

"You mean like a bullet hole or stab wound?" Alex asked me.

"Well, you would've seen blood if that happened," I replied. "Maybe there was a needle prick you missed or something."

"We need to check him," Axel said, looking at his body under the sheet. "Alex was shocked when he found him and probably wasn't thinking clearly. Give the boy a break."

"Who's going to do it?" Alex asked, terrified. "I, I just can't."

"I'll look," I said, wondering how those words left my lips. "Axel, will you help me?"

"Yes."

Everyone stood back as Axel and I walked over to Sherman's lifeless body under the crisp white sheet. I was shaking internally, but didn't want anyone else to know how terrified I was. Axel noticed my shaky hands as I lifted them to take hold of the sheet. He gently grabbed my hands and helped them back to my side. "I'll do it, Ruth Ann," he whispered. "You stand here, and if it's too difficult to see, then go back by the others."

"I'm fine," I said, lying a bit. "I will let you pull the sheet down however. Once I've seen his face for a minute I think I'll be okay."

Axel stood near the top of the side of the bed and I stood next to him. We were blocking the other's view. They were several feet behind us. He grabbed the sheet and slowly pulled it down so that it was folded in half displaying Sherman from his waist up. "He looks peaceful," I said, sadly. "I don't see anything right off the bat," I said, checking Sherman's head and neck down to his waist area. "But, it's hard to tell with his clothes on."

"What did you just say?" Carlos yelled from behind us. "Did you just say Sherman has his clothes on?"

"He's right!" Axel hollered. He turned to Alex and quickly asked, "Was he in his clothes when you found him?" Alex nodded. "But, I thought Sherman went to bed. Wouldn't he have changed into his sleep shirt and pants?"

"You're right!" I said, excited. "That means Sherman didn't die here in his sleep. He must've been awake and somebody murdered him!"

"Not again," Inga muttered. "Just like Bert!"

"No, it's nothing like Bert," I said, remembering the disgusting burnt body of Axel's former butler. "Bert was brutally murdered and burned, and then dropped from a ceiling to terrify everyone at the Halloween party."

"We don't know how Sherman died, Ruth Ann," Axel reminded me. "We can only hope he wasn't in any pain."

"Keep looking for any signs," Carlos said from afar. "Maybe

a needle prick. Pull down his collar or roll up his sleeves."

"Maybe if you have such good ideas you should come over here and do it yourself!" Axel snapped. "Give us a minute. We're trying to be thorough without disturbing the crime scene."

"It is a crime scene now," I said. "We need to call John and get him back to the house."

"Judy took off and went back to town and left us here alone," Inga stated. "I thought they were going to protect us."

"Judy?" I said, laughing. "We seem to have a habit of protecting her!"

Axel looked serious and said, "We do need to call them, but first, let's see if we can find any clues before the cops come and kick us out. This is personal. We need to find that woman and take care of her ourselves!"

"Whoa," Carlos bellowed. "You want *us* to go chase after Cassandra and the twins?"

"You bet I do," Axel answered. "Are you with me or not?"

"I'm in," Inga replied first, very eagerly. I nodded, even though I felt a twinge of guilt for not contacting John immediately.

Carlos did come over and help Axel search Sherman's body. I stepped aside to make room for him, but didn't go far. I wanted to be close in case they uncovered something. They worked in tandem unbuttoning Sherman's black vest and then his white collared shirt. If Sherman could come back to life he would be mortified at what we were doing to him.

"Look for tiny pin pricks around the neck," Isabella called out. "It wouldn't surprise me if Cassandra injected him with something fatal. She's vicious, but I remember her not liking blood."

"You mean like her sister, Martika?" Carlos asked, sarcastically.

She didn't reply, but I noticed she quietly snuck around to the other side of the bed. She leaned over as Axel was meticulously looking over Sherman's bare chest and arms. "You see anything?" Axel asked her.

"I'm looking," she replied, leaning way over to look. She pointed to a few areas, but shook her head. "No, nothing so far."

We waited while Isabella did her own thorough search. Just when I thought she was going to stand back, she lifted her finger and reached toward Sherman's neck. "Look."

Axel, Carlos, and I tried to get close enough without shoving the other out of the way. "Look at what?" I asked, frustrated that I couldn't get close enough to see.

"There's a tiny red spot right here," she said, almost touching his neck on the side that was closest to her. "I think it's an injection site."

"We didn't see it because we're on the other side of him," Axel mentioned. "I'm glad you came over here, Isabella."

"That confirms it," I said, after seeing the tiny injection spot. "Sherman was murdered with a fatal injection. I'll bet he was poisoned."

"We don't know what was injected, Ruth Ann," Axel said. "But, I feel fairly confident he was killed, and didn't pass away in his sleep."

"Somebody needs to call the police, now," Alex said. "This is a crime scene and we're all going to be suspects since our fingerprints are everywhere."

"None of us had any reason to kill Sherman," I said to Alex.

Inga got impatient. "What are we going to do now? We need find that

'X 'on the map. If we have to wait for the police, they'll get away!"

"OK Inga," I said. "I think we leave a note explaining what happened, and I'll call the police station to alert John. I'll just tell him that he needs to get up here immediately and go to Sherman's bedroom."

"We're just going to leave a note?" Isabella asked, curiously.

"Yes. I'm not waiting around for them to drive up here, and then answer all the questions they'll have for us. We'll never be allowed to pursue them once John hears our story."

"So, we're not going to tell the police where we're going?" Alex asked, stunned. "But, what if we need back-up?"

"We have guns, and plenty of people," Axel answered. "With me, Carlos, Alex, Inga, Ruth Ann and Isabella, we're a big enough group."

"But, none of us are the police!" he cried. "We can use all the help we can get. They'll be able to raid the cabin or wherever they're staying and keep everyone alive."

"We don't know that," I said to Alex. "I think we need to go and check out where this map leads. We have to do it for Sherman's sake. Especially if Prunella was responsible."

"Nonsense!" Inga hollered. "She didn't do it, but I agree we need to clear her name. Let's go!"

"We have to explain as much as we can in the note first, Inga," Axel said. "But, what do we say about us being gone when they get here?"

"We don't tell them," Inga snapped. "They should've been here to protect Sherman in the first place! Judy left without leaving any other officers here."

"She's right, Ruth Ann," Axel said, noticing my hesitancy. He wasn't wrong. I was internally going over our choices and possible consequences as fast as I could think.

"Fine," I said. "We really don't have any other option. If we wait, or even one of us stays here, it'll take too long. They could've left the area by the time we get to wherever it is we're going."

"The 'X' on the map is where we're going, Ruth Ann," Carlos reminded me, even though I knew that.

"Who's going to write the note and who's going to call the station?" Inga inquired. "I'm not a writer, and calling the station should be Ruth Ann's job."

"Me?" I asked, even though it made logical sense. "Fine, I'll call, but each of us contributes to the letter."

"Sounds like a plan," Axel said. "I'm not comfortable leaving poor Sherman here alone with a note pinned to him. It's so harsh and disrespectful, but as Ruth Ann stated, we don't have any other option."

We walked over to Sherman's old writing desk under the window. Inga opened the desk as if she knew where he kept pen and paper. "Have you looked in there before?" I asked, curiously, hopefully not accusingly.

"Yes."

Axel was surprised at her abrupt answer. "You mean when Sherman was in here with you, correct? I'm assuming you didn't snoop into his private effects."

Inga turned her head from the desk and stared at her employer. "If you're accusing me of snooping, you are correct! I looked in here before when Sherman and I have been at odds. He is, excuse me, *was* a peculiar fellow and even though I've known him a long time, I still didn't know much about his past."

"But if he didn't want you to know, then you should have respected his privacy," I said, changing her attention to me now, and not in a positive way.

"Like you haven't snooped into most of our lives, Ruth Ann!"

"Inga," I cried out. "Stop behaving like a brat. You know we weren't trying to get on your case. Can we just write the note?"

"Fine." Inga grabbed a loose piece of paper and a large, fancy pen. She held the pen up and asked, "Who's doing the writing?"

"I'm stuck calling, so one of you write," I replied.

Isabella grabbed the pen and sat down on the little wooden chair at the desk. "Okay, tell me what to write."

This is what we collectively came up with. Nothing we could write would take away the pain, but it was time for retribution. We needed to find Cassandra, the twins and Prunella.

John,

We tried to leave the crime scene as untouched as possible. Unfortunately, we have been in this room and we had to check Sherman for a pulse to see if he was still alive. Alex was the first to find Sherman. He came and found the rest of us immediately. Carlos, Axel and I did unbutton his vest and shirt. Isabella was the one who discovered the pin prick, red spot on his neck.

Sherman was clearly murdered. We assume it was Cassandra who struck again. Please don't be mad at us. It was of the utmost urgency that we left and followed our instincts to check out various places in town. They're probably long gone, so we don't feel like we are in any danger. If we find anything out we will contact you immediately.

As you read this and your anger builds, which I'm pretty sure it will, please remember that Sherman was our friend and family member. Prunella is pregnant and being held by a lunatic. We aren't thinking rationally ourselves, but if we waste more time waiting here for you or your officers to arrive, we might risk never finding them.

Please forgive us,
Ruth Ann (Axel, Inga, Carlos, Isabella, and Alex)

P.S. We're all fine by the way.

EIGHTEEN

"Wow. That is quite a note," Carlos said, taking the piece of paper from Isabella and reading it.

"I didn't like the way it read as if I wrote it," I stated. "You guys are cowards when it comes to John. However, it was good to mention Alex came and found us immediately after discovering Sherman was dead."

"He is the chief of police, Ruth Ann," Axel said. "I've been in enough hot water with the police."

"So, let's throw Ruth Ann under the bus!" I thundered, angrily.

"Can we go now?" Inga asked impatiently, as she walked over to the bed and said a quiet good-bye to her friend. I felt tears well in my eyes, and my anger subsided as she gently touched the sheet we had pulled over him. She didn't look under it, but turned and headed into the hallway.

It was so final. We would never see Sherman alive again. I know I hadn't known him for long, but so much has happened from the minute I met him back in Sweden. He was a proper, but grumpy, butler who respected his employer and actually, all of us. He was brave, yet a coward in many ways. No matter what he was, he would've given his life to protect his great niece, Prunella. This was personal more than ever now. We had to catch that evil witch, Cassandra!

"Who's going to drive?" Inga inquired, looking at Axel and

me.

"I will," I said first. "I know the town best."

"But that means you should be looking out the window and guiding us, Ruth Ann," Axel said. "Let me drive. You sit in the front and the rest of them can squeeze into the back seat."

"Fine," I said. "That's probably best anyway."

We headed down the stairs and grabbed our coats before heading out the kitchen door and down a brick path that led to the massive garage. It was morning. The sun was glistening on the fresh snow. I had to cover my eyes for a second to adjust to the brightness. "It's going to invigorate us!" I called out to the rest of our group.

"It's freezing!" Carlos yelped, tugging his coat a little tighter. "I'm not used to this cold air."

"How are you doing Isabella?" I asked. "It's got to be quite the shock being in this frigid climate."

Isabella had been awfully quiet. I wasn't sure if she was uncomfortable being around us after finding poor Sherman. I knew she sensed something horrible was still going to happen, but I could only hope and pray that Sherman's death was the worst thing she dreaded.

"Isabella?" Carlos asked, nudging her as they walked side by side on the way to the garage. "Did you hear Ruth Ann's question?"

She woke from her trance and said, "What question?"

"She asked you if you're doing okay in this cold weather?" Carlos stammered. "What were you thinking about?"

"Everything. I was going over in my mind how my grandmother warned me not to try saving Cassandra. I failed miserably and now look what she's done. She's killed an innocent man, but for what?"

"She's got a good point," Axel said, turning around from being in the lead. "Why did they have to kill Sherman?"

"Maybe he ran into them while we were in the basement or tunnel," Alex suggested. "If they felt threatened they would've had to stop him."

"They didn't just stop him, Alex," Inga snapped. "They murdered him for no reason. Sherman is and never was a threat to anyone!"

"Well, I don't know, but when I got into his room, they had obviously already killed him and were placing him back in his bed."

"You think Prunella was involved killing her great uncle, don't you?" I asked Isabella.

"I'm afraid I do. She's not in her right mind. That's why we have to find her, and quickly so she doesn't do any more harm."

"You think she's going to hurt somebody else?" I asked, stunned.

"All I can tell you is that I don't think this is anywhere close to being over. There's a lot more to come," she said with such conviction in her voice that it scared me.

"We're here," Axel said, walking to the door of the massive garage housing several cars. "Let's take that big black one," he said, pointing to a large, luxurious sedan with a shiny Viking ship adorning the front hood.

We piled into the sedan. Axel and I were in the front seat, and Carlos, Inga, Isabella and Alex were in the back. They were tightly crammed in, but not uncomfortably. It was a large sedan with black leather seats. Axel turned on the car and the front and back seat heaters. "We'll be warm in a second."

"Turn mine off, please," I said, dreading the heated seat. "I don't need mine." I didn't say why, but most women of my age would understand that extra heat was not needed!

Axel opened the garage door with a push of a button on his visor. The sun shone in and he pulled onto the gravel road that led to the one and only road in and out of town. I knew it took approximately twenty minutes to get back to town. I pulled out my cell phone because I still had to call the police station. "It's dead," I said, foolishly shaking my phone, thinking I could get it to work.

"Here," Axel said. "Let me call from the car. You can speak, and the rest of us will remain quiet. We don't want him to know that we've left the house."

"Good call," Carlos said from the back seat. "Are you going to ask for John?"

"No way," I answered swiftly. "If I had to speak to him, he'd force too much information out of me. It's best that I speak to the new receptionist. I think her name is Chris."

I waited for Axel to call the station and the voice that answered threw me. I whispered, "Oh, no. I think it's Lou, one of John's detectives."

"Hello, is anyone there?" the strong male voice called out through the car's speaker.

"Lou, is that you?" I asked without telling him it was me.

"Ruth Ann?" he replied, obviously recognizing my voice. "Is everything okay? I know John was about to head back to Eklund's estate, let me go get him."

"No, wait, Lou," I said, quickly. "Everything's fine. I was just calling to find out when someone was coming back up to Axel's estate. Now that you told me John's about to come back, I don't need anything else."

"Okay, suit yourself," he said, and then the phone went dead.

"He hung up fast enough," Axel said. "That seems odd, doesn't it?"

"Maybe he was busy at the station," Inga mentioned from the back seat.

We descended the mountain into our tiny valley town in no time. There was no ice or snow on the road because the plows in the area kept the road impeccably clear. Main Street is the only major road that runs from our town into the larger town of Grand Junction. It had snowed a little overnight, but an inch or two is nothing in our climate.

"We're entering the outskirts of Deer Creek," I called out to everyone. "We'll be going by my daughter's bakery and..." I stopped, realizing I made a serious error. "I forgot it's Monday, and my antique store is due to open soon."

Axel quickly said, "Call Meme, your assistant, and ask her to open the store. Tell her you're not feeling well." Before I could respond how I despise lying, he added, "I know you don't want to do that, but what else could you say?"

"He's got a point, Ruth Ann," Inga said from the back seat. "It's not exactly a lie. You *don't* feel good. Your close friend was murdered and your cousin has gone crazy because of a lunatic!"

"You're right, Inga," I cried. "I don't feel good. I'm sick and devastated about Sherman. We need to do whatever it takes to catch Cassandra and those twins."

"Call her," Axel said. "Just type in her number on the screen. I don't know it."

I pushed in Meme's cell phone number on Axel's touch screen. Within seconds, Meme answered, "Hello?"

"Hi, Meme," I said, holding my finger up to my mouth so nobody else would speak.

"Ruth Ann, is that you?"

"Yes, Meme," I said, suddenly realizing the number that popped up on her phone wasn't my own.

"Where are you calling from? I didn't recognize the number when it showed up."

Think fast, I said to myself. "I, I let my cell phone go dead so I borrowed Prunella's phone."

"Oh, that's too funny, Ruth Ann. You have a history of that happening. Are you up at Prunella's place right now?" she asked, obviously wondering why I wasn't at my store.

"Yes, that's why I'm calling you. I just woke up and realized it was Monday and I wanted to ask if you could run the store today because I'm feeling a bit under the weather." There was silence on the other end. I added, "If not, we can keep the store closed today. It's okay, really."

"No, no, Ruth Ann. I'll drop Elijah off at Kiddie Care right now. I'll get over to the store as soon as I can. Feel better!" Meme hung up before I could respond. I told myself I had to give her another raise just for being so nice and accommodating.

"Good, that's taken care of," Axel said. "Now, what about your daughters?"

"What about them?" I asked, confused. "They don't need to know anything yet."

"What if they call your store or worse, go over and find you're not there," Alex said from the back. "You know your daughters. They'll think you're up to no good."

"She is," Isabella replied smiling, even though none of it was very funny.

"I didn't think of that," I said, worried. "Maybe I should leave them a message."

"No!" Inga hollered from behind me. "Lynne or Nancy might actually pick up their phone, and then what will you do?"

I thought very carefully about my answer. Finally, I said, "Nancy won't answer. It's Monday and she's teaching. Lynne is too busy at her new shop in the resort. It just opened and she's running her bakery, too. She won't have time to answer my call."

"You better hope not," Axel muttered.

I glared at him and snapped, "You have any better suggestions?"

He shook his head as he came to the only stoplight on Main Street. We were stopped at the intersection where turning left would take us into Deer Creek Resort's parking lot. Lynne's new shop was located there. I glanced at the massive log cabin themed resort.

I had to risk it. I punched in Nancy's cell phone first on Axel's car screen. "Shhh, the phone is ringing." I held my breath hoping her voicemail would come on. "Yes! It's her voicemail." I left a brief message saying I was up at the estate and decided to relax up there today.

"As long as Nancy doesn't communicate with Meme. You told her you were sick," Inga said.

"There's no reason for those two to talk. However, Lynne could be a bigger problem. She has a tendency to pop into my store when she hasn't heard from me. I'm just hoping the new store and bakery is keeping her occupied."

"Risky, but you don't have a choice right now," Axel said.

I took a deep breath and called Lynne. She was the one who had the biggest chance of picking up her phone. I looked at the clock on Axel's dashboard and it was 9:30 in the morning. "Voicemail." Phew, I got lucky. I left the same message on Lynne's phone that I left on Nancy's just in case the two talked.

"Good, we should be okay now," Axel said, pulling around a curve that took us just past the high school lot. "We're almost to the spot on the map, Ruth Ann. Does it look familiar now?"

"No," I said, truthfully. "I've never been past the school complex."

"Great," Carlos mumbled sarcastically from the back. "What do we do now?"

"We follow this road and see where it leads," Axel replied very matter of factly. "We don't have a choice, do we?"

"No," Carlos answered, discouraged.

"I'm scared," Isabella said softly from the back. "We're rushing into a situation we know nothing about."

"Just like Axel said. We don't have a choice," Inga said, sitting next to her. Poor Isabella looked so tiny next to Inga's large, middle-aged body.

Axel spoke specifically to Alex and Carlos as he tossed the map into the back seat. "Look closely at the map. Do either of you see anything besides an 'X' behind the school complex?"

I was momentarily offended, but I had just admitted I didn't recognize anything over here. "All I've ever seen from the back of the school was woods."

"Maybe there are cabins in the woods back here," Carlos suggested. "But, wouldn't you know that Ruth Ann? You've lived here for years."

"The only cabins I know aren't located this way. I thought it was just wilderness and mountainous terrain."

"Well, we're about to find out," Axel said, veering the car around another curve."

"I didn't know the road went this direction!" I cried out.

"It's not much of a road anymore," Axel said, holding on tightly to the steering wheel. It's a gravel road, I hope it doesn't scratch my car!"

"Forget about your car, Eklund!" Carlos bellowed. "You have enough money to buy another one or have this one detailed."

"He's right," I said to Axel. "Just keep watch for any cars or cabins once we enter these woods."

"It looks pretty dark in there," Isabella said in a trembling voice. "I don't like how I'm feeling right now."

"What's that supposed to mean?" Inga snapped at the poor girl. "Are you saying you know what we're getting ourselves into?"

"No, no, Inga," she replied immediately. "I just am scared, that's all."

"We're all scared," Alex said, reassuring her. "I'm starting to regret ever coming to this town!"

I wasn't going to dignify his remark with an answer. If it wasn't for us, Alex would have no family at all. "Look," I called out to Axel. "The road ends at the edge of the woods."

"Not exactly, Ruth Ann. It doesn't look like much of a road, but there are tire tracks that have worn down the grass."

"It has to be them!" Inga exclaimed. "They're back here!"

"We don't know that for sure, Inga," Axel said. "We don't know who's been here, but we're about to find out." Axel slowed down to a crawl as his automatic headlights turned on. "It is dark in here," he said, gripping the steering wheel even more tightly.

"Everyone keep a lookout," I said, looking from side to side in the woods. It was so thick with trees and bushes that I couldn't see past the narrow opening Axel's car was driving through. "It's really eerie in here. No wonder I've never explored this place."

We traveled deep into the forest before Axel noticed the matted down tire tracks disappear. "If they kept going, why did the tire tracks stop?" he asked, confused.

"Did we miss an opening off one side or the other?" Carlos

asked.

"I don't think so, but it's so dark I can't say for sure."

I suggested we back up a bit and see if we missed anything. Axel agreed, but maneuvering the car in the dark, thick woods wasn't easy. Carlos was yelling from the back to "Watch out" constantly, and Inga was draped over poor Alex who was next to the other back window.

"Inga, back off!" Alex snapped, shoving her off him. "I'm trying to look too, but you're hovering over me."

"I can't see from the middle, Alex. We all need to be looking."

"Don't bother," Axel said, suddenly. "I think I just spotted where their car pulled off the road."

I looked Axel's direction as his car came to a complete stop. He turned off his headlights. "Hey, I can't see anything, Axel," I cried.

"We can't risk being seen from this road, Ruth Ann."

"I get it, but are you sure you spotted another road?" I questioned him.

"Just let him turn on the road, Ruth Ann," Carlos said, irritated.

"It's not exactly a road," Axel corrected Carlos and me. "It looks like a wide trail."

"Maybe that's all it is," Inga said.

"Nope," Axel replied. "I saw matted down grass again."

"What are we going to do?" Isabella inquired, looking scared, her eyes staring toward the dark trail. "Are we going to drive from here or get out and walk?"

"That's what I'm trying to decide right now," Axel admitted. "I'm not sure how far down they went or *if* this is where they went."

"I say we drive," Carlos suggested. "It's freezing cold out there and we might have to walk for miles!"

"It wouldn't be miles, Carlos," I said. "There's not much room back here. "Deer Creek is in a little valley surrounded by the largest mountain, Deer Creek Mountain, and several smaller ones."

"But, we really don't know how far back they went, Ruth Ann," Axel said. "I say we drive, but I'll have to go in there without my lights on."

"How are you going to see where you're going?" I inquired.

"Very, very slowly."

We agreed because there was no other alternative at the moment. Axel backed up so he had room to make the tight right turn. It was quite bumpy, and when he went over a small rock, he sputtered a word not appropriate for anyone to hear. More than likely he was worried about his car. He apologized quickly, adding, "I can't risk blowing out a tire. What if we need a fast escape?"

We didn't get very far before the darkness enclosed us and the only light we had was the glow of Axel's dashboard. He wasn't happy about the light, so I pulled off my scarf and held it over the glowing dashboard. "Thanks, Ruth Ann," he said. "That was a great idea."

"Do you see anything up ahead, Axel?" Carlos asked, peering out the side window. "All I see from the side of the car is blackness, and sporadic branches banging the car."

"Nothing yet," Axel replied. "We haven't gone a hundred yards yet. It's really slow going. I'm terrified I'm going to run into a rock or worse, a human being!"

"Who would be out here in the dark?" Inga exclaimed. "Plus, it's got to be ten degrees out there."

"Not quite, Inga," I answered for Axel. "It's cold, but not that cold yet."

"Inga," Axel started to say. "The obvious answer to who could be out here is my wife or one of her kidnappers."

"They wouldn't be hanging out on some unknown trail waiting for us," Inga said.

"Yes, they would and could," I said. "If they realized the map was left behind they could be watching for us."

"Exactly," Axel agreed. "I'm sure Cassandra has one of the

twins in the cold as a lookout."

"Then it doesn't matter if you run him down!" Carlos bellowed from the back of the car.

I turned around and glared at him. "Axel doesn't want to run anybody over, even one of the twins."

As I turned my head around, I caught site of Axel's gaze. He had a look of..." Are you kidding me! Of course, I want to run them down!" I guess I didn't blame him. One of those twins was more than likely the father of his wife's baby. I chose to let it go and focused on looking out the front windshield.

A few minutes later, Alex cried out, "Stop, Axel!"

We turned to see what Alex was hollering about. "What is it?" Axel asked, halting the car. "Do you see something?"

"Look in the woods. There's a sliver of a light peeking through. I see it, do any of you?"

I couldn't see anything from my viewpoint, but Alex was looking to the side. "Maybe the trail turns and we're about to find a cabin," Alex said.

"Keep going, Axel," Carlos suggested. "If we keep the lights off and don't make too much noise, I think we could get closer to see if it's anything important."

Axel slowly moved forward over the frozen, crackling ground. It was difficult to know if we were making too much noise or not. Axel was doing a great job, but being out in the woods with no other noise around could make us a dangerous target.

"I see it!" Inga hollered, hanging over poor Alex again. "It's definitely a light of some kind."

"It's getting larger as we move," Alex said. "Keep going."

Carlos and Isabella were staring out the back window since the light was coming from Alex and Inga's side of the car. I still was in the dark, so to speak, and waited for someone to tell me exactly what they were seeing. I felt Axel was oblivious to the light also, but he put his trust in the four in the back seat and kept moving slowly ahead.

About five painstaking minutes, Carlos said he saw the light.

We were moving in the right direction now since the trail did curve a little to the left. I finally saw the light straight ahead in the distance. "Maybe we should stop the car and a couple of us go check it out," Axel said. "I'm afraid we'll make too much noise if I keep going."

"I agree, Eklund," Carlos said, calling Axel by his last name. I noticed many men did that. John, for one, called Axel by his surname. I don't believe I've ever done that, so it was kind of strange to me. Maybe it was a guy thing and...no, I'm wrong. Judy, the pain in the butt detective, called him Eklund, too. I wondered what they were thinking right about now? Once again, we had dodged them and gone rogue. John would be furious right about now, and wondering where we went.

"Who wants to come with me?" Axel asked.

"I will," Carlos answered instantly. "I think the two of us should go and leave Alex here to protect the others."

Inga almost threw herself over poor, dainty Isabella. Her anger-filled eyes said it all, but she couldn't let Carlos' words go unnoticed. "You think I need protecting?"

Carlos regretted the words right after he said them. Quickly, he tried to recover. "I didn't mean it that way, Inga. I just meant we need to leave Alex here...along with you, to make sure nobody sneaks up on you all."

"Oh," Inga replied, relaxing a little. However, now I was peeved.

"Inga isn't the only one who doesn't need protecting!" I stammered. "Isabella and I are perfectly capable of handling anything you can."

"Enough!" Axel roared. "Can we just decide who's going with me?"

"I'm okay with you and Carlos going," I said pleasantly.

"I think I should go with you, Mr. Eklund," Inga chimed in. "Carlos isn't used to this harsh cold weather. He may freeze and not be able to react."

Axel shook his head in frustration. "Okay, Inga, Carlos and I

228

will go and leave Alex, Isabella and Ruth Ann here in the car." He added, "Everyone happy with that?" he asked, irritated.

"Yes," we replied in unison.

They put on their coats, bundling up as much as they could. The lights didn't appear too far away, but that could be deceiving. Just like on a beach. I've spent many vacations walking on a beach and what appeared to be close ended up being quite far away.

"Ruth Ann, I'm leaving the keys in the ignition. If it gets too cold, start it up and turn on the heat."

"Fine," I replied, watching him step out of the car.

"Also, if you hear or see anything that seems off, just leave. We'll fend for ourselves."

"Ruth Ann can't leave us out here alone!" Carlos snapped.

"Yes, she can if she feels they're in danger," Axel said, firmly.

I turned to Carlos and tried to assure him. "Carlos, I'm not going to take off. I promise it would have to be extremely dire circumstances that would force me to leave."

Carlos seemed appeased. The three of them left and carefully walked down the trail. I watched as far as I could see until they faded into the darkness. Alex was silent, Isabella looked terrified. I asked, "Are you okay?"

"No."

"I'm sure they'll be fine," I said.

"I just have a bad feeling."

Alex and I both quickly demanded, "Why?"

"I, I don't know why exactly."

"You're thinking about Cassandra," I suggested, hoping it wasn't another premonition of hers. "She's betrayed you and you're angry."

"Angry?" she hollered, startling Alex and me. "I'm way more than angry. She's evil and I'm terrified of what she's done with Prunella and what she could do if she catches Axel, Inga and Carlos."

"They can handle themselves," Alex said quietly, as he stared out the window.

"Alex's right," I agreed. "I don't want to worry about them. I'm focusing on finding Prunella and getting her away from that woman to get her help."

"I know, Ruth Ann. You're right, but I'm worried there's been too much damage done."

"What do you mean by that?" Axel snapped, turning his attention back to Isabella.

"I... I'm worried, that's all," she said, refusing to say any more.

"Let her be for now, Alex," I said, dying to know what she meant, but now wasn't the right time. I was also worried about my cousin and if we could save her and the baby. If she's truly been brainwashed and tried to kill (or she actually killed) Sherman, I don't know if she'll ever be the same.

Alex went back to staring out the window and I let my mind wander. I went back in time to when Prunella and I first met. She was held captive in an attic at Axel's Stockholm estate, just lying in a bed looking helpless. Axel thought she was fighting a terminal illness, but Prunella came up with that farce because she thought Axel wanted to kill her for our necklace, Blue Ice. However, Axel never intended on killing her. He was a different man back then, but I find it impossible to believe he would've ever turned into a cold-blooded killer. I convinced them all to come and live in Deer Creek with me once we settled our affairs in Sweden. Axel ended up in a Swedish prison for his numerous crimes, but he managed to get pardoned for every single one of them. I never really understood how that happened, but in the end, I was glad. Prunella and Axel reunited and I thought they were living as a happy couple near me. Boy, was I wrong! Now, Prunella is acting oddly, and Axel is flirting with me!

Now we wait. We wait to see if Axel, Inga and Carlos find a cabin where Cassandra is holding Prunella prisoner. But, how did she find the cabin and who was with her and Prunella? These are the questions I needed answered immediately!

NINETEEN

"What is taking them so long?" Alex demanded.

"They haven't been gone that long," I replied. "It's only been about ten minutes."

"I thought they were just going to check it out and see if that's where Prunella's being held prisoner?" he asked.

"Maybe it's taking longer to get to the cabin," I answered.

"Give them a little more time," Isabella said, quietly. "I don't believe they're in any danger *at the moment.*"

There was another one of her intuitions, I whispered to myself. I knew Alex was worried so I didn't want to ask her about it, even though I was aware Isabella had very strong powers just like her grandmother. Alex might push her too far and she would crumble before ever telling us anything. I thought going about it at a slower pace might let her relax and reveal her fears were about what was about to happen.

"You're awful quiet, Ruth Ann," Alex snapped. "You know that she (eyeing Isabella intently) knows more!"

"I do not!" Isabella cried, loudly and forcefully. "I'm just as scared as you both are. Stop trying to get me to tell you something I don't know anything about."

"Isabella," I said calmly, trying to reassure her. "Alex isn't trying to force any information out of you. He's just very concerned and scared. I know that when you're ready and have something to tell us you will, right?" Hopefully, that would calm her nerves and let her speak freely to us.

She took a deep breath and said, "I'm too nervous, Ruth Ann. I, I can't understand my feelings when I'm so scared!"

"Take your time," I said, but Alex interrupted and retorted, "We don't have time!"

I glared at Alex and really tried hard to keep my patience. "Alex, the more you yell and push Isabella, the less likely she'll be able to help us. *Do you understand*?" I said those last three words slowly and with clear, precise annunciation.

He didn't say a word, but turned his attention back to staring out the window.

"Thank you, Ruth Ann," Isabella said sweetly, sitting on the opposite side of the back seat from Alex. "I promise you once I know anything for sure, I'll tell you."

"Thank you," I replied, knowing those words meant she had *some* idea of what was going on.

The next several minutes passed agonizingly slowly. I was about to suggest turning on the car to get warm. It was cold and dark in these woods, even though Axel's dashboard clock was illuminated it was only around noon on Monday. I had pulled my scarf off the dashboard because I was freezing. I wrapped it around my neck and part of my head. I didn't have the car on, but I could see what time it was.

I turned my attention to Isabella. She was sitting far away from Alex with her knees pulled up to her chest shivering, even though she was wearing a warm long parka. "You have to be freezing! I forgot you're not used to the Colorado climate. Why don't I turn on the car and blast the heat for a little while?"

"It is very cold in here, but I don't want to risk being heard."

"I'm sure it'll be fine as long as we don't turn on the headlights," I replied, reaching for the button that starts the car.

"Wait, Ruth Ann!" Carlos bellowed from the back. "I think I see something coming toward us."

"I really wish we had something to protect us," I said, searching the meticulously clean black leather seats.

"I'm here!" Alex barked.

"I meant a weapon," I snapped back. "Can you see anything else?" I asked, turning to look out the front driver's seat window.

"No," he said, glued to the window. "But, I swear I saw something coming toward us."

"Maybe it was an animal and it went off into the woods," I suggested.

Isabella's baby blue eyes opened wide enough to pop out. "What kind of animal?"

"Probably a moose or deer," I answered, calmly.

"Oh, I guess we're safe in here."

"There!" Alex hollered. "Look out the window, quickly!"

I turned and looked down the narrow trail. "I don't see anything...wait!" I cried out. "I think someone is running toward us. Yes, I'm sure of it!"

"But who?" Isabella asked, terrified.

"We'll know in a minute," Alex responded, glued to the window. "Ruth Ann, are the car doors locked?"

"Yes," I said, pushing the button on the door to double check. "Yes, we're locked in."

"Be ready if it isn't Axel, Carlos or Inga."

"I will," I said, placing my hand near the ignition button.

Isabella had moved over so she was almost on top of Alex. She was looking intently out the window when the dark shape came into focus.

"It's Inga!" Isabella screamed, happily. "Unlock the doors so she can get in."

I immediately pushed the button and the locks clicked open. "Lock it as soon as she's inside," Alex demanded.

"Inga," I shouted loudly after she jumped in the front passenger's seat. "You're back."

She was too out of breath to respond. The three of us wanted desperately to know what they found out when she finally spoke. "They're in there, Ruth Ann!"

"Who's in there, Inga?" I asked, eagerly.

"Well, I didn't actually see Prunella or Cassandra, but those goofy twins are standing guard. One's walking around the cabin, and the other is just inside the front door."

"How do you know that?" Alex asked, curiously. "It sounds like you didn't get close enough to the cabin."

Inga glared at him. "We were close, but every time we tried to get on the front porch, one twin would make his way around the cabin. We didn't want to get caught! That wouldn't do us any good."

"Inga," I said, trying to get her to focus. "Please tell us what happened from the beginning. Unless, Axel and Carlos are in danger right now."

"No, no, they're hiding in the bushes near the front of the cabin trying to look inside and spot Prunella or that nasty Cassandra."

"Tell us quickly what happened," I asked calmly, but very, very anxiously.

She sat back and relaxed ever so slightly. I knew she had a horrible day. Her precious Prunella was a prisoner so close by, and her best friend (yes, I believe he was), Sherman, had been brutally murdered. Possibly by Prunella.

"We left you, Alex, and Isabella in the car and marched over toward the light. It's definitely a log cabin set deep in the woods. Nobody could spot this place from the road or whatever you want to call what we drove on." She stopped, looked out the window to make sure nobody was sneaking up on us. "Good, we're still okay. I don't know how long we can keep this car here, though."

"Why?" I asked, confused. "Nobody can spot us back here."

"What if they try and leave?" Inga exclaimed. "I saw a car sticking out from the back side of the cabin."

"Did you recognize the car?" I asked curiously, wondering if it was the car Cassandra had rented.

"No, it's too dark and the car was hidden by the cabin. They must've pulled on the small grassy area behind the cabin so if anyone ventured back here, they wouldn't see it."

"Like us," Isabella said.

"Probably. They must be on the lookout for us by now," I said.

"Maybe they don't know we found the slip of paper with the map on it," Alex said.

"Who cares?" Inga snapped. "Can I go on?" she waited until we shut our mouths. "We made our way up to the cabin, but immediately saw one of those huge twins walking out from the front door and pacing around the front for a while. Then, he walked around the cabin, but not for long. He was back in the front really fast."

"So, that's why you didn't get time to get too close, right?" I asked.

"Yes. That and the fact that the other twin was standing inside the front door looking out most of the time."

"Wasn't the door closed? It's cold outside," I asked.

"The door is framed in wood, but the entire middle of the door was glass."

"That's not a typical door for our climate," I said. "It gets really cold and most people want a sturdy door, not a pretty glass one."

"Once again, who cares?" Inga snapped. "The one twin did disappear every so often. That's when Mr. Eklund and Carlos tried to get a closer look." She waited for us to interrupt, but this time we didn't. Honestly, I wanted to ask why she didn't go up to the porch to look, but thought it wouldn't be wise.

"I know what you're thinking, Ruth Ann," Inga said, grinning deviously. "Why didn't I go with them, right?" she looked only at me, with her accusing glare.

I wasn't going to dignify her question with a response. She was correct, but I didn't want her to know that! "No, Inga, I was just waiting for you to continue. I thought you didn't want any further interruptions."

"Oh," she said, confused, but happy. "Sorry, I'm under a lot of stress and I shouldn't have accused you."

"That's okay, Inga. Please continue."

"Yes, um, well, we tried several times to get close enough to go in, but failed. But, it doesn't really matter, does it?" she said, excited.

"Huh?" Alex asked, confused that Inga was fine with not seeing if Prunella was actually in the cabin.

"Think about it. Why would the twins' stakeout the cabin if Cassandra and Prunella weren't in there?"

"You have a point there, Inga," Alex agreed. "What are we doing now?"

"Mr. Eklund told me to come back and tell you three what was going on. I'm going to head back to see if they were able to get any closer." Inga was about to head out when I grabbed her arm.

"No way, Inga," I bellowed. "We go with you this time."

"I was given explicit instructions to tell you not to try and follow in case you said that."

"By whom?" I insisted, angrily.

Isabella, who was awfully quiet in the back seat said, "I bet Axel and Carlos said it, didn't they?"

The three of us turned our attention to her. "Why would you say that?" Inga asked, suspiciously.

"I finally don't feel as threatened. Don't ask me why, but suddenly I'm not afraid anymore," said Isabella.

"Hey," I exclaimed. "Maybe that's because before you were worried for Prunella's life."

"And she's not now?" Inga asked, baffled that I would suggest we weren't in any danger.

"No, no, that's not what I'm saying Inga. I think Isabella couldn't sense what was happening because she was so stressed out about Sherman." I looked back at Isabella and she was smiling.

"Yes, Ruth Ann." Isabella directed her explanation to Inga. "I wasn't thinking clearly, but maybe Ruth Ann said it better than I could. I've been very foggy lately, and now I'm not. I feel like I'm getting a good reading on what's happening right now."

"Do explain," Alex suggested, impatiently.

"I don't feel that Carlos or Axel are in danger right now. I'm not saying things won't change quickly, but if you're worried about them, don't. I think they've made progress too."

Inga got excited and wanted to bolt out of the car. She wanted to be there when any progress occurred. "I've got to go!"

"Hold on Inga," I said, stomping on her enthusiasm. "You're not going without us now that Isabella feels were not in danger."

"But, Ruth Ann," Isabella cried out. "I also said things could change very quickly."

"But right at this moment, we're safe. So, I'm going." I zipped up my long, down coat and slipped on my gloves and hat. My scarf was neatly tucked underneath my coat for extra protection. "Let's go," I said to Inga.

"You don't think you two are leaving Isabella and me here, do you?" Alex barked, trying to get himself bundled up.

"Somebody has to stay with the car and be ready to get out of here in a hurry if we come running back," I said.

"It won't make any difference, Ruth Ann," he said. "If we're in that much of a hurry, one of us will be able to get the car running so we can back it out of here."

"Fine," I said, not that Inga ever had a chance of leaving any of us behind!

"Let's go. Get bundled up because it's cold out there," I said, looking at the clock noticing the time was now an hour past noon.

Once we were out of the car, Inga ordered, "Nobody can talk once we get closer. We can't risk the twins hearing us."

Inga led the way down the narrow grass trail. I was behind her with Alex and Isabella walking side by side behind me. It was eerily dark even though it was early afternoon. I suddenly felt as if I was a character in a horror movie, walking in the woods waiting for a psychopath to jump out of nowhere waving his dagger and itching to bludgeon me to death. A chill ran up my spine and it wasn't from the cold air.

"Okay, look to the right," Inga whispered. "Can you see the

cabin?"

Alex, Isabella, and I stood together looking down the path. It had grown wider as we walked and I could see how a car would make it back here. "Yes," I said, catching sight of the light, and that's when the cabin came into focus. "I see it!"

"Me, too," Isabella answered.

Alex nodded, but didn't speak. I could tell he was taking it in and searching the surrounding areas as much as he could. There wasn't much to see. Just evergreens and barren bushes with their branches poking out ready to stab whoever got too close.

"I'll take you to where I left Mr. Eklund and Carlos. Maybe they won't be there because they were able to get closer."

"Great, let's go, I'm really cold," Isabella said, willingly.

Inga veered off the trail as the cabin grew near. She made her way just a few feet into the woods so we wouldn't be spotted by one of Cassandra's guards. She stopped suddenly, looked aggravated, and spat out, "They're not here, and I don't see them on the porch!"

"Maybe they found a better place to see inside the cabin," I suggested.

"Or maybe they got caught!" Alex said, irritated. "If they got too close or made their way on the porch, I'll bet they were spotted and dragged inside."

"Geez, Alex," Inga said, exasperated. "They're smarter than that. I think what Ruth Ann said makes more sense."

"Let's hope so," he mumbled, but we heard him.

"What are we going to do?" Isabella inquired. "Are we going to look for them?"

"I, I really don't know. They told me to come back to this spot and wait for them."

"Well, then we wait," I replied.

"For how long?" Alex asked, anxiously. "Maybe they got caught in this very spot."

"We don't know anything for sure, Alex," I said, becoming irritated with him now. "I say we give it a little while and keep our own watch. I haven't seen any movement from inside the front door or noticed the twins walking around the place."

"One walked around the cabin and the other one stood in front of the front door, remember?" Inga said, questioning my memory of what she told us in the car.

"I do remember, Inga. I'm just saying I haven't seen either twin."

"We shouldn't talk so much," Inga snapped. "If they got caught, they may come out to look for us."

"They don't know we came with Axel and Carlos," I said.

"C'mon, Ruth Ann, they're smarter than that. Even Cassandra would figure out we'd stay together," Isabella said.

"You're probably right," I admitted, hoping my bickering would waste time.

Isabella smiled, even though her face was frozen and looked pained as she tried to position her mouth into a smile. I knew she was back to her old self by the way she was reading each of us. She had me worried that she was too frightened to let her natural born powers shine through.

I stood staring at the empty front porch of the cabin. It was an old, abandoned vacation cabin, and although it looked like it had been here for decades, I noticed it was in pretty good shape. The winters were harsh on cabins in this area, but why did this one look so good? It must have been built very well and, judging by the quality, probably by a rather wealthy person. The wooden porch was large, but devoid of furniture. and the massive front door was located smack dab in the center of the one-story cabin. From where I stood, I could see a thick wooden frame with a large plate of glass so whoever was inside could see out, and whoever was outside could see in. There were two sets of double windows on either side of the front door. I noticed those had window coverings. I couldn't tell if they were blinds or curtains, but whatever was covering the windows was very dark. I wondered if Prunella was being held inside one of those rooms? I wish I could get closer so I could take a good look, but that would be very dangerous. If one of the twins caught sight of me, I would definitely be sacrificed without a blink of his eye. He could be the father of Prunella's baby. It was either Jacob or his twin brother, whose name we don't know yet. I knew one of them was the father, but the others didn't have that information yet. Only Axel and I knew, unless Isabella had figured it out by now.

"Ruth Ann!" Inga whispered, emphatically. "What is wrong with you? We've been talking to you, but you're staring blankly into space."

"No, I'm not," I wailed back.

"Shhh, not so loud!" Inga grumbled.

"Sorry," I said, sarcastically. "I was just thinking to myself. What did you say to me?"

"We said a lot!" she replied, irritated.

"Well, we're just standing here, why don't you tell me again."

Alex's hand slapped against my mouth, startling me. He held a finger of his other hand to his mouth. I was about to pull his hand away and complain, but figured something was happening. I whirled around and noticed a figure coming out of the cabin. It was Axel!

TWENTY

He ran down the three wide wooden stairs and through the small front yard toward the spot he told Inga to wait. "Axel!" I exclaimed.

Inga was able to get the words out I wanted to, but didn't have a chance. "Mr. Eklund, how on earth did you walk out of the cabin without being caught?"

Axel had a slight grin on his face and said, "Carlos and I were able to sneak inside."

"But how?" I asked, wondering if we were too late and Cassandra, Prunella and the twins had left. But, that was impossible! They would've had to drive past us. I was so confused.

"Listen, I don't have a lot of time. I need to get back to Carlos."

"He's inside with those killers?" Isabella cried out, horrified.

Axel put his ungloved hand on her shoulder and gave her a slight squeeze. "Don't worry, Isabella, he's fine. We were well hidden."

I couldn't wait to hear his explanation of how they were able to get inside, so I rushed and asked the obvious question, "Did you find Prunella?"

Axel told me to wait a minute and let him explain what happened. I nodded, even though all he had to do was answer yes or no.

"After Inga took off to the car, Carlos noticed the twin keeping watch outside went inside the front door. He walked right past his twin and then they both disappeared from the door. Carlos and I hurried to the door and stood on either side of the glass and looked in. The cabin has a small, tiled foyer, and then wide planked floors run straight back down a hall. We also spotted two halls that went to the right and left."

"Don't tell me you and Carlos went in and hid yourselves down one of the hallways?" Alex asked, excitedly.

"That's exactly what we did," Axel said, glaring at Alex for ruining the climax of his story.

"You two are crazy!" Alex said. "If one of those twins got sight of you, I bet you and Carlos would be dead right now!"

"We didn't have a choice, did we?" he asked, rhetorically. "I need to find my wife to make sure she's not hurt or her..." he stopped speaking before he mentioned the baby.

"Your baby," Inga said, sympathetically, in a tone not typical of her usual tough demeanor

"Yes, Inga," Axel said, solemnly. "Prunella's baby, too."

I could see Inga wanted to protest the way he avoided saying ''my baby'', but I grabbed her arm and shook my head. I hoped she would drop it. This wasn't the time or the place to bicker about semantics.

"Carlos was the one who suggested we go inside and find a place to hide. He didn't wait for me to object, so the minute, or I should say the second he noticed an opening, he opened the door, grabbed my arm and pulled me down the hall to the left."

"Why left?" I asked. "Did you know bedrooms were down that way?"

"No, it was just a guess. We only had a split second before one of the twins could come back to stand guard at the front door. Carlos opened the first door on the left and we practically threw ourselves inside."

"Was it a bedroom?" I asked, feeling exhilarated with anticipation.

"Nope, it looked like a den." he replied. Carlos told me to check the room out while he kept watch at the door to make sure we were still safe."

"Did you find anything?" Inga asked, desperately. "Any sign of Ms. Prunella?"

"No, it was just an empty room with a writing desk, a stool and some

old books scattered on the floor. That cabin was probably abandoned ages ago."

"That's why I didn't know it existed," I said. "It's was probably built long before I moved to Deer Creek."

"I'm not done," Axel said, glancing back at the cabin to make sure there wasn't any commotion happening.

"Go on, then," Alex said, annoyed.

"I filled Carlos in on what I saw in the den. He whispered that we should try another room the minute we got the chance. We waited for what seemed like hours when the twin standing guard at the front door left and went down the hall toward the back of the cabin. Carlos grabbed my arm and we went to the next room on the left. Both of these rooms faced the front of the house."

"This one had to be a bedroom!" I said, hoping.

"Yes, it was," he answered with a grin. "But," he held up his hand to keep our questions to ourselves. "It wasn't where Prunella was being held."

"Was somebody else staying there?" Inga asked, anxiously.

"Yep," he said, smiling. He was riding this out as long as he could before I finally broke.

"Axel! Just tell us without the pauses, please!" I bellowed, allowing Inga to place her hand over my mouth again, rather forcefully.

"Sorry, I know we're on limited time. The bedroom we were in was Cassandra's."

"Cassandra's?" Isabella cried out, but not nearly as loudly as I had.

"Yes. It was clearly her room. We entered just in the nick of time because one twin returned, but with Cassandra alongside of him."

"Oh, no," I said, worried. "Did she come to her room?"

"Hold on, Ruth Ann. Let me tell you what Carlos and I overheard." I nodded with intense eagerness. "The door was closed when we entered so we had to keep it closed after we went in. We didn't want her to look down the hall and notice something was off. So, Carlos opened the door at most an inch. We stuck our heads as close as we could so we could listen to their conversation. Here's what we picked up. It wasn't a lot, but enough. Here it goes..."

Cassandra said, "There's no sign of anyone!"

Twin said, "Nope. I've been here the whole time. Jacob was in and out patrolling the cabin. He said he hasn't heard a sound outside."

Cassandra cried, "That's impossible! They had to have found that map by now. They can't be that stupid, can they?"

The twin asked, "Should one of us go back to the estate and leave another, more obvious, clue?"

Cassandra slapped him in the face. "Are you stupid, too? No, I don't want you or your clunky brother to leave the cabin." With that Cassandra slapped the twin's face.

"Hey, you didn't have to hit me!"

Cassandra replied, "I had to wake you up! You were being an imbecile. Let me think a minute. You stay here," she said, and looked out the front and then down the hall to where Carlos and I were hiding. "I'm going to lie down for a few minutes and try to think of something."

The twin nodded, and Cassandra turned to go to her room. She stopped when she was halfway down the hall and ordered, "Tell Jacob to come inside and check on the women. I don't trust either one of them."

Twin replied, "What could they possibly do? They're tied up in there."

Cassandra, rubbing something bulging in her back pocket, my guess a gun, said, "They're more resilient than you think,

244

Johann. Keep an eye on them, but don't leave your post. I want
Jacob to come inside and check on them. I want your eyes peeled
toward the road and anything that's moving out there."

Johann responded, "Fine, I won't move."

Axel stopped and said, "That was what she said, and then she
marched down the hall to where Carlos and I were hiding."

"Oh, no," I cried out. "You two were about to get caught!"

"Well, obviously, Ruth Ann," Inga stated, very sarcastically.
"But they didn't get caught or Mr. Eklund wouldn't be standing
here telling us what happened."

I felt like the stupid one. "Oops, you're right. I got caught up
in the story."

"It's not a story, Ruth Ann," Axel said. "It really happened!
We were terrified that we were going to get caught."

"Please go on," Isabella begged. I glanced at her distressed
face. Cassandra was once close to her, and now she was utterly evil
and willing to kill for whatever it was she wanted. I knew she
originally wanted Blue Ice, but she had that already. Why keep
Prunella and lead us on this wild goose chase?

"Carlos and I turned and looked at the disaster in her room.
There were clothes and garbage spread over the floor and bed.
She's a slob! I then spotted two doors next to each other. Carlos
opened one and it was a bathroom. He immediately stated it
wouldn't be wise to hide in there, so he waited as I opened the
other door. It was a walk-in closet. I figured by the size of the
room, the bathroom and the walk-in closet, that it was the master
bedroom. Plus, let's face it, why would Cassandra take any other
room!

"Please, don't keep us in suspense any longer. Did Cassandra
come in here?" Inga begged.

"Yep, but we were safely tucked away in the large closet
behind a pile of boxes. She did have a few clothes hung in there,
but not very many."

"Did she open the closet door?" I asked, eagerly.

"No," he answered, but then slowly asked us, "I know you were wondering what happened to Carlos and me, but didn't any of you catch what was said between Cassandra and Johann?"

Alex, Inga, Isabella and I looked at each other and shook our heads. We had no idea what he was referring to. "Come on, think..." he said, frustrated.

"Wasting time again, Axel," Alex said. "Just spill."

"When Cassandra told Johann to have his twin, Jacob, come inside to check on Prunella...didn't any of you catch what I repeated?"

"No!" Inga barked, exasperated.

"She told Johann to tell Jacob to check on the *women, not woman.*"

None of us understood, until suddenly it dawned on me. "What do you mean by *women*? Who else is in there?"

"Exactly," he said, smiling that I was the one who figured it out. "Cassandra said she didn't trust the *women* being held prisoner in another room."

"I'm confused," Inga said, rubbing her frozen forehead with her gloved hand. "Do you even know what room they're in?"

"We were kind of busy trying not to get caught at that moment, Inga," Axel answered. "Cassandra was inside the very room Carlos and I were hiding."

"What happened in her bedroom?" I asked, keeping the other subject on the back burner for the moment.

"She marched inside and slammed the door shut, startling Carlos and me. We were lucky that the closet door was louvered so we could see out without opening it. Our only fear was what to do if she would come in the closet. But, we were lucky. She plopped herself on the bed and this is where it got even stranger."

"What, what?" Inga demanded.

"She started talking to herself. I'll try and repeat as much of her conversation with herself that I can remember. Here goes..."

"I can't believe what is happening to me! Why? I've been a

good girl, Momma...why are you punishing me? I did what you asked and got rid of Martika, but these other people are making it too difficult for me. How am I supposed to complete the tasks you've asked of me?"

"What on earth is going on here?" Inga bellowed. "This woman is totally loony. She's talking to her dead mother about killing her sister and some task Cassandra was supposed to pull off for her!"

"Yes, that's what it sounded like to Carlos and me," Axel replied. "But she didn't kill Martika. She wasn't even there when she was killed."

"I know," I said, looking over at Isabella, who had turned white as a sheep. "Are you okay, Isabella?"

"No," she replied, horror stricken. "Cassandra isn't crazy. I think her mother really did put things in her mind and she's trying to fulfill her wishes, even though she's dead."

"Are you saying you believe her mother is talking to her from the dead?" Alex inquired, confused.

"Yes, well no. I mean, when Cassandra was young, I think her mother put words into her head about how horrible her older sister was. I'm a bit confused about the task she referred to. What could her mother want her to do?"

"Steal my necklace!" I cried out.

"But she has that, Ruth Ann," Inga interjected. "There has to be something else to this, but what?"

"Would you like to hear what else she said to herself while lying on the bed?" Axel asked, waiting patiently for us to finish talking out our scenarios.

"Of course," I said. "Why didn't you just tell us there was more?"

"Here goes," he said, ignoring my question.

"Momma, please tell me what to do next. I'm stuck with Johann and Jacob, and they're dumb as rocks. If I'm to pull off the

rest of my mission, I need help. Please, send me help."

Axel added, "she paused for a moment to let her mother 'talk' to her. Then, she continued, as if answering her."

"Ah, so I need to use the woman with Prunella to help me. But she won't! She's too old and stubborn to see my side. I've lost you and everyone I've ever loved. How can I do this alone?" Cassandra paused, waiting for her dead mother to respond. A few seconds later, Cassandra continued, "But she's not really our family, how can I convince her to help? She's related to my lying friend!"

Isabella, listening intently, caught on. "And I am that 'lying friend'!"

"I think so," Axel said, staring at the young, terrified girl. "Who is she referring to, Isabella? Do you have another relative with powers?

Isabella thought long and hard. She shook her head vehemently. "I, I don't know anyone else!"

"Think, Isabella," I said, eagerly. "Did Meme or your mother ever talk about a family member with the same powers?"

"No, no," she babbled, baffled. "Maybe she's talking about another family. I'm sure Cassandra had other friends who lied to her."

"It's too much of a coincidence, Isabella," Axel said. "I'm pretty sure she was talking about your family. Martika, you and Cassandra are half-sisters."

"I know that, Mr. Eklund," Isabella said, angrily.

"He didn't mean to disrespect any of your family, Isabella," I said gently, trying to calm her nerves. I turned to Axel and asked, "Did Cassandra say anything else?"

"Yes."

Cassandra waited for her mother's reply. "Momma, I hate

her! She left me alone and came to this country. I won't ever trust her again!" She began sobbing, and then sat bolt upright and shouted, "I WILL NEVER TRUST ANYONE EVER AGAIN!" Silence, as she stared up at the ceiling. "Don't make me talk to her, Momma. I hate her and the family she's with now. Prunella gave me the necklace. She didn't even fight for it. Why can't I just take it back home and then I can sell it and make enough money to live on for the rest of my life. I won't need anything from anyone else once I have lots of money."

"So, she wants to sell my necklace," I said, furious. "Who would buy something so rare and valuable down in Jamaica? She comes from a tiny village, and nobody has that kind of money."

"Not exactly, Ruth Ann," Isabella replied. "We actually have some very, very wealthy people in our country."

"Really?" Alex asked, curiously. "How did they make so much money?"

Axel glared at Alex. "Who cares? Can we get back to what's going on right now?"

"Yes, we need to figure out what's going on. I'm pretty confused, I have to admit," I said. "We know Prunella is being held prisoner with another woman who we think is related to Isabella's family. My assumption is she has some kind of powers." A lightbulb went off in my head. "Hey, maybe this woman was brought in to rid the gem of the curse, but..." I looked at Isabella, who looked saddened by my remarks. "I'm sorry, Isabella. I'm not saying your grandmother didn't break the curse. Maybe, there's some other curse or...what if they're trying to place *another* curse on it?"

"That's it!" Inga exclaimed. "That makes sense."

Isabella looked from me to Inga. "You both could be right. Why else would Cassandra be hanging around if she already possesses the gem?"

"Axel, what happened next?" I asked, seeing if there was more to Cassandra's weird experience in her bedroom.

"Not much of any importance. She went on for a little while muttering to her mother about how nobody has ever appreciated her and loved her...it got to the point Carlos and I didn't know how long she would go on. Finally, she dozed off and Carlos suggested we sneak out."

"You didn't!" I exclaimed.

"No, that would be stupid. We went and leaned against the wall near the door and waited for her to leave."

"You must not have had to wait too long," Inga said. "I wasn't gone that long getting Ruth Ann, Isabella and Alex."

"Nope. Suddenly, she shot up and ran out of the room. Carlos and I hurried out of the closet and checked the hall. We needed to go to the opposite hallway to see if we could get closer to Prunella and this mysterious woman."

"But, there was a guard at the front door. You couldn't get past him," Alex said.

"No, but we went back into the den, and then into a hall closet near the front door where Johann was stationed. We stayed there because we could hear if any of them walked away." Axel turned to look toward the cabin to make sure he still didn't hear any commotion. "Still quiet," he said. "My guess, Carlos is still hiding."

"Is he in the hall closet?" I asked, curiously.

"No. Jacob came back to his twin and said Cassandra was inside the room with the women. Jacob could tell it was going to be a while so he suggested they hurry into the kitchen and grab something to eat."

"So, they left their post?" Inga asked, surprised. "Weren't they afraid of the wrath of Cassandra if she didn't see them in their posts?"

"My guess is those twins aren't the brightest. They risked it, and left the foyer. Carlos and I hurried down the other hall and spotted two doors on each side of the hall. We knew Prunella had to be in one of them. We figured one of the two rooms facing the front were bedrooms. We hurried to the first door and placed our heads against it to listen. We didn't hear anything from the first room so I opened the door. It was a small bedroom with two old iron twin beds on each wall. We noticed men's clothes lying neatly on the perfectly made beds. What surprised us the most was that it had to be the twins room, but compared to Cassandra's room this one was immaculate! Funny, the twins were neat as could be while Cassandra's was a total mess!"

"So, Carlos is hiding in the twin's room?" Alex asked, amazed. "One of those guys could go in there at any time for any reason."

"Don't worry, Alex," Axel said. "He's not in there, either."

"So, where is he?" Inga demanded.

"He's in the hall closet right across from where Prunella's being held."

"How do you know that?" I asked, confused.

"Because I left him there," he replied.

I gave him a nasty look. He raised his hand before I could make a snotty remark. "I was with him before I headed outside to find all of you."

"You had that much time to get out?" Isabella asked, surprised. "Wasn't one of the twins back guarding the front door?"

"Nope. Those two were stuffing their faces in the kitchen."

"How would you know that?" I asked, repeating my last question.

"Because, when I left Carlos, I made a quick turn away from the front door to investigate the rest of the cabin."

"You're nuts!" Alex exclaimed. "You just put yourself in danger of getting caught."

"No, I didn't. I heard their voices laughing from the kitchen. I also heard Cassandra's voice in the bedroom across for the closet."

"What did you hear?" I asked, desperately wanting to know if he heard Prunella's voice. I really wanted to know if she was safe and uninjured.

"First, let me finish what I saw with the twins." I nodded, and he continued. "When you walk in the front door you're standing in a large foyer. There is a hall that goes to the left and the right. We were hiding in the hall to the right of where the women were being held. If you enter the front door and go straight, it takes you down a wide hallway that opens into a large great room and kitchen area." He paused, waiting for any comments, but we stood staring at him waiting to hear what was most important...if he heard his wife's voice. "When I left Carlos back in the closet, I thought it was prudent I knew the total layout of the cabin, just in case. I felt temporarily safe because Cassandra was busy and so were the twins. I quickly went down the main hall to the great room and could hear the twins laughing and chowing down on food."

"Those women are becoming real pains," Jacob declared with a full mouth of food.

"All women are pains!" Johann exclaimed.

"Well, most women," Jacob agreed. "But, not that pretty one we have tied up. She's mine!"

"Who says you get to have her!" Johann snapped. "Maybe she would prefer me."

Axel chimed in, "It took every ounce of my power not to rush in and strangle the two of them!"

"Nonsense!" Jacob said. "I already have a relationship with her!"

"What are you babbling about, Jacob? We haven't had a moment alone with her since we arrived in this pit of a town."

Jacob didn't respond to his brother, but flashed an evil smile.

"Hey, you never told me you and her hooked up!"

Jacob didn't reply again, but stuffed a fried chicken leg into his mouth.

Uh-oh, Jacob pretty much admitted he and Prunella had been intimately connected. Axel's look in my direction was for a desperate plea of assistance. Was he about to admit what he and I already knew? I didn't have to wait too long because Alex and Inga picked up on it.

"Mr. Eklund," Inga began. "Are you telling me that Jacob and Ms. Prunella were having some sort of affair?"

"Not exactly, Inga," Axel replied.

"Exactly what then?" Alex demanded.

"It's a long story, and until I have the truth, I won't talk about it anymore. I will say this, Prunella did not have an affair with that criminal!"

"Well, that's good enough for me. For a moment, I thought you knew something we didn't," Inga said, eyeing Axel and me suspiciously. I was afraid it was written all over my face that Prunella's baby was not fathered by Axel.

TWENTY-ONE

"What happened next?" I asked, trying to get us off that fragile topic. I knew Isabella sensed what was going on by the look she was giving me. It was one of those 'I know what you're thinking looks', and I chose not to look directly at her.

"I was at the end of the hall watching the two of them stuff their mouths with fried chicken and biscuits. They had no idea I was there. The kitchen was on the far-right side of the room and there was an open area with an old, but rather elegant mahogany table with a couple chairs in front of where I was hiding. On the other side of the room was a large living area and a massive floor to ceiling stone fireplace. One of the twins was sitting while he ate, and the other was near the kitchen sink."

"You must've stayed there for quite a while since you can describe the place with so much detail," Inga said, surprised.

Axel shrugged his shoulders and replied, "Not really. Once they finished eating, I rushed out the front door and met up with all of you. I was furious when I left, but I kept reminding myself that what is important is getting Prunella out of there unharmed."

"Exactly!" I proclaimed. "We can work everything else out once we've saved her."

"Work what out?" Inga asked, baffled. "Hey, you two know something you're not telling us. That's not fair! How are we to help if you won't be honest?"

"Nothing else is going on, Inga," I lied. "It's been a horrible twelve hours or so with Prunella being captured and Sherman getting murdered."

"I won't ever believe that Prunella had something to do with that!" Inga bellowed. "Nobody will ever convince me."

The rest of us didn't say a word. I wasn't so sure, actually. If Prunella wasn't in her right mind, then maybe she did have a part in Sherman's death. Maybe she injected Sherman with a poison that killed him. Once we get her healed and back to her old self, I knew she would never forgive herself. I don't know what the future holds, but whatever it was, I knew it was going to be a tough road.

Alex brought us back to the present. "So, you left Carlos in a closet across the hall from Prunella and some stranger, right?" Axel nodded. "You haven't told us what you overheard."

"Ah, yes," Axel said, nodding again. "When I looked out of the closet to make sure the coast was clear, I told Carlos what my plans were. First, I needed to get out of there safely, and second, I had to find Inga. Carlos suggested I listen at Prunella's door to see if I could hear Cassandra in there."

"So, you did," I said, even though we already knew.

"I tiptoed to the door and was about to lean my head against it. However, I didn't have to. I could hear Cassandra loud and clear."

"Was she threatening Ms. Prunella?" Inga demanded, furious.

"No, no, it wasn't like that," Axel answered. "She was goading them. She was telling Prunella that she has her whole family cornered, and if she didn't cooperate she would kill each one of us."

"But, she doesn't have us," Inga roared, indignantly.

"Prunella doesn't know that," he replied.

"What was her response?" I asked, worried about her welfare and what Cassandra would do to her if she didn't cooperate with her.

"She didn't reply. Or, she couldn't," Axel said. "I only heard faint muffled sounds that had to be hers. My guess is she's got a gag in her mouth and can't speak."

"That's it!" Inga yelled, not caring who heard her. "I'm going to go in there and rip that woman's head off!" She started to march in the direction of the cabin when Alex took a firm grip on her arm.

"No, you don't, Inga," he said, firmly. "We won't risk any more lives."

"That's right," I said. "Let Axel continue, please."

"I will try and repeat what I heard Cassandra spouting out at the women."

"Now, now, Prunella," Cassandra said, intimidatingly. "Why won't you just help me? I won't hurt you any further if you cooperate. I need you to give the nice lady next to you some crucial information. You don't want me to kill her in front of you, do you?" Mumbled groans and protests came out of the stranger's mouth.

Prunella must not have believed Cassandra, because Cassandra became irate. "Listen to me you little bitch. If you don't do as I say, I will kill...let me see, who first...Ruth Ann! That's who I'll bring in and I'll murder her with my own two hands right in front of you! Is that what you want to see?" Cassandra must've been satisfied with Prunella's response. "There, that wasn't so difficult, was it? I'm coming back soon to get everything that old woman needs to finalize the transformation."

"I had to get out of there immediately, because I could hear Cassandra's footsteps moving toward the door."

"But, I thought you went to the kitchen *after* you listened at the door?" I asked, confused. Maybe I misunderstood and he went to the kitchen and then back to listen at the door.

"I did. As I rushed down the hall to get outside, I heard Cassandra's voice yelling from inside the bedroom again. She was furious at something, but I don't know what. I didn't think she was going to hurt Prunella or the mysterious old woman because she needed them for something. We just don't know what yet. That's why I stopped to check on the twins, and then I got myself out of there and came here to meet up with Inga, but all of you were here, too."

"Oh," I said, wondering if Axel was telling us the entire story. I had a feeling he was lying about something, but I didn't know what or why.

"So, all you know is that Cassandra needs Prunella to give or do something with this old woman that will help Cassandra?" Inga asked, sounding unsure of the words the minute they left her lips.

"I guess so," Axel said. "I have no idea what Prunella could have that Cassandra needs."

"Cassandra already has the necklace, right?" I asked, wondering if Prunella pulled a fast one and hid it, and then refused to reveal the location.

"I thought so," Axel said. "I'm starting to think she doesn't. Maybe Prunella hid it. Or, maybe she's wearing it and won't take it off!"

"That's not it," Alex said, frustrated. "If Prunella was wearing it, Cassandra or those twins would've ripped it right off her neck."

"If they could," Isabella mumbled, staring into space.

"What does that mean?" Axel asked her.

Inga, Axel, Alex, and I waited for her response. We became quite impatient when Isabella realized we were staring at her with annoyed expressions. "Sorry," she said, quietly. "I don't want to scare any of you, but there is something I heard long ago from my grandmother."

"Scare us!" Inga bellowed. "What are you babbling about?"

"Tell us, Isabella," I begged. "We don't have a lot of time."

"Years ago, when I was just a young girl," she said, but I couldn't help but think...young girl? She still was young! "I was only about eight at the time when my grandmother tried to help another woman, about her same age, rid herself of a piece of jewelry that wouldn't or couldn't be removed."

"That makes no sense!" Inga spat. "Just break the chain then.

Were they worried about the value of the piece and didn't want to break it?"

"No, Inga. That's not what I'm saying. My grandmother *couldn't* get it off. It was stuck on her. I can't explain it, but I remember sneaking a peek inside the room they were in, trying desperately to remove the...necklace! That's it. It was a necklace of some sort."

"Didn't you get a good look at it?" I asked, very curiously. Please don't tell me it was like our Blue Ice!

"Just a peek," she answered. "It was red, *blood red*, in color. It frightened me so that I ran back to my bedroom and closed my eyes wishing I had never seen it."

"But, why?" I asked, baffled. "It was just a gem. It can't hurt you."

"But, they can, Ruth Ann. Haven't you learned anything after everything your family has gone through with your own necklace?"

"Yes, but it was never physically impossible to remove. I hardly think that's what's happening now," I said, doubting what I just said. Anything could be true since Blue Ice entered my life. It was one thing after another with that gem. Truly, becoming very tiresome!

"Don't be so close-minded, Ruth Ann," Isabella said. "You were skeptical about it carrying a curse, too."

"Good point," I admitted.

Axel chimed in, "Who was the woman your grandmother was trying to help?"

She shrugged her shoulders and said, "I have no idea. I never saw her again."

"Didn't you ever ask her about it?" I asked, interestedly. "I mean, it scared you so much that you ran and hid in your bedroom."

"No. I heard things about the red gem and that it wasn't supposed to be that color, but..." she stopped, turned pale white and swayed, forcing Alex to grab a hold of her. "No, it couldn't be," she muttered to herself.

"What, what?" Inga demanded. "What can't it be?"

I noticed Isabella was shaking. "Isabella, what's wrong?"

She rambled so fast none of us could decipher what she said. "Slow down!" Axel ordered, exasperated.

"I'm sorry," she said, taking a breath. "I just had a horrifying thought. What if that's what's happened to Prunella's necklace? What if it's turned red, *blood red*, and won't come off her neck!"

"Nonsense," Axel snapped back at her.

"What would cause a necklace to turn colors?" I asked, just out of curiosity.

"Not colors, Ruth Ann, only red, *blood red*."

"Oh," I said, not fond of her answer. "Blood red sounds so...chilling."

"Yes, Ruth Ann. I agree," Isabella said. "I never saw that necklace again, but my grandmother and mother would bring up the topic from time to time. I was very young, but I was also a curious child. I never wanted to see that kind of curse again, but it's starting to make sense to me now."

"How?" I asked, holding my hand in the air to stop the others from speaking. I wanted her to spill everything she knew before she closed up again or passed out.

"I overheard my grandmother explain that a cursed gem could turn red, *blood red*, if someone is trying to be re-curse it."

"Re-curse?" Inga said, mockingly.

"Yes, Inga. It happens. My grandmother said sometimes a curse can be put back on the item or the item can reject another curse."

"I'm so confused," Inga said, rubbing her head.

"So, you think our necklace is stuck on Prunella's body because Cassandra is trying to use this old woman to place another curse on it?" Axel asked, fully understanding what Isabella was explaining.

"Yes."

"But, why and for what purpose?" he asked, seriously.

"We don't know," she answered, truthfully.

"But, who is that old woman?" I inquired. "Did she bring her here from your village back in Jamaica?"

"That's a very good question, Ruth Ann," she said. "I doubt anyone around here would be able to handle this level of a curse."

"None of this makes any sense!" Alex hollered. "If Cassandra wanted the necklace, why didn't she just take it back to Jamaica to the old woman?"

"If she can't get it off of Prunella, then she would've had to kidnap her to Jamaica," I explained.

"So, you believe me?" Isabella asked enthusiastically.

"You've never lied before," I said, trying desperately to accept her words. "I'm not sure that's what is happening, but it's a strong possibility. Otherwise, Cassandra would just have taken the necklace and left."

"Exactly," Isabella said. "There's something else Axel told us that changes things."

"What now?" Inga demanded, throwing her arms in the air out of frustration.

"We originally thought Prunella was brainwashed or controlled by Cassandra, and that's why she acted so strangely." Inga glared at the Isabella.

"I'm sorry, but we have to face the fact that Prunella might have had a hand in Sherman's death. But, there's a positive side to this, I think..."

"What? What could possibly be positive?" I asked, stunned by her comment.

"If she's tied and gagged along with the old woman, then she's fighting back. Cassandra has to restrain her."

"Ah," Axel said, understanding her point. "If Prunella was a willing participant, she wouldn't have to be restrained, right?"
"Yes."

"I get it now," I said. "But, we don't want Prunella fighting back too much. She'll risk her own and the baby's safety!"

"Let's go get her!" Inga announced, willing and ready to fight her way to her favorite person on the earth.

"Hold on," Axel said, waving his hand up to stop her. "We need a plan. Carlos is stuck in a closet, and Prunella is locked in a room with a total stranger. Plus, those twins and Cassandra are guarding them."

"Maybe Carlos was able to free them," Inga said, hoping that was a possibility.

"Then they would've found us by now," Axel said, crushing Inga's hopes.

"What do you want us to do, Axel?" Alex asked. "Should you and I go in and find Carlos and break into the bedroom?"

"Hey, wait a minute!" Inga said, furious at Alex's suggestion that only Axel and he go back to the cabin.

Axel immediately squashed Inga's protestations. "Don't worry, Inga," he said. "I definitely want you with us. You're a force to be reckoned with, and we might need your strength and persistence."

"Thank you, sir," she replied, giving Alex a mocking smile. "Nobody wants to rescue Prunella more than me."

"Well, I'm not going to argue that, but you know we all want her back with us," Axel replied.

"How are we going to pull this off?" I asked.

"Isabella," Axel said, turning to her for some help. "Is there anything you can tell me about Prunella?"

Isabella's eyes moved toward the cabin not so far away. "I don't feel that she's in any imminent danger, however, Carlos might be in trouble."

"Why didn't you speak up before?" I cried.

She looked so pathetic and innocent. She explained that she didn't feel either Carlos or Prunella were being harassed while we were talking, but it might have just changed.

Axel whipped his head around and motioned for us to get down. "There are loud noises coming from the cabin, don't you hear them?"

We kneeled as low to the frozen ground as possible, hidden

by the bushes on the side of the grass road. "Somebody's yelling!" Inga whispered, fear in her voice. "I can't make out the words, though."

"Carlos was just caught!" Axel said, horrified. "I just heard one of the twins yelling at him, asking how he got inside the cabin."

"Did Carlos respond?" Isabella asked, worried for her dear friend.

"No, not that I can make out. I think they're trying to get him to speak," Alex said, eyeing Axel with a worried look.

"How do you know that?" I demanded.

"I heard a few noises, probably from Carlos. Maybe they slugged him and he fell to the ground," Alex said.

"We've got to save him," Inga said, standing up and trying to march toward the cabin, but Axel grabbed her ankle halting her.

"No, sir," she said, reaching down and trying to release his grip. "We've got to get in there. We have more people than they do. I can take one twin, and Alex can take the other. That leaves the rest of you to deal with Cassandra."

"They have guns, Inga," I said, realizing Inga was serious. "All it takes is one shot and one of us could be dead."

"Yeah, and now they know we're here," Isabella announced. "I think the twins are going to search the grounds for us."

"What are we going to do?" I asked, worried for our safety.

"I can't risk your life, Ruth Ann," Axel said, mentioning only my name. "Maybe you and Isabella should get back to the car and go to the police station. There's a slight chance we can hold out until you get back here with the police."

"That's not going to happen!" I cried. "By the time we go there and come back, too much could've happened. I think we need another plan, and quick!"

"Give it up, Mr. Eklund," Inga said. "She's not going to give in. I think we go around back and try and see what's going on back there. They'll probably check out front first, and that's where we are right now."

"Good point, Inga," Axel responded. "Follow me."

We nodded and stood up. The arthritis in my knees and the extremely hard frozen ground made it hard for me to straighten. I didn't take long to loosen up though. We hurried around the right side of the cabin just in time. One of the twins threw open the front door and started yelling, "We know you're out there! You might as well turn yourselves in. Maybe we'll spare *some* of your lives."

"Did you hear him?" I asked, becoming extremely angry. That just spurred me on to go after them and finish them off! That arrogant, young twin was not only unintelligent, but a big bully. I will not allow someone like that to win!

"Yes, he's trying to goad us to come out of hiding," Axel said.

"Ignore him, Ruth Ann," Inga whispered. "They won't see us coming."

We made our way to the back side of the cabin. I spotted a broken screen door with a solid door behind it. "There," Axel announced, making his way to the back door.

"You'd think they'd guard that door, too," Inga said, dumbfounded. "I hope we're not walking into a trap."

"I can hear both of the twins out front now," Alex said, standing behind the rest of us looking out in every direction for possible attackers. "They would've found us if we stayed where we were."

"If they come up empty, they will definitely search out back. We need to get our butts inside and hide somewhere." Axel said.

"Where are we going to hide?" I asked, worried. "You described the inside as one large great room with a kitchen."

"I'm sure there's a pantry or some other door we can go through," Inga answered for Axel.

"We'll find out," he said, opening the screen door as gently as possible.

He disappeared in the cabin leaving the rest of us wondering what we should do. "Follow him," Inga spat at me.

I would have loved to remind her about respect, but it clearly wasn't the time. I stepped up two narrow wooden steps to the door. I noticed Axel didn't close the door all the way. I reached up and opened the door. I saw the grand old mahogany table Alex had described. In a moment of utter fantasy, I imagined what that table could look like in my shop after it had been repaired and refinished.

"Come on, Ruth Ann," Alex said from behind. "Go inside, please."

I woke out of my dream state and stepped inside. I looked from right to left to forward. Where did Axel disappear? I turned around and shrugged my shoulders at Alex. "Where'd he go?"

Alex came in, and then Isabella and Inga. "This cabin is misleading," Inga said, eyeing the expansive great room. "It looks so small from the front."

"Who cares about that?" Alex barked. "Where's Eklund?"

"Shhh," a male voice called out from nowhere.

"Where is he?" I asked, whipping my head around looking for Axel.

"I'm right here," he said, sticking his head out of a door near the kitchen. "I'm inside the biggest pantry I've ever seen."

Inga marched over with no regard for her safety. "What do you mean the biggest? The one back at the estate is huge."

Once I made sure the coast was clear, I ran over to the pantry and hurried inside. I knew Cassandra and the twins were searching for us. Hopefully, they wouldn't think to look *inside* the cabin. "There's not much in here," I said, looking at all the empty shelves.

"I doubt they've used it much, Ruth Ann," Inga said, snottily. "Cassandra's only been here a short time."

"Good point," I admitted, dismissing her haughty attitude.

We were all inside the pantry with plenty of spare room. "What now?" Alex asked, eagerly.

"I think I should sneak over to the closet where Carlos was," Axel suggested, not looking at me because he knew I would object.

"But, he was caught in there," I exclaimed.

"Exactly," he said with an evil smirk. "They've already checked in there. Why would they look there again?"

I wanted to tell him they might check to see if any of us were able to get inside, but I refrained. "We need to find out what happened to Carlos, so you should probably go. We're not going to do any good waiting in here."

Axel was about to open the door to head to the front part of the cabin when he quickly shut the door. "They're coming!" he whispered, turning back to us.

There was nowhere to hide inside the pantry. If they opened it up for any reason, we were doomed. I held my breath as the sound of Cassandra's voice creeped closer to the kitchen. She was shouting at the twins. I wasn't sure from where, since the great room was so large the sounds could be reverberating from anywhere.

"You stupid fools!" she hollered. "Where'd they go?"

"We don't know," one of the twins answered. "We caught one trying to get in the room where the two women are being held. That doesn't mean the others are even here."

Cassandra didn't respond immediately. My guess she was glaring at them waiting to pounce. Finally, "You think only Carlos, yes, that's his name, came all the way up to this cabin to rescue the precious Prunella alone?"

"Possibly," a twin replied, cautiously.

"Not possible. I'm sure they're all around somewhere. Go back outside and find a car. They had to have driven up here. Go to the main entrance to the cabin and see if there's a car on the side of the gravel road."

The twins left without another word. We heard the front door slam, and Cassandra started her own conversation, again.

"How did I get stuck with these two imbeciles?" She began pacing near the pantry. "What am I supposed to do with her if she won't cooperate? Am I supposed to kill her to get that necklace off of her?"

We were shocked. "I knew it!" Isabella whispered. "That is

what's going on. Until the curse is broken, only Prunella can remove that necklace."

We turned our attention back to Cassandra's conversation. "Momma, please tell me what to do! I can't do this alone!" Silence for a few seconds, and then she said, "I will keep trying. I need to get that gem back in my hands so I can return home and put this curse to good use."

"What curse?" I asked Isabella, wondering what Cassandra meant by that.

"I, I don't know, Ruth Ann," she said, very distressed. "My grandmother got rid of the curse."

"Could there be another one she missed? Or maybe the old woman with her right now placed a new one on it!" Inga questioned, worried for her best friend and employer.

"Impossible," Isabella replied, ardently. She paused for a second while we stood in the dark pantry staring at her. "Well, I guess it's possible a new one was created, but really?"

"Obviously, Cassandra wants the gem for a purpose. She came all the way here to retrieve it and brought some witch with her!" Alex protested. "We have to discover that purpose and rescue Prunella."

"I agree," Axel quietly replied. He had been very quiet listening at the door waiting for Cassandra to leave so he could take off to the closet where Carlos was last was seen.

Suddenly, Cassandra said in a loud voice, "I get it! I'm going to finish her off no matter what I have to do to her. Now," she paused for a moment. "Now, I need something strong to drink."

"Uh-oh," Axel said, backing away from the door. "I hope she doesn't come looking for her alcohol in here."

We held our breaths as Cassandra started rummaging through the cabinets looking for a bottle of something. "There has to be some rum or vodka in here!" she bellowed, angrily. Just as she was marching near the pantry, Axel suggested we grab whatever we could that could knock her out.

I grabbed a five-pound bag of flour, Inga picked up a wooden rolling pin, Isabella grabbed a full jug of water and Alex lifted a two-slice toaster in the air high above his head. I looked over at Axel and noticed he had the best weapon of all, a large serrated knife. "Wow, you're not going to stab her, are you?" I asked, curiously.

"If I have to, yes," he answered.

"Only if you absolutely have to, Axel," I begged. "We're not murderers."

"Ruth Ann," Inga interjected. "If he doesn't kill her, I will!"

"Shhh, we don't have time for this," Isabella chimed in. "Is she going to open the door?"

We stood frozen, waiting as we heard Cassandra grab the handle of the pantry door. "Oh, no," I said to myself.

Just as the door inched open, we were saved. The twins returned yelling and screaming that they found something. Cassandra released the handle and stepped away from the door. "Phew," I said, wiping my damp forehead. "That was really close."

"Too close," Axel said, lowering the knife to his side. I noticed as he lowered it, his hand was trembling slightly. It actually made me feel better knowing that he wasn't without a conscience, even if it was a woman threatening Prunella's life.

"What are you two yelling about?" Cassandra barked just as the twins entered the kitchen.

"We found it!" one of them shouted, proudly. "We found their car. They're here, somewhere."

"But, you didn't find any of them along the way?" she asked, stunned at the twin's ineptness.

"No, ma'am, but now we know they're here, somewhere."

"Search the grounds outside. I don't want one inch left undisturbed, got it?"

"What if they already got inside somehow?" a twin bravely suggested.

I looked at Axel, terrified they would start a search on the inside of the cabin, but thankfully, Cassandra snapped back, "Don't you think we would've heard them you fool!"

267

"Yes, but..." he was abruptly cut-off. "No buts! Go outside and search every inch of these grounds. They'll eventually freeze, and need to come inside. We'll be watching for them to come in."

"It's getting dark outside," a twin said. "We're going to have a hard time searching."

"Grab the flashlights. I think I put them in one of these drawers or..."

"Oh, no, what if she thinks they're in the pantry!" I cried out softly.

"No, no, I think I put them in my bedroom," she said, starting to walk away leaving the twins alone in the kitchen. "Wait here," she ordered them.

When she was out of earshot, one of the twins spoke up. "That woman's seriously becoming a pain!"

"I agree, Johann. But, we've got ourselves in too deep. We need to keep playing this charade of acting stupid and foolish. She'll never guess that we're actually smart enough to plot taking that necklace for ourselves."

"Jacob, we can never speak those words again. If she ever heard us, I think she'd actually murder us on the spot."

"With what?" Jacob asked.

"She's got the power to curse us so we end up like her father did," Johann reminded him.

"I forgot about that," Jacob said, irritably.

"Let's just remember that when, not if, we get our hands on the necklace, we take it directly to our Uncle and he'll know how to sell it. He promised he would split the profit with us."

"You trust Uncle Steven?" Jacob asked, surprised at his brother's naiveté.

"More than that crazy bitch!" Johann answered in a loud, angry voice.

"Shut-up!" Jacob snapped. "She'll hear you, and that'll blow our plans."

"Unbelievable," Axel muttered to himself. "Steven's alive and not in prison. How'd that happen?"

"We suspected, but now we have proof," I said, just as devastated as he was.

"You don't think he's hanging around here, do you?" Inga asked, horrified with the news. "Ms. Prunella will be in even more serious danger!"

"We know that!" Axel snapped at her. "Shhh, I think they're talking to each other again."

"In between stuffing their mouths with food," I mumbled, listening to their disgusting crunching and slurping sounds.

"You know," Jacob said. "I'm not sure I'd let her hurt that young woman."

"Why not?" Johann asked after a loud burp.

"Because we had kind of a thing."

"I told you to shut up about that!" Johann barked, pounding his beer bottle down on the counter. "Nothing actually happened between the two of you. You're just imagining things."

"No, I'm not!" he fiercely replied. "Her and I slept together in Martika's house in Jamaica. I didn't even have to force her to sleep with me. She was willing and very enthusiastic."

"You're just as nuts as Cassandra," Johann said, laughing. "Hurry up and finish your beer, she's bound to come back with those flashlights."

He was correct. Cassandra came stomping back just in time. Axel was about to leap through the door and attack Jacob. Not only did Jacob taunt Axel without knowing it, but he admitted to everyone in the pantry that he had slept with Prunella. Now, whether they believed him or not is yet to be determined. I wasn't sure if once Axel calmed down he would choose to come clean and tell the truth or continue lying. I needed to know because I wasn't sure what I was supposed to say *or not* say on the extremely delicate topic.

Once Alex got a good grip on Axel, he strongly, but quietly, suggested he calm down or risk the lives of the rest of us inside the pantry. Axel, being the intelligent man he is, nodded and agreed to behave. I wanted to console him, but that could give away the fact we were hiding something. I chose to stand as far away from him and ignore what was said. Unfortunately, Inga wasn't going to accept this.

TWENTY-TWO

Inga pushed her way in front of Isabella, who nearly fell into the shelves, and shoved Alex to the side. "What was he talking about, Sir?" she asked, emphasizing 'Sir' with a bit of disdain.

Axel tried to catch my eye, but he was on his own with this one. I wasn't going to say anything. Usually, if I'm lying (which I don't promote!) it is written all over my face, which makes me a horrible poker player!

"He's crazy, Inga," Axel replied, furious. "They're all crazy!"

"He was awful specific, Mr. Eklund," she persisted.

"Inga, he was bragging to his brother. Why would Prunella 'willingly' and 'enthusiastically' participate in such a vile act?"

She thought about that for a short moment. Finally, a tiny grin appeared on her face. "I guess you're right. That would never happen. She's loyal to a fault."

Phew, she bought it for now. I was dreading the day the truth came out. Unless, Axel was planning on keeping that secret hidden forever and let everyone, except Prunella, Isabella and me believe that he was the father. But for now, we had more important matters. We needed to get out of the pantry and into the bedroom to save Prunella and Carlos. I wasn't sure if the old woman was in the room against her will or voluntarily waiting to help Cassandra. I doubted the latter, since I heard she was also tied up.

I turned my attention back to Cassandra's rant at the twins. "Here," she said. "I found two flashlights. Now, go and find them."

"But," Jacob started to say, but Cassandra cut him off

immediately.

"No, buts, Jacob. I don't want either of you coming back without them. Got it?"

"Yes, ma'am," they both replied. I heard their loud clomping footsteps depart down the hall and out the front door.

We waited to see what Cassandra's next move was going to be. Was she going to start another conversation with her dead mother or go to her room to rest? She could go to Prunella's, Carlos', and the old woman's bedroom, too. We heard her open a cooler and pop a can of something, more than likely a beer. "Ah, that's what I needed," she said with satisfaction. "Now, if those imbeciles can just carry out my task, I'll feel better when the rest of them are taken care of." Another swig of beer ended with an unladylike burp. "Do I have to do everything myself? They better hurry-up because it's awful dark and cold outside. I don't want them freezing to death before I get a chance to kill them myself!"

Our silent, but horrified reactions inside the pantry said it all. She was planning on killing us! I wanted to speak, but was too afraid she would hear me. Axel turned to find me at the back of the long pantry. He shook his head and placed a long, well-manicured finger to his mouth. He didn't want any of us tipping her off that we were actually inside the cabin. Finally, after she finished her beer, she declared, "I'm exhausted. Maybe I'll go lie down for a little while. Those two shouldn't be gone long, and they'll come find me once they have the prisoners." She started to march out of the kitchen, her footsteps echoing on the wood floors. "Ah, I better check on our current prisoners first," she muttered as her voice trailed down the hallway toward Prunella's and Carlos' rooms.

"I think it's safe to talk now," Axel said. "We heard enough to make sure we don't make any mistakes."

"We need to hurry and get to Prunella and Carlos," Alex said, anxiously.

Axel glared at the young man and said, "You heard her. She was going to check on them first, and then go take her little nap."

"So, we wait a minute or two and then go," Alex responded,

irritated.

I interrupted and said, "I'm sure we'll hear her marching down the hall. These old wood floors make a lot of noise."

"That means we need to be very careful how *we* walk around, too," Isabella suggested, looking down at Inga's cloddy, black work shoes.

"Hey," Inga bellowed, catching her eyeing her shoes. "I'm on my feet all day long. I need supportive shoes!"

"I'm not cutting them down, Inga," Isabella said, quickly. "I just noticed they're heavy shoes and could make a lot of noise when you walk."

"I'll manage," she replied, derisively. "Are we going?"

"Once we hear her go to her room," Axel replied. "I'm going to open the pantry door so we can listen better." He reached and slowly opened the door. The LED lantern on the island temporarily blinded me as I looked at it. That was the only light in the back of the cabin. It was a bright light, but only in the kitchen. The other side of the room was very dark. "I'm going to sneak around toward the hall. Stay back until I give you a sign it's clear."

We waited inside the pantry while Axel tiptoed over to the hall that leads into the front foyer. It didn't take long before we heard Cassandra marching toward her bedroom. Axel didn't have to spy on her long because we could hear every detail up until the slamming of her door. Was she mad after her visit with Prunella and Carlos or was there another reason for her slamming the door? Maybe, it was just her rotten disposition.

Axel waved us to follow him. We rushed out of the pantry in single file and headed down the hall, through the foyer, and into the linen closet across from Prunella's bedroom. We didn't hear any voices coming from inside the room, most likely because they were gagged. I was hoping Carlos was in there with them. We didn't know that for sure, but where else would he be?

Once safely inside the closet, Axel said, "Okay, they checked in here when they captured Carlos. I doubt they'll think to look in here again, but if they do we need a plan."

"We tackle her to the ground!" Inga suggested willingly, slapping her fist in her other hand.

"If it's just her," Alex replied. "If those twins come with, we're screwed, they won't think first, they'll probably just react."

"You think they'll kill us on the spot?" I asked, wondering if that's what he meant.

"Yes. I'm sure Cassandra has told them to kill us if they have the chance," Alex said.

"I don't agree," Axel chimed in. "I believe she wants to kill us herself. It'll give her the satisfaction and closure she obviously needs so desperately."

"I think Axel's right," I said, agreeing wholeheartedly. "Is there anything in here we can use to defend ourselves?" I looked at the shelves and noticed the only items in sight were extra sheets, towels, and toilet paper.

"I still have the knife," Axel announced, holding it high for us to see.

"That's a start," Alex said.

"There are cleaners in here we could use to throw at their face. It might temporarily hold them back long enough for us to get out of here," Inga said, picking up a bottle of toilet bowl cleanser.

"Could work," Axel responded. "But, that won't buy us enough time to get Prunella and Carlos, too."

"We need to find out if Carlos is actually in there," I said. "How are we going to do that?"

"I say, while Cassandra's napping and the twins are outside, we try and get inside," Axel suggested. "Alex and Inga, are you game?"

"Just those two?" I asked, curiously. Did he want Isabella and me to stay in the closet while they tried to free the others?

"Yes," he answered, but quickly added, "Just until we get inside and free them."

"I guess that's alright," I said, looking at Isabella and she was nodding in agreement. "I'm keeping the door open, though. And, if Cassandra opens her door, we'll be able to warn you."

"Let's go," Inga said, opening the toilet cleaner and squirting it on a nearby pile of paper towels to test it. "All good," she said, smiling and appearing very eager to move.

Isabella and I stayed back while Axel, Alex and Inga walked out into the dark hallway. "Don't make any noise or scare them so they scream," I called out.

"They can't scream if they're gagged, Ruth Ann," Inga snottily reminded me.

She had a point, but wow, she's been acting obnoxiously lately. Once we were safe, I think I should have a little talk with her. Not that I had any right to put her in her place, but just a reminder to treat people with respect. I turned my attention back to the three of them standing outside the door desperately trying to get inside the bedroom. I could see the frustration on Axel's face. He was feverishly pulling at the door knob, but finally, he came back into the closet.

"It's no use." he said, exasperated. He needed a break while Alex and Inga continued to try and unlock it.

"Why?" I asked.

"It's got a lock that requires a key. Without bolt cutters, we won't be able to get in there."

I felt the hysteria building inside of me, but forced myself to stay calm. In a quivering voice and gritted teeth, I asked, "What are we going to do? We have to get them out of there!"

"I'm thinking, Ruth Ann," Axel said, frustrated. "I'm so tired I can't think straight. I don't know what to do!"

He wasn't a young man any more. He was about ten years older than me, and I was exhausted. I can't keep going through these all-nighters. "Hey," I said, excited. "What if we went in through the window outside?"

Axel popped his head up, looking like new man. "That's a great idea!" He stormed out of the closet and whispered something to Alex and Inga. They nodded and walked inside the closet.

"Great idea, Ruth Ann," Inga declared, actually giving me credit for my idea.

"Thank you, Inga," I said, smiling. "We only have one tiny, minor problem..."

"What?" Inga barked.

"The twins are searching for us outside. Don't you think it'll be obvious if we're standing in front of the bedroom window trying to break in?"

"She's got another good point," Axel said, deflated. "But, I don't see an alternative. We've got to risk it."

I quickly replied and stipulated, "Oh, and there is no way Isabella and I are going to remain inside this closet while you three head outside!"

Inga was the first to react, "But, we can't have five of us standing in front of the cabin!"

Axel quickly responded to Inga *and* me, "We will not leave them inside, Inga. What if we need to make a quick escape? I say we stick together."

Why didn't he suggest that before? But, instead I replied, "Thank you."

"Here's the plan," Axel said, taking charge. "I'll make sure the coast is clear. It's dark outside so we can hide near the front of the cabin. If we stay low, and I mean almost flat on the ground, they won't see us."

"I noticed earlier that there are overgrown shrubs in the front, so that'll help too," Alex added.

"Yes, and only one of us at a time should stand and work on opening the window. I'm sure it's locked, they wouldn't be that stupid keeping it unlocked. We need to hurry outside so we can see what we need to do about opening that window."

I slipped my coat on quickly. Inga, Alex, Axel, and Isabella were still wearing theirs, but there was no way I could've stayed inside with a heavy, long coat. I would've passed out by now with the heat. I buttoned it up as high as it went and pulled out the hat and gloves I had stuffed inside the pockets and put them on. Thankfully, my coat and accessories were black so they would keep me hidden.

Axel took off toward the front door. The rest of us stuck our heads out of the closet and watched him enter the foyer. There was nothing coming from Cassandra's wing of the cabin, so he waved us to hurry to him. However, Axel didn't wait for us, but opened the front door and stepped on the front porch. I knew what he was doing. He wanted to be the one caught if Jacob and Johann were waiting there. Inga and Alex didn't hesitate for long. They rushed out the front door without looking back at Isabella and me. I wasn't going to be caught inside, so I grabbed Isabella's gloved hand and pulled her out on the porch.

"Ruth Ann," a quiet voice called my name. "We're over here."

I turned toward the direction I thought the voice was calling and saw Axel ardently waving his hand for us to get over to them immediately. We hurried to a small area under the window to Prunella's room. He motioned for us to get to the ground as stay as low as we were able. "I heard one of the twins nearby. I can't tell where they are right now, so stay low."

There wasn't a lot of room because small yews formed a semicircle in front of the windows. The ground was covered with frozen mulch that was quite sharp as I made my way to the ground. "Ouch," I heard Inga gasp, angrily. "I think I just cut my knee open!"

"Don't worry about that now," Alex snapped, lying flat on his stomach on the cold ground. "Just get down here. I can hear them coming!"

We didn't waste time and dropped down on our stomachs. We were practically on top of each other as we tried to fit our bodies as close to the log cabin as possible.

Suddenly, the twins appeared out of thin air standing on the frozen grass in the front yard. "We can't go in there, Johann."

"It's freezing! I'm not staying out here all night. I think they took off on foot to find help. Maybe we need to leave before they come back with the police!"

"We're miles from that crappy little town," Jacob said,

shivering. "If their car's still here, then they are around ... somewhere."

"We've searched everywhere, you fool. It's pitch black in those woods and I don't want to get attacked by a bear!"

"Shut-up," Jacob hollered. "We need to come up with a lie to tell her."

"Like what, Jacob?" he asked, baffled.

Jacob rubbed his hatless head and said, "I know! We tell her they took off to get the police and we need to get out of here right away."

"What good will that do?" Johann asked. "If we have to leave in a hurry, where will we go? And, we can't ditch her yet because we still don't have the necklace for Steven to pawn."

"Yeah, well, let me think a minute," Jacob replied, wracking his brain for a better plan. "I've got it! We tell her we need to move to another location because we heard sirens coming this way, and it won't be long before they find us. Then, we load up the truck with Prunella and that old woman. Before Cassandra and her new prisoner get in... we take off and leave them here to get caught."

"That's brilliant!" Johann exclaimed. "She goes to prison, and we don't have to deal with her anymore. We get to keep the necklace! Plus, we don't have to answer any questions about why their car is still parked down the road."

"And the girl," Jacob added with a devilish grin.

From the bushes, Alex suddenly grabbed Axel's leg just as he started to rise to attack Jacob. "No, Axel, let it go for now."

Axel nodded and fell flat to the ground again. I knew it had to be painful listening to Jacob talk about Prunella that way. I highly doubted Prunella would want to be with Jacob so Axel needed to be patient until we got her away from them.

"But, what if she questions the lack of sirens and orders us to remain at the cabin?" Johann asked, worried. "I can't take much more of her. I'm about to commit murder and it's not even against those prisoners!"

"Easy, Johann," Jacob said, laughing. "She'll get hers. Just give it a little more time."

With that, the twins marched up the steps and headed inside the cabin.

"Now what?" Inga said, anxiously. "We can't let them take Ms. Prunella out of here. We've got to save her first!"

"And Carlos, Inga," Isabella said, calmly, but seriously.

"Of course, we rescue Carlos," Inga snapped. "What are we going to do?" she asked Axel.

"I'm thinking, I'm thinking," he said, frustrated. "We haven't even looked inside the window to see if Carlos is in there with Prunella!"

"Where else would he be?" I questioned him. "You've been in all the rooms, but this one," I said, pointing at the window above my head.

Alex kneeled, feeling safe he wouldn't be seen. "I think we hurry and get inside the room. The twins still have to tell Cassandra their lie. I feel fairy confident we'll hear her response."

Axel nodded, got on his knees with a little moan, and stood up. He noticed me staring at him and quickly said, "It's cold, my bones aren't as agile as they used to be."

"I hear you!" I said, grinning. I pulled myself onto all fours and then slowly rose to standing. Axel and Alex were about to complain, but chose to focus on the window in front of them. "Can you see anything?" I asked, anxiously.

"The blinds are closed," Alex replied. "I'm going to try and pull the window up."

"How?" I asked, curiously. "There's nothing to grab from the outside."

"I'll figure it out," Alex said, reaching up with bare, flat hands against the cold window.

We watched as he used every ounce of strength to slide the window open. "I can't get it to budge."

"It's probably locked," Axel said, trying himself, but getting nowhere.

"Break it!" Inga demanded, now standing next to me right behind Axel and Alex. She tried to push her way to the window, but the men didn't budge.

"It'll make too much noise," Isabella said, still lying on the ground.

"I agree, but we don't have a choice," Axel said.

"What if we bang a little on the window?" I suggested. "Maybe Prunella or Carlos can reach the window and unlock it for us."

"I thought they were tied and gagged?" Inga asked, confused with my suggestion.

"Maybe if they hear us, they'll figure out a way to get over to the window," I replied.

"We can try," Axel said. "If either of them don't respond, we'll have to try and break it."

"Wait for her to start screaming at the twins," Isabella suggested. "They won't hear you break the window if you do it at the same time."

"Well, we know she'll be screaming soon, so hurry up and bang on the window," I said.

"Hopefully, Cassandra won't be inside the room when we do it," Inga said, bursting our hopes.

"She was napping," I reminded her. "And, I'm sure as soon as she gets up, Jacob and Johann will be waiting to pounce on her with their plan."

Axel didn't wait for any further discussion. He reached his shivering, bare hand to the window and tapped it lightly. "Let's see if we hear anything from inside." He leaned close to the window. His chest reached the bottom of the window, so his head was fully against the frozen glass. "I don't hear a thing."

Alex was as tall as Axel, both a little over six feet tall. "Let me have a listen," Alex said. We waited as both of them placed their ears to the glass. "Nothing," Alex said, confirming with Axel.

"Do it a little harder," Inga demanded. "I barely heard a

thing."

I nodded in agreement, and Alex raised his fist this time and banged rather loudly. "Uh-oh," I said. "That was really loud."

"Shhh," Axel said, placing his ear against the window, facing the front door just in case Cassandra or the twins heard the bang.

"Something's happening in there!" Alex exclaimed in a low voice. "I hear rustling noises."

"Like a chair moving across the floor?" I asked, anxiously.

"It's too difficult to be specific, Ruth Ann," Alex answered.

Axel said, "I hear it too! I think someone's trying to get to the window!"

We waited, watching the front door and the window. Suddenly, we heard loud screams coming from somewhere inside the cabin. "It's her. She's awake," Inga said.

"She's really mad at the twins," Isabella said, watching the front door intently. None of us wanted to get caught standing underneath the window. "Maybe, we should get back down to the ground again."

"That's a really good idea, Isabella," Axel said. "Alex and I will remain standing while Inga watches over you two on the ground."

"Once again, I do not need protecting!" I was sick and tired of them treating me like I was a fragile flower.

Nobody dared say a word. I scowled as I knelt to the ground and Isabella joined me. Inga kept standing, straddling Isabella and me. It was ridiculous. What would she do if they came out and found us? Sit on us! "Anything from inside the bedroom?" I asked, wondering if they still heard movement.

"Hold on, Ruth Ann," Axel said, excitedly. "Look, the blinds are moving!"

I wanted to stand, but Inga's large body blocked me. She took her role as protector very seriously. I tried rolling to get away from her sturdy legs, but there was nowhere to go. Isabella was on one side of me, and the small bushes were on the other. I was about to pinch one of Inga's leg, when Axel cried out, "I see a hand!"

"Whose hand?" I bellowed from the solid ground.

"Alex, can you see it any better?" Axel asked, nervously.

Suddenly, Alex jumped back from shock. "Whoa!" he hollered, loudly.

"What, what?" I begged, trying to get past Inga's solid frame.

"Stop fighting me!" Inga snapped. "I'm not budging until they tell me to."

Isabella caught Inga off-guard and snuck out from underneath her legs. She was like a tiny wild woman, twisting and rolling and jumping to her feet. If I was in my twenties maybe I could've done that, too. "Hey," Inga said, trying to grab her legs or arms. "What are you doing?"

Isabella didn't respond, but rushed to the window and tried to get close to the glass. She wasn't tall enough to see inside after shoving poor Alex out of the way. He was so stunned by her behavior he stayed back as we watched her jump up and down trying to see in.

"Isabella," I said, now on my knees trying to get to a standing position. "What's wrong?"

"Nothing," she said, out of breath and very excited. "I think I know who's in there with Prunella."

"We know, it's Carlos," I said, trying to understand.

"No, no," she said, stepping onto a rock that was off to the side. She spotted it, rolled it over and stepped on it, balancing perfectly. She stared at the window waiting for the hand to appear again. Alex, recovering from what he saw filled us in.

"It wasn't Prunella's or Carlos' hand I saw."

"Who else could it be?" I asked, confused. "Oh, wait a minute. Are you saying the hand you saw was..."?

"Old," Alex finished my sentence.

"You're saying the old woman inside the room made it to the blinds and put her hand through the slats?" I asked, surprised.

"Yes," Alex replied. "I saw the hand and it scared me to death! I wasn't expecting that. This withered, dark hand poked through one of the slats."

"Isabella?" Axel turned his attention to her. "You said you think you know who the old woman is? I thought you had no idea."

"It's too hard to explain, but if you just trust me a moment," she said, putting her hand to the window and laying it flat against the glass. Suddenly, she cried, "Look, she's got her hand flat against mine!"

"What's happening?" Inga asked. "You two know each other?"

"Not exactly," Isabella said, smiling. "Let me try and explain."

"Please, but hurry-up!" Axel said, looking at the front door in a panic.

"Can't we wait for explanations until we get them out of there?" I asked, nervously. "Can she open the window from inside?"

Isabella's eyes closed and she squeezed them tightly. I think she was trying to communicate with the woman inside. We waited as patiently as we could when we heard a click and a tiny movement with the window. "She's doing it!" I cried out. "The window just moved a little."

Axel and Alex tried desperately to get their fingers in the sliver of an opening at the bottom of the window. Finally, Isabella was able to do it. Her tiny hands opened the window about an inch or two. Axel and Alex took over and raised the window as high as they could. "I'm going in," Alex said, moving the blinds away from the glass and shoving the upper half of his body through the opening.

"I hope Cassandra or the twins aren't in there," I said, trying to get close to the window, but with Axel, Isabella and Inga's bodies front and center I didn't stand a chance.

"I don't hear anything," Axel said, reaching in and moving the blinds away after Alex disappeared inside.

It was torturous waiting for Alex to report back to us. Axel decided not to wait and hoisted himself up and inside the bedroom so fast none of us had time to object. "Hey," Inga bellowed. "He didn't even tell us he was going in!"

"He's anxious about Prunella, Inga," I said, finally able to get close to the window. I stood on tippy toes trying to see in, but the blinds fell back against the window blocking our view.

"How come we can't hear anything in there?" Isabella asked, worried.

"Where did that old woman go?" Inga asked, reaching in and trying to push the blinds away. "I'm going to go in and see if they need help."

Just as Inga was about to pull her large body up and over the window sill, I pulled her down by the back of her coat. "Hey, what'd you do that for?"

"There's enough of them in there!" I snapped. "You can't just leave Isabella and me out here alone."

Suddenly, we heard loud screams and banging noises coming from inside the cabin. We didn't think it was from inside the bedroom, though. "Something's happening, Ruth Ann," Isabella said, her eyes so large I thought they were going to pop out of their sockets. "Maybe we should call inside and see if they're okay."

I wasn't sure what we should do. Inga, Isabella, and I were sitting ducks in front of the cabin. Just as I was going to suggest Inga take a better look in the window, Axel's head popped out and scared us to death. "Ruth Ann," he said, out of breath and panicked. "Prunella's not in here!"

"What?" I cried. "Where is she?"

"I don't know, but something's happening in another part of the cabin. There's screams and lots of loud noises. Alex is trying to get out of the bedroom, but the lock is on the outside of the door and we can't break it."

"Is Carlos in there?" Isabella asked, worried. She was trying to see around Axel and the blind. "I don't hear him!"

"No, he's not in here either," Alex said from the other side of the room. "Just the old lady."

"We're coming out and we'll have to make a quick decision about what we're going to do," Axel said, hopping out of the window back on the frozen ground. He reached his hands up and called to Alex, "Okay, pick her up and I'll grab her from my end."

"Inga, help him," Isabella said, watching Axel take a hold of two tiny, old hands and pulling her out of the window opening. The woman didn't speak, but I finally got a glimpse of her head as she exited the window.

Isabella stood back, but kept a close eye on the front door. Axel was worried they were going to hear us and come flying out the front door just as we were getting Alex and the old woman free. "All clear still," she said, holding on to the wrinkled hands tightly.

"She's out," Axel said to Alex. "Get out of there now!"

Alex hopped out of the window with ease and we dropped to the ground just in time. The front door whipped open nearly taking the hinges off the frame. It was one of the twins. He looked furious! I was thankful that the sky was pitch black, and we shouldn't be spotted.

"Johann," the male twin, Jacob hollered. "Bring them out!"

I looked at Axel and he looked confused. "Bring *who* out?" he whispered very carefully.

We waited. I looked over at Isabella who was protecting the old woman with her body. I felt a different wave of emotion hit me. Isabella knew her, I was sure of it! But, why didn't she tell us about her in the first place? I knew I would get the truth out of her eventually. Hopefully, this woman would be able to tell us what's going on with Prunella and now Carlos.

We lay on the ground and watched as Johann dragged a person out of the front door. It was Carlos! "Oh, no," Isabella muttered. "They're hurting him!"

"Shhh," Axel whispered. "He's alive and able to walk on his own. That's a good sign."

We watched poor Carlos get socked in the stomach for not obeying his captor. He was fighting with all his might, but he had his wrists tied behind his back and his mouth had a large piece of tape over it. He tried to kick Johann, but that didn't make the twin happy. He raised his arm to punch him in the face when a loud shout from a woman ordered him to stop.

What stunned us was that the voice wasn't Cassandra's.

TWENTY-THREE

"Look, it's Prunella!" I exclaimed loudly, terrified that I had just given our location away.

We looked on, horrified as Prunella marched out the front door screaming at Johann. "Don't touch him again!" she barked, with authority. "He's not going to fight us anymore, right Carlos?"

Carlos shook his head vigorously. I watched, shocked, as Prunella grabbed Jacob's hand and they hurried down the front steps and around the side of the cabin. Fortunately, the stone path leading to the back of the cabin was on the opposite side of where we were hiding.

Her coat was unbuttoned and flapping in the night air. I couldn't see too well, but saw an expression on her face that I'd never seen before. She looked ruthless, cruel, almost as if she was in charge instead of Cassandra. I noticed Isabella's and the old woman's heads had popped up, staring at Prunella. I reached out and touched Isabella's arm. "What, Ruth Ann?" Isabella quietly demanded, irritated at me.

"You two are staring at Prunella strangely. Why?"

She shook her head. "Not now."

"Yes, now. I know something else is going on. I can see it in your eyes."

Isabella made sure no one else was listening to us. "Look at her neck, Ruth Ann."

I lifted my head and tried to catch a glimpse of Prunella's

opened coat. I squinted, but couldn't make out what Isabella was referring to. "What?" I asked her, confused. "I can't see. It's too dark and too far away for me to see anything."

Before Isabella could answer, Inga let out a loud gasp. "Look at Ms. Prunella! Her neck is red!"

Everyone looked at Prunella. Inga was right. That's what Isabella must've been staring at so intensely. But, wait, her neck wasn't red...it was the necklace, my necklace! My beautiful, blue aquamarine had turned a deep, dark red!

"Maybe it's not the same necklace," Inga desperately suggested. "Something very strange is happening! I think Prunella's turned...turned evil."

"Nonsense," Axel snapped, watching the four of them disappear around the side of the cabin.

Axel popped up and ran around to the opposite side of the cabin. We were so stunned by what we had just witnessed that we remained frozen on the ground. Finally, Inga snapped out of her stupor. "What are we waiting for?" She jumped to her feet and took off after Axel. Isabella rolled her protective body off the old woman, and with Alex's help, they had her on her feet. I watched, still in shock, until Alex held his hand out to help me to my feet. I didn't know what to do or think. I noticed Isabella speaking to the old woman in a soft, caring voice, but I had no idea what she was saying.

"Come on, let's catch up with them," Alex said, waving his arms trying to get us moving.

"What did you say to her?" I asked Isabella. "You haven't told me if you actually know this woman?"

Isabella wanted to answer, but there wasn't time. Axel, Inga, and Alex disappeared into the darkness and around the side of the cabin. I grabbed Isabella's arm and she held onto the old woman's arm. We weren't as fast as the others, but we made our way to the back side of the cabin just in time to see Jacob shove Carlos into the back seat of a small black sedan. "Easy with him, Jacob!" Prunella hollered. "We need him for insurance."

"What's she talking about?" I asked confused, and out of breath.

"Shhh," Axel replied, holding his finger to his mouth. "We need to listen to see if they mention where they're going."

Carlos was jammed into the middle of the back seat with Prunella on one side and Jacob on the other. Johann was the driver. He started the car with ease. The car was spotless and appeared to be a new luxury sedan with all the bells and whistles. As the engine roared, so did the loud, banging music from within. The volume of the music not only made us jump, but also jolted the passengers inside. I noticed Jacob slap Johann's head from the back seat.

"What are they doing?" I asked.

"They're obviously about to leave," Axel said.

"But, what about Cassandra?" I asked, baffled. "She hasn't come out yet."

"No idea," he responded.

"You don't think they killed her so the twins could take the necklace for themselves, and their uncle, do you?" I asked.

"Steven's very dangerous and he'll kill anybody to get what he wants," Axel replied, answering my question.

"How did he get back here in the first place?" Inga demanded. "He was supposed to be in jail for the rest of his life!"

"He obviously escaped," Alex replied.

"We have to follow them," Inga insisted.

"There's one thing you all are forgetting," Axel said, solemnly. "My car is blocking the road. They'll have to drive on the edge to get past it. I'm not sure if there's enough room for both cars on that narrow road, if you call it a road."

"You think they'll come back to keep looking for us?" I asked, terrified.

"Nope. Cassandra already ordered them to look, and they came up empty. Now, with Prunella at the helm, I have no idea what their plans are," Axel said.

"Prunella's not in charge!" I snapped. "She's going along

with them so they can lead us to wherever they're going. I bet she knows about Steven Svenson and where he's waiting for them. We have to follow and call the police so they can take them down!"

"We will, but we need to check inside first," Axel said.

"What for?" Inga demanded.

"First, to see if Cassandra's alive or dead, and secondly, to see if Prunella left us a clue."

"Who cares?" Inga replied.

"I'm not going to leave her here if she's alive and hurt," Axel insisted. "I'm evil, but not that evil. Or, at least not any more. In the old days, I wouldn't have cared what happened to her."

Thoughtful of him, but I was with Inga. Who cares what happened to Cassandra. She was wicked and once we got into town we could tell the cops where she is. Let them deal with her. I was about to suggest that when a loud scream howled from inside.

"That's her!" Inga bellowed.

"Maybe she got her gag off," I suggested. "If she was gagged, that is."

"Let's get inside," Axel said, turning and running toward the door.

We watched the black sedan turn around in the gravel driveway of the cabin and head down the road. Once it was out of sight, we ran to the back door of the cabin.

"It's open," Alex said, reaching and turning the handle. "I'm going in."

"Wait," Axel shouted. "It could be a trap."

"But, the others left," he replied, confused. "I think she's been restrained and heard them leave."

"That must've really made her furious," I said with a grin.

"Be careful," Axel said, waiting just steps behind Alex. "She's sneaky, and who knows what she's capable of doing."

Alex opened the door and stepped inside the cabin. Axel followed, then Inga and me. Isabella and the old woman stayed on the back stoop. I turned and asked, "Why aren't you going inside?"

Isabella answered, "She won't go in."

"Why?"

"She's terrified of Cassandra," Isabella replied.

"She won't hurt her anymore," I said. "The twins must've restrained her or she would've chased after them when they took off with Prunella and Carlos."

"She still won't budge," Isabella said, shaking her head. "I'll stay with her. You go with the others." She quickly added, "Just don't leave without us."

"Of course not," I said, thinking that was a foolish remark. I headed inside the cabin and didn't see any of the others. I looked to my left at the empty kitchen, and then to the right at the open great room. "Where'd they go?" I said to myself. I rushed straight down the hall toward the front foyer. Once I stood in the foyer, I tried to hear which direction they went. To the right was Cassandra's bedroom. To the left, was the room where Prunella and the old woman were held captive.

Suddenly, a thought popped into my head. If Prunella was in charge, why was she locked in that room? She had to have played a part with the twins, telling them that she was on their side and would go with them to meet Steven Svenson. How else could she have been freed? The disgusting fact that Jacob was the likely father of her baby could also play a part. Maybe she was able to convince them that they would be a couple, but she had to take over for Cassandra as their leader. Seems incomprehensible, but who knows what she was capable of doing.

I was awakened from my thoughts by noises from the hall to the right. "Cassandra's room," I said, and rushed down the hall. What I found shocked me and forced me to freeze at the doorway.

"Stop!" I screamed. "Get your hands off her!"

Inga, Alex, and Axel jumped at my shouts from the door. "Ruth Ann," Inga shouted. "We had to restrain her so she couldn't pull a fast one."

"You don't have to throw her to the ground so forcibly."

"She was about to hit Mr. Eklund over the head with a fire poker!" Alex exclaimed, holding it to show me.

"Oh," I said, not realizing what happened before I arrived. "I guess you had to act quickly."

"Yes, Ruth Ann," Axel answered. "I'm thankful Alex and Inga tackled her before she whacked me. I could've been killed."

"Sorry, tell me, what happened?" I asked, looking over at where Inga was sitting on top of her.

"I'll explain quickly," Axel said. I nodded and let him continue. "We ran inside the cabin and heard her yelling so we knew she was in her bedroom. The door was jammed shut with that chair from the outside." I looked to my right and noticed a broken dining room chair lying on the floor.

"I guess I didn't notice it. I was too busy trying to find you."

"When we were able to open the door, she was waiting inside. She grabbed me by the neck," Axel took his hand and rubbed his bare neck in disgust. "She tried to strangle me, but I grabbed her and threw her on the bed. Alex and Inga jumped on her, but she's really quick. She rolled to the other side of her bed and stood waiting for our next move. When I ran around to grab her, thinking she didn't stand a chance with the three of us in here, she reached down to her nightstand and pulled out a fire poker. She was about to wail it at my head when Inga and Alex flew to my aide and wrestled her to the floor. That's when you entered the room."

"Oh, I guess I shouldn't have jumped to the wrong conclusion."

I noticed Inga using all her might to keep the woman face down on the floor. She was kicking and screaming into the rug where her head was jammed. The fury was undeniable, but with Alex and Inga restricting her movements, she didn't stand a chance.

"Did she say anything?" I asked, curiously.

"Oh, yes, she did!" Inga said, turning her head my direction. "But, she has her filthy mouth taped now."

"That's why I only heard muffled screams from her," I said.

"When I broke the door and rushed in," Axel started to say.

"The look in her eyes caused me to freeze. It was just long enough for her to grab my neck and begin strangling me."

"What look?" I asked, curiously. Were her eyes red like Prunella's had been earlier?

"I know what you're thinking, Ruth Ann," he said. "Her eyes weren't red. They just gave off such an evil glare that it actually scared me for a moment."

"Oh," I replied, relieved. "What did she say to you?"

"When she had her hands around my neck, she told me she would personally kill my wife! She said those idiot twins tried to fool her, but they're dumb as rocks and won't last a minute without her running the show."

"Really?" I asked.

"She didn't exactly use those words. Her words were, let's just say, a little more colorful," he said.

Alex stood up after they had tied her hands and feet together so she couldn't kick them anymore. "What're we doing with her?" he asked.

"Yeah," Inga chimed in, wondering herself. "I'm not taking my eyes off of this one. She's as sneaky as they come."

"I agree," Axel said. "I think we need to keep her with us."

We looked at him as if he was the crazy one now. "Are you kidding?" I bellowed. "She'll never cooperate with us."

"But, she might be able to help us find them," Alex said, agreeing with Axel.

"No way!" Inga barked. "She's not going to say a word to help us."

Axel stared at Cassandra on the floor and said slowly, "If she knows what's best she will."

Cassandra moved violently on the floor, forcing Inga to pounce on top of her again.

"I don't think she likes your threats, Axel," I said. I walked to the woman on the floor and knelt down. Her head was on the side and her eyes were glaring daggers at me. "How does it feel now, Cassandra?" I asked her sarcastically.

She tried to come after me, but she was stuck with Inga on top of her back and her hands and ankles tied. "Doesn't pay to be so nasty, does it?" I asked, standing up and sitting on the edge of the bed.

"We need to get out of here and find Ms. Prunella and Carlos," Inga said, anxiously. "It's been too long. They could've gone far away from here."

"I don't think that's going to happen, Inga," Axel said. "I think they're still around town waiting to meet up with Steven."

"Where do you think he is?" I asked.

"I have a couple ideas," he replied, secretively. "Let's figure out how we're going to get this woman to cooperate first."

I suggested we find a sedative. "There has to be something around here, don't you think?" I didn't wait for an answer, but walked into her bathroom.

I opened the door and found a disgusting mess. "What a slob!" There were towels strewn all over the floor, and her toiletries took over the small sink counter. The caps were off of her hair products, the mirror was covered in toothpaste splashes and water spots. I didn't want to touch the quilted makeup bag that was on top of the toilet basin, but figured she might've kept a stash of drugs inside. I stepped over a pile of clothes and grabbed the red bag. It was quite heavy. I unzipped it and peeked inside.

The woman was loaded with creams for the face, hands, and body. Obviously, being in a tropical climate did havoc on one's skin. I dumped the contents into the sink and rummaged through it. There were several pill bottles, but not like the kind you or I would pick up at a local pharmacy. The bottles were small and made of clear glass. I picked up and investigated four of them. One bottle had tiny red pills, another had white ones, and the other two had round, yellow pills. None of them were identifiable. I took the bottles in my hands and walked back into the bedroom.

"Look what I found," I declared, dumping the glass bottles on her unmade bed.

"What are they?" Axel asked, walking to the bed and

grabbing the bottle with the red pills.

"I have no idea, but maybe Cassandra would be willing to tell us," I answered, looking down on the floor and noticing that Inga had pulled Cassandra to a sitting position. Her legs were straight in front of her and her arms were tied behind her back. She had a scowl on her face that suggested she wasn't going to be cooperative.

I noticed behind her grimace, that she was a pretty woman probably about my daughters' and Prunella's age. I wasn't sure of her age, but she was beautiful. Her dark skin and tiger-colored eyes were stunning, despite the evil they were spewing at the moment. It was so unfortunate that her upbringing caused such hatred and the need for revenge. A glimmer of reforming her passed through my head. If she understood we weren't the people Martika said we were, and Isabella wasn't the 'chosen' child of their father's, then maybe they could have a relationship. However, she's committed too many crimes. She's probably going to spend the rest of her life in prison.

"Ruth Ann?" Suddenly, I heard Axel calling my name. "What are you thinking about?"

"Nothing," I said, admitting the defeat of reformation. "I'm going to try and get through to her," I said quietly to Axel.

"Good luck with that!" he replied. "Just make sure you don't get too close. She may lunge or spit at your face."

"That's disgusting, Axel," I said. "But, just in case, I'll keep my distance."

I picked up the glass bottles and carried them over to where Inga was kneeling right next to the rigid form of Cassandra. "Let's take the tape off her mouth."

"Are you serious?" Inga asked, surprised at my request.

I observed Cassandra watching me get a little closer. I had to admit, I was a little nervous, but, I wasn't going to let her see that. I lifted up the pill bottles so she could see what I had in my hands. Her furious glare told me she probably wasn't too thrilled that I had rummaged through her personal belongings.

"Look, Cassandra," I began. "This doesn't have to be this way if you cooperate with us. I'll take the tape off if you agree to answer some questions." I waited for her response, which didn't come too swiftly. I could almost feel the wheels turning in her mind as she went over different scenarios of how this could play out. Finally, after a minute or two, she nodded. I took it as a sign of cooperation, but not without extreme caution.

"Be careful, Ruth Ann," Axel called, not too far behind me. He didn't want to crowd her. Alex and Axel stood a few feet back near the bed. Inga however, was ready to pounce if she tried any funny stuff.

"I'm going to reach up and pull off your tape. It may hurt, so please don't lash out."

I slowly set the pill bottles on the floor as she attentively watched. I reached with one hand and peeled a tiny bit of the sticky tape away from her cheek. "You got to pull it off quickly, Ruth Ann," Axel suggested. "Otherwise, it's more painful."

I ripped the tape off, and Cassandra let out a wail. "Ouch!" she snapped, angrily.

"Sorry, no other way to do it," I said, even though I kind of liked it.

"What are you going to do to me?" she barked. She was irate, and probably figured she didn't have anything to lose. She was under our watch now, and probably thought we'd kill her or turn her over to the police.

"We're asking the questions!" Inga snapped.

Cassandra slowly turned her head toward Inga and glared at her. "I don't have to answer any of your stupid questions. You're just going to get rid of me anyway."

"Cassandra," I said, trying to get her attention back to me. "Let's begin with what we know. You came here to attack my family and steal our necklace, right?"

No response. "You kidnapped Prunella, brainwashed her or put a curse on her to get her to go along with your plan, right?" No response, again. "You killed our close friend and family member,

296

Sherman, didn't you?" I was shaking as I asked the last question. She was a murderer!

"No, I didn't kill your butler!" she howled. "Your precious Prunella did it!"

"That's ridiculous! You either drugged or forced her to do it, didn't you?" Inga demanded, her face reddened with rage.

"So, what if I did?" she asked, mockingly. "I didn't have to do much. She was a willing participant. And now look at her! She's taken over the whole operation!"

Axel couldn't take her insults us any longer. He came a little closer and I noticed how livid he was. He placed his face within inches of hers. "How dare you say that? She's not a murderer. What did you do to her?" He backed up before she could react and stood over her. Clearly, not helping my chances of getting her to cooperate.

"Why don't you take one of those little red pills and see what *you'll* do," she said, spitting on the ground very close to Inga. Inga quickly raised her arm away from the spray and shot Cassandra a look that made me shiver!

"Wait!" I cried. "Are you saying those red pills are what you gave my cousin?"

"I'm not saying a thing," Cassandra replied, smacking her lips shut, but then added, "I just suggested taking one of them."

I grabbed the red pill bottle on the floor. I held them close and examined them. There was no stamped numbers or letters on the little pills. I unhinged the metal clasp and was about to dump one in my hand. "Stop!" Axel shouted, almost causing me to dump the pills on to the ground.

"What was that for?" I asked, irritated.

"Don't touch them," he answered. "We don't want any residue on your hand. What if you got some of that in your mouth?"

"Oh, I guess that could be a slight possibility," I admitted, placing the hinge tightly back in place, securing the bottle.

"You all are chickens!" she spat. "What about those yellow

pills? Or the white ones?" she teased. "Maybe one of those pills would sedate me like you want to do."

"We wouldn't have to do anything if you acted like a decent human being!" Alex snapped, finally coming closer. "Just tell us what you gave Prunella!"

"Sorry, you'll have to try each pill!"

"That will never happen and you know it," I said, exasperated. "Can you at least admit Prunella took one of these pills?"

"Possibly," she replied. "Or...maybe that old woman put a trance on her. Or...maybe she hypnotized her!"

"Stop playing games, you bitch!" Axel hollered. "You know she's pregnant and anything you forced down her throat could jeopardize the baby!"

Cassandra's face turned an ugly shade of gray. I think from her reaction she wasn't aware Prunella was pregnant. "No, she can't be," she mumbled. "I, I would never hurt an innocent baby. That's what happened to me! I don't want anyone to turn out like me!"

TWENTY-FOUR

"What are you saying, Cassandra?" I asked, suddenly feeling a twinge of empathy. "You really didn't know about the pregnancy?"

Her head raised to meet my astonished stare, and I could swear her demeanor changed completely. "No. I didn't know she was pregnant. But," she paused and thought a moment. "But, that might be why I overheard Jacob discussing his plans with Johann to raise a child far away from here with his girlfriend."

"What?" I roared.

"I figured they were just bragging. I thought they were going to take the money they earned and go back to Sweden and start a new life. Maybe, get married and have some kids." For a moment, it sounded like she was speaking as a normal person, but sadly, we were mistaken. Her face turned a nasty shade of red, and she took a deep breath and began spewing vile words at us once again.

"How dare you? You think you can come here and take me down! Never! I will kill each and every one of you before I admit defeat. I will find those idiots and take them and your pretty little wife down. Once and for all! I will seek my revenge and nobody will ever catch me!" She held her gaze on each one of us for seconds. The point was taken. I thought we had a slight breakthrough, but it didn't last long.

Inga burst out laughing. "You're a fool. You're the one tied and restrained. How do you think your plan will work?"

Cassandra glared at Inga, but didn't say a word. She turned

her gaze back to the glass bottles on the ground. Here we go again... "So, let's get back to these little pills." She became eerily calm and continued, "You need to know what your precious Prunella ingested. You can't do anything to me without knowing how to get her back to normal, right?" We didn't respond. "Only I know the antidote that will return her to you. If you don't do as I say, I will never fess up."

"Shut up, Cassandra!" I barked, surprising even myself. I turned to Axel and stood up. I held the bottles and asked him if there was a way we could find out what was inside these without her help.

"How?" he asked quietly. "She probably brought them with her or..." Axel turned and ran out of the room down the hall as fast as he could. Inga, Alex, and I stood staring at the empty door.

"Hey, where'd he go?" Inga asked, stunned.

"I think I know," I said, figuring it out. "I think he ran out of here to speak to that old woman. She refused to come inside the cabin. Isabella was staying with her."

"They have to be frozen!" Alex said, alarmed.

"I bet they've stepped inside the kitchen by now," I said. "Let me check. You two stay close to her. Don't let her move an inch!"

"You bet!" Inga said, shoving the tape back across Cassandra's mouth. I noticed she wasn't gentle with her as she forced the tape on. I didn't care if Inga hurt her a little; she deserved it!

I rushed out of the bedroom and past the foyer. I made a jolting left turn and entered the great room where I spotted Axel forcibly trying to get the old woman to come with him toward the front of the cabin. Isabella was crying, trying to help the old woman, but Axel didn't care. "Please leave her alone, Axel!" Isabella begged, tears streaming down her cheeks. "She doesn't understand what you're doing."

I rushed to Isabella's and the old woman's sides and pulled Axel's arm as hard as I could to get him to release the grip he had on the older woman. "Let go, Axel," I demanded. He turned and released immediately.

"What are you doing, Ruth Ann?" Axel shouted. "She knows what's in those bottles!"

"What bottles?" Isabella asked, confused. "He keeps shouting at her, but she doesn't understand him!"

"I found some unidentifiable pill bottles in Cassandra's personal things. She taunted us by saying Prunella took some of them, but she won't tell us what they are, and now she's threatening to not give us the antidote unless we let her call the shots!" I took a deep breath. "Axel rushed to you thinking she," I subtly nudged my head in the old woman's direction. "She might know what they are. Maybe she even brought them!"

The old woman turned toward Isabella. Their eyes met and somehow, I knew the older woman understood what I just said. "She does know!" I yelled. "Isabella, get her to admit it, right now!"

Isabella looked desperately into the old woman's eyes, leaned over and whispered inaudible words in her ear. "What did you tell her?" Axel demanded. "We don't have time for this."

"She understood some of what Ruth Ann said about the bottles of pills. She said she wants to be taken to them."

"But, Cassandra's still in the room," I said, confused. "I thought she wouldn't go near her because she was so afraid of her."

The old woman whispered additional words in Isabella's ear. "She said it's more important than her fears right now."

"Let's go," Axel said, finally getting what he wanted in the first place.

The four of us hurried back to Cassandra's bedroom. The glass pill bottles were carefully set on a small table near the door. I picked them up and held each one for her to see clearly.

"No, no, no," she mumbled repeatedly, terror in her eyes.

"What's she saying?" I asked, looking to Isabella. The old woman was rambling words none of us understood. Well, none of us except Isabella.

"Isabella," I screamed, terrified. "Why is she saying that?"

Isabella held on to the old woman's shoulders trying to calm her down. The woman was holding the bottle of red pills in her withered hands, rocking back and forth. I noticed tears streaming down her face, terrifying me further. "Please, tell me what they are!" Isabella begged of the woman. "We can't let Prunella die!"

"Die?" Axel bellowed. "Why would she die after taking these? She just walked out of here on her own free will."

"I don't know, Axel," Isabella replied, trying to get the old woman to speak to her. "Let me calm her down first, and then maybe she'll tell me why she's so upset."

"Hurry," I begged. "Ask about those yellow and white ones, too?"

The old woman heard my question. She stopped crying and stared at the pill bottles. She slowly reached her free hand and grabbed the bottle of yellow pills. She raised them close to her face and smelled the closed bottle. "Open it for her," I said to Isabella.

"No, no, no," the old woman cried. I watched as she set the bottle back down and grabbed the white bottle of pills. She did the same thing. Smelled and then set the pills back down. She grabbed Isabella's arm and pulled her into the hallway, never looking at Cassandra on the floor. I followed them into the hall, but Isabella shoved me back inside the bedroom. "Please, Ruth Ann," she said, letting go of my arm. "Give me a moment with her, alone."

I stepped back inside the bedroom and stood next to Axel. I turned my attention to Inga. She was sitting on the floor next to Cassandra. She had allowed Cassandra to sit up, but Alex was on one side and Inga on the other. I couldn't help but notice the intensity in the room. Cassandra was staring toward the door, waiting for the old woman and Isabella to return. Finally, after a few intense minutes, Isabella and the old woman re-entered.

"It's bad, Ruth Ann," Isabella announced, causing Axel to come closer. "Those red pills are very dangerous."

"How dangerous?" I asked, holding Axel off with my arm. I knew he was dying to interrogate Isabella, but he would just make matters worse. He was a terrified husband, trying to find his pregnant wife. Even though they were having troubles in their marriage, I still believed he loved her deeply.

"There's no easy way to say this," she replied to me, ignoring Axel's impatience. "All it takes is one pill, and the person who took it could die."

"Die?" Axel shouted. "But, we just saw her walk out the front door!"

"It isn't fatal to everyone after the first pill, but," she stopped, turned toward the old woman who was staring at her. She nodded her head, prodding Isabella to tell us more.

"Please, just tell us," I pleaded.

"The second pill or third pill could kill her. Eventually, one of them will be the fatal dose."

"How many has she taken?" I demanded, grabbing the bottle from the grasp of the old woman's hands. She resisted and held the bottle close to her chest, but I forced it out of her hands. She shook her head vehemently, trying to keep me from taking them, but she was fragile and weak, allowing me to take the pills from her easily.

"No, no, no," she cried, again and again. "No touch!"

"She spoke in English," Inga shouted from the floor.

"She understands a little," Isabella replied. "She doesn't want Ruth Ann to touch any of the pills."

"I won't," I answered the old woman. "Please, Isabella, what else did she tell you about the pills?"

"Prunella has taken only two pills. At first, Prunella acted as Cassandra wanted, but it obviously backfired on Cassandra, and now Prunella has taken control of the twins."

"I'm confused," I said, trying to follow Isabella's explanation.

"Cassandra brought the pills and the old woman with her from Jamaica. She wanted to get Prunella to go along with her plans, but when she resisted, the pills had a much stronger effect on Prunella's personality than Cassandra expected. The first pill turned Prunella's into a ruthless, remorseless killer." Isabella paused, watching us figure out in our own minds that she had the capability of murdering her Great Uncle Sherman.

"However, the second pill made her stronger and even more ruthless. Prunella was able to overtake Cassandra and convince the twins that they needed to follow her and dump Cassandra. She promised to take them away and give them a wealthy, luxurious life."

"Of course, Jacob and Johann agreed," I mumbled.

"So, that's when they planned to overthrow Cassandra, and leave her here to die," Axel said.

"Yes," Isabella replied.

"Did the old woman know of Cassandra's plans with those pills?" Axel asked, turning his anger toward the trembling old woman.

"No, no, no," she rambled. "She...she made me."

Isabella stepped in between Axel and the old woman. "Don't blame her!" she argued, holding her arms out to her side shielding him from the woman. "She didn't know anything about Cassandra's plans. She was forced to come here."

"Didn't she know that giving Cassandra those pills was dangerous?" I asked.

"No, well, yes," Isabella replied, still protecting the old woman with her own body. "Cassandra didn't ask for the pills. She stole them and kidnapped the old woman. She figured if she went along with Cassandra, she would be able to help whoever took the pills."

"Really?" Axel asked, doubting her word. "Then why did she let Cassandra give her two pills? I know she's weak, but couldn't she have helped Prunella?"

"Look," Isabella began to say, exasperated. "I don't know the whole story. She just told me that Cassandra marched into her home and took her and the pills."

"How did she know where to get those pills?" Inga asked from a distance.

Isabella turned to the old woman and whispered in her ear. I could see the old woman frantically returning Isabella's questions. I didn't understand a word, but she was clearly defending herself.

"She told me that she dabbles in medicine back home, and unlike American medicine, it's full of natural ingredients that have been passed on from generation to generation. She was the doctor back in her village. That's why, and how, Cassandra found her. She knew she could get some good drugs to conquer Prunella or whomever she wanted."

"I guess that makes sense," I said. "Didn't she have anyone living with her who could've stopped Cassandra? Like a son or grandson?"

"No," Isabella stated without concurring with the old woman. "She lives alone."

I noticed a strange look on Isabella's face. I saw her catch my stare, and she quickly said, "I never met her before, Ruth Ann."

"Why would you say that?" I asked, even though it's exactly what I was thinking.

"Because I could tell by your expression that you doubted my words."

"I haven't doubted anything you've said!" I retorted. "I just don't understand how you knew she lived alone."

"That's how it is back in our villages. If she was the medicine woman of the village, then she probably lived all alone without any family."

The old woman grabbed Isabella's arm and whipped her around to face her. I was amazed at the strength she displayed. Isabella was stunned by her action, but let her whisper words in her ear.

"What is she saying?" Axel demanded.

Isabella turned back to us and said, "It was nothing."

"Knock it off, Isabella!" Axel said, irritated. "She obviously didn't like your comments about her being the medicine woman or having no family. Which is it?"

Isabella caved and replied, "The no family part. I guess she abandoned her family when she was a young woman. She still has family from what she just told me, but the ones who are still alive don't know she exists."

"That's horrible!" I declared. "Why wouldn't she tell them?"

Isabella remained silent. I had a funny feeling this wasn't the end of it. Somehow, someway, this woman had a bigger role in our lives than the rest of us knew. Well, everyone but Isabella.

"Enough!" Alex yelled from the window. "We need to get out of here. It's getting late and it's dark outside." He walked up to Axel and asked, "Axel, you said you know where they may have gone. Let's get out of here!"

"We need to bring her with," Axel responded, pointing to Cassandra.

"Just leave her tied up," Alex said. "Have Ruth Ann call her cop boyfriend to come and get her."

"Hey," I said, realizing I had totally forgotten about John. "He's probably furious with us anyway. I should call him, but I really don't want to hear him scream at me. Maybe we should check out Axel's idea of where he thinks Steven Svenson is hiding. I bet Jacob, Prunella, Johann and Carlos are there by now."

Axel walked over to Cassandra and easily knelt on the floor next to her. He asked Inga to back off a little, and she did. She didn't go far, but enough for Axel to get nice and close to Cassandra's face. "I'm only going to ask you this once," he said so close to her face I was worried she would bite him. "My wife is pregnant, and you forced an illegal drug down her throat. I need to save the baby so...if you have any human emotion in you at all...you will help us track down the twins." He waited to see her expression. I really thought I was witnessing her warming up a tad. "I know your plans were to get the money from Steven Svenson for the necklace, but you've been duped. You'd think you would want to get revenge on him, so why not help us?"

He waited for her reaction, but she only appeared mildly curious, so he continued. "I wasn't sure if you wanted the necklace for it's 'believed' powers or its financial rewards. I really don't care, Cassandra. I just want to get my wife away from those lunatics. I'm ready to make you a deal..." he cut off his words, hoping they got her full attention. They sure did.

Her eyes popped wide open, and she nodded. Axel obviously thought it was time to for her to speak so he ripped the tape from her mouth. "Ouch!" she shouted, but quickly recovered.

"So, I got your attention?" he inquired, and she nodded. "Good. Let's see how we can work together so it not only benefits us, but you."

"I'm listening," Cassandra replied, and it was the first time I felt she was ready to work with us.

"You lead us to them, and we'll bring you with us. You won't be restrained, unless you try to hurt or overthrow us, got it?"

"I'm still listening. I'll tell you my decision when you're finished telling me how this will benefit *me*."

"You stay with us, on our side until we get my wife and necklace back. If you play nice girl, I promise you will get to keep the necklace."

"WHAT?" I shouted. "It's not yours to bargain with, Axel!"

I instantaneously regretted my words. Axel turned to me with such an enraged gaze that it could've burned through my eyeballs. "Ruth Ann," he tried to say calmly, through gritted teeth. "If that's how we can be sure we get Prunella back safely, then it's a small price to pay."

"Oh, yes, I agree," I quickly replied, sincerely hoping he was lying.

Cassandra watched our exchange closely. I hoped I didn't blow it, because she could back off considering to help. She looked from Axel to me, and then back to Axel. "You aren't trying to fool me, are you?" she asked him. "I'm not someone you want to deceive. I can't wait to get my revenge on those twins, and Svenson!"

"No, Cassandra," Axel said in an even-tempered tone. I knew he was using every ounce of his strength to not lunge and strangle the woman.

"What are you going to do to the twins and their uncle?" she asked, eagerly.

"We'll turn them in," Axel replied. "But, I'll tell the police that you were a victim, and the twins and Steven Svenson planned the whole thing."

"You would do that for me?" she asked innocently, which surprised me.

"Yes."

"Hmm, let me think a moment," she said, looking away from Axel and the rest of us and gazing out the ice-covered window.

Inga, Alex, Isabella and the old woman stood near the door. Axel and I were the only ones near Cassandra. We didn't want her to feel like we were hovering, but we didn't have the time to wait for her to ponder all her options, so Axel asked, "Do we have a deal?"

"Yes."

"If I release your hands and feet, you won't try any funny stuff?" Axel asked, probably not trusting her response anyway.

"No, if you mean by *funny stuff* that I would try and run or grab one of you?"

"Yes," I answered. "We're not vicious people. We just want my cousin back, and her baby."

"The baby," she mumbled. "I don't want to be responsible for her baby's death. We do need to help her."

"Really?" I asked, hesitant about her turn around.

"Of course!" she said. "I was out for revenge, but I never wanted anyone to get killed."

"Sure didn't seem like it," Inga said from the doorway.

"Inga," Axel quickly interjected. "Cassandra seems to be on a path of redemption. I was given a second chance, so let's give her one."

"But she killed Sherman!" Inga exclaimed.

"I, I didn't mean for that to happen!" Cassandra yelled. "Prunella and that pill killed him. I didn't know she would react so powerfully."

"But, you knew those pills could be fatal and change her

personality," I said, questioning her supposed redemption.

"I wanted her to become ruthless, like I was. I wanted revenge, and I was terribly, terribly hurt in my past. Martika and my family abandoned me."

"But, it doesn't give you the right to hurt other people, Cassandra," I said calmly, trying not to fuel her fire.

Cassandra, probably for the first time in her life, lowered her head and sobbed. Everything horrible she had done exited my brain, and I reached over to console her. I put my arms around her shoulders and gave her a hug. At first, she resisted. But, once she realized what I was doing, she returned my hug with her own, strong arms and grasped as if she'd never let go. I couldn't help but say, "It'll be alright now. Let us help you."

She released my hold, wiped her wet eyes and did something that shocked all of us, she smiled at each one of us. "I... I've been horrible. I know I'll never be forgiven for what I've done, but I will try. I'm not good at being kind or helpful...maybe you can teach me. I promise I'll work very hard to change."

I sat on the floor, stunned and exhausted. Was my mind playing tricks on me or did I just hear the evilest woman I knew apologize and promise to be a good person and help us? Time would tell.

TWENTY-FIVE

Axel untied the ropes on her wrists and ankles. She immediately leaned over and grabbed her ankles and rubbed. I noticed they were red, but she hadn't been tied up long enough for them to be too bruised. "Thank you," she said, sweetly.

"I really hope your words are true," Axel said. "I would hate it if you were trying to fool us."

She looked into his eyes and said, "I'm done seeking revenge. I've spent my whole life trying to come up with the perfect plan to get my revenge. All those years, and I still failed."

"You didn't fail!" I cried. "You won, Cassandra! Don't you get it?"

She looked at me oddly and said, "I don't understand."

"By giving up your criminal ways, you've won. You want to be a good person. That's worth more than any necklace or revenge."

She smiled, and nodded. "I know you promised me the necklace. I don't think I'm that good, because I still want it." She hesitated and said, "Actually, it's not that I want it, I need it."

Axel stood and held out a hand to help her stand. She willingly grabbed it as he gave a little push for her to get to her feet. "What do you mean you *need* it?" he inquired, curiously.

"I spent every penny I've ever had on this plan. I don't have any money left. I need the necklace to survive."

"Don't worry about that now, Cassandra," Axel said. "Let's worry about getting the necklace and Prunella away from the twins and Svenson."

She nodded and started to walk toward the door. The old woman, who was carefully watching, screamed and ran down the hallway.

"Isabella," Axel called out quickly. "Go after her. Don't let her go anywhere."

Isabella rushed after the old woman while we let Cassandra grab a few personal items. Inga, being suspicious, demanded, "What are you taking?"

Cassandra glared at her, but not like she had before. It was more of an annoying glare than an evil stare. "I need my personal belongings. My passport, and I have a knife and..." Axel immediately cut her off.

"No way, no knife," he insisted, holding out his hand. "I heard everything you said, but I'm not that naïve. What if you were playing me?"

"I said I wouldn't," she snapped, handing over the knife she stuffed inside her back waistband of her pants.

"I'm sorry, but you understand, don't you?" he asked her.

"I guess I wouldn't trust me either," she laughed, but quickly became serious. "We'll need more than one knife to overthrow them."

Alex asked, "Do you have anything we could use?"

"Yes. Follow me," she said, and marched out of the room with all of us trailing behind. None of us wanted to let her out of our sight for even a second.

She walked into the kitchen and opened a drawer on the island. She pulled out two guns, and another small, but dangerous knife. "Here," she said, holding the weapons for Axel and Alex to grab. "This should show you I'm trustworthy."

Inga was offended she didn't get a gun. She snatched the knife out of Cassandra's hand and stuffed it inside the apron of her uniform. At the same time, she pulled out the voodoo doll that she had been carrying since we were in Deer Creek.

"What about this doll Cassandra? Can it hurt any of us?"

Cassandra laughed and said, "No, it's not real. I just planted that doll in the tunnels to scare you and throw you off my trail."

I was about to say something sarcastic when Axel said to Cassandra, "Any ammo?"

Cassandra reached inside the same drawer and pulled out a box of bullets. She handed it to Axel and he divided them between himself and Alex. "Do you know how to use this?" he asked Alex.

"Yep," he replied, expertly filling the cartridge with ammunition.

"I don't want to know how you know how to use a gun," I said, but afterward I probably will question the young man.

Isabella showed up holding the old woman's arm tightly. "She was trying to escape out the window."

"Why?" I asked, confused. "Didn't she hear Cassandra say she wants to make amends?"

"I don't know if she believes her," Isabella said quietly, trying not to upset Cassandra.

Cassandra heard her anyway and said, "Maybe we should tell the truth about this old woman."

"What are you talking about?" I asked, perplexed. I looked over at Isabella's shocked face and knew there was more to this woman than she had divulged.

"No!" Isabella snapped. "Later, not now."

"Why not?" I asked. "I, for one, want to know."

"Me, too," Axel said. "Spill," he requested, firmly.

Cassandra opened the cooler and grabbed several bottles of water. She placed them on the island and opened one for herself. She took a long swig, and said, "I think Isabella can tell you what I know, too."

We turned to Isabella and I replied, "Really?"

Isabella retorted, "I don't think Cassandra's as reformed as she says she is."

"Yes, I am," she bellowed. "You know who she is, just tell them!"

Isabella looked terrified. She refused to speak, so Cassandra spoke for her. "The old woman has a name. It's Mattie."

"Mattie," I repeated a couple times. I looked over at her and held out my hand. She reached out and I grabbed it and held it gently. "Hello, Mattie. I'm glad to know your name. My name is Ruth Ann."

She smiled for the first time, and I noticed the missing teeth in her mouth. The teeth that were left were yellowed and crooked. I didn't want to look disgusted, so I grinned and turned my attention back to Cassandra.

"Mattie," she continued, "is related to someone you all know."

"Who?" I asked, anxiously.

"Meme."

"Meme?" I questioned. My mind went immediately to the assistant manager at my antique store in town.

"Meme, Isabella's dead grandmother."

"Oh," I said, slowly. "Wait, what?"

"Yes," Isabella said, taking over. "She's my grandmother's sister. I never met her before."

"Then how did you know she was her sister?" I asked, curiously.

"Mattie told me."

"When did she tell you?" Axel asked, suspiciously.

"When we were outside the front window trying to get inside to rescue Prunella and Carlos. I had a sudden surge of energy run through my body. I knew at that moment, that something, or someone, would change my life." She quickly added, "I didn't know what it meant then. I didn't know until I looked inside Mattie's eyes, that we were somehow connected."

"So, you never knew this woman entered the states and was in our town?" I asked, even though I knew the answer. I wanted to clarify for Axel and the others.

"No. It wasn't until we were hiding on the front lawn that I found out the truth. Remember, I was protecting her. We were very close, and she told me the truth."

313

"And you believed her?" Alex asked, doubting the old woman's truth.

"Yes, Alex," Isabella said. "I told you that I knew we were related after looking in her eyes. She has my grandmother's eyes."

Isabella looked pleadingly at me for help. I closed my eyes for a second and tried to picture Meme's eyes. I didn't know Meme for long, but she made a huge impact on my life, and I will never forget her or what she did for our family. I popped open my eyes and... "Yes!" I exclaimed. "They are the same."

"Ruth Ann," Axel said, doubting my announcement. "You can't possibly know that for sure."

"I had very close encounters with Meme. She changed my life, and I will never forget those intense, yet gentle brown eyes." I glanced at Mattie and pointed, "She has the same eyes. Look!"

"Whatever, Ruth Ann," Inga said. "Can we figure out our next move, please?"

Cassandra agreed. "I'll tell you where they went. I think we should get moving. That is...unless you don't want my help anymore."

"Of course, we do!" I cried. "Tell us."

"Well, first, Mattie needs to understand that I'm not going to hurt her or threaten her anymore." Cassandra walked closer to the old woman who rapidly threw her hands to her face and keeled over as if Cassandra was going to hit her. "Hey, I'm not going to hurt you!"

We watched as Cassandra gently removed the old woman's hands from her face and held them. "I'm very sorry, Mattie. I wasn't myself, and you know that, don't you?"

"What's she talking about?" Inga whispered to me.

"No idea," I replied. "Let's listen."

Mattie raised her head and looked into Cassandra's eyes. She held the gaze for too long if you ask me. Suddenly, the fear drained from her eyes and a toothless grin appeared. Mattie took one of her hands and touched Cassandra's face. She rubbed her young, brown cheek and then released. "Yes, I believe you," she said in English.

"I think you are better."

"It's out of my system, yes?" Cassandra asked, confusing the rest of us.

"Yes. If it wasn't, you would still be evil."

"Enough!" Axel bellowed. "Explain what you two are talking about."

"Fine," Cassandra responded. "I'll just say it. I've been taking the yellow pills."

"You have?" I asked, stunned. "Wait, what color did Prunella take?"

"The red ones," Axel answered for the two women.

"Yes. I took the yellow ones to help me because they were supposed to give me the power and confidence to pull off this plan. However, they had side effects that made me very cruel." She held up her hand to stop our objections. "I was angry and out for revenge most of my life, but these pills, according to Mattie, would give me the self-assurance to pull it off. I planned for years and years to get revenge on Martika and Isabella, but, I never had the courage to take action. That's what those pills were for."

"Did you plan on giving Prunella the red ones or did that happen after Prunella resisted?" Axel asked, curious and turning angry.

"No. Originally, I thought I'd kidnap her and use her for ransom. However, she fought and fought hard. I forced Mattie to tell me what the different pills could do to her. I knew the yellow ones gave me the power to carry out my plan, but I wasn't aware how nasty I was becoming. I didn't want Prunella to have power because that could hurt me. So, I thought the red ones would subdue her. I was terribly wrong. The red ones can be fatal, and cause irreversible damage."

"Irreversible?" I questioned. "Are you saying Prunella may never return to her normal, sweet self?"

"I really don't know, Ruth Ann," Cassandra answered.

I could tell Axel wanted to murder her. His face was red, and he started pacing around the island. "Then, why did you give them to her?" he yelled.

"I, I wasn't myself, sir," she replied, truthfully. "I was on a drug that changed my personality. I'm so sorry. I couldn't get a straight answer from Mattie, so I just gave her a red pill. At first, it didn't do much. She was still fighting us, so that's when I gave her the second pill. Almost immediately, she turned on me and convinced Jacob and Johann to side with her."

"This is absurd!" Axel bellowed. "My wife may be a monster, forever!"

"No, no," Mattie blurted loudly. "I can fix her."

Everyone went silent. I asked, "How? You have the antidote for the red pills?"

"And why didn't Cassandra need an antidote?" Inga inquired, also pacing right behind Axel waving her arms in the air in exasperation.

"The yellow pills aren't as lethal."

"Why did you bring those pills in the first place?" Alex asked.

"I forced her to," Cassandra admitted. "It was me who sought out Mattie. I found out she was related to Isabella and Martika, and I took full advantage of it. I knew she was the village's medicine woman. She would have all sorts of concoctions I could use. It was all me, don't blame Mattie."

"I'm glad you're coming clean, Cassandra, but Mattie could have lied and given you placebos," I said.

"Placebos?" Mattie and Cassandra repeated, confused.

"Fake pills. Sugar pills, basically," I answered.

"Oh, well, I didn't give her the chance. Before I forced her to come with us, I went inside her home and asked tons of questions about medicines and which ones were safe and which ones were not."

"So, Mattie had no idea why you were asking all those questions?" I asked.

"None."

"Forget about it," Axel said, exasperated. "Tell us where *you* think they went, and I'll tell you my thoughts."

"Jacob and Johann were originally told by their uncle to meet them at some local airport. I believe the name of the town was Grand Junction."

"Why would they meet at an airport?" I asked, frantically.

"To fly back to Stockholm, I guess," she answered, matter of factly.

"Are you saying they're leaving the country?" Axel shouted. "Why wouldn't you tell us that earlier? We've been wasting so much time at this bloody cabin."

"I was trying to convince you all to trust me."

Inga snapped, "You also took a lot of time fighting us."

"I'm sorry," she said, again.

"Why didn't you tell us you were taking pills when you decided to work with us?" Alex inquired.

"It took a while for me to feel myself again. Plus, I wanted to check with Mattie to make sure I wasn't going to start acting like that terrible person again."

"This is all too much to take in *or* believe," Inga said. "How do we know either of you is telling the truth?" Inga directed her question to Mattie and Cassandra.

"They are," Isabella answered for them. "We don't have any other choice but to believe them."

I turned my attention to Axel. "You said you had an idea about where they are... where?"

Axel rubbed his aching head and replied, "If they went to the airport, then we'll have to follow them to Sweden. But, we have to go back to my estate to grab our passports and whatever else we need. I can check the other place I think they might use to hide out." He added with emphasis, "We have to do this quickly. I will call ahead and have my pilot on standby. If we need to get to the airport and take-off, he'll have the plane ready. Agreed?"

We agreed, and headed out the front door and down the frozen path to the car. It was a very full car with Cassandra and the old woman now, but we needed them. I was worried our car would be smashed from Johann squeezing past it, but it was untouched. They must've had enough room to get around our car to escape.

"Hurry, Axel," I called out from the middle of the back seat. I was stuffed in the back with Isabella, Inga and Mattie. In the front was Axel, Alex, and Cassandra. "I can't breathe back here."

"I'm going as fast as I can, Ruth Ann," he answered, heading through town.

"What time is it?" Inga asked from the back.

"It's just before ten at night," Axel replied.

It took about thirty minutes to get to the estate. Axel drove past the covered fountain and pulled right up to the front door entrance. We quickly piled out of the car and agreed to go our separate ways to grab our personal items. I was thankful everything I needed was here at the estate. I even kept my passport in the library safe along with Axel's, Inga's, Prunella and Sherman's. Poor Sherman. I wondered as we drove up the mountain if any police would still be around. I crossed my fingers and toes that John and Judy had left.

Thankfully, there were no police cars out front as Axel pulled up. I shouted to everyone, "I'm glad they're gone, but that must mean Sherman was also taken away."

"It's been a long day, Ruth Ann. I'm sure Sherman was gone quite a while ago. I'm kind of surprised John didn't station a cop here, though."

"It looks deserted, doesn't it?" Inga asked as she opened the front door and rushed inside. "I'm going to head upstairs first. I want to see if Sherman really is gone."

I didn't want to say she was being silly since there would be no way the police would leave a dead body for this long. "While you're up there, pack a little bag, Inga," I called out as she flew up the stairs.

She didn't reply, but disappeared onto the third-floor landing. I turned to Axel and asked him to grab all our passports from his safe. He nodded and disappeared inside his library. Isabella, Mattie, Cassandra, Alex and I stood alone in the foyer. Alex broke the silence and said, "I'm going to my room. I'll get my passport and pack a few items."

"Don't be long," I said, watching him head up the stairs.

I turned to Isabella and said, "Why don't you take Mattie and go in the kitchen. Give her some tea and then hurry and grab what you need. I assume you have your passport in your room?"

"Yes. I'll get what I need after I bring Mattie into the kitchen. Hey," Isabella said. "What about Mattie's papers?"

Cassandra replied, "I have everything we need."

"Good," I replied. "Cassandra, do you want to come with me while I pack a bag?"

"I guess I should. I figure nobody trusts me enough to leave me alone," she said, solemnly.

"It's not that, exactly," I answered. "But, you do see our side, right? It hasn't been that long since you vowed to kill everyone."

"It was the pills, Ruth Ann," she replied. "I don't feel that way anymore."

"That's good, but," she cut me off and agreed to come with me.

We trudged up to the second floor and down the hall to my room. Cassandra plopped down on the sofa and shut her eyes. I wished I could join her. I was exhausted. The only positive about flying to Stockholm was we could get some sleep on the trip over. I went into the closet and grabbed a large overnight bag. I filled it with clothes and headed into the bathroom and packed my necessities. Once I was done, I woke Cassandra and we headed downstairs to the kitchen. Inga, Isabella, Mattie and Alex were already there eating the food that Inga had prepared and set out on the island.

"I'm starving," I said, grabbing a piece of cold turkey.

We spent the next fifteen minutes stuffing our faces with turkey, stuffing, and rolls. "Where's Mr. Eklund?" Inga inquired.

"He had more to do than us, I guess," I said, a little worried he wasn't in here yet. "I knew he had to get papers from his library, pack a bag, and he had to check a place or two to see if

Prunella and the others were hiding there."

"Like where?" Alex asked, curiously.

"My best guess would be the guesthouse, and the basement," I answered, shuddering at the thought of the room in the basement where I was held as a prisoner months ago. So much has transpired since then, but I was still terrified of the room where Helena was murdered and shackled to the wall.

"I'm here!" Axel called out from the butler's pantry. He was out of breath, but was able to tell us that he had checked the basement, and ran through the tunnel to the guesthouse. "Empty."

"So, that means they headed to Sweden," I said, happy I'd get some rest, but terrified of what was happening to Prunella.

TWENTY-SIX

We all piled back in Axel's over-sized black sedan. Our bags were stuffed into the trunk, and we headed down the frozen highway to Axel's plane. "I bet they took off from this airport, too," Inga said from the back.

"It's a private airport so I'm sure they did," Axel replied.

"Can you ask someone when we get there?" Alex inquired.

"I already did."

"And?" I asked, not happy I had to pry the information from him.

His hands were tightly gripping the steering wheel as he maneuvered the slippery roads to the airport. "My pilot will give me that information when we get there. The jet is fueled and ready to go."

"Good," I said, sitting back and trying not to feel claustrophobic with four people in the back seat.

Once we arrived at the airport, Axel pulled his sedan right into the hangar. The plane's lights were on and the stairs were out. "Let's go!" Inga said, eager to get back to her old estate in Stockholm.

I looked at Isabella, Cassandra and Mattie. They didn't look as excited. I doubted they had ever been on a private jet. I told them it was safe, and we would be very comfortable. Mattie didn't understand what was happening most of the time. She was an older woman who had lived in the same village most of her life.

"It'll be alright," I said to them. "Cassandra, are you okay?"

"Yes. I'm good. I've traveled before as you know, but never on such a small plane."

"You'll like it. Plus, we can eat and sleep while we fly."

"I need some sleep," Cassandra said, holding on to the rail and stepping into the plane.

"We all do," I replied, yawning. I was worried that they had to be in the air by now. Hopefully, once we landed, Axel would be able to tell us where Prunella, Jacob, Johann and Steven went.

A short thirteen or so hours later, we landed in Stockholm. We were well rested and fed, but with the time change, we landed in Stockholm also at night. Axel had a car waiting for us and said, "Let's head to my estate just outside of town. We can come up with a plan there."

We hurried into the large SUV, and noticed that Axel had hired a driver. It didn't take long to re-familiarize myself to the estate where I was a prisoner at not too many months ago. It was a strange feeling walking up these steps. I remembered that I was free to roam inside, yet also a prisoner in the house. Prunella was a prisoner of sorts, too. She was hidden away in a comfortably renovated attic pretending to be seriously ill so Axel wouldn't kill her. So much had transpired, but in the end, Axel and Prunella made up. Many lives had been lost, and a baby was conceived in a brutal way, but we remained close and together. Well, all of us except Prunella. But, I planned on fixing that, soon. Once I heard those red pills she was forced to take could permanently change her personality, I had my doubts to our future. Fortunately, she was still alive, and hopefully her unborn baby was safe.

"What are we supposed to do here?" Isabella asked, anxiously. "This looks just like your house back in Colorado."

"Similar, but there are a few differences," Axel answered, leaving out the 'differences' he referred to. "I'm going to make some calls and see what I can uncover about Steven's whereabouts."

Inga marched past us and headed down the hall into the kitchen. The estate had been shut down for a few months and only checked infrequently by Axel's employees. I suggested we follow Inga and talk in the kitchen. "What are we going to do? We need to find where Steven took Prunella and the twins," Alex said, anxiously.

"We have to wait for Axel," I answered. "We have no idea where to start."

Once inside the kitchen, Inga was busy wiping down the counters and appliances. She opened the large refrigerator and was astonished to find it stocked. "How did this happen?"

"Axel obviously called ahead and had someone stock the refrigerator," I said.

"Hmm," Inga mumbled, and rummaged through the refrigerator. She appeared satisfied, and then headed into the large walk-in pantry. We've hidden in there, too, I thought to myself. A few minutes later, Inga reappeared and said we could live here for quite some time with all the food in there.

"Great, anyone hungry?" I asked, looking at Cassandra, Isabella, Mattie, and Alex who were sitting around the large rectangular kitchen table.

"No," Alex replied. "We ate on the plane."

I plopped down on a stool at the island and asked Inga if she could make a pot of tea. She mumbled a few words, my guess, unkindly, and filled the teapot and placed it on the stove. Then she pulled out a large glass urn that was next to the massive stove and placed it on the island.

"Biscotti!" I exclaimed with joy. "I love these."

"Somebody else knew that too," Inga replied, suspiciously. "Who would fill the jar with them?"

"I don't know, but I sure am glad!"

I hopped off the stool and grabbed a large plate from the cabinet. I placed a pile of almond biscotti on it and set the plate on the kitchen table. Once the tea was whistling, I rushed over and filled the cups for those who wanted tea. Mattie accepted a cup, so did Isabella and Cassandra. I sat down with them at the table and enjoyed my favorite biscotti and tea. "Now, if Axel could walk in here and tell us where Svenson is keeping Prunella, we could rescue her and get our lives back to normal."

That was the last I remember until...

TWENTY-SEVEN

I woke up in the dark, disoriented for only a moment when I realized something was wrong. "I don't remember going to sleep," I whispered to myself.

"Ruth Ann," a female voice called from nearby. "Are you awake?"

"Yes," I replied, trying to figure out who just asked me.

"It's me, Cassandra," she replied in a strong, but quiet voice.

"Where are we, and what happened to us?" I said, feeling foggy and confused.

"I've been wondering that myself," she replied. "Someone drugged us."

"How?" I asked, trying to sit up, but realizing I was restrained. "Hey, there's a belt tied around my waist. I can't sit up!"

"I know," she said. "I can't either."

"What's going on?"

"I think something was in the tea or the biscotti. They're the only things we've drunk or eaten since we arrived."

"But, you and I weren't the only ones who drank the tea or ate a biscotti."

"Isabella did, too," she answered. "She may be in here with us, but not awake yet."

"It's so dark in here," I said. "Isabella? Isabella? Are you in here?" I called out, a little louder each time I asked.

"Nothing," Cassandra replied. "Maybe she's not in here. She

325

could be in another room."

"Didn't Mattie drink the tea, too?" I inquired, curiously.

"I believe she did, but I didn't see her eat a biscotti."

"Someone *drugged* the biscotti?" I asked, rhetorically. "How could that happen?"

"Who knows, Ruth Ann," Cassandra replied. "But, we're the only ones we know of who blacked out and ended up in this room."

"What room?" I asked, trying to adjust my eyes to see if any sign of where we were was coming into focus.

"I think we're in a bedroom."

"I'm on the couch and somehow strapped in. I've been working on releasing myself, but it's not budging, yet."

"I'm in a bed, but it's not my bed."

"Do you think we're still in Axel's home?" she asked in a shaky voice.

"I have no idea," I answered, truthfully. "Until we get ourselves freed, we have no idea."

"Shhh, Ruth Ann," Cassandra called in a quiet voice. "I think I hear someone jiggling the door knob."

"If someone comes in, pretend to be unconscious," I replied quickly. "We need to see who comes in and if they're here to check on us or rescue us."

"Yes, I think..." Cassandra's voice cut out just as I heard the door slowly begin to squeak open.

A bright light flicked on, forcing me to close my eyes. However, I needed to open them slightly to see who entered. I waited a moment, and then pried one eye open. I couldn't make out who was there, but he was standing over Cassandra sprawled on the couch.

"Still out, hey?" a male voice said. "Wake up!" he shouted. I opened my eyes a little more since the man was concentrating on Cassandra and his back was to me. He bent down and grabbed her by the shoulders and shook her forcefully. Somehow, she remained limp. It looked painful as he shook her back and forth. "Wake up, you bitch!"

Whoa, I knew who it was. It was Jacob. Where were we? I watched until Jacob gave up trying to wake Cassandra. Uh-oh, he backed away and started to turn toward my direction. I promptly closed my eyes and waited for the shaking of my life. I could hear his footsteps get near the side of my bed, and I anticipated strong, rough hands grabbing my shoulders, but there was nothing. I could hear him breathing close to my face. I had to remain as still as I could. I refused to let him intimidate me into opening my eyes. He didn't say a word, but suddenly, I couldn't feel his hot breath on my face anymore. He must've backed away.

As he walked toward the door, I opened my eyes long enough to see the room. It was a small bedroom, and I was strapped into a twin bed. Against the opposite wall, Cassandra was tied onto a small loveseat, and it looked painful. I wondered how she could breathe with all the rounds of rope around her waist and chest area. Without any notice, the lights went out, plunging us back into darkness.

The door shut, and I waited a moment before calling out for Cassandra. "Are you alright? I saw him shake you so hard I thought he hurt you."

"No, I'm okay. A little bruised, but okay. Did you see who it was?"

"Oh, yes," I replied. "Jacob. He put you in the worst of our two positions. I'm only strapped in with a large piece of leather. You've got ropes wrapped around you several times."

"I know, I can feel them," she said, wincing in pain. "Can you try and free yourself. I'm afraid I won't be able to."

"I'll try," I said, wriggling around to see if the leather strap would loosen.

"Try pulling it with your hands and feel around for the buckle," she suggested. "Maybe you can release it."

I pulled with all my might, but I couldn't get it to loosen. I kept trying since I was our only hope for getting us out of here. There was no way Cassandra could untie her ropes. I squirmed, twisted, and pulled, and finally I heard a snap.

"You did it!" Cassandra cried from the other side of the room.

"I did," I said, excited. "Let me get to you."

I ripped off the strap and threw it on the floor and slid my legs to the side of the bed. I stood as fast as I could, but my legs felt a little wobbly. Once I felt fairly stable, I hurried to her. "They definitely drugged us."

"Take deep breaths, Ruth Ann," she suggested. "Get oxygen moving through your body."

I took in a few deep breaths, and quickly felt better. I hurried to the couch, still in the dark, and felt for the loveseat. "I need to turn the light on to see how I can release the ropes," I said, reaching the wall and feeling for a switch. "Got it!"

The lights shone brightly, blinding us momentarily, but making us feel confident we had a chance to get out of this room. "Wow, they really tied you up," I said, trying to find if there was a knot I could undo.

"They hate me, Ruth Ann," Cassandra replied. "They think I'm their biggest enemy right now."

"They're the ones who betrayed you, Cassandra," I said. "I know it's sounds crazy, but you were the victim this time." I thought about my words for a moment as I tried to loosen the ropes. Becoming a victim after everything she's done seemed preposterous, but that's what happened. Jacob, Johann and Prunella overtook Cassandra, and poor Carlos was stuck with them, somewhere.

"Is there anything in here you can use to cut the ropes?" she asked me, impatiently.

"I'll look." I rushed to the nightstand next to the bed.

"Hurry, Ruth Ann," she cried. "They could come back any second."

"I'm trying," I said, opening the drawer and finding it empty. I ran into the closet and hit jackpot! At the back of the closet was a tool box. I bent down and opened it and saw exactly what I needed, a pair of scissors. Not only would that free Cassandra, but it could be a valuable weapon if necessary.

"Great!" Cassandra exclaimed, as I cut her free. She quickly unwrapped the ropes from her body and said, "Now, let's get out of here!"

"Where's here?" I asked, wondering where we were. "We need to think for a second before we run out of this room. What if there's a guard outside the door or waiting for us down the hall?"

"We can't stay in here."

"No, but we should make sure we have coats in case we make it outside. It's freezing outside."

I rushed inside the closet and pulled our coats down from the hangars. I spotted them when I grabbed the scissors. "They were hanging inside."

"So, weird," she mumbled.

We stood against the door and put our ears flush with the door. I whispered, "I don't hear anything."

"Either do I. I'll open it." Cassandra reached and grabbed a hold of the doorknob. "It's locked."

"Of course, it is," I said. "We need to break out. I can do it."

"You?" she asked, stunned. "You're kind of a goody-goody, aren't you?"

"*Me*? Not, really. You just see it that way. If you knew me, you'd know I've gotten into quite a few sticky situations the last few months."

"Prove it," she said with a smile. "Pick the lock."

I ran back in the closet and looked inside the tool box again. I grabbed a small pick and knew I could get us out now. "Give me a second," I said, inserting the tool into the tiny hole. I moved it, jiggled it, forced it, until I heard a slight click. "Got it!"

"Wow, I have to admit I'm impressed," she said, turning the knob to see if I really did unlock it. "Yes, you did."

She slowly opened the door after I turned off the lights. We didn't want anyone seeing a light shining from inside the room just in case we weren't alone in the hall. "Nobody," she said, sticking her head out the door. "It's deserted out there."

"Out where?" I asked, wondering what was on the other side of the door.

Cassandra grabbed my arm and forced me down the hall at an extremely fast pace. "Slow down!" I whispered, out of breath as we went past several closed doors in the darkened hallway.

"I don't even know if we're on the first, second, or tenth floor!" she replied, frustrated.

We came to a stop at the end of the long hall. "Are we in an apartment or an office building?" I asked, confused. The doors we flew by had numbers on them, but no windows. "Maybe it's a hotel."

"We're at a dead end, Ruth Ann," she said, turning around to see if there was anywhere we could go.

"Look," I called out pointing to the last door on the end of the hall. "I think it's a staircase." I walked over and grabbed the knob. "Locked!"

"Why would they lock a staircase?" she asked, baffled. She turned away from the door and faced me straight on. "Do you still have that tool?"

I was briefly confused, but then it dawned on me. "Oh, you want me to break this lock, too?"

"Uh-huh."

I kept the tool in my coat pocket, just in case. I grabbed it and started to work on the door. "I wonder where the others are?" I asked while frantically jiggling the lock. "I'm surprised Isabella and Mattie weren't with us. They drank the tea."

"I don't know, Ruth Ann. I think you and I are the ones they want."

"Want for what?" I demanded, frustrated that I wasn't getting anywhere with this lock. It couldn't have been beginner's luck on the last door. I had to prove to Cassandra I could do it, repeatedly if necessary.

"The others are sort of disposable in my opinion. Prunella knows you're the most valuable hostage, and I'm probably the most dangerous in their eyes."

I thought about it for a second, and came to the conclusion Cassandra was probably correct. "You think Prunella wants to hurt me?"

"In her current state, yes, Ruth Ann. I'm so sorry I ever brought Mattie and those pills to your town."

She was right. If she had controlled her urge for revenge, none of this would've happened. However, my words didn't agree with my thoughts. "We can't go backwards, Cassandra. I know you weren't in *your* right mind either."

"You can say that!" she answered, ready to take the pick out of my hand and try herself. I yanked her hand away, mostly out of aggravation, and told her to give me a minute longer. "Fine, but this may not be a lock that can be undone with a little tool."

"Got it!" I exclaimed, loudly. "Sorry, I got excited. Let's get out of here."

I threw open the door and just as we were about to step in the stairwell, a strong hand wrapped around my waist and shoved me to the ground. I was about to yell at Cassandra for knocking me down, when I realized it wasn't her hand that held me. "What the?" I snapped, and looked up at the growling face of Jacob (or was it Johann?). I hadn't seen either close enough to tell them apart.

"Well, well, well," he started to say in a sarcastic tone. "Where do you think, you're going?"

Cassandra was plastered against the wall by the other twin, and yelping in pain. "Stop it!" she barked at him. "You're hurting me."

"You deserve a lot more than I'm doing to you now," he answered, squeezing her tighter against the wall.

"Leave her alone!" I shouted. "You two are making a huge mistake. Prunella isn't thinking clearly. Stop following her, she'll betray you both!"

They looked at each other for a moment, and then laughter belted out of their Scandinavian mouths.

"You think I don't know her?" I asked, hoping to throw them

off. "She's my cousin, and I've seen her work over many fools smarter than the likes of you." I watched and waited to see if they took my bait. If I could put even the slightest doubt in their minds about Prunella's trustworthiness, maybe Cassandra could fake her way back in with them.

"Shut-up!" Jacob snapped. I knew it was Jacob because Johann was mad that Jacob had reacted to me first and told him he was always beating him to the punch. "Johann, not now!" Jacob snarled at his brother. "This old woman is trying to con me."

Old woman! I wanted to reach up and belt him! How dare he call me old! I didn't show any anger. I replied, "Fine, trust Prunella. You'll see. I'll be the one laughing all the way to the bank while you two rot in jail!"

Jacob was about to slap me when a female's voice screamed, "Stop!"

Cassandra and I looked at Prunella's rigid form marching down the hall toward the four of us. She grabbed Jacob's arm and forced him to release Cassandra. He didn't let go easily. Before he released his hold he threw her to the ground next to me like she was a rag doll. "Hey, you didn't need to do that," I shouted. "What is your problem?"

He shot me a brief, nasty glare, but directed his attention to Prunella. "Why'd you make me let her go?"

Prunella looked intently into Cassandra's eyes, as she answered Jacob with, "She'll get hers soon enough. We have other pertinent matters to get ready for."

"What?" I asked curiously, not expecting an answer, so when she spoke, I was shocked.

"Ruth Ann, I might as well tell you since you'll drive us nuts until we do." I shot her a hurt look, but she stayed cold as ice. "Knock off the puppy eyes. It won't work on me anymore. You're dead to me, so don't bother trying to win my affection back."

"What did I do to deserve this?" I asked, terribly offended by her remarks. "I've given you everything since we met."

"*Everything*?" she quizzed. "My life has been in constant

upheaval since we met back in my husband's estate near here!"
Ah-ha! Finally, our first clue. We were near Axel's estate.

"I think you have things backwards, Prunella. I was the one who rescued you from the attic. Have you forgotten?" I asked, feelings my anger rising rapidly. How dare she accuse me of making her life worse. I was losing my patience, hoping and hoping she was just playing a part. What if she wasn't, and this was her new personality?

She ignored my comments, and turned her attention to Jacob. "Take them into my office. I'll handle them myself."

Jacob reached down to grab my arm, but Prunella pulled him back. "Hold on, Jacob, dear, let me help my precious cousin up from the floor." She bent down, and looked deeply into my eyes as we came intimately close. I could swear I saw a glimmer of hope in her eyes that my sweet cousin was still in there, deep down. I might've imagined it, but when I noticed a quick wink, I felt reassured she was play acting with the twins. But, for what end? This couldn't be about the necklace, could it?

"Johann, take Cassandra back to their bedroom."

"No!" I shouted. "We stay together!"

Prunella eyed me oddly, "Wait, you *want* to be with her?"

"Yes."

"She killed your friend, and initiated her revenge on our family."

"She wasn't herself," I responded, not saying a word about the pills. I didn't want to find myself back in that bedroom. I hoped going into another room might give us an option for escaping.

"Fine. Have it your way," Prunella answered. "Johann, bring her with us." She motioned for him to pick Cassandra up from the floor. She winced as he grabbed her arm and yanked her to standing.

"She's hurt!" I exclaimed.

Cassandra quickly said, "I'm fine, Ruth Ann."

Prunella took a gentler hold of my arm and helped me to stand. As she stood up, I noticed her hand grab a hold of her stomach. It wasn't obvious, but I saw her do it. I was about to react when she pulled me so quickly I practically fell into her. "Hey, that wasn't necessary!" I snapped. "I'm going willingly."

"You'd better," she said, walking rapidly down the hall. I did all I could to keep up with her. I was practically jogging by the time we went past the bedroom where we had been detained a few minutes ago. I was relieved because I momentarily thought she was going to put us back there instead of going to her office.

"Where's this office of yours? And," I added, "Where are we anyway?"

My questions were ignored. We marched down to the middle of the hall, and came upon a single door elevator. "We're going inside an elevator?"

Cassandra gave me a little kick. When I looked at her, she was shaking her head slightly. She mouthed, "stop", and I figured she wanted me to keep my mouth shut. If she only knew me better!

Jacob gave me a push from behind, forcing me inside the elevator. Prunella had already stepped in, leaving me in the hall. I wanted to turn and give him a big shove, but I restrained myself. Cassandra stepped in before her escort, Johann, did. There wasn't a lot of room inside the tiny, elevator. I was feeling a wave of claustrophobia run through me, but I closed my eyes for a moment and took a deep breath. After calming down a little, I opened my eyes and examined the panel to distract my mind. I noticed there were buttons for four floors. 'B' for the basement level, 1, 2, and 3. She hit the '1' and the elevator jolted and started to move shakily down. I concluded we were on the third floor.

The elevator halted and the door slowly opened. I wish I could've run and gotten out of the building, but that would only put me in more danger since Jacob and Johann were loose cannons. They might react first, and think later. Prunella would be forced to restrain me or worse, so I waited until I was ordered to move.

Prunella was the first one out. She told Jacob and Johann to stand back and let her lead Cassandra and me in her office. I stepped out of the elevator and entered an ornately decorated circular room. I tried to get my bearings, but it was difficult. The round room was dark, with deep red paint on the walls and richly framed landscape oil paintings on the walls. There were several closed doors. The floors were a black, shiny marble which echoed with each step we took. I watched as Prunella whispered something into Jacob's ear. She smiled as he gently squeezed her shoulder and took off across the room with Johann. They disappeared into one of the five doors. We were now alone with Prunella. Odds were in our favor that we could overtake her, but I had a feeling her bodyguards were close by.

Prunella said, "Follow me." She started to walk across the spotless, gleaming floor and turned and told us, "No funny stuff."

Cassandra grabbed my arm as we followed Prunella into a room to the right. "Hurry up!" she ordered, from inside the room.

"We're right behind you," Cassandra barked. "What is your problem?"

Prunella ignored Cassandra and waited for us to get all the way in before slamming the door shut. I jumped at her impulsive action, but didn't say a word. Prunella marched across the large room and sat behind a beautiful writing desk. The room seemed very familiar. It was oddly furnished just like Axel's library rooms in both of his estates. Her desk wasn't as bulky or massive, but there were bookshelves behind the desk against the wall, and two wingback chairs were placed in front of the desk. The colors were definitely brighter than Axel's dark, warm colors. I continued to survey the room and noticed the large fireplace against a side wall. It wasn't stone, but a sleek, clean neutral colored marble. There was a fire blazing, which made the room quite warm. There was a long, leather sofa and two chairs set in front of the fireplace. Quite similar to Axel's set-up.

I was confused. Prunella seemed very comfortable here. As if she had been here before, and actually furnished this place, but that would be impossible. We were back in Stockholm, and she hadn't been here in months. Not since we left together, so how did she do all this? I didn't realize how long I had been staring at the room when Cassandra cleared her throat, bringing me back to the present. "Oh, sorry, it's just that..." I stopped, because I didn't want to mention my thoughts. Prunella wasn't herself, but when and if she ever was, I had a lot of questions to ask.

"Sit down, Ruth Ann," Prunella said from behind her desk. Cassandra had already taken a seat in one of the chairs facing her desk. I sat down slowly, and then waited for Prunella to speak.

Prunella opened a drawer and pulled out a black velvet box. "Uh-oh," I mumbled to myself. I really hoped it wasn't what I suspected was in that box. Boy, was I sadly mistaken!

TWENTY-EIGHT

Cassandra's and my eyes were glued to that velvet box. Prunella teased us by stroking it over and over with her pale and delicate fingers. Finally, she looked up and stared me straight in the face. "What do you think I have in here?" she asked, mockingly.

"I have no idea," I said, with a firm voice. "Why don't you open it and show us?" I asked her, sarcastically. "You're obviously relishing for our reaction."

She threw me a wicked eye, scaring me a little. I wiggled in my seat as I noticed the irises of her eyes. They were blood red, just like they were back at Axel's estate in Deer Creek. "What is wrong with you?" I demanded, stupidly. Cassandra reached over and swatted me in the arm. She whispered with gritted teeth, "Will you shut up!"

"Sorry," I sighed, quietly. "It shocked me, again."

"What are you two whispering about? Stop talking unless I ask you a direct question."

Cassandra looked away from me and concentrated on Prunella and that velvet box. I could see the greed in her eyes as she watched Prunella pick up the box and use her dainty hand to flip it open. I thought she was going to finally disclose what was inside, but she slapped the box shut. "Why'd you do that?" Cassandra yelled, angrily. "You're very naïve if you think we don't know what you're doing. You think we'll do or say anything to get our hands on that necklace in there."

Prunella slowly lifted her head and took her eyes off the box and concentrated on Cassandra. "You think you're so smart but you were fool enough to lose Jacob's and Johann's loyalty and respect."

"What do you know?" Cassandra shouted.

"I know they tricked you because you were so self-obsessed and hell bent on revenge, that you didn't see them coming after you!"

"They wouldn't have betrayed me if you didn't *entice* them."

If Prunella had a weapon near her, she would've used it on Cassandra. "Shut up!"

Cassandra could barely hide her smile when the door to library, or as Prunella called it, her office, flew open. Jacob was out of breath and bellowed, "He's gone!"

Prunella shot up and ran to the door. "What do you mean...he's gone?" she asked, grabbing his shoulders and shaking them. "You fool!"

"Hey, knock it off," Jacob retorted. "It wasn't my fault!" She took a deep breath and asked, very slowly and concisely, "Then how did he escape? And, shouldn't you be looking for him instead of standing in here?"

"Johann's checking the entire building," he said, anxiously. "I was looking too, but figured I'd better come in here and tell you."

"Yes, yes, that's good, Jacob. I'm sorry for yelling at you."

"I'm going outside to see if I can find any footprints."

"Report back to me as soon as you have news," she said, waving him away and marching back to her chair at the desk.

I couldn't take the suspense any longer so I blurted out, "Who escaped?"

Prunella appeared ready to answer me, and then she closed her mouth, smiled and replied, "Never mind. He won't be free for long."

"Then why can't you just tell us?" I asked, adding, "It's Carlos, isn't it?"

Her laughter howled throughout the room. "No, it's not

Carlos. You don't need to worry about him any longer..." she hesitated and added, "He can't save you now."

I stood rapidly and was about to lunge across the desk at my cousin when Cassandra yanked me back and tossed me into my seat. "Stop, Ruth Ann."

Prunella looked furious. "Were you about to attack *me*? How dare you!"

She stood and stomped out of the room. Before closing the door behind her she ordered, "Don't move an inch!"

Once she was gone, Cassandra jumped up and ran to the door. I tried arguing with her, but she whipped her hand in the air motioning me to stop speaking. "I want to see if I can hear anything. Can you please just shut your mouth for a minute!"

"Hey," I replied, offended. "I'm just," I stopped and put my hand over my mouth to prevent myself from speaking. Sometimes, it was impossible for me not to talk. This was one of those rare times I really needed to keep quiet.

"She's out there," Cassandra whispered. I stood and walked closer to her, against protests to stay in my chair in case Prunella surprised us. "She's talking to a female, I think."

"A female?" I questioned, surprised. "Who?"

"How am I supposed to know?" she snapped. "Shhh, let me listen."

Cassandra kept her ear against the crack of the door hoping to get more information. She shook her head and said, "They're not out there anymore."

"Did you get any information?"

"Just Prunella ordering this woman to get her some tea and something to eat."

"No," I said, dazed. "It couldn't be..."

"Who?" she demanded as she rushed back to her chair and sat down.

I followed her, and after I plopped myself down, I answered, "It could be Inga."

"Inga?" Cassandra asked.

"You know, Inga. She's our, or rather Axel and Prunella's friend and housekeeper."

"Oh, the big, clunky woman who was with all of you."

"Yes, but why would Inga be roaming free in this place?" I asked, starting to wonder who I could trust.

"Maybe she's one of them."

"No way!"

"I think she's coming back in," Cassandra whispered. "Stay quiet, and don't jump at her again!"

We watched as the doors flew open and Prunella sauntered in, holding her black velvet box. I didn't even notice her carry it out. Smart, though, otherwise we definitely would've opened it. She didn't sit in her chair, but hopped on the desk near Cassandra and me. "So, have you calmed down, Ruth Ann?"

Me? Of course, I was calm considering the conditions. "I'm fine, Prunella. Why don't you stop beating around the bush and tell us what's in that box, and who Johann misplaced?" I quickly added, "And your plans are for us."

I didn't give away my rage, just said it plainly and simply. "Well, well, you're calling the shots now?" she inquired with a sinister laugh. "Let's get one thing straight. I'm not the sweet, innocent, dutiful wife and cousin you and Axel once loved. I've changed, for the better, I might add."

"And how is murder and kidnapping better, Prunella?" Cassandra asked, interrupting our moment.

"Shut up!"

"Then answer her," I insisted. "Do you know what you've done? You killed Sherman!"

Prunella's reaction wasn't what I expected. For a split second, I thought I spotted her eyes moisten, but the red irises reappeared, and if steam could've poured out of her ears, it would have. "He deserved it. He was dead weight."

"YOU'RE NUTS!" I shouted. "He was your great uncle, and devoted friend and butler. How could you do such a despicable thing! You'll go to jail for the rest of your life when you get caught."

"I don't plan on getting caught, Ruth Ann," she said, calm and coolly. "He didn't suffer. He just fell asleep and never woke up."

"So, you just confessed to killing him," Cassandra announced. "There's *two* witnesses to testify against you."

"HAHAHA," she laughed, vigorously. "And why would you assume there would be two witnesses left to testify?"

Stunned and sickened, I replied, "You plan on killing us, don't you?"

"Yes, Ruth Ann. I can't have any witnesses if I want to stay a free woman."

"Even if you kill us, you won't get away with it. There are too many others who know what you've done!" I yelled.

"I'm aware of that, Ruth Ann," she replied. "You don't need to worry about that, anyway. I've already taken care of one of them."

"Carlos," I mumbled.

"Yes, your new boy toy, Carlos, is no longer," she said, smiling.

"What did you do to him?" Cassandra pleaded, terrified.

"He was a pain. He wouldn't stay calm and let us leave the cabin to fly over here."

"You killed him back in Deer Creek?" I asked, curious and worried his body was dumped on a road.

"No, no," she said. "We flew him here, and then...let's just say...he disappeared."

"Disappeared where?" I asked, wondering if there was a chance he was still alive.

"None of your business!" she snapped, hopping off the desk and walking toward the door. "Stay here. I'll be right back," she ordered, and stepped out of her office.

"He's not dead, Ruth Ann," Cassandra quickly said to me. "She's just trying to get a rise out of you. Don't play into her act."

"You don't think she or one of those twins killed him?" I

asked, suddenly feeling some hope for poor Carlos.

"No. I don't even think she personally killed Sherman. She just wants you to think she's a hard-ass now. The best reaction from you is none."

"Don't say or ask anything?" I inquired, confused.

"Yes. Let it go. We'll get out of this somehow, but not if you force her hand. She might do something to us just to prove she can."

"Oh, I get that," I said, feeling better. "I promise to *try* and keep my mouth shut. When she comes in, we need her to open that velvet box." I said, as I pointed to the box Prunella mistakenly left on the desk.

"Hey, Ruth Ann!" Cassandra said, excitedly. She stood up and reached her arm to the desk and snatched the black box.

"Hurry," I said, anxiously. "She did say she'd be right back."

I watched as Cassandra placed her delicate hand on the clasp and then...she stopped. "What are you waiting for?" I demanded.

"You do it, Ruth Ann," Cassandra said, shocking me. She wanted that necklace so badly that I was stunned when she handed me the velvet box.

I grabbed it and said, "You don't have to ask me twice."

Cassandra said, "You don't think she left it here on purpose, do you?"

"I highly doubt it," I said, taking the brass clasp and turning it so I could open the box. "Here goes..." I pried the box open gently and finally, after what seemed like an eternity, I was able to see my Blue Ice again. But how did Prunella get it off her neck? I was utterly perplexed.

TWENTY-NINE

"It's not my necklace!" I declared. "It's a knock off, I know it!"

"Let me see, Ruth Ann," Cassandra demanded.

I turned the box so she could see it. "It certainly looks like your necklace, Ruth Ann."

"No, this one isn't blue and Isabella told us that no one could remove the necklace from Prunella's neck."

"No one EXCEPT Prunella can remove it. Think about it, Ruth Ann."

"Oh, no," I replied, looking closely at the jewel in the box. "It's RED!"

"Blood red, Ruth Ann," she corrected me. "That necklace is blood red, like Prunella's eyes. It's been tampered with, but not intentionally.

"What on earth do you mean?" I asked, confused. I reached to touch the gem, when Cassandra swatted my hand away.

"Don't touch that!"

"Why not?" I asked, angrily.

"It's cursed or worse."

"What's worse than a curse?" I asked, mesmerized by the sight of the bright red gem gleaming up at me.

"I told you, Prunella has changed. The old woman, Mattie, must've placed another curse on it. She isn't as trustworthy as Isabella thinks she is. I used her, too, remember!"

"I thought you said you *forced* her to help you?"

"Yes, well, I did, but why do you think I went to her in the first place?"

"Tell me, but hurry!"

"She dabbles in dark arts, voodoo and witchcraft!"

"I knew she wasn't as innocent as she appeared. Poor Isabella wants her to be like her grandmother, but she isn't, is she?"

"No, she's nothing like Meme. Meme knew all about her. She was banished from Isabella's family's village."

"That's horrible. Where is she now?"

"Probably using Prunella."

"That makes everything much worse, doesn't it?" I asked, horrified by this revelation.

"I think so. She'll keep Prunella under her spell. I don't think those pills did as much damage as I was originally told. I think Mattie used me too."

"She's old, Cassandra. How could she have that much control?"

"She may be weak and old, but she has powers that could make Prunella and those twins very dangerous people."

"We've got to get out of here," I said, panicking. I wanted to run out as fast as I could and bulldoze anyone who got in my way. I felt trapped, claustrophobic and filled with anxiety. I closed the velvet box and tossed it on the desk. "I don't want this anymore!" I was about to take off for the door when Cassandra pulled me down.

"Don't move," she said, quietly. "She's coming."

I turned my head to see the door opening. I returned my gaze to the desk, not wanting Prunella to think I had been staring at the door waiting for her to return. "Well, you two are still sitting," she barked. She marched over to the desk and stared at the box. She picked it up and said, "So, you looked inside, didn't you?"

"Nope," I said, nonchalantly.

"DON'T LIE TO ME!" she screamed.

Cassandra looked furious. I have to admit, Prunella's outburst made me jump, but I tried to appear unaffected. "What is your problem?" I asked angrily, but calmly. "You know you left it here so we'd look. What's the big deal anyway? It is partially mine."

"HA!" she cackled. "That necklace doesn't belong to you anymore. It's not even the same." She grabbed the box and flipped it open. "See," she tilted the box so we could get a glimpse.

I didn't want to have any response. I wanted her to see me cool and calm, even though on the inside, I was a mess. "So, what," I said, looking at my poor necklace. "I can get that fixed."

"Fixed!" she hollered. "This isn't a broken piece from your stupid little antique store that can be reset! This is my new, re-invented Blood Ice! Say goodbye to your precious Blue Ice forever!"

Cassandra discreetly tapped my elbow. I knew she wanted me to remain calm and unaffected by Prunella's rants. Actually, I wanted to scream that my cousin was crazy, but instead, I took a deep breath and responded with one little word, "Whatever."

That infuriated Prunella more than I hoped. She walked around the desk and stood directly over me as I sat in the chair. "Whatever?" she questioned, extremely close to my face. "Did you actually say that?"

I didn't give in. "Yes, Prunella. I said whatever. If you want to rub it in my face, go ahead. I don't care anymore."

"That's a joke, Ruth Ann," she said, sitting on the arm of my chair and laughing at me. "That necklace means more to you than it ever did for me. I only wanted it once I knew it could control people's lives."

"It can't do that," I said, mistakenly giving her the satisfaction. "People control people, not things."

"This isn't a thing," she said, reaching over at the desk and pulling the necklace out of the box and holding it inches from my face. "Go ahead, Ruth Ann, touch it."

"No thanks," I said, turning my head away from her and the cursed gem.

"I said touch it!" she demanded.

Cassandra shook her head vehemently. "No, don't do it!"

Prunella turned around and shot daggers at Cassandra. "Shut up! It's none of your business. You lost out, so you're persona non-grata now."

"Prunella, you're the one who'll be sorry," I said, trying to get her attention back. "Just admit what you've done and we can get you help."

"HELP?" she laughed, wildly. "I'm about to start a wonderful life with Jacob and our baby."

I forgot about the baby. I can't believe that slipped my mind. But, wait a minute, she just admitted that Jacob was the father. Even though I knew the answer, I asked, "What if Axel's the father?"

"You and I know that's impossible, Ruth Ann," she said, calming down and talking civilly. "Why would you ask me that?"

"Axel would be a great father to your baby. Even if he isn't the biological father."

"He's old!" she howled.

"You fell in love with him despite your age difference," I answered. "The old Prunella wouldn't be so nasty."

"She's long gone, and stop trying to get her back," Prunella spat. "We're wasting time. Where is she with my tea?" Prunella stood, about to head to the door, when the office door opened and her tea arrived.

"Inga!" I bellowed. She walked in carrying a silver tray with tea and chocolates. "What are you doing?"

Inga ignored me, and carried the tray and set it on the desk. "Would you like me to pour?" she asked Prunella, in a much kinder, high-pitched voice than she normally used.

"Of course, you fool," Prunella answered, rudely.

Inga reached for a tea cup, and I noticed her hands shaking. She lifted the porcelain tea pot and tried to pour the steaming liquid, but she spilled a little on the saucer. It assured me that Inga wasn't under Prunella's control. Finally, I thought we had a chance of getting somewhere.

"You fool!" Prunella snapped. "Wipe it up!"

"Yes, Ms. Prunella," Inga answered, obediently. She pulled a towel from her apron pocket and wiped the mess on the saucer. She carefully picked it up and placed it in front of Prunella who was now sitting behind her desk. "Anything else?" she asked.

Prunella looked at me and actually asked if I would like a cup of tea since she knew I loved it. "That would be nice," I answered, wondering if it was a peace offering.

"Pour her some," Prunella ordered Inga.

Inga gingerly poured me and Cassandra tea, even though Cassandra was never asked. She walked the cup over and handed it to me. I looked at her expression of fear, and knew we had to figure a way out of here. "Thank you," I said, grabbing the cup, without a saucer from her. She placed the other cup of tea on the edge of the desk without handing it to Cassandra. Cassandra shrugged her shoulders and chose to ignore the tea.

"So, what am I going to do with you, Ruth Ann?" Prunella asked, not intending for me to answer. "You have been fairly kind to me, so maybe I won't torture you too long." She turned her attention to Cassandra, "You, on the other hand, I could care less about. I'll get Jacob or Johann to kill you right away." She took a dainty sip of her tea, and reached for a foil wrapped piece of chocolate. "Mmm, these are my favorites," she said, opening the dark chocolate candy. She passed the crystal bowl across the table and said, "Go ahead, I know you love your chocolate, too."

"I do, but if you're going to kill Cassandra now, then you might as well kill me too." I noticed Cassandra's horrified look on her face, but I ignored it and continued. "However, my last request is to have *you* kill me, not your hired killers."

"Me?" she laughed. "I'm not going to get my hands dirty."

"Your hands are filthy already," Cassandra responded, bitterly. "What's one or two more deaths?"

"Shut up!"

"No," Cassandra replied, smiling back at her. I started to think that her advice of sitting back and not letting Prunella see our emotions just went out the window.

I asked, confused, "Cassandra, what are you doing?"

"If she's going to have one of the twins kill me, what do I have to lose?"

"She does have a point," I said, looking at Prunella. "Where are Axel, Isabella, Alex and Mattie?" I added, "I would say Carlos, but you claim he was already taken care of. And I know where Inga is."

"Inga is my loyal servant, Ruth Ann. She always has been. Just like Sherman was, before he..." she stopped, swallowed hard, and said, "But, things have changed. I have to live my life now, without all of you!"

"Why?" I asked, wondering what changed in the last few days to make her hate us.

"Mattie, through Isabella, explained what I'm turning into. I have become a strong, wealthy woman who doesn't need anyone."

"But, that's what you were before those pills," I said, slipping about her taking the red pills.

"Pills!" she bellowed.

"It was me that forced those two red pills down your throat, Prunella," Cassandra said. "They are dangerous, and Mattie should've never given them to me."

"They aren't dangerous, Cassandra. Mattie has been giving me one of those pills twice a day now."

"Really?" I asked, realizing Mattie wasn't a prisoner like the rest of us.

"So, you've employed Mattie now, huh?" Cassandra inquired. "She's an old, evil witch. What do you need with her?"

"She transformed me into a powerful woman. Plus, look at this beautiful gem now!" She held the red, emerald shaped gem in her hand and it gleamed as streams of light flickered around her. "It's so much better than that ugly, blue color."

"No, it's not!" I hollered. "It's cursed, and Isabella needs to break it. That blood red piece is evil, and whoever touches it becomes evil."

"Nonsense, Ruth Ann," Prunella responded, chuckling at me. "Isabella already knows all about the change in our necklace. She sensed it long before you laid eyes on it. Plus, she's willing to take Mattie and go back to their village in Jamaica and never set foot anywhere near Deer Creek."

"I thought you were going to kill *all* of us," I snapped.

Prunella stood, and leaned over the desk toward us. "I could care less what happens to Isabella or Mattie. If I chose to let them live, then sending them to their village would be my only option."

"Is that what you did to Carlos?" Cassandra asked, raising a good point. "You said he was taken care of. You never said he was killed."

"Ah, the difference was he put up a fight. A valiant fight, but Jacob and Johann had to handle him a little differently than the old woman and poor, weak Isabella."

"You had him killed, then," I said, somberly. "He was a good man, and that wasn't necessary. Just like Sherman. He was your family, and the mere fact that you would want him dead sickens me, Prunella. How dare you think you've become a better woman. You're despicable!"

"Get out!" she shouted, and rushed to the door to call for someone to come and get Cassandra and me.

"Where are you taking us?" I asked, as Jacob entered and Prunella whispered something in his ear.

"Really?" he asked, confused with Prunella's request.

"Yes, I just want them away from me for a moment. Just do it."

Jacob walked over and grabbed my arm and Cassandra's arm. We were dragged out of the office into the circular foyer. He pointed to a door on the other side and let go of our arms. "Don't try any funny stuff," he said, pushing us in front of him. "I'm watching every move you make."

He led us through a closed door and down a short, dark hall with no windows. We pushed open the only door at the end and entered into a bright, sunny kitchen. Inga was standing at the sink washing dishes.

I wasn't going to ask Jacob any questions since he took us to Inga, without realizing that with her, we would definitely figure out an escape plan.

"Stay here," he said, directing us to a round, wooden table. "Sit."

Cassandra and I sat down without saying a word. Inga froze as she spotted us. I caught a slight turn of her mouth, knowing she was trying to hide a grin. Jacob walked over to the sink and told Inga to heat up more water for her boss. "Yes, sir," she said, following his order and setting the tea kettle on the stove with fresh water.

"Keep an eye on those two," he said, obviously thinking Inga was trustworthy.

He told her he'd be back in a few minutes to get the hot water, and headed into the hall.

I was about to stand and rush to Inga, when Inga said, "No, stay where you are!"

"Hey, don't tell me they've brainwashed you, too?" I asked, irritably.

"No, Ruth Ann," she answered, reassuringly. "That big goon could come back here any second. There's too much to say, and I don't have enough time."

"Tell us what you know, and hurry," Cassandra insisted.

"I'm glad you two are unharmed," she started by saying. "I can't say the others are quite as lucky."

"Where are they?" I asked, worried.

"All I know is that old woman isn't on our side."

"We heard," I said. "Go on."

Inga eyed me suspiciously. "How do you know?"

"Prunella told us. Don't worry, I'm not in her good graces. She was bragging about Mattie and how she's in control of everyone."

"Not everyone," she muttered. "I'm playing along for now. Once I figure out where everyone else is, then we'll overtake her."

"Remember, its Prunella, Inga," I reminded her. "I have to believe she can't help herself. Once we get a hold of Mattie, then we can force her to stop giving Prunella those red pills and tell us if there's an antidote."

"She will never return to her normal self. The pills cause permanent personality changes." She added, "And not for the good!"

"I won't believe that until we've tried every last thing to save her," I said.

Cassandra huffed, and said, "Give it up, Ruth Ann. Prunella is lost to you and your family. All we can do now is try to save the rest of us who are still alive."

Inga looked horrified. "What do you mean *still alive?*"

"She claims Carlos was 'taken' care of," Cassandra answered.

"You mean killed or something else?"

"We don't exactly know, Inga," I replied. "She said Carlos was putting up too much of a fight and the twins 'took care' of him. She implied that he was no longer with us."

"That could mean plenty of things!" Inga bellowed. "They could've sent him somewhere remote or shoved him in a hole in the ground!"

"I wish I had the feeling there was still hope, but the way she described it..." I stopped and Cassandra reminded me that Prunella was trying to get on my nerves and make me think the worst.

"Inga, tell us what you've heard since we've been separated," I asked. "And, where are we?"

"You, Isabella, and Mattie drank the drugged tea," she began, but I interrupted and added Cassandra's name. "No, Ruth Ann. Cassandra didn't drink the tea."

"Then how did I end up with Ruth Ann upstairs in that bedroom?" she asked, confused.

Inga looked at her oddly. "You don't remember?"

"No, why?"

"After Ruth Ann and the others passed out, you lunged at Ms.

Prunella when she came into the kitchen. The twins had already overtaken Mr. Eklund and Alex and took them away. She was waiting for everyone at Mr. Eklund's estate here in Stockholm."

"Then what happened?" I asked, anxiously.

"Jacob or Johann, who knows which one, clocked Cassandra in the back of the head. She went down cold."

Cassandra rubbed the back of her head. "That's why I had such a terrible headache when I woke. I thought it was from the drugged tea."

"You didn't drink any tea," Inga reminded her.

"I can't remember if I did or didn't."

"So, that tells me what I already know, Inga," I said, frustrated. "I know where Cassandra and I ended up. What about Isabella, Mattie, Axel and Alex?" I also mumbled, "Carlos, too."

"Carlos, I have no idea about him." She turned and walked to the door to make sure no one was listening. "Mr. Eklund and Alex are in this building."

"What building are we in?" I asked.

"One of Mr. Eklund's abandoned buildings down at the docks."

"Really?" I asked, surprised. "You mean we're at his company where we were months ago?"

"Yes, and no." Inga replied, confusing me. "This building isn't used anymore. It used to house employees when they worked and lived on his property. The rent was so cheap that his workers felt obligated to stay with his company."

"I never heard about this place before," I said. "Good in theory, but then why would it be abandoned?"

"When he lost everything, they shut the place down. Most workers found others jobs in the area or were forced to move."

"That's terrible!" I said, disgusted.

"He's hired many of them back, Ruth Ann," Inga said, knowing way more than she should.

"How do you know all this?" I asked.

"Some from Ms. Prunella, and some just by listening when I

would bring Mr. Eklund coffee or food in his library back in Deer Creek."

"Oh, that makes sense."

"Let me continue," Inga said, worried we were going to be interrupted soon. "I don't know exactly what room or what floor Mr. Eklund or Alex are in. There are four floors in this place. That much I know. Also, from what those twins bragged, they had to put them in their place several times."

"What does that mean?" I asked.

"Obviously, Axel and Alex gave them trouble, so they probably beat them up a bit. My guess, is that they're tied to a bed in one of the rooms. The problem is going to be finding them. There are a lot of rooms here to check!"

"But, I bet there's a guard standing outside *their* room," I said, smiling at my quick thinking.

"Good point," Cassandra admitted. "What about Isabella and Mattie, Inga?"

"Isabella was drugged like you two. I thought you three would be together, but obviously, you weren't."

"Maybe she was in the room next to us!" I exclaimed. "We gotta go check."

"Not yet, Ruth Ann," Inga said. "They told you to stay put and not try anything."

"I forgot for the moment. But, we have to figure out a way to get to them."

"And, if you want to know, the old witch, I mean, Mattie," Inga said, sarcastically. "She's as free as a bird."

"You mean she can roam the entire building by herself?" Cassandra inquired, irritated. "She could be listening to us right now!"

"I don't think she hears very well, or understands English," I said.

"Don't underestimate her, Ruth Ann," Cassandra answered. "She's old, but evil. She could care less that Isabella is her great niece."

"Poor Isabella," I said. "She had a light in her eyes when she heard Mattie was her cherished grandmother's sister. She really wanted to have part of her family with her."

"Don't count on Mattie," Cassandra said. "When I hired her, she was a willing participant and, even though I lied before about how I found her, I knew exactly who I was hiring to get those pills and place curses on people. Mattie has quite the reputation back in her village. Residents are terrified of her, and will do anything to keep away from her."

"But, why?" I asked, perplexed. "What made her so evil?"

"Who knows," Cassandra replied. "She was ousted from her family just like I was."

"Sorry, Cassandra," I said. "However, now you understand it doesn't pay to seek revenge, maybe we can do the same with Mattie."

"Doubtful," Inga muttered. "Can we come up with a plan before you two are taken away from me?"

"First, we need to find everyone," I said. "But, how? Cassandra and I aren't free to roam."

"Maybe they'll put you two back in that bedroom. Then, you can sneak out and check to see if Isabella's nearby. Oh, and maybe Alex and Mr. Eklund, too."

"That would be ideal, but I don't know what she's going to do with us," I answered, worried. I suddenly felt a pang of hunger. I looked at Inga, and before I asked, she pulled open the refrigerator and grabbed a plate of cheese and cold cuts. "Here, eat these quickly." I grabbed a hunk of Swiss cheese and a few pieces of chicken. It was exactly what I needed. I looked over at the closed drapes and asked, "What time of day is it? I have no idea how long we were out with the drugged tea."

"It's mid-morning, Ruth Ann," Inga answered. "You and Cassandra should be well rested. I didn't get much sleep because I was trying to convince Ms. Prunella that my services would be best used in the kitchen. Finally, after a long battle, she conceded and let me work in the kitchen for her and those goons, Jacob and

Johann."

I noticed a funny look on her face. She hesitated a second, but finally curiosity won out. "Ruth Ann, I have a question for you and I'd like you to be honest with me. Please."

"Of course, Inga," I replied, wondering where this was going.

"I overheard some really strange comments from those twins."

"Such as?" I asked.

"The one, I think Jacob, kept bragging about winning Ms. Prunella over." She looked at me and asked, "Do you know anything about that?"

"I haven't overheard anything about that," I said, fairly truthfully. I actually hadn't heard them brag about that, but they did mention the baby and who the real father is.

"Oh, well, then the next thing you definitely wouldn't know about."

Uh-oh, I thought to myself. "What wouldn't I know?"

"Johann slipped and told his brother that he's too stupid to be a father. He wouldn't even be able to keep a monkey alive, yet alone a tiny infant."

Cassandra's mouth dropped open, and I felt cornered. Do I finally tell the truth? The truth that isn't mine to tell? I must've taken too long to respond, because Inga called me out. "Ruth Ann! You know something! I have a right to know."

Cassandra, who had been sitting back at the kitchen table, stood up and came next to me on one side of the island. Inga was directly opposite of us now with glaring eyes, demanding I spill whatever I knew. "I, well, I was sworn to secrecy, Inga."

"Don't you think it's a little late for that!" She snapped. "We've been taken prisoner by your cousin, and my dear friend and employer." She banged her hand against the marble counter, swearing under her breath after hurting her hand. "I knew something was up! You, Ms. Prunella and Mr. Eklund have been acting goofy since Thanksgiving dinner. The three of you were creeping around that estate, trying to hide things from us." She paused, and a look of horror appeared on her face. "Wait a minute! Don't tell me that whatever it is you're hiding from the rest of us could've prevented poor Sherman's death?"

"No!" I exclaimed. "Sherman's death had nothing to do with the secret."

"Secret?" Cassandra muttered, quietly, but very curiously. "Why don't you tell us your little secret."

"It's not so little, actually," I admitted. I only thought a second before realizing I didn't have a choice. Axel would understand under these circumstances. "Okay, here goes," I began. "We know Prunella is pregnant..."

"Yes, we know that," Inga snapped, hands on waist waiting for bigger news.

Aggravated, I blurted out, "Well, what you don't know is that Axel *cannot* be the baby's biological father!"

The information didn't take long to sink in when the lightbulb went off inside Inga's and Cassandra's brains. Cassandra was the first to respond, "Ooh, that's juicy news, Ruth Ann. Are you telling me your precious, perfect Prunella slept with Jacob?"

I shot her a nasty glare. "No, that's not what happened."

Inga remained silent, which was very unusual for her. I wanted to reassure her that Prunella wasn't cheating on Axel. "It wasn't consensual, Inga," I said, carefully. Her eyes opened wide, and the fury I saw building inside her scared me. I waved my hands rapidly in front of me and said, "Wait, wait, Inga. Let me explain."

"You better do it fast or I'm going to track that, that, disgusting fool down and murder him with my own two hands."

Quickly, before Inga burst a blood vessel, I explained. "When we were in Jamaica, Martika kidnapped Prunella and held her prisoner in her house. Jacob and Prunella...well...they conceived a baby. I really believe Prunella didn't have a choice. She was most likely drugged, and pretended to like the guy. I haven't heard the whole story from Prunella."

"That's nonsense!" Inga barked. "He took total advantage of

her, plain and simple!"

"I'm sure he did," I agreed. "However, she was a prisoner of Martika's, and we don't know what she forced down her throat. I'm sure if it was some weird hallucinogenic, Prunella wasn't in control of her actions."

"But Jacob was," Cassandra added, disgusted. "I wondered why they were so willing to help me after that whole Martika fiasco."

Inga eyed Cassandra suspiciously, "You really had no idea that Jacob was the father of Prunella's baby?"

"None, honestly."

Inga shrugged her shoulders, and I was relieved that burden was off my own shoulders. Axel may be furious with me, but I was cornered, and I wasn't going to keep that secret any longer.

Before I could say any more, the kitchen door swung open and Prunella marched in. "Well, well, well," she said, strutting over to the island and leaning against it near me. "I knew you'd try to convince Inga to be on your side." She smiled, and requested a bottle of water from the refrigerator. Inga quickly did as she was told, and placed a cold bottle of water on the island. "Anything to eat, Ms. Prunella?" Inga asked in the most disgustingly sweet voice.

"No, thank you, Inga," she replied, kindly, turning to me and mockingly adding, "It's no use, Ruth Ann. Inga will never betray me. She's known me longer than you have, and she will always be loyal to me."

"So, you think," I snapped quietly with gritted teeth, but loud enough for her to hear.

Prunella turned to Inga and smiled, "You would never pick *her* over me, would you, Inga?"

Inga shifted nervously and replied, "Never, ma'am."

I watched Inga after Prunella turned back to me and grinned. She carefully shook her head and rolled her eyes. "Whatever, Prunella." I added, "Can you tell us what's going to happen to us? It seems to constantly change."

"For the time being, I will let you live." She turned to Cassandra and said, "You, on the other hand, I will gladly give you to Jacob and Johann. They can do what they want with you!"

"No!" I shouted, angrily.

Prunella eyed me oddly. "What, you two are besties?"

"I never said that," I retorted. "Those goons will try and get their own revenge on Cassandra, and, and, I think we should leave her for the police."

Cassandra's hurt look shown across her face. As Prunella looked at Cassandra, I tried to show her I was lying about the police. Ever so slightly, I shook my head side to side, hoping she would catch on. She caught my action and she flashed a slight grin to acknowledge she understood.

Cassandra decided to play along. "Who cares what Ruth Ann wants!" she blurted out. "The police will never catch me, and you'll never keep me here, either. I'm smarter than all of you!"

"Really?" Prunella asked, intrigued. "And how do you plan on getting out of here? You're *my* prisoner this time."

"Not for long," she mumbled.

"We'll see about that," Prunella spat, walking to the door and calling for Jacob. Seconds later, the big, blonde, bully of a Swede stumbled in.

"Yes, Prunella," he said, grabbing her hand and giving it a squeeze.

His action sickened me. This whole thing was absolutely ridiculous and I was done with it! Something had to break so we could get out of here and take Prunella home to get the help she needed to get back to her normal, sweet self. I returned my attention to the two of them.

Prunella leaned over and whispered in Jacob's ear. A huge grin appeared, and he said, "Of course I can do that."

"Thanks, sweetie," she said, planting a kiss on his cheek. "I'll be there to check on them in a little while."

Jacob marched over to the island, and without speaking, grabbed Cassandra's and my arms. "Hey," I bellowed. "Not so hard!"

"Where are you taking us?" Cassandra demanded, angrily.

"You'll find out," Prunella said from the doorway. She held the door open as the three of us left Inga and Prunella alone in the kitchen. I quickly turned and saw Inga's terrified eyes staring back at me wondering what she was supposed to do now.

He led us back into the foyer and walked us to the elevator. He pushed the button and the single door opened slowly. He gave us a shove and we piled into the elevator. I watched as he pushed the number '4' on the panel. I think he's taking us back to the bedroom where we were before.

Cassandra smiled, knowing we could escape from there much more easily than from the kitchen. "So, Jacob," Cassandra began. "What's the deal with you and Prunella? I thought you wanted to be rich, and independent. But, now you're just Prunella's little puppet doing anything she asks."

"Shut up, Cassandra! You don't know anything about my relationship with her."

"Relationship!" Cassandra mocked. "You're a fool if you think she's doing anything but using you."

"That's not true! We're in love and we're going to have..." he shut his mouth and glared at Cassandra. "No more talking!"

Cassandra didn't listen to his order, and kept antagonizing him. "Have what, Jacob? A life or a... a baby!"

He raised his hand high and slowly, methodically, swung it at Cassandra's face. I jumped in front and blocked his arm, but took a hit in my stomach. I keeled over and nearly fell to the floor, but Cassandra took hold of my arm and kept me upright, well, almost upright. "What'd you do that for?" he bellowed. "She deserved it. Why would you stick up for her?" he asked, curiously. "She was ready to kick you and your family to the curb! All she wanted was your bloody necklace!"

I didn't want Jacob to think I was friendly with Cassandra so I pretended to turn on her. "I'm not on her side. I was stupid to stop you from swatting her in the face. She deserves what she's got coming!"

Cassandra didn't flinch. I knew she understood what I was doing, so I continued. "Go ahead, lock her away and throw out the key. But, why are you holding me? I have nothing to do with you or Prunella anymore."

"Oh, you still have an important part in this," he said, accidentally.

"Really?" I asked, more curious than ever. "What do I have to do?"

Jacob realized he said too much. He told me to shut up, too, and we waited for the very slow elevator door to open on the fourth floor. He marched us down the hall, and as we walked, Cassandra and I tried to hear for any sign of life in the doors we passed. He stopped at the door we were in not long ago. He pulled out a chain full of keys and grabbed one. He unlocked and kicked the door all the way open. "In," he said, pointing.

Cassandra marched in without saying a word, so I followed her. He slammed the door shut, and we were alone again.

THIRTY

"This is great!" Cassandra declared, smiling as she walked away from the door and plopped herself on the bed.

"Are you being sarcastic or are you really happy we're back in this room?" I asked, confused.

"No, this is a good thing, Ruth Ann. I think Isabella's right next door!"

"How do you know that?"

"Didn't you hear the noise coming from that room?"

"No, I tried listening at each door as Jacob led us down the hallway, but I didn't hear a thing."

"I did," she said, disappearing into the walk-in closet where she thought she heard noises coming from the other side of the wall. "Hey, can you hear me, Ruth Ann? You're not talking, and that's not like you."

"Ruth Ann," she called again from deep inside the large closet. "I'm going to bang on the wall and see if I get a response from the other side."

Finally, I answered after wondering how I missed hearing noises from the room next door. "But, what if it's not Isabella, and the person inside tells on us?"

"Really?" she said, laughing. "Whoever is in there is just as much a prisoner as we are! This is an abandoned building, remember?"

"Oh, yeah, I guess you're right." I went inside and stood near

Cassandra just as she picked up a loose piece of metal shelving. She lifted it and banged it against the wall.

"Listen, Ruth Ann," she said, quietly. "I think I can hear someone in there."

"What do you hear?" I asked anxiously, putting my ear against the wall next to Cassandra.

"I think it's Isabella, and she's crying!"

"I can't hear a thing!" I said, irritated. I took the piece of shelving away from Cassandra and started beating the wall. My overwhelming strength, I say that in jest, broke a hole in the wall!

"Ruth Ann!" Cassandra yelled, excitedly. "That was fantastic!" She whipped the piece out of my hands and started expanding the hole. "I can see through it now. Let me look and call out for Isabella."

"You'd think she'd be right on the other side with all the noise we've made," I said, worried it wasn't Isabella waiting on the other side.

"Maybe she was afraid, and stood back until she knew who was breaking through the wall," Cassandra suggested, making a lot of sense. "I'd stand off in case I was in danger."

Cassandra dropped the shelf and used her hand to break away the loosened drywall. I joined in, and in no time, we had a hole the size of a cantaloupe. "Look, Cassandra," I told her, giving her a little shove.

She coughed from the dust, and leaned in to take a look. Suddenly, a hand reached out and pulled Cassandra's long, dark hair. Her head went flying against the wall and she screamed in pain. "Stop!" she yelled. "Isabella, is that you?"

The hand released its grip, and Cassandra pulled her head back inside the closet. "What the..." she was about to swear, but then Isabella's hand and head appeared inside our closet.

"Hey, it's you two!" she said, joyfully. "I'm sorry, Cassandra," she said. "I didn't know who was coming through the hole. I was about to clunk you with a lamp!"

"Well, thankfully, you didn't," Cassandra said, rubbing her

head.

"Sorry, I didn't know," she said, remorsefully. "Let's make the hole bigger so you can get into my room."

I told both of them to back away as I picked up the metal shelf and used it as my sledge hammer. Within a few minutes, the hole was big enough that we could climb through. "We have to be careful," Cassandra said as she stepped inside Isabella's room. "We need to find a piece of furniture big enough to block the hole in case someone comes in and we haven't figured out how to escape."

I stepped on a stool in the closet and climbed through the opening. It was easier than I thought. I was happy to see Isabella's smiling face on the other side. Her face was tear stained, but she was happy to see us. "Finally," she said. "I didn't know where anyone was or if any of you were still...alive."

"We're fine, Isabella," I said, reassuring her with a gentle rub on her back. "How are you?"

"It was horrible, Ruth Ann," she said, tearing up, again. "That horrible Prunella told me I was worthless and weak, and that I'm only alive because I inherited my mother's and grandmother's powers. What does that mean?" she asked, sobbing into her hands and covering her face.

I said, "Don't listen to her and prove her point, Isabella!"

She removed her hands slowly, and gave me a nasty little stare. "Are you agreeing with Prunella?"

"No, of course not," I said, immediately. "But, you can't let them see you falling apart when they humiliate you. You have to come across cold and uncaring. I know it's difficult to act that way, but you have to remain unemotional."

"Maybe I am a weak woman."

"No, you're not!" Cassandra snapped. "Stop being a baby and help us get out of this mess."

"You're right," she said, drying her tears and standing up strong.

"Tell us what happened to you. We ran into Inga down in the

kitchen and Prunella believes she's on her side, but Inga told us she's just pretending."

"I saw Inga when Prunella and Jacob brought me in this room not long ago." She looked around the shabby bedroom and said, "It's a depressing room to be stuck in." I had to agree with her. The room smelled musty from lack of use, and the brown and tan striped wallpaper was peeling off the walls. The brass light in the middle of the ceiling was rusting and only three of the five bulbs were still lit. I looked at the twin bed and noticed there was no bedding, just a beige sheet thrown across of it. Isabella had used her coat as a blanket while she slept after being drugged.

"They drugged me, just like you two," she said, angrily. "I drank that tea, and then Inga told me you two were together. I didn't know where, she wouldn't tell me that."

"Wait, you spoke with Inga alone?" I asked, baffled.

"Yes, but very briefly." She added, "It was when they dumped me in here. Jacob told Inga to get me settled, and I pretended to still be knocked out, but I wasn't. I was faking at first, but I really did pass out after I was alone. When Jacob left and Inga carried me to bed, I opened my eyes and nearly scared her to death. She dropped me, but luckily, I was over the bed, so I landed on a soft mattress."

"Thankfully, you didn't land on this hard floor," I said, looking down at the scraped and worn wooden floor.

"Inga was furious at first, but I told her I had to pretend or they'd give me more of the drug."

"What did she say, exactly?" Cassandra asked.

"Inga told me the only reason she wasn't considered a prisoner was because Prunella believed her when Inga said she was and always will be loyal to her."

"She believed that?" Cassandra replied, laughing. "How gullible."

Isabella shot her a nasty glare, "Stop it, Cassandra! Prunella can't help how she's behaving. She's had a total personality change."

"And not for the good," I added. "Go on."

"Inga said Prunella didn't take much convincing. She told her to resume her normal housekeeping and cooking routines. There's only one kitchen here, and three upper floors with bedrooms."

"We noticed that," I said.

"She told me she overheard Prunella and the twins talking about what to do with Axel and Alex. Inga thought she heard they were thrown in the basement. It sounded horrible, Ruth Ann," she said, shivering in fear.

"Why?" I asked.

"She heard Jacob or Johann tell Prunella that they're restrained and they won't be able to free each other. She said they're on the cold cement floor without anything. Inga heard one of the twins say that they tied their hands and feet, and gagged their mouths."

"But, if they're just in the middle of a cement floor, they can probably hop around and figure out a way to get up and out of there," Cassandra said, confused.

"No, no, Cassandra," she said. "They are tied from the rafters above them down to the floor. They aren't within reach of each other, and they can't move from their spot at all."

"Oh, that's different," Cassandra said.

"Inga thought Prunella and the twins didn't even notice her when she was cleaning up some dishes in the office. Inga told me that's how she always gets her information. By sneaking in a room and quietly doing her job. Most of the time, nobody even notices her."

"Obviously, this was one of those times," I said, well aware of Inga's little secret.

"So, we know where Axel and Alex are, so that leaves Mattie and Carlos, right?" Cassandra inquired, even though we knew Mattie's whereabouts, and well, we weren't sure about Carlos. "Mattie, the witch, is around. She keeps handing Prunella pills, according to Inga. She wants to swat them out of her wrinkled, old, nasty hands, but can't or it would give her away. She's hoping I can help and find a cure or antidote for Prunella."

"Can you?" I asked, curiously.

"I don't know, Ruth Ann," Isabella said, honestly. "I need to know what's in those pills."

Cassandra chimed in and said, "Remember, I had the antidote for those in my hands, but when they overtook me, they took them. I'll bet anything that Prunella or the twins have them."

"And if the twins have it, they won't give it to her. They want her in control because it benefits them," I said. "I highly doubt Prunella has them, that makes no sense."

"We're forgetting about someone, Ruth Ann," Cassandra said.

"Who?" I asked, wondering to whom she was referring.

"That Svenson guy, Steven."

"I totally forgot about him. I bet he's the one in charge of everything, don't you think?"

"Probably, but with Prunella's personality disorder, she thinks *she's* in charge and holds all the cards with Svenson," Cassandra said.

"He's a murderer," I said, despising that man for everything he'd done. "He's the one who killed poor Bert and Helena, and my guess, Sherman."

"Prunella had a hand in Sherman's death, Ruth Ann," Isabella reminded me, sadly.

"It wasn't her fault!" I exclaimed, furious at everything that had happened lately. I was so happy when I found out about my extended family, and now, well, I wish it never happened!

Isabella grabbed my hand and gave a gentle squeeze. "You really don't mean that you wish you never met Prunella. You're just angry and hurt. If you hadn't, you wouldn't have met Inga, Axel, Alex, my grandmother and me!

I stood back from her and was about to answer, when it hit me. I didn't say out loud that I wished I had never met Prunella. She was doing it again. She read my mind. "It's okay, Ruth Ann. It's part of who I am, so you might as well get used to it."

"I just hope I never think anything badly of you!" I said, jokingly.

"You wouldn't."

"Can we get on with this, please?" Cassandra barked. "Enough of the love fest, we need a plan."

"I think we find a way to get to the basement and free Axel and Alex," I suggested.

"Maybe Prunella will send Inga in with a tray of food for us," Isabella hoped.

"That's not a bad plan, Isabella," Cassandra said, excited. "We have to eat at some point, right?" she continued, without waiting or wanting an answer to her question. "Inga will tell us the easiest way to get to the basement, and then, once we free them, we'll grab Inga and get out of here."

"And go where?" I asked, ruining her moment of excitement.

"Home, or I should say, your home," Cassandra said, deflated. "I don't know what you're going to do with me. You might want me in jail for everything I've done."

"We told you that's not going to happen, Cassandra," I said.

"Yeah, we forgive you," Isabella said, smiling at her friend and half-sister. "Martika died because of her need for revenge. But you've stopped, and we can move forward now. It's just you and me left."

"You're right," Cassandra said. "I will prove to all of you that I can be a good person. I don't want to go to prison."

I wanted to change the subject. I was hopeful we could keep Cassandra out of prison, but if John got his hands on her I wasn't sure what he would do. Until then, we needed to free ourselves, but, I wasn't going to leave Prunella here and fly back to Deer Creek without her.

"Once we hear someone coming, we'll see where they go. Hopefully, it'll be Inga," I said. "But, it could be one of the twins."

"Or Prunella," Cassandra added.

"If it's not Inga, what do we do?" Isabella asked, worried.

"We knock them out, and get out of here as fast as we can,"

Cassandra replied.

"With what?" I bellowed, surveying the lack of weapons in our rooms.

"We'll have to get creative," she said. "We broke through that wall between our rooms with a piece of shelving. I think we can figure something out."

"Isabella," Cassandra said, turning serious. "Ruth Ann and I have to go back to our room. When we leave, push that dresser in front of the hole." Cassandra walked over to a beaten, old wood dresser and gave it a little shove. It appeared light, so it shouldn't be a problem moving it to cover the hole we made. "You're leaving me alone?" she asked, terrified.

"We have to!" she answered. "They can't know we've communicated, and worse, broke through a wall to get to you."

"I guess so."

"If they come to us first, you can hear everything through the hole. And if they come to you, we do the same. We have to hope it's Inga that comes into our rooms. That will make this much easier."

The way my luck ran, I doubted Inga would be the one to enter our room.

Cassandra and I climbed back through the hole, and watched as Isabella slid the dresser in front of the hole. It didn't quite cover the top of the hole, but I didn't think it was that noticeable. "We can keep talking, but if we hear any noise from the hall, go back to your bed and pretend to be asleep," Cassandra told Isabella. "Ruth Ann and I will be doing the same thing."

We spent our time going over possible scenarios for our escape. I refused to agree with leaving Prunella behind. "She's not your sweet cousin anymore, Ruth Ann," Cassandra reminded me.

"But, if we give her the antidote, she'll go back to her normal self, eventually."

"You don't know that for sure," Isabella said, solemnly. "There's no guarantee."

"Thanks for the optimism," I said, bitterly. "I have to stay hopeful."

I climbed out of the closet, leaving Cassandra with Isabella. I knew it was going to come down to Prunella. My conscience would not let me leave Prunella behind. It wasn't who I was. I would rather tie her up, gag her and drag her onto a plane to bring her back home than leave her here alone or with Jacob, her new 'man', according to her. Did she forget she was already married to Axel? I knew they were having marital problems, but legally, they were still married.

What would Axel want to do? He had made it abundantly clear that he had formed romantic feelings for me. At first, I was shocked and refused to believe it, but if I was *truly* honest with myself, I think Axel and I fit together better than Prunella and he ever did. Banish the thought, Ruth Ann!

THIRTY-ONE

"Shhh," Cassandra cried, running out of the closet. "Isabella's doorknob jingled. I told her to run to her bed, fast!"

"Let's go look," I said, anxiously. "We can watch from our side of the closet."

Cassandra and I rushed back inside the closet and watched, and to our dismay, one of the twins entered. But, he wasn't alone.

"Who's that?" Cassandra whispered. "He's in a suit!"

"This is bad," I mumbled, terrified at the sight of this man. "It's worse than we could ever imagine."

Cassandra threw me a nasty look. "Just tell me so we can figure something out!"

"It's Steven," I replied.

"Steven?" she asked, at first confused. "Wait," figuring it out. "*That's Svenson?*"

"Yes."

"What's he doing here, and in Isabella's room?"

We turned our attention back to Isabella's room. We watched as Svenson shoved Johann over to the bed where Isabella pretended to be asleep.

"Wake her up!" Svenson ordered Johann.

"And how do you want me to do that, Uncle?" he asked, looking down at the frail woman, covered with her coat.

"I don't know and don't care. Throw something at her!"

"No, that's cruel," Johann said, surprising Cassandra and me.

370

Steven eyed him suspiciously." Why not? You have a little crush on the pretty, young thing?"

"No!" he replied turning red-faced, embarrassed. "Why can't we wait and let her wake up on her own?"

"She should've already woken up. We didn't give her that much of the drug."

"Then she should be waking up soon. Why don't I stay here and wait? I'll call you when she's alert."

"Fine," he barked. He turned to walk out of the room, but stopped and snapped, "No funny stuff, Johann."

"No way."

"I'm serious," he said from the doorway. "You're the softy in our family, and you can't let her sweet talk you into helping her. Do you understand how important it is that I question her?"

"Yes, Uncle."

"Then contact me the minute she wakes up." With that, he marched out of the room and slammed the door. That alone should've woken her, but it only made both of us jump inside the closet.

"What does he mean by that?" I whispered to Cassandra. "Isabella must have some information they need."

"Or, she's the only one who can perform for them."

"Perform?" I asked, confused. "What do you mean?"

"Isabella has unusual powers, remember? Her grandmother, Meme, was notorious for placing and breaking curses on people."

"You think Steven wants to use Isabella to place or remove a curse?" I asked.

"Yes, Ruth Ann. Think about your necklace. How did it look down in the office?"

I immediately thought of my beautiful aquamarine stone, and how it's turned that horrible shade of red. "Blood red," I murmured.

"Exactly. Svenson doesn't want a blood red stone! He wants it restored to its original beauty, and Isabella might be the one to do that for him."

"So, he can sell it at a high price, I bet," I said, disgusted.

"An *extremely* high price."

"I was told that it was priceless since there are no others as large and brilliant as ours."

"I know," she said, suddenly looking ashamed. "I feel like such a fool. If I would've known better, and not let my need for revenge cloud my judgement, we would never be in this position." She lowered her head, and if I didn't know better, I thought I saw a tear roll down her cheek. "Also, Prunella would never have taken those pills and turned into the evil person she is right now."

"We can't go back, Cassandra," I said, patting her arm. "We can only move forward and get Prunella the help she needs. That's why I'm not willing to just leave this place and her behind. I can't do that. I don't care if we have to drag her kicking and screaming. She will get the help she needs."

"I don't think modern medicine can cure her, Ruth Ann. I believe the only one who can bring your Prunella back is Mattie."

"I thought Mattie's pills can help Prunella."

"Yes, but I bet there's more to it. I think the curse has to be broken, and either Isabella or Mattie need to do that."

"I understand that the curse has to be taken off the gem, but I don't see how removing a curse will help Prunella's personality change."

"I think both things need to be accomplished, Ruth Ann. I think Svenson knows that, and don't ask me how. Maybe he's got control over Mattie now. She might've told him that Prunella has power over the gem.

"So, what you're saying is that Prunella is sort of cursed, too. The stone is cursed and turned blood red, and Prunella turned evil. Both are dark and dangerous, and both Mattie *and* Isabella are needed so that Blue Ice can go back to its original state. Then, Steven can sell it and live a wealthy life. Right?"

"Yes. That's my take on it."

"Wow, that's a mouthful!"

"Let's see what's going on in there," Cassandra said, stepping to the hole and peeking in."

I followed suit, and we watched Johann pace and Isabella lie on the bed pretending to be passed out. Suddenly, a horrible thought came to me. What if he noticed the dresser and the hole we made? All hell would break loose, and Cassandra and I would be caught. However, what could they do to us? We're already their prisoners!

"Look, Ruth Ann," Cassandra said, excited. "Isabella just rolled over and moaned!"

We watched as poor Isabella rolled from her back to her side, facing us. She opened one eye carefully, and looked in the direction of the dresser. I watched Johann as he paced away from her. She must've sensed he wasn't looking at her and wanted to see if we were still watching.

Cassandra told me to watch Johann while she tried to communicate with Isabella. I was thankful Johann had his cell phone out and was typing away on it as he stood near the door to the hall. He completely ignored the still figure lying on the bed at the moment. Cassandra stuck her head in as much as she could and mouthed some words for Isabella. I had no idea what she was trying to tell her, but figured it was something on the order of "hang in there," and "we're still here."

Out of nowhere a blast of loud noise came from Johann's phone startling not only us, but him. "What the?" he blurted out, answering the phone. "Who is it?"

A moment later, Johann said, "Oh, sorry, Uncle." He paused, and said, looking over at Isabella, "No, she's still out." His free arm went in the air and he bellowed, "I won't do that! She's not hurting anyone. Why should I treat her so severely?"

Obviously, Steven was demanding Johann do something to Isabella to waken her. I noticed Isabella's frightened look, and realized we couldn't let him hurt her. We waited as Johann and Steven fought back and forth for several minutes. Finally, Johann said, in a bitter tone, "Fine. I'll get her awake one way or another. What should I do with her then?"

Cassandra and I looked at each other trying to figure out our next move. "He's not going to touch her, Ruth Ann." I nodded, and turned back to Johann.

"You want me to bring her there?" he asked, baffled. "It's your call. I'll be down soon."

He started to walk toward the bed, mumbling along the way. "I'll see if I can gently wake her. I don't want to do that to her, she's so pretty."

"What does Svenson want him to do?" Cassandra whispered. "It sounds violent."

"I think so, too. Why else would he say he doesn't want to do it because she's so pretty."

"We have to stop him."

"How do you plan to do that?" I asked, worried.

"I'm thinking, I'm thinking," she muttered.

I felt a rush of panic run through my body. I didn't want us to get caught, yet I didn't want Johann to hit Isabella. What could we possibly do to stop him though?

Cassandra's head was glued to the hole. Her hands were to the side of the hole as she leaned in as far as she could go. "Let me see," I asked her, trying to push an arm out of the way. She wouldn't budge. I stood back trying to listen to Johann, but couldn't hear anything. I couldn't take it any longer. I grabbed her arm and shoved it back at her side and stuck my head next to hers. "Sorry," she said, giving me a little room. "I was too absorbed in watching what Johann was going to do next."

We waited as he paced around her bed, mumbling incoherent words. Finally, he stopped and bent over her side and gently nudged her. "Please wake up. I don't want to force you awake." Nothing. Isabella was going to an extreme with her *fake* sleeping. It would be better if she just woke up.

"Look," Cassandra said, excited. "She's coming to!" I wondered if Cassandra believed she was really still asleep.

"Shhh," I said. "Let's see what she does."

We watched Isabella slowly open her eyes, and sit upright,

terrified. The fear in her eyes looked real, but she knew he was in there waiting for her. She could easily win an acting award at the moment. She tried to speak, but nothing came out of her mouth.

Johann took over, "Please, it's okay. I won't hurt you!" he said, waving his arms in the air. "I, I have to take you somewhere, though."

Isabella got her voice back. "Where? Where are you going to take me?"

Johann looked around as if he was being watched, and said, "We have to go meet someone. I wish I didn't have to do this, but if I don't, I'll be in big trouble."

Isabella ran with it. "You don't have to do anything you don't want to...um," she stopped and waited for him to say his name. "Johann," she repeated in as sweet of a voice she could muster. "Who is giving you orders?"

Johann obliged and answered, "My uncle. It's complicated."

"Why?"

"If I don't follow along, everyone will think I'm weak and dumb. They already call me that, but I'm way smarter than my brother, Jacob."

"Jacob," she said, as if pondering the name. She knew well enough who both of them were. "He's your twin, right?"

"Yes!" he said, happily. "You must be coming out of your funk. Your head is clearing."

"I am still a little groggy."

"That'll go away." He looked around and bent over close to her face. "Please, just do what they want. I promise I will protect you after that."

"You will?" she asked confused, yet pleased.

I looked at Cassandra and noticed her smiling. "I think we can get him to come to our side," she whispered, without looking back at me.

"I do too! He seems awfully concerned about Isabella."

We watched as Johann reached his hands out to help her stand. "Wait, Johann," Isabella said, retreating from him a little. "I need you to tell me why I should trust you."

"Because, I didn't want them to take you prisoner in the first place. They just want to use you for your...you know," he said, stopping mid-sentence.

"My what?" she asked, innocently. I felt fairly certain she knew that they wanted her for her powers.

"You have certain abilities they need at the moment. I begged Jacob and Uncle Steven to let you go, but they wouldn't. They want to make as much money on the thing as they can."

"What thing?" she asked, pretending she didn't know what he was referring to.

"That ugly necklace!" he blurted out, angrily. "They need you to return it to its original state."

"But, how am I supposed to do that?" she asked, innocently.

"I don't know. They told me that you and your grandmother have supernatural powers, and made me promise to bring you to them so you can fix the dumb thing."

"It's not dumb, Johann," she said sweetly, hoping to win him over. "My grandmother's last breath broke the curse that had been on it for over a hundred years. I can't imagine it has another curse on it."

"But it does," he replied, anxiously. "It even turned another color!"

"Blood red, right?" she asked, slipping.

He eyed her suspiciously. "How do you know that?" Uh, oh, she blew it, I thought to myself. Cassandra stepped back from the hole and raised her arms in the air out of exasperation.

"Why did she say that?" she asked me, rhetorically. "She had him going, and then she blew it!"

"Wait, let's see what happens," I said, hoping Isabella could reel Johann back.

"I asked you how you knew it was red, blood red?" he repeated, becoming irritated with Isabella's reluctance to respond instantaneously.

Isabella reacted quickly. "I, I saw it on Prunella back at the cabin in the woods."

"You did?" he asked, puzzled. "When?"

"When you, Jacob, Carlos and Prunella were leaving. I saw a flash of red on her neck and was shocked!"

"Oh, yeah," he said, relieved. "She was wearing that ugly thing." He stood back a couple feet, and watched Isabella closely. "You're not playing me, are you?"

"How could I play you?" she demanded.

"Forget it," he said, clunking his hand on his forehead. "I guess that makes sense."

"Are you going to take me to them?" she asked, harmlessly.

"I told you I don't have a choice."

"Yes, you do," she said, slightly turning her head toward the hole in the wall.

"Tell me," he asked, curiously.

"If you can trust me, I will make sure you don't get into any trouble."

"Why would I get into trouble?" he asked, a little irritated with Isabella's words.

"No, no, that's not what I mean. I meant, if you could help me and my friends, we would promise to protect you from your uncle. He sounds rather cruel, don't you think?"

"He's a jerk," Johann replied. "My parents couldn't stand him, but when they died, he took in Jacob and me and raised us since we were teenagers." He thought about that for a moment and continued, "However, he did get a huge chunk of money after my parents died to take care of us until we were old enough to be on our own."

"He did?" Isabella asked, intrigued. My mind immediately thought that Uncle Steven killed off the twins' parents to inherit the large sum of money!

"Yes, it does cost money to raise kids you know."

"Oh, I understand," she said, hoping to keep him calm. "What exactly is a large sum of money?" she asked.

"Millions," he replied, as it suddenly dawned on him that he might've gotten screwed by Uncle Steven. "You know, come to think about it, I don't know why Jacob and I haven't taken control of the rest of the money. You don't think..." he stopped, turned to Isabella with a desperate look.

"You think it's possible your uncle took advantage of you and Jacob and spent *your* money?"

"That louse!" he shouted. "I'll kill him if he did! That wasn't his money to spend. It was supposed to be used for Jacob and me."

"And whatever was left, you and Jacob would inherit, right? I'm sure there was an age when you would take control of the money."

"I think so."

"You don't know the age?"

"No." He stomped away from the bed and started pacing the room, mumbling incoherent words. Isabella looked at our eyes popping out from behind the hole. She quickly gave us a thumb up. I nodded back to her, hoping she would continue to win Johann over.

"It's okay, Johann," Isabella said, getting his attention back to her. "You're an adult now. You don't need their approval on anything. I know you're not dumb so don't listen to them anymore!"

"You're right, Isabella!" he exclaimed, slapping his hands on his thighs. "I'm going to march into my uncle's place and demand my portion of the money from my parent's heritance."

"No!" Isabella shouted. "You can't do that!"

"Why not?" he asked, confused. "It's my money, not his. I'll give Jacob his portion so he can raise his..." he clasped his lips shut tightly, and turned away from her.

"It's okay, Johann. I already know."

"You do?" he asked, surprised.

"It's those powers of mine. I had the feeling Jacob was the father of Prunella's baby."

"Wow," he said, impressed. "You really do have supernatural powers!"

"Yes, so let's use them the right way. Are you on board?"

He didn't respond, but rushed to her side on the bed and sat down next to her. "How?"

"I have an idea," she said, excited. "We can get your money and the necklace away from them."

"How?" he asked, again. "I don't want to hurt my brother. I know he's a bully, and pushes me around a lot, but I don't want him hurt."

"He doesn't have to be hurt. Why can't we use my friends to help get back what's rightfully yours?"

"Hmmm," he mused, his tiny brain working hard to understand. "It might work."

"Great!" Isabella bellowed, but quickly calmed herself down. "Are you willing to help the others though? I can't leave here without Ruth Ann, Cassandra, Axel and Alex."

"What about your friend from your homeland?" he asked.

"Carlos?" she asked, confused. "I thought he was, you know..."

"He's not dead."

Isabella jumped on her feet and was about to hug the huge twin, when she pulled back. "I'm sorry. I didn't mean to get so excited. I just thought you or Jacob killed him."

"I haven't killed anyone."

"You haven't?" she asked, surprised.

"What about Martika, and the others?"

"That was my uncle and..." he stopped, swallowed hard and finished. "Jacob."

"That's too bad," she said sweetly, hoping to curtail his anger from rearing its ugly head. "How do you feel about that?"

"I tried to keep them from doing it. I'm not a murderer. I know I've done a lot of bad things, but I won't ever kill a person."

"I'm really glad to hear that," she said, reaching down and patting his hand. She sat next to him while Cassandra and I watched stunned, but hopeful. There was a long moment of silence before Johann stood up and made a decision.

"I'm with you."

Isabella stood up next to him with her tiny body only coming up to his chest. "I'm very happy to hear that."

"What's our plan? We have to have a plan."

"I think we'll have a little help with that," she said, turning toward the dresser, smiling.

"What are you talking about?" he asked, baffled.

"It's time," Isabella called out loudly. "You can come out now."

Johann watched as Cassandra moved a lamp that was blocking the hole so nobody would see us. She stuck her head through the hole and his shocked look scared me. "What the?" he said, stopping before his profanity took over.

"It's okay, Johann," Isabella said, quickly. "It's Ruth Ann and Cassandra. They were being held in the next room."

"I know that!" he barked, angrily. "You all tricked me!"

"No, no, we didn't!" Isabella exclaimed. "I was thrown in here after being drugged, and so were they. They heard me crying through the walls, and broke a hole in the wall to save me. Nobody was tricking you. We want you to help us. Can you do that, Johann?"

"I don't know," he said, rubbing his chin.

I called out from behind the hole, "Johann, could you please move the dresser so we can come in and talk with you? I promise we're not planning any funny stuff."

"I guess so," he said, marching over to the dresser and shoving it to the side with ease. He was amazed at our accomplishment, almost smiling at our effort. "Let me make it a little bigger so you can fit through."

I wasn't about to tell him that we had already come through the hole, so we let him rip off a few more pieces of drywall and reach inside the hole to give us a hand.

"Thanks," I said, allowing him to practically lift me up and over. "Whoa," I said, as he plunked me on the ground.

"You next," he said to Cassandra.

"You hate me," she said. "You think I betrayed and used you and Jacob."

"You did," he replied, still holding his hand out for her to grab. "However, circumstances have changed, and I'm willing to cooperate if you are."

"Yes, I agree. Circumstances have changed."

"You seem awful chummy with Ruth Ann and Isabella, so I guess you came to your senses, too."

"I did, Johann," she said, accepting his help climbing into the room. "I wasn't in my right mind most of the time. I spent way too many years plotting my revenge."

"You were very angry, Cassandra. I hope that's not the case anymore."

"I'm angry, but only at your uncle, and..." she hesitated, but added, "and, your brother."

"I don't blame you. He's a jerk, and hopefully he'll come to his senses, too."

"You did, Johann," I added. "Maybe you can get through to him."

"Actually, I don't think Jacob will be willing to help us. We're on our own."

"Not if we get Axel and Alex," Isabella said.

"And don't forget about Inga," I added. "Oh, and you said Carlos wasn't dead. Where is he then?"

"I'll have to get him myself," he replied. "I'm going to have to pretend I'm still working with them. That's the only way we can get you all out of here, alive."

"That would be nice," I said. "I'd like to stay alive."

"What's our plan?" Cassandra asked. "We don't have a lot of time. Right now, your uncle and brother are waiting for you to bring Isabella to them."

"But, I can't do that. They'll force her to help them," he said, worried. "And they'll stop at nothing."

"But, they can't kill me if they need my powers, right?" she asked, anxiously.

"I guess not, but," he looked at Isabella with adoring eyes. "But, they might hurt you."

"We don't have any choice," Isabella said, strongly. "Johann, you take me to them, and we'll pretend that you're still working with them. Ruth Ann and Cassandra can grab Inga and get Axel and Alex. They can wait for us to be done with your uncle and then we can escape!"

"Nice plan, Isabella," Cassandra said. "But, we can't risk you being left alone with Jacob and Svenson."

"We don't have a choice!" she declared. "I'm willing to risk it." She turned to Johann and said, "You won't let them hurt me, will you?"

"I'll kill both of them with my own two hands first!"

"No more killing anybody!" I said, loudly. "Enough. We need to get out of here, with Prunella too." I quickly added, "And my necklace!"

"Good luck with that," Cassandra said. "Prunella won't go easily. She's still on Jacob's and Svenson's side."

"We'll see," I said. "I think we need to find Mattie, too. She can be forced to help us, right?"

"Definitely," Johann agreed. "I'll shake her until she spills about her antidote."

"We have a lot of obstacles to conquer, but if we get the others, we can figure it out as we go," I said.

"Uh-oh," Johann said, looking down at his hand. "My brother is calling me."

"Answer it," Cassandra said. "Tell them you finally got her awake, and you're about to carry her down to them."

He shakily answered the call, "Yes, Jacob." Pause. "I'm coming, lay off! She just woke up after I shook her." Pause. "She wasn't happy if that's what you want to know." Pause. "I didn't have to hit her!" he said, angrily. "I'm coming, I'm coming." He tapped the phone roughly and shoved it into his pocket. "That brother of mine was mad that I didn't have to rough her up!"

"That's pretty sick," Isabella said. "I'm sure glad you didn't!"

"I couldn't. You're too pretty and nice for me to hurt you. I hope you can forgive me one day and look at me like a friend or ..."

His face reddened as he lowered his head toward the floor. Isabella went over and grabbed his hand. "Let's get through this, and then we'll see."

"Thanks."

"Can we get moving, please!" Cassandra demanded. "We don't want Jacob to come in here because you're taking too long."

"Okay, here's our tentative plan," I said, taking the lead. "Johann and Isabella will go to Steven's office. We'll follow to make sure we know where they are. Then, we'll grab Inga and head to the basement to release Axel and Alex. After that, we'll come back to the office and make sure you're safe and unharmed."

"All along making sure nobody else pops up and deters us," Cassandra mentioned, bursting our bubble.

"Who?" I asked her. "Only Mattie and Prunella are left, and I feel fairly confident Prunella will be with Jacob and Steven."

"Don't forget Carlos," Isabella said.

"He's not exactly in the building," Johann replied, carefully. "We have to get him on our way out of here."

"Wait a minute," Cassandra said, worried. "Are you telling me Carlos is being held somewhere else?"

"Yes, but it's not far from here. I know the way."

"Let's get going," I said, anxiously. "We have to get out of here. All of us!"

"We'll try, Ruth Ann," Cassandra said. "I know you're hoping we can get Prunella too, but if we can't, we will drag *you* with us kicking and screaming."

"You'll have to," I said, knowing there was no way I was leaving without Prunella.

THIRTY-TWO

Johann and Isabella headed for the door. After they were out, Johann waved that it was clear for Cassandra and me to follow.

Johann carried Isabella to keep up the charade she was still drugged. He carried her like he was carrying a sack of potatoes, with hardly any effort at all. "Follow me," he said, hurrying past the elevator.

"Aren't we going down to the first floor?" I asked, curiously.

"Yes, but not on the elevator. If they're waiting in the lobby and the elevator doors open to find all of us, we'd be in big trouble," he said, smarter than he looked.

"Good point," Cassandra said.

He went to the end of the hall, opened the door and descended the brightly lit stairwell. Before we stepped through the door, Johann told Cassandra and me to wait. "Let me make sure the coast is clear in here."

"Here, where?" I inquired.

"This door opens into the kitchen, and I want to make sure Prunella or Jacob aren't hanging around inside there."

"That's great!" I bellowed, forcing nasty looks my way. "Sorry," I said, much more quietly. "Inga will be in there and we can fill her in."

"Hopefully," Johann said.

Cassandra and I stayed back and waited as Johann carried Isabella over the threshold and into the kitchen. It didn't take long before a hand reached through the cracked door and waved us in.

"Inga!" I cried, never happier to see her in my life. "We have so much to tell you."

She looked at us curiously, as Johann held Isabella. I had to stop her before she went after Johann. "No, he's on our side, now."

"You've got to be kidding, Ruth Ann?" Inga asked, sarcastically. "He's not. He's fooling you so you all can be killed."

"No, no, it's true," Isabella said, finally opening her eyes. "He really is going to help us."

"Explain, quickly," Inga demanded, walking away from the sink and toward the large table where we stood.

Johann temporarily set Isabella down, but he insisted we tell Inga later because he had to take Isabella into his uncle's office. "No, you can't!" Inga bellowed. "They'll hurt her."

"We've got it covered, Inga," I said, filling her in on our plan to follow them to his office. "Once Johann and Isabella are inside Steven's office, we'll go free Axel and Alex."

"Risky, but it might work," she said, pacing around the table and thinking about it. "We'll have to arm ourselves with weapons."

"What weapons?" Cassandra snapped. "It's not like they're leaving guns lying around."

Inga glared at Cassandra. "I'm still not sure I trust you."

"This isn't the time, Inga," I said, trying to diffuse her anger. "What do you have in mind?"

Inga disappeared into the walk-in cooler and came out wielding two handguns. "Holy cow!" Johann exclaimed. "Where did you get those?"

"That's none of *your* business," she snapped at him. "I was waiting for a plan so I could pull these out."

She put one gun in her apron pocket and handed the other one to Cassandra. "Hey, I thought you didn't trust her!" I argued. "What about me?"

"You can have this pocket knife," she said, dropping a small piece of metal in the palm of my hand. "You open it, and it's a knife, Ruth Ann."

"Gee, thanks," I said, a little disappointed.

"I gotta go!" Johann said, anxiously. "Isabella, are you ready?"

Isabella held her arms out for Johann to pick her up. "Let's get this over with."

Before I could protest Isabella's safety, Johann turned to me and promised no one would put a hand on her. "If you're sure you can protect her," I said, still not completely confident with our plan.

"Only option," Isabella said, smiling. "I'll be fine. Remember, I have special powers!"

"Not the kind that won't get you killed!" I replied, terrified. But, I had to sound positive. "We'll be right behind you. Once you're inside, Inga, Cassandra and I will hurry and get Axel and Alex. We'll be right back waiting to pounce and rescue you and Prunella."

"And Johann," Isabella added.

"Yes, Johann will be coming with us, too."

We followed Johann since he knew the way. Inga told Cassandra that the gun was loaded and to be careful. Johann led us through a different door that took us back inside the lobby. He headed directly to another door and without hesitating, opened it up. "We go down this hall and his office is on the right." He made sure nobody was lurking, and waved us to follow. "Here, he said a moment later. "This is the door. Now hurry and go get your other friends. I'm going to knock and take Isabella in."

We stood back, behind a corner and watched as Johann knocked on the door and carried Isabella inside. I felt my heart pounding and adrenaline rushing through my body as I watched the door close behind them. I hurried to the door and put my ear against it hoping I could hear inside, jackpot! I heard Prunella's voice yelling at Johann about taking so long, and Steven agreeing with her. That meant the only person wandering around was Mattie.

"Let's go," Cassandra said, pulling me away from the door.

We rushed back to the kitchen and let Inga lead the way to the basement. The stairwell was pitch black. "They're down there in the dark," I said, worried.

"Shhh," Inga said, heading down a long set of narrow stairs. "I've got a flashlight."

We followed Inga and her stream of light into the deep, dark basement. Inga suddenly stopped at the bottom of the stairs. "I'm going to pull the string to turn on the lightbulb." She added quickly, "and before you ask, I've been down here before to get supplies for the kitchen."

"So, you've seen Axel and Alex?" I asked, excitedly.

"No. They're in another location. Just follow me and don't ask any more questions, please."

I didn't understand her abruptness, but followed anyway. Once there was light, I could see a large room filled with boxes and shelves. Inga marched to the opposite side of the massive room and stood in front of a door. "This has to be it," she said. "When I went down here earlier, Jacob told me to stay away from here. That made it abundantly clear they were in there."

"Open it," Cassandra requested.

"It's locked."

"How are we going to get in?" I asked, anxiously. "We need to get back to Isabella and Johann."

"Hold on. I came prepared. I noticed the lock earlier, and grabbed a tool to get it off."

Inga pulled out a long, skinny metal pin and grabbed the old-fashioned padlock. Almost immediately, the lock released, and Inga tossed it on the floor making a loud echoing noise. "Oops," she said. "That was really loud."

She grabbed the handle and pushed open the heavy, metal door. She stood in the doorway for a second, and then turned toward us with her mouth wide-open.

"What, what is it?" I asked, panicked. "Don't tell me they're..."

"No, Ruth Ann," Inga responded immediately, knowing what

I feared. "They're not dead, injured or anything!"

"What does that mean?" Cassandra asked, shoving me aside and pushing her way inside the room. "You've got to be kidding me!"

"What, what?" I asked, eagerly.

"They're not in there," Inga answered. "I don't get it. Why the lock and orders not to go near here?"

I walked in to have a look. They must've been in here. "Maybe they escaped," I said, wondering if there was a way out other than this door.

"How?" Cassandra asked, roaming around the empty cement room.

"There's no window well or anything," Inga said, confused. "What happened?"

"We need to get back upstairs," Cassandra said, suddenly. "We can't leave Isabella alone too long."

I hesitated, hoping to find a clue, but Inga grabbed my arm hastily and pulled me to the stairs. "Let go, Inga!" I demanded, rubbing my sore arm. "You didn't have to bruise me."

"Sorry, but I know you. You would've spent too much time in that room. I told you, they *were* in there. *Were* being the key word."

"I don't get it, where are they and how are we going to save Isabella now?" I asked, anxiously. "We need Axel's and Alex's help overtaking Jacob, Prunella, and Steven."

"We'll be fine, Ruth Ann," Inga answered, feeling her apron pocket. "We have a little help."

I felt my own pants pocket for the tiny knife I hid. I doubted my weapon could do any damage to a huge Swedish man! I followed Inga up the stairs as fast as I could. I was out of breath, and generally exhausted. Cassandra was standing in the kitchen waiting for us.

"Come on, we've got to get back to Isabella and Johann."

Inga marched past an irritated Cassandra and took us to the hall outside Steven's office. I had to admit that I wouldn't have found it. Prunella has an office off the foyer, too, and the doors all looked alike. The only distinct door was the elevator. I tried to memorize my surroundings a little better this time, hoping it wouldn't be necessary.

"Shhh," Inga said, turning around once we reached our destination. "I don't hear anything."

"Why would you?" I asked, finally catching up. "They're inside that room."

"I think I would feel better if I heard yelling. The quietness bothers me."

She was right. It was eerily quiet and dark. I was subconsciously hoping Axel and Alex were here already, but the hall was devoid of anyone except the three of us. "What now?" I whispered. "Should we go in?"

"NO!" Cassandra yelled in a whispered voice. Her look made me feel stupid, but what else were we going to do? Just stand outside the office and wait for someone to catch us?

"Give it a minute or two," Inga said. "Maybe they're still in there."

We waited outside of the door, but ready to flee if necessary. "Nothing's happening," I said, anxiously. "I can't take this anymore."

Just as soon as my words left my mouth, we heard voices coming toward us from the foyer. "Oh, no," Cassandra said. "There's nowhere for us to hide."

We tried several doors previously, wondering if we could hide in another room. None were open, so we knew we were dead meat. "We don't have a choice," Inga said. "We've got to go inside that office of his and hide."

"If we can," Cassandra added. "We're doomed."

"Stop it!" I snapped. "It's not over yet." I reached and grabbed the door handle and luckily, it turned. I pushed it open a little and took a peek inside. I couldn't see anything, and then Inga shoved me into the room.

"They're coming," she said. "Get in there!"

I stumbled into the office. Inga and Cassandra hurried in and shut the door. We immediately found out why it had been so quiet.

"Isabella!" I cried, running to a twin cot in the middle of the room. Her eyes were closed, and her hands were lying on her stomach as if she was laid out to rest. I quickly took her pulse, and was relieved to find one. "She's alive," I said, thankfully.

"Johann's over here," Cassandra called out from behind a large, executive desk near the back wall.

"Where?" Inga asked, waiting by the door in case they came in. Her gun was in her hand aimed directly at the back side of the door.

"He's been knocked out," Cassandra said, dropping to the floor and disappearing behind the desk. "I think I can rouse him, but we have to hurry."

We didn't have time. Inga told us they were close, and we had to take cover. I spotted a pile of boxes along the side of the far wall and the three of us rushed over and hid behind them. I prayed they wouldn't notice us.

We waited patiently until the door opened and Prunella and Steven Svenson entered. Where was Jacob? Maybe he had tried to protect his brother and was punished for it. I dismissed that thought because if Jacob was able to protect Johann, he would've been on the floor, unconscious, like his twin.

"Shut the door!" Prunella demanded.

"Don't you dare order me around. You work for me, remember?"

"I don't work for anyone!" she spat, red eyes glaring his direction. "I'm the one who saved your ass!"

"Shut up, Prunella. We don't have time for petty bickering. They've escaped and are probably lurking around ready to save her," he said, pointing to the still figure lying on the cot. "We're not done with her yet. I think the medicine Mattie injected has finally taken effect. Go and try to rouse her."

Prunella didn't argue and marched toward Isabella lying on the cot. She stood staring at the motionless figure. She reached her arm in the air and just as she was about to slap Isabella's face, Steven yelled, "Stop!"

Prunella turned slowly and asked, "Why? You told me to wake her!"

"You're a mean one, aren't you? Just shake her a little. I want her to cooperate, not cower and flat-out refuse to assist us."

"Then we'd have to kill her," Prunella said, without any human compassion. What happened to her? I was amazed at the behavior of this new woman, drugs or no drugs.

She did as Steven asked. She grabbed Isabella's shoulders and gave them a hearty shake. "Nothing." She tried harder, almost knocking Isabella off the cot. "You think she's faking?"

"Not the way you're shaking her," he snapped.

"Maybe we should come back," she suggested.

"I think we need that witch. We need her conscious, but able to submit to our needs. We need that stone to be revived, not remain that horrid red color."

"Blood red, as they're calling it," Prunella said with a sick laugh. I think she actually enjoyed the eerie change in the stone.

"Who cares? I need to find that old witch." He told Prunella to stand guard while he went and found Mattie, and if she heard any noise to contact him immediately. She held up a tiny gadget and said, "Will do."

It looked like she was holding a walkie-talkie. He left and slammed the door behind him.

Inga, Cassandra, and I watched through cracks in the stacked boxes as she paced around the cot. She began singing a disturbing little tune while watching Isabella sleep:

Wake up, wake up, sleepy little witch.
We need your help or I'll make you twitch.

If you don't wake up, Mattie will come,
And give you more drugs so you can hum...

Your little tune or chant we need,
So, the bloody red gem will suit my greed.

Steven wants the gem to be blue,
I don't care, just want to be with Jacob and my little baby, too.

I watched in horror as she repeated the tune over and over. "She's lost it," Cassandra murmured.

Inga elbowed her side, causing Cassandra to blurt out in pain. "Uh-oh," Inga said, watching as Prunella's hypnotic state came to a halt.

"Who's there?" she hollered, standing frozen next to the cot.

None of us responded. Why did Inga do that? Cassandra reacted without thinking, and we were now caught. I made a foolish decision. I jumped to my feet and went around the boxes so Prunella could see me.

"Ruth Ann!" she yelled. "What...how did you get in here?"

"I'm here to rescue Isabella. You don't need her. Leave her alone!"

Prunella let out a howl of laughter, surprising me. What was so funny? I noticed Inga was about to reveal herself, but I kicked my leg her direction as subtly as possibly. I didn't want Inga or Cassandra to show themselves yet. If I could persuade Prunella that I was alone and here to help not only Isabella, but her, maybe she might cooperate. I knew it was a long shot, but it was my only choice at the moment.

"Get over here!" Prunella ordered.

I walked toward her, not looking behind me hoping the two of them would stay hidden. "Let her go, Prunella. We can figure something out without using her against her will."

"It's too late, Ruth Ann. I'm in too deep, and can't go back to my old life. I want to stay here in Sweden with Jacob. I know you think I was forced here, but I wasn't. I agreed to work with Jacob and his uncle. Actually," Prunella looked around as if she didn't want anyone else to hear her. "Actually, Jacob and I plan on fooling his uncle, too."

"Really?" I asked, stunned. "So, you don't want Blue Ice to return to its original state?"

"I could care less," she replied, shrugging her shoulders. "It's more valuable this color anyway," she said, opening her crisp white button down shirt and displayed our necklace. "It's stunning, isn't it?"

"No, it's not, Prunella," I said, honestly. I knew I risked her wrath, but I was furious. "It's fake, not real."

"Of course, it's real. It's been beautifully transformed, that's all."

"It's ugly, and represents evil, Prunella. I don't care what you say to me, you're not yourself and I can help you. Won't you let me? I want you to come home with us. Are you willing?"

"Home?" She bawled. "That place isn't my home. It never was. My home is here, in this country. I don't plan on ever going back to that boring, little town of yours. You go," she stopped, and thought a moment. "No, wait. You're not going anywhere."

I walked closer to her, and angrily, I said, "What, Prunella? What are you planning on doing to me?"

"You'll have to wait and see," she said, turning her attention back to Isabella. "Ah, look, Ruth Ann," she said, smiling. "The little witch is beginning to rouse."

"Leave her alone!" I yelled, shoving Prunella away. She landed against the wall, but on her feet.

"How dare you push me! You'll pay for that one." She reached in the back pocket of her jeans and pulled out the walkie-talkie. As she pushed a button, I turned to Isabella and mouthed, "Stay asleep." She nodded, and closed her eyes. I was thankful she recognized me, after Mattie loaded her with drugs.

"Get back here," she snapped into the device. "We have a situation."

I heard a muffled voice coming out of the speaker, but couldn't tell if it was Jacob or Steven. I knew we had only a matter of minutes before whoever it was came back in the room. I made a quick decision, hopefully a good one, and rushed after Prunella. As I ran into her, shoving her against the wall, I yelled, "Inga, Cassandra, now!"

The two women sprinted to my side, forcing Prunella not to move. I ran to the desk and frantically opened drawers, looking for tape to cover her mouth. We didn't want her scream. I got lucky, and found a roll of masking tape. I hurried back to Cassandra and Inga. "We need to keep her quiet for a while," I said, reaching into Inga's apron pocket and grabbing the small towel I knew she always carried. I shoved it partially into Prunella's mouth and started wrapping the masking tape around her mouth and back of her head. Once I felt it was secure, I said, "That should hold for a little while."

"Why did you do that?" Inga asked, confused why I was being so cruel to her loyal friend and employer.

"This is why," I said, grabbing the walkie-talkie and stepping back a few feet.

Prunella was kicking and fighting us, but Inga and Cassandra were able to overpower her. They watched me carefully as I made a surprising move. I pressed the side button and spoke into the device.

"Jacob, you there?" I said, disguising my voice to make it sound a little younger, hopefully, and muffled. I needed this to work, because I was making a risky move trying to fool her beloved Jacob.

I got extremely lucky when a voice returned my request. "Prunella, is that you?" Jacob said, fairly clearly. "You sound funny. I'm almost there, so hang on."

"No, no, it's okay, Jacob," I said, hoping he would fall for this ploy. "I need you to go to the fourth floor and search their rooms. I think they left a clue behind telling us where they were hiding. I'm okay in here. The girl's still out cold. I need you to make sure the other rooms are safe. Can you do that for me?"

There was no response from Jacob. I crossed my fingers,

praying Jacob would fall for my scheme. It would buy us time to come up with our own plan. Finally, he answered. "Okay, I'll do that. Do you need my uncle in there?"

"No, no, I'm good. Where is he?"

"He's on a call with a prospective buyer. He's trying to convince the man that he's willing to fly to Rome to hand deliver it." Jacob added, "It's a heavy conversation. It might take a little while."

"I'm fine, Jacob. Just go and make sure the other floors are safe."

He agreed and we ended our conversation. Prunella's horrified look revealed that she had lost this round. She relaxed, and melted against the wall. "What's next, Ruth Ann?" Inga asked, excited. "I think we can carry her out of here. We should go now!"

"What about Axel, Alex and Carlos?"

"And don't forget about Johann," a quiet voice called from the middle of the room.

"Isabella," I said, happy to see her sitting upright on the cot looking alert.

"Are you feeling okay? I heard Mattie injected you with a drug."

"She did, but it wasn't what Prunella and the others thought it was. It was only an herb that wouldn't hurt me."

"Wait," I said, confused. "Are you telling me Mattie is on your side now?"

"She always has been, Ruth Ann," Isabella answered. "She played along with Prunella until she's able to inject *her* with the antidote."

"You've got to be kidding," Cassandra said, laughing. "There have been twists than I can't even keep up with."

"Tell me about it," Inga said, still grasping Prunella's arms against her back.

"Let's go home," I announced. "I bet Axel, Alex and Carlos are waiting for us wherever Carlos was hidden."

"We need to help Johann. He's the only one knows where

Carlos is."

Isabella stood carefully and walked over to the desk. She bent down and we waited as she miraculously revived Johann. "I'm okay," he said, rubbing the back of his head. "I have a lump, but that's all."

"Good," I said relieved, knowing we needed his help. "We need to get going."

"I'll take us to the other hiding place," Johann said, wobbling toward us. Isabella held his arm tightly as he leaned against her. "Just give me a moment. I'm getting my bearings."

We waited as he took a bottle of water from one of the shelves behind the desk and chugged it. "Okay, let's go."

Finally, a glimmer of hope that we could be going back home to Deer Creek!

THIRTY-THREE

Johann helped Inga hold down Prunella until I was able to tie her hands behind her back. Cassandra wanted me to tie her ankles and let Johann carry her, but I disagreed. "She can walk like the rest of us."

Prunella was eerily calm. I wasn't sure if she would walk out of here with the rest of us, but we had Johann and Inga as back up. Johann grabbed Prunella's arm, but Inga swatted it away. "I'll take her." I watched her, waiting for resistance, but it didn't happen. We were able to get into the hall without being seen or heard.

"Hurry," Johann said, anxiously. "I know how to get out of here without being seen."

"Seen?" I questioned. "Are you telling us that there are cameras watching the place?"

"Yes, in some areas. They're old, but my uncle got a few running. Fortunately, there weren't any working ones in these offices, and the camera at the back door is also broken."

We followed him into the foyer and he suddenly bolted across the room to one of the doors we hadn't explored before. He held the door open and waited for Inga to take Prunella, and then Isabella, Cassandra and I to get through the door. "Follow the hall to the end. It'll take us outside."

We hurried down the dark hall. The only lights in the hall were dimly lit sconces along the walls. When we reached the end of the hall, Johann called for us to stop. "Don't open that door!" he bellowed. "If they noticed we're gone, someone could be waiting outside for us. I'm going first."

He pushed his way to the front of our group and slowly opened the door to the back of the building. "It's getting light out," he said, covering his eyes from the light. "We could be easily spotted."

"Hurry up, then," Cassandra snapped. "Where are we going?"

"Follow me," Johann said, grabbing Prunella's arm to help Inga. We rushed across the parking lot and spotted two parked cars. "My uncles, and Jacob's," he informed us.

We didn't have far to go. I recognized where we were now. We were heading straight for Eklund Industries. "We've been here before," I said, recognizing exactly where we were from my previous trip. "Are you telling us that Carlos is in there?" I asked, pointing to the entrance that would take us to Axel's office.

"Yep. He's up in her husband's office."

Prunella's reaction startled Inga who was trying to keep a tight grip on her arm. She started to kick, and fight desperately to escape. "Knock it off!" Johann shouted, just getting a hard kick in his shin. "I agreed to keeping your legs free, but if you try that again, I'll tie you up myself and carry you the rest of the way."

She calmed down, but looked furious. Her eyes looked wild, and the red glare coming not only from her eyes, but also from our necklace was terrifying. She had to know where Carlos was taken. Maybe it was her idea in the first place! We entered glass doors that open into a beautiful lobby with a massive, old replica of a Viking ship displayed. Johann hurried to a separate set of elevators that would take us directly to Axel's office. I remembered it well, but last time we were trying to capture Axel, and now we were hoping he was safe with Carlos.

"Shhh," Cassandra said. "The door's opening." We dreaded hearing the ding the elevator made as it reached its destination. The door opened, and we stepped into the outer reception area of Axel's suite of private rooms. I knew there was a secret room where his vault was, and I was wondering if that was where Carlos was being held prisoner. Johann and I walked side by side as we entered Axel's main office.

"They're not in here," Isabella cried out, disappointed.

"Don't worry, this isn't the end," I said, leading the way with Johann right behind me.

"You know where you're going, Ruth Ann," Johann said to me. "Obviously, you've been here before."

"Yes, and I didn't plan on ever returning, but here we are."

I found the entrance to his secret office and opened the door. The small room was just off Axel's vault room and it was brightly lit. "There he is!" Isabella squealed, spotting Carlos sitting in a desk chair smack dab in the middle of the room. "He's alive, isn't he?" she asked, running to him and touching his face with her tiny hands. "Yes, yes, he is!"

"He's been drugged," Johann stated. "By that witch, again."

"Can we rouse him?" I asked, worried. "We need to waken him and then find Axel and Alex before we get caught."

"There's more of us than them, Ruth Ann," Inga reminded me. "They've lost."

Prunella shook her head, obviously disagreeing with Inga. "Take her tape off," Cassandra requested. "I have a few questions for her."

"But, we don't want her screaming," I said, questioning Cassandra's intentions.

She insisted, and watched as Inga unwrapped the tape and pulled the thin towel out of her mouth. "Finally!" she barked, moving her mouth around trying to get the numbness to dissipate. She turned to Cassandra and spat, "What do you want from me? You've already figured it all out!"

"Not exactly, Prunella," Cassandra replied. I was watching, confused by Cassandra, while Johann and Isabella were busily untying Carlos and trying to revive him.

"I have nothing to tell you."

"Where's Mattie?" she asked Prunella.

"How would I know? I've been with you!"

"She's not on your side, is she?"

"Of course, she is!" Prunella demanded.

"She gave Isabella a placebo, you fool," Cassandra informed her. "That means she isn't working with you, but *against* you."

Prunella's expression changed, and she became extremely agitated. "You're lying! I watched her inject Isabella and she immediately passed out. That's what we were waiting for. We needed her to be semi-conscious so we could force her to take that bloody curse off my necklace."

"Our necklace, Prunella," I added.

"Whatever," she said, sarcastically.

"So, what you're saying is that the only person who could remove this evil curse is Isabella?" Cassandra asked, finally making me understand what her intentions were.

"Yes," she said, realizing she said too much. "Well, no, Mattie has to help her, Isabella is just a back-up."

"Really?" Isabella asked, lifting her head from working on Carlos. "You're lying, Prunella! I know exactly what you're thinking, so say your words very carefully."

Prunella's nasty glare made Isabella smile. "Go ahead, Prunella, try me."

"If you think you're so smart, tell me what I'm thinking right now!"

"You're hoping I don't walk over and take the necklace off you."

"But, that's not true!" Prunella replied, suddenly feeling the walls closing in on her. "You can't take it off me. It's stuck now."

"It's not stuck," I said. "You just won't take it off."

"Yes, Ruth Ann," Isabella said. "And *we* can't get it off until I break the curse."

"That's ridiculous," I said, marching up to Prunella and reaching up to touch the stone.

"Stop!" Isabella cried, rushing to my side. "Don't touch that!"

"Why not?" Inga asked, holding Prunella still.

"If Ruth Ann touches it now, she'll have the same hatred,

400

anger and thoughts for revenge Prunella has. The pills aren't the only thing changing Prunella, it's that stone!"

All of us stopped and looked at Prunella and her blood red gem flickering in the bright lights of the tiny outer room outside of Axel's vault. Prunella was looking down at her necklace, smiling away. "You'll never get it off me. I won't let you."

"You won't have a choice," I said, feeling calmer than I had in a very long time. "I actually know that Isabella will be able to help you. Finally, this will end the way I want it to."

"I hope so, Ruth Ann," Isabella said. "Where is Mattie? I need her."

"I'm here, Isabella," a voice called from the doorway. "I've been listening all along, and you're right."

"Wait!" Inga bellowed. "You speak *English*?"

"Yes, yes," the old lady answered. "I've been pretending for a long time."

"But, how, why?" Cassandra asked, confused. "When I hired you back in your village, you were pretending there, too?"

"Yes," she said, walking to Carlos and placing her hand on his head and muttering a few incoherent words. He immediately woke up, and looked around at our group.

"Well, it's about time," he said, shaking off the cobwebs in his head.

"Carlos!" Isabella cried, joyfully.

Mattie held her withered hand in the air to stop us from speaking. "We need to get this done, Isabella. Time is of the essence."

"I know."

"We know what we need to do?" she asked her great niece. Isabella nodded, and walked to Prunella. "Ruth Ann, Inga, step away from Prunella now, please."

"But, she'll take off," Inga argued. "I'll hold her while you do whatever you need to do."

"No," Mattie said with authority, causing Inga to back away.

We stood near Carlos while Isabella and Mattie turned the

lights down and circled Prunella. She started to fight, but then suddenly stood silent, watching in horror. "She'll be okay, won't she?" I asked from the other side of the room.

"Shhh, Ruth Ann," Isabella said with a calm, even voice.

We watched as the two mumbled words, sang a serene tune, and waved their arms in the air. I felt a chill run through my body as a not so distant memory rushed through me. I stumbled, but Johann grabbed me just in time. "I'm okay," I whispered.

Shadows of people flowed out of the blood red necklace and danced on the walls and ceiling of the room. The whole event took only a few minutes. Everyone watching was in awe as Mattie and Isabella chanted to rid the precious gem of its evil curse. Finally, a bright light flashed and Prunella dropped to the floor.

"Grab her!" I exclaimed, rushing to her aide. I reached down to check on Prunella when I noticed the miracle on her neck. "It's, it's done! You did it!" I cried in joy.

Cassandra turned on the lights, and the others came to help Mattie, who was crumpled on the ground. "I'm okay. It just takes a lot of energy out of a very old woman."

I took Isabella's arm, and she smiled. "No, Ruth Ann. Mattie isn't going to die like Meme did."

"Good. What's wrong with Prunella?"

She was lying on the ground curled in a fetal position. "Give her a few minutes," Mattie said. "Her body's been through a huge transformation."

"Will she wake up and be herself?" I asked, curiously.

"Hopefully," Isabella replied.

"*Hopefully?*" I shot back. "What else could be wrong with her?"

"The lasting effects of the pills she's been ingesting," Mattie answered.

"Why didn't you give her fake pills?" Johann asked.

"Cassandra gave her the pills, remember?" I answered for Mattie.

Carlos was on his feet and wondering what had happened.

We didn't have too much time to fill him in when Johann told us we had to get out of here.

"But, where are Axel and Alex?" I asked, frantically looking around the room. "We can't leave without them."

Mattie answered that question for us. "They're fine. They're on their way, but I sense something else is going to happen."

"What?" Inga demanded, holding Prunella's head in her lap.

Mattie couldn't tell us, she was struggling from the loss of energy it took to break the curse. She looked pleadingly at Isabella, who was also pale and drained of energy. "I feel it too, but, but I have a feeling something's wrong."

The rest of us went into panic mode. "We have to carry Prunella and get out of here!" Cassandra insisted.

Agreeing it was time to go, even though we didn't know what was happening to Axel and Alex, we headed through the hall into Axel's main office. Unfortunately, we didn't make it past there.

THIRTY-FOUR

"Don't move another step," Steven Svenson ordered, holding a very large gun in our direction. Jacob was standing near him holding a knife to Axel's throat. Poor Alex was on the floor next to them, very still.

"Is he dead?" I couldn't help but ask.

"Who cares?" Steven barked, laughing. "I doubt we're that lucky, but if he is, I could care less."

"You're sick!" I hollered.

"Would you like to join him?" he asked me. "I can make that happen very easily."

"What do you want from us?" Johann asked.

"You're a traitorous piece of dirt" his uncle yelled. "How dare you turn on your family."

"I'm tired of all the murders, and running around the world chasing after some stupid necklace!"

"Shut up!" Jacob cried. He noticed that Prunella was in Johann's arms and ordered him to give her to him. Johann refused, and Jacob kicked Axel away from him, knocking him into the wall where he fell unconscious. He started to march toward his twin brother, with fury in his expression.

Johann handed the limp Prunella to Inga as fast as he could, and before his brother could react, Johann reached in his jeans pocket and pulled out a gun. Jacob didn't see it coming. Johann pulled the trigger and his brother was thrown to the floor from the force of the gunfire. "You killed him!" Steven shouted, holding his own gun, but not firing back at Johann. "Why did you do that? He's your twin brother."

"He's evil, uncle. You need to drop your gun before you get shot," Johann said, holding his gun steadily in his uncle's direction.

Steven looked down at his gun, and aimed it at Prunella and Inga. "Stop!" Johann screamed, charging his uncle before he could shoot any of us.

Steven's gun discharged into poor Johann's body as he was about to take down his uncle. The force took Johann and his uncle to the floor. Steven's gun dropped to the ground, and before he could retrieve it, Axel rolled over and took it. He hopped up, having pretended to be knocked out and hollered, "You're through, Svenson!"

"Axel!" I shouted, thrilled he wasn't hurt.

"Ruth Ann, check on Alex."

I rushed to him and felt for a pulse. "I can't find one!" I said, horrified. "What's wrong with him?" I frantically looked for someone to help me, but everyone stood frozen. "Please, what happened to him?"

"Jacob injected something into him as we headed in the office. He dropped immediately," Axel answered. "Call for help, maybe his pulse is just weak."

Isabella rushed to Johann and turned the heavy man over on his back. "He's gone," she said, tears streaming down her face. "He died, saving me...saving all of us."

"Yes, he was a hero," Mattie said.

Carlos ran to an empty desk and asked how to call for help. "I already did," Axel said, holding his cell phone in his hand.

"Don't worry," a loud, male voice hollered from the hall about to enter the office.

"Uh-oh," I muttered. "I know that voice."

"Yes, you do."

"John!" I exclaimed, jumping to my feet.

"I can't believe you did this to me, again," he said, furious.

"Judy, the coast is clear."

"Oh no, she's here, too," I said, stunned. "How did you find us?"

"It took a while, but we figured it all out. You didn't give us much to work with, and as usual, took it upon yourselves to solve the crime."

"We didn't have the time or the choice," I said, pleadingly.

"We don't have time for this now. I want everyone to go into the outer office and wait for us to question each and every one of you."

"But, what about Johann and Alex?" Isabella asked, crying hysterically.

"Ambulances are on their way," Judy answered, leaning down and taking Johann's pulse first. "Nope, he's dead." She crawled over to Alex, and spent a little longer on him. "He's alive, but his pulse is extremely weak."

"The ambulance needs to get her fast!" I shouted.

"Everyone out!" John ordered, loudly. "Judy, follow and take them, one at a time, and question them thoroughly."

Judy grabbed me first, of course, wanting to get my statement before I had time to talk with the others.

It took a couple hours before Axel, Carlos, Isabella, Inga, Cassandra, Mattie and I were able to leave Eklund Industries. We had a van waiting for us to take us to Axel's estate. "Prunella will be fine," Judy said to me, after complaining I wanted to go in the ambulance with her. "Once she's awake, I need to interrogate her. She's in for some trouble, you know."

"She had no control of herself, Judy!" I explained. "It's not her fault."

"And this Cassandra woman is also in a heap of trouble. She's coming back to Deer Creek with us and probably spending time in prison."

"She's not a criminal," I said, knowing full well that Cassandra did break a lot of laws.

"We'll see," Judy answered, getting into one of the local cop

406

cars and following behind the ambulances carrying Prunella and Alex. Johann and Jacob's bodies were taken to the morgue.

"I'm exhausted, "Axel said, leaning back in the van."

"We all are," I said.

Cassandra added, "I'm surprised they didn't take me to jail. After everything I've done, I'm sure that's where I'm headed."

"We'll see about that!" I said, smiling at her. "We're all going to testify in your defense. Maybe we can use those dreaded pills as our defense?"

"Yeah," Cassandra said, turning hopeful. "They didn't start my original path for revenge, but they sure enhanced it."

The policeman who drove the van dropped us at the front of Axel's estate. We dragged our exhausted bodies into several of the bedrooms and dropped off into a well-deserved sleep. I wasn't sure what the future had in store for us, but one thing for sure, I was a little sick of that Blue Ice! I held the necklace in my hand, staring at the beautiful, yet troubled gem. I closed my palm and formed a tight fist. Nobody was going to touch it again and have a chance of putting another ridiculous curse on it!

I awoke to the sun shining through the window. I sat up in bed and noticed Inga and Cassandra sitting on the couch whispering. I took a big stretch and smiled. It was a new day. "Hi!" I called out happily.

"Ruth Ann!" Inga bellowed. "It's about time you woke up!"

"What on earth are you talking about?"

"You've been asleep for over twelve hours!" Isabella cried. "I was really worried about you."

I stood and walked over to them. I sat between the two and placed my hands on their legs. "I'm totally fine. I was sleep deprived, that's all."

"Phew," Inga said, hopping up. "I'm going to fix a huge breakfast, so don't take so long."

"Wait!" I said. "Any word on Alex and Prunella?"

Isabella and Inga exchanged funny glances. "Tell me," I ordered. "Whatever the news is, I need to hear it right now."

"Well, um, Prunella is alive and has a strong pulse, but Alex," Inga stopped speaking and did a hard swallow.

"No, are you telling me Alex didn't make it?" I asked, terrified to hear the answer.

"He's still alive, but barely, Ruth Ann," Isabella said, a tear falling down her cheek. "The policeman, John, said he never regained consciousness. He wasn't in pain, just fell into a deep coma."

I felt sick. The young man that recently came into our lives was gravely ill. It was all my fault and I'll never forgive myself for it! Why did I push people to get involved in things they didn't want to? He had no other family, and the one he just discovered could be sending him to an early death.

"It's not your fault, Ruth Ann," Isabella said. "It's horrible, but you didn't cause it."

"Jacob and Svenson did," Inga snapped. "Jacob got what he deserved, and this time, that Svenson lawyer better stay in prison!"

"He'll be in maximum security," I said, still feeling sick to my stomach about Alex. "Hey, what about Prunella? Is she awake and talking?"

"No, Ruth Ann," Isabella answered. "She's not conscious yet. They say she's also in a coma and they're not sure if or when she'll come out of it."

"Oh, no," I said quietly, feeling my body begin to shake. "I have to get to the hospital."

"Axel's there right now," Inga answered. "There's more."

"The baby, right?" I asked, knowing the answer before they informed me. "It didn't survive, did it?"

"No," Inga said.

"This is horrible. We've lost too many of our friends and family because of this," I said, pointing to the Blue Ice in my hand. "I think we should get rid of it. Our family can't afford to lose any more members!"

"No, Ruth Ann," Isabella replied. "You can never get rid of it. It's part of you, now."

"Not if I sell it!" I exclaimed, suddenly feeling anger rise in my body. "I hate it!"

"No, you don't," Inga said. "It's the circumstances surrounding it. Listen to Isabella, we'll make it work."

"It's too hard," I said, lowering my head in my hands and sobbing.

THIRTY-FIVE

Then next few days were hectic. I spent most of my days at the hospital watching Prunella and Alex waste away. Axel was right by my side, along with Inga. John and Judy took Cassandra back to Deer Creek as their prisoner. I promised Cassandra that as soon as Prunella and Alex were awake, I'd be there fighting for her. She took it fairly well, but I could see the terror in her eyes. Isabella, Mattie and Carlos went with her for support. They would all be staying at Axel's Deer Creek estate for an extended time. I was hoping forever!

Inga, Axel and I were the only ones left. His Stockholm estate was cold and empty.

I didn't know what the future held with all our losses, and Prunella's and Alex's uncertain futures. But, I felt stronger each day, and I would not let this family crumble. I had two wonderful daughters waiting for me back home, and a thriving business. A few questions regarding my future with John kept popping up in my mind. Were we meant to be together? Only time will tell. Axel and I have been spending countless hours together forming an even closer bond. What was this connection we had with one another? I was confused, but we decided our full attention had to be getting Prunella back to us, and making sure Alex woke up.

All I wanted to do was go back home to Deer Creek. I've never wanted anything more in my life!

If you want the read more about the characters from Deer Creek, Colorado, check out Richardson's other mysteries;

BLUE ICE

Meet the residents of the small Colorado town and join them on a journey from the mountains of the sleepy little town of Deer Creek, Colorado to the icy fjords of Sweden on the track of a mythical aquamarine necklace called Blue Ice.

ICE QUEST

Just when they thought the mystery was solved and life in the peaceful little town of Deer Creek could settle down, the rare aquamarine necklace called Blue Ice disappeared AGAIN! Now Ruth Ann and her friends must race to solve this new mystery before someone else is killed.

CURSED ICE

It started as a wonderful vacation in Jamaica for Ruth Ann and John, until a monster wave dragged him away! Was this all some terrible dream? Or was it an ancient voodoo curse on the necklace, Blue Ice? Once again, Ruth Ann had to solve the mystery, but right now it looked impossible. She was all alone in an unfamiliar land, with nothing but miles of empty beach around her.

And then the old woman's voice whispered on the breeze; *"It's too late! The curse has begun ..."*

ABOUT THE AUTHOR

Karin Richardson graduated from The University of Iowa with a communications degree. She currently resides in a suburb of Chicago with her family.

Richardson's aspiration has always been to complete a series of mystery novels for readers of all ages. *BLOOD ICE* is the fourth book in this Deer Creek Mystery Series. Look on Amazon for the first three books, *BLUE ICE, ICE QUEST, & CURSED ICE.*

When she's not in the Dominican Republic admiring a pet monkey, Richardson is hard at work on the next book of the Deer Creek Mysteries.